HENRIK IBSEN

THE MASTER BUILDER

AND OTHER PLAYS

TRANSLATED BY
Una Ellis-Fermor

PENGUIN BOOKS

PENGUIN BOOKS

Published by the Penguin Group
Penguin Books Ltd, 27 Wrights Lane, London W8 5TZ, England
Penguin Books USA Inc., 375 Hudson Street, New York, New York 10014, USA
Penguin Books Australia Ltd, Ringwood, Victoria, Australia
Penguin Books Canada Ltd, 10 Alcorn Avenue, Toronto, Ontario, Canada M4V 3B2
Penguin Books (NZ) Ltd, 182–190 Wairau Road, Auckland 10, New Zealand

Penguin Books Ltd, Registered Offices: Harmondsworth, Middlesex, England

This translation first published 1958
19 20

Printed in England by Clays Ltd, St Ives plc
Set in Monotype Bembo

All applications for licences to perform plays in this volume should
be made to the International Copyright Bureau Ltd, 26 Charing
Cross Road, London WC2

PENGUIN ✶ CLASSICS

THE MASTER BUILDER

AND OTHER PLAYS

Henrik Ibsen was born at Skien, Norway, in 1828. His family went bankrupt when he was a child, and he struggled with poverty for many years. His first ambition was medicine, but he abandoned this to write and to work in the theatre. Of his early verse plays, *The Vikings at Hegeland* is now best remembered. In the year of its publication (1858) he married Susannah Thoresen, a pastor's daughter.

A scholarship enabled Ibsen to travel to Rome in 1864. In Italy he wrote *Brand* (1866), which earned him a state pension, and *Peer Gynt* (1867), for which Grieg later wrote the incidental music. These plays established his reputation. Apart from two short visits to Norway, he lived in Italy and Germany until 1891.

From *The League of Youth* (1869) onwards, Ibsen renounced poetry and wrote prose drama. Though a timid man, he supported in his plays many crucial causes of his day, such as the emancipation of women. Plays like *Ghosts* (1881) and *A Doll's House* (1879) caused critical uproar. Other plays included *The Pillars of the Community*, *The Wild Duck*, *The Lady from the Sea*, *Hedda Gabler*, *The Master Builder*, *John Gabriel Borkmann* and *When We Dead Awake*.

Towards the end of his life Ibsen, one of the world's greatest dramatists, suffered strokes which destroyed his memory for words and even the alphabet. He died in 1906 in Kristiana (now Oslo).

DAME UNA ELLIS-FERMOR was Professor of English at Bedford College, University of London, until her death in 1957. Her translation of *Hedda Gabler and Other Plays* has also appeared as a Penguin Classic

CONTENTS

Owing to the death of Una Ellis-Fermor while this book was in the early stages of production, it has been seen through the press by Miss Margaret Cardwell.

INTRODUCTION

THE first volume* of Ibsen's plays in this series contained three plays, *Pillars of the Community*, *The Wild Duck*, and *Hedda Gabler*, all representative of that phase of Ibsen's thought and art in which he was concerned primarily with the relation of the individual to the community, with his social and personal morality, with the effects of his conduct upon the world about him, with the judgement delivered upon that conduct at the bar of public opinion and to a greater or less degree also by his own conscience. The group of plays chosen for the second volume come from the later and final phase of Ibsen's work in which, though his characteristic belief in the validity of truth, in every operation of life and in every process of thought, is as clear as ever, his concern is rather with the inner experience of the individual, with his often unaided exploration of that experience, with the re-assessment and revaluation of his past at some ultimate turning-point of his soul's pilgrimage. If these last plays are still, as in some sense they all are, studies of conversion, of the crisis in which a man is brought face to face with himself, the overruling agencies are no longer now the criticism of the world but the visions released from the depth of the soul in hours of lonely reflection; the characteristic predicaments are not those of Karsten Bernick faced with Lona Hessel's demand for repentance and confession nor of Hjalmar Ekdal before Gregers Werle's 'claims of the ideal', but, instead, of Rebekka West's self-discovery, prompted as often by the implications as by the intentions of the other characters' words, or of John Gabriel Borkman's heroic delusion, maintained in the face of fact, yet already ripe for collapse at the touch of a truth he has long secretly acknowledged.

Rosmersholm, finished in 1886, is the first of the final group, following immediately after *The Wild Duck*, the last of the earlier. Six years later, the interval being filled by *The Lady from the Sea* and *Hedda Gabler*, comes *The Master Builder* in 1892, the second play in this volume. This was followed, after the normal interval of two years, by *Little Eyolf* (1894), our third play and by *John Gabriel Borkman*

*I would refer readers to the first few pages of that volume for a few general, introductory comments on Ibsen's thought as it is reflected in the prose plays.

(1896), our fourth. After that, only one, *When We Dead Awaken*, remained to be written and as this was unfinished at Ibsen's death, the series of his plays may in a sense be said to end with the last three in the present volume. But in fact all four, including *Rosmersholm*, are closely related in ideas, in form, and in style; they represent between them some of the noblest thought and the finest dramatic art in the whole of his work.

Yet a change has come over both thought and art, for, as I have suggested, Ibsen is no longer concerned so much with man in relation to society as with man alone with his own mind and with the consequences not only of his actions but of his dreams. The cardinal points of his philosophy are not changed. Truth is still sacred and the man who betrays it in his heart will still destroy himself and maim the lives of those who love him. But the recognition of truth, and of certain supreme values now seen to be inseparable from it, generally takes the form of self-discovery after a long and lonely exploration prompted in part at least by some spontaneous impulse from within the mind. Confession is made only to the judge in the man's soul and to the single individual whose spirit is linked closely with his own. The community has lost or is losing its hold upon him.

The absolute demands of truth are recognized, as in all Ibsen's plays from *The Vikings* to *When We Dead Awaken*, but now truth is seen to be linked inseparably with the cardinal virtues or values, of freedom, responsibility, love, innocence, and joy. Freedom of the spirit, freedom to live and to act is, in all Ibsen's work, intimately dependent upon truth in the heart and the relationship was already suggested in *Peer Gynt* and in *Pillars of the Community*. The recognition of responsibility, without which there can be no growth to adult stature, is also present, if only by implication, in *Peer Gynt*; but it first finds overt expression in the late plays, where it forms one of the main themes in *The Lady from the Sea* and *Little Eyolf* and is implicit in the last scenes of *Rosmersholm*. Again, in all these, it is the recognition of truth that sets the characters free for growth and responsibility. Love itself is so close to truth as to seem almost an aspect of it in the earlier *Peer Gynt* and the later *Little Eyolf*; the theme of the loveless marriage, begun in *The Vikings* and a subsidiary theme in *Pillars of the Community*, becomes again the centre of the action in *John Gabriel Borkman*, where Ella Rentheim's words are an echo, after some forty years, of Hjørdis's in *The Vikings*. Joy, again, which is killed by 'the lies and the shams' and lives only in the light of truth and of that innocence which is the sign of truth, comes into full possession of its rights in these late plays. The problem of its nature lies, it is true, behind many of the later passages in *Emperor and Galilean* and its ghost walks, along with others, in Mrs Alving's memory of her dead husband; but in nearly all the late plays there is at one point or other a deliberate contrast between those who have 'the joy of life' and those who kill it in the name of duty. Rebekka, Hilde, Rita, Mrs Wilton, Maja, all bear triumphant witness to its power at some phase of the spirit's growth; but in *Rosmersholm* the intricate relation between joy, nobility, innocence, and truth is so analysed by the two chief characters as to illuminate all the passages in the earlier plays, while in *The Master Builder* Mrs Solness, with her morbid yet pathetic clinging to 'duty', calls forth from Hilde at once the sanest defence of the righteousness of joy and some of the most irresponsible deeds committed in its name.

Truth, freedom, responsibility, love, innocence, joy, these are among the dominant themes of the late plays and their evaluation by the characters is a large part of the subject-matter; events, deeds, and motives are read and re-read in the light of these values and the light itself increases as the significance grows clear. But because all the others derive from or depend on the first, upon the practice of truth in the heart, there is continuous self-examination, not only of the deeds and motives of the moment but of those of the past and of a past that recedes ever further and further until the initial act or thought is disclosed that has set the whole process at work. If we had to describe in one phrase the subject-matter shared by all these late plays, we should probably call it spiritual exploration; it is in fact, in most cases, an examination of conscience without benefit of clergy.

This spiritual exploration dictates the form characteristic of these late plays; the long journey back into the past that is to be revalued, the slightness of the action in the present, the imminence of the spiritual climax, and the intimacy of the thought to be revealed determine at once the sparsity of event and the rich and subtle implications of the dialogue. Since Ibsen's plays, from *Brand* onwards and to some degree before it, had been concerned with the assessment of conduct, with the judgements of the characters upon each other and the implicit judgement of the play itself, the habit of reflection had been early established among them. But reflection, not upon the deed of the moment but upon the whole course of the man's life, first finds full expression in the apocalyptic fifth act of *Peer Gynt*. In the plays that follow, from *Pillars of the Community* onwards, the re-assessment has to be transferred from the domain of some visionary Last Judgement to that of the immediate world in which the plays of social criticism are set. This is done, perhaps can only be done, by translating vision into the form of some overt confession, declaration, or defence made by the character who is brought to judgement; he must, that is to say, render some account of his life to himself or to his confessor and to do this he must look back upon his past, disentangle motives, and acknowledge the bearings of his action. Such discussions of past acts and conduct form some of the most memorable scenes of *Pillars of the Community*, *A Doll's House*, *Ghosts*, and in some degree of *The Wild Duck*. Now, in the later plays, where the active agency is within rather than outside the man, the impulse of his own conscience rather than an incursion from the world of men, the problem of revealing these findings in dialogue becomes one of manifold difficulty and complexity. Here the dramatist must depend often upon half-unconscious disclosures, upon those overtones of thought that suddenly reveal the travelling mind and the point it has reached in its pilgrimage. He must prompt or evoke the discoveries and elicit their disclosure partly by the words of the other characters, often by phrases used by chance, without any specific intention of evoking the images or releasing the memories that follow from them. He must give over this dialogue, with its potentiality for many-dimensional travel, into the hands of characters who are, to themselves and to each other, unknown worlds of thought and motive. And by their very doubt and questioning of each other's motives and meanings they must find their way back, through paths less visible to themselves than to the readers, to the origin of their actions and to the perception of their guilt. *Rosmersholm* is perhaps the supreme example of the dramatic technique that lifts veil after veil from the past both of action and of motive, and, while the events move forward in time, leads us further and further back into that hidden world. And so, as the play progresses from cause to effect, the characters, on their spiritual exploration, and we with them, regress from effect to cause.

But *Rosmersholm*, if it is the finest of its kind, is not alone; for all the late plays are to some extent related to it in technique as they are all (with the exception of *Hedda Gabler*) related in content. *John Gabriel Borkman* perhaps stands next to it in the final and finished simplicity with which it uses and modifies this technique. Here the problem of disclosure is made easier by the character of Borkman, a man of genius wholly preoccupied with his inner world and fully articulate, but the problem of revealing the self-discovery before he has himself acknowledged it becomes correspondingly more intricate. Beside these two, the techniques of *The Master Builder* and *Little Eyolf* seem at first of a different order; but this merely because we are not solely concerned in either play with the revaluation of the past under the shadow of imminent catastrophe. There is a future in *Little Eyolf* and the play travels forward into it; the elucidation of the past is there to serve that future almost as in *Pillars of the Community*. There might have been a future for Halvard Solness and I think we are never wholly convinced that the end, though a true image of the probable effect of Hilde's fantasies, is necessarily an inevitable effect. But *Rosmersholm* and *John Gabriel Borkman* stand upon the very edge of doom; beyond that black curtain no future is possible in this world. A terrible dilemma, logical as it is relentless, and deriving directly from Rebekka's sin against truth, makes it impossible for Rosmer to trust her except in death. And the last hours of Borkman's illusionary life have already begun when Ella Rentheim breaks in upon his retreat bringing in the death-dealing air of truth together with the icy wind from the fjelds.

Perhaps it is inevitable that technical problems of such intricacy as these should be solved or appear to be solved in part by the use of what is often called symbolism.* I prefer to regard this rather as imagery and I believe that in all these plays it has only a subsidiary part, often comparable to that of iterative verbal imagery in Elizabethan drama. That it is there is undeniable; it guides us and illuminates our reading of meanings often hard to discern; the white

---

* This question has been treated most interestingly and in much detail by John Northam in *Ibsen's Dramatic Method* (Faber and Faber, 1953). I refer my readers to it for a full study of this aspect of Ibsen's technique.

horses of *Rosmersholm*, the weather, the lighting are all touches that guide us as they have done since the earliest of Ibsen's middle plays. But to suggest that there is a mystery or a stubborn refusal to serve the ends of the play in the imagistic material in, say, *The Master Builder* is, I think, to mistake Ibsen's intention here and to lose sight of his lifelong habit in using this sensitive medium for cross-lighting.* Solness, to continue the instance I have chosen, has a liking (which is almost an obsession) for certain delusions such as the presence at his elbow of mysterious powers that pander to his craving for dominion; it is part of his psychological condition and he betrays that fact by his evasions when Hilde pins him down in the matter of the crack in the flue. If he had had the stature of a Borkman and fourteen years of solitary brooding to confirm him, he too would have built himself an impregnable image, as unshakeable as the spirits of the mine. But this imagery is all within his own mind; inconsistent, obscure, and obsessive as it is, it is not Ibsen's, as are the coffin ships of *Pillars*, and whatever havoc it plays with Solness's imagination, it does not damage the structure of the play. One dominant piece of imagery we may legitimately trace through the last three of our four plays, that of the mountains, which play a formative part in the thoughts and emotions of Alfred Allmers, Hilde Wangel, and John Gabriel Borkman, becoming a force beneficent or destructive in their lives as in those of Brand and Peer Gynt before them or of Arnold Rubek after them.

Rosmersholm, the first of our group, belongs to that relatively small group of plays (the *Prometheus Bound* of Aeschylus being the earliest) in which the events that form the plot are crises or conflicts in the minds of the characters rather than actual happenings; to the drama, that is, of inward rather than of outward event. Admittedly no tragedy, nor any other kind of serious play, can exist without both an inward and an outward sequence of events, but the interreactions

* His control of the medium may be traced from an early stage of Ibsen's work; certainly by the time of the writing of *Pillars of the Community* he had subordinated imagery completely to the service of the play. The 'coffin ships' there fulfil three functions; they are agents in final stages of the plot, they stand out as representative instances of the unscrupulous dealings of Bernick, Vigeland, and Sandstad, and they are finally – but only in the last place – images of the moral rottenness of the community of which these three are the 'pillars'. In all the later plays I find the same threefold and wholly functional use of visual imagery and not even *The Master Builder* is an exception.

and the relative proportions of the two may vary widely. In Shakespearean tragedy, there is both balance and intermixture; the mind of Hamlet makes a long and lonely pilgrimage marked by successive stages, but the series of coordinated events in the world that surrounds him affects and is affected by this inward progression; there is continuous interplay between them and, though each affords matter for a continuous story, neither escapes for long the influence of the other. But in plays like *Rosmersholm* the outward plot is reduced both in dimensions and power throughout the greater part of the play, so that it becomes a mere vehicle for the significant, inward plot. To attempt to describe what happens on this outward level would be to record a number of visits and conversations unaccompanied by deeds or, until the end, by decisions that lead to deeds. The main plot of the play is to be found instead in the series of hard-won victories by which Rebekka's soul affirms its allegiance to the conversion it has experienced, defining it ever more clearly, until the final perception demands expression in the outward drama, overwhelming her own life and the House of Rosmer.

We have already noticed that the play leaves the impression of moving at once forward and backward in time, but in fact, this is not precisely what happens, for the regression is more natural and less systematic than this; neither the order in which the past facts are disclosed to us nor the order of Rebekka's exploration is a precise reversal of the past order of events. But our impression is just in so far as we travel further and further into the past and nearer and nearer to the roots of her problem with the movement of the main subject, the revelation of Rebekka's own nature to herself. In fact, in the second and third acts, the significant events are revealed to us (and sometimes, simultaneously, their meaning to her) in an order which is approximately the reverse of their original progress, so that her exploration of her past and her revaluation of it do thus travel backwards in time. After this has been disentangled there follow Rebekka's two confessions, which describe the main phases of her mental progress in their original order: the half-true, half-false confession made to Kroll and Rosmer at the end of Act III and the final and wholly true one made to Rosmer at the end of Act IV. At this point and not until this is her self-knowledge complete.

Moreover, each of the characters in this drama has its own past

13

and its own soul's tragedy brought about by the past actions of one or more of the other four characters. And so each, even of the subordinate figures, turns out upon inspection to be studied with an intimate sympathy. The domineering Kroll whose judgements are so often right but whose very virtues alienate, the man who, in any committee meeting, could be relied on to lose ten votes for his cause every time he spoke for it, suddenly checks our exasperation by a moment's reference to the love he once felt for Rebekka; in that clumsy, shame-faced recollection he becomes a living being. Brendel is a study of a rarer kind. On one side he is the eternal beach-comber, the man who has refused the compulsions of society and had the courage to live life in his own way; it is this side which makes the deepest impression on Rosmer, so that after Brendel's departure, he suddenly takes the initiative in his talk with Kroll. But the other side is a brief but penetrating study of the half-artist, the man who pretends to know the 'mysterious rapture of creation' in its 'rough outline', but cannot stoop to the dull task of 'writing it down'. Brendel has, in fact, some notion of the first stage of the artistic process, that of imaginative conception, but none whatever of the strenuous task of communication which alone makes the process complete. The world knows plenty of these self-deceivers, but not all of them are as gorgeous in their protective colouring. And Ibsen, who gave us, in Rubek, a study of a genuine artist who ultimately betrayed his art, knows well the complementary character of Brendel, who mistakes fantasy for creation. His precise opposite is Peer Gynt, the genuine poet *manqué*, who evades his desperate calling and chooses fantasy to avoid the discipline of the imaginative life. Paradoxically, Peer's is the more reverent attitude, for he has not destroyed his vision by putting it into 'common words'. Rebekka is deceived by Brendel's rhetoric, which poses as poetic experience, and accepts his magniloquent claim as something fine. A poet would have judged him more sternly. But Brendel does not escape with his delusions. When we meet him for the second time, something – and surely not the contact with the gutter, which must have been familiar? – has shown him that his horn of plenty has all along been empty and has made him homesick for 'the great nothingness'. He too has suffered a conversion by a vision of truth; for him as for Peer Gynt, the first stage of that is perhaps Yeats's recognition that 'Where there is nothing there is

God'. His renewed contact with Rosmer has not been without effect
and he is ready to perish into reality. The Rosmer way of life has
ennobled him too. For it does ennoble, even if it 'kills joy'.

Each of these characters has his own distinctive language; syntax,
vocabulary, and rhythms all image the mind. Rosmer speaks the
grave, natural prose of an old-fashioned gentleman; Kroll passes,
when roused, from his slightly pompous manner, with its occasional
German constructions, into the language of the platform and sometimes to that of the hustings; Mrs Helseth's idiom is homely and
wholesome; Brendel's a bewildering confusion of the colloquial and
the inflated, full of clichés and imperfectly remembered foreign
phrases; Mortensgaard's a flashy mixture of the colloquial and racy,
but, when he is strongly moved, plain and manly; Rebekka's is at once
the easiest and the most direct, changing from fluency to terseness as
the tension grows.

Through this play, as through most of Ibsen's prose dramas, runs
that pattern of words which serves some of the evocative purposes of
imagery in poetic drama. The recurring references to the mill-race, to
the House of Rosmer, and to the Rosmer view of life keep certain
significant facts before us; the constant repetition of words like 'apostate', 'emancipation', 'innocence', 'nobleman', 'joy' serves to define
the points of balance and of tension in the world of ideas. The white
horse of the first two acts and the white horses of the third have the
same effect, but their function is half that of true images; the silent
messengers of death, rushing out of the darkness, belong to the hidden
world of strange thoughts and untamed passions that lies close about
the new Rosmersholm, with its light, its joy, and the freedom of its
liberal thought. Ibsen first called his play 'Hvide heste', but the title
he finally chose lays the emphasis on the more potent spiritual force.

It is this emphasis laid on the House of Rosmer by the title of the
play that points also to the Rosmer way of life as its centre. 'The
Rosmer view of life does ennoble ... but it kills joy.' True. But in
our first tragic bewilderment we sometimes forget the obverse of
this truth: if it kills joy, yet it does ennoble. The play, for all the
delicacy of its poetic structure, is as stern as any that Ibsen wrote.
What a man sows he must reap. 'Where I have sinned, it is right I
should expiate.' The final suicide is not merely the solution of the
pitiless dilemma in which Rebekka's lies and Rosmer's impercipience

have entangled them both; it is an atonement for their sins which, even if mistaken, is made joyful because it at once expiates and unites. 'Nu er vi to *et*'; on no other terms could they be one. That these were the only terms is the result of the working of a stern moral law. But of their duty under that law they have no doubt and of the nature of their acceptance there is no question. Here at last Ibsen speaks clearly with Wordsworth's voice: 'Nor know we anything so fair As is the smile upon thy face.' Their solution has not the sanity of Rita's and Alfred's, nor the radiance of Peer's and Solveig's, still less the sublimity of Rubek's and Irene's; thus far they are, indeed, 'sinful creatures'. But upon it are inscribed nevertheless the words which go in truth to the heart of them all: 'Nu er vi to *et*'.

In *The Master Builder*, as in *John Gabriel Borkman* (or, for the matter of that, *Brand* and *Peer Gynt*), our imaginations are filled by the central character who gives his name to the play. All four men have in greater or less degree what we may fitly call genius; with all four Ibsen himself has a peculiar sympathy, close, and personal. And in all four the genius is in some degree thwarted, twisted by fate or by something alien in the character; and so in all four there is some perversity, obsession, or delusion which serves at once to compensate for the frustration and to perpetuate it. Brand and Borkman are the heroic members of this fraternity; Peer Gynt and Solness (who have here something in common with the wholly unheroiç Hjalmar Ekdal) choose delusions that spare them encounters with those implacable facts upon which Brand and Borkman make war.

But whereas Peer Gynt evades the claims of his genius, Solness has prostituted his. He seems to have yielded early to the temptation to win his way in part at least by the compelling power over other minds which is an incidental accompaniment of genius. We meet him in middle-life when the exercise of this power has become almost automatic; he imposes his will without scruple upon the impressionable Kaja, absorbing her life for his own purposes as he has done long since with Aline, as he once did casually, in a forgotten moment, with Hilde. But he himself has not escaped unharmed; to avoid the plain admission of his ruthlessness he has built a myth and has succeeded in half-convincing himself that he is at once the director and victim of strange, daemonic powers, a kind of modern practitioner of white magic whose servants have ended by dictating their own terms. The myth has no foundations (hence perhaps his obsession with the 'foundation' of Hilde's castle in the air) and he betrays himself helplessly when Hilde's common sense attempts to pin him down to fact and expose his theory as nonsense.* Certain of his other superstitions, though they too are a part of his punishment, are in fact only reasonable deductions which reveal, by way of contrast, his fundamental, harsh good sense; he has richly deserved the assault from the younger generation and is quite right in expecting it to be ruthless when it comes; he has in truth injured Aline, not, indeed, through causing her house to burn down by ill-wishing it, but by such ruthless acts as cutting up the garden of her estate into small holdings.

But if Solness has ruined his moral fibre by yielding to the temptation to exploit the effect of his power over his fellows, the very taking of this road has been in part the result of his circumstances. He tells us that he was a boy from the country and we realize that he is a gifted artist, with a powerful imagination, who has never had contact with his peers or enjoyed the stimulus of fair chances. He is not an architect because he had never learnt enough; he is only a master builder. Characteristically, he never blames this homely circumstance for his conduct; he hides from himself in a myth of daemonic powers and strange compulsions. Where John Gabriel Borkman had national pre-eminence and dreamed, not unjustifiably, of international fame, Solness remains one of Ibsen's small-town men, with great local success, like Karsten Bernick, but, unlike Karsten, with an avid imagination. He is the only major figure in the four plays of this volume who makes no self-discovery; the others all pass from self-deception into a measure of self-judgement, while he goes to his death in pursuit of a vain image of himself. With bitter irony and with absolute fidelity to fact, Ibsen leads him to destruction by the agency of the only one of his victims who had strength enough to challenge him to make good his pretensions.

For Hilde Wangel's is no submissive spirit; she has courage, an unbroken will, and a faith in the righteousness of joy which is more

* He escapes by changing the subject, swiftly but not very adroitly, when Hilde (in the second act) follows up too closely the relationship between the crack in the flue and the fire which broke out in a quite different part of the house.

than mere animal spirits. Like Regine before her, she recognizes the claims of joy, but what was housed coarsely in Regine is in Hilde part of a character which, though weak in imagination, is yet sensitive, and though eager and impetuous, is yet generous. Halvard Solness's careless words of ten years before have determined the direction of her dreams and in reaction against the traditions of her world she can fancy herself a troll and a bird of prey. But pity and tenderness are still there, uncorrupted and unperverted; her innate and impulsive affectionateness overcame Aline's long habit of silence and once this has happened the troll and the bird of prey vanish. When Aline has become a living person to her she can no longer take Halvard away; she cannot do it – not 'to a person I *know*'. She does not balance the relations between the principles of 'joy' and 'duty' as Mrs Alving had done; youth is still too strong in her to do more than protest against the sacrifice committed in the name of duty, but no character but Hilde's could have stood between Aline's and Halvard's so clearly illuminating both and the relationship between them.

For Aline Solness is, as we have suggested, in some sense a complementary study to Mrs Alving, a picture of the principle of duty exerting unchecked control. At no time can she have had a tithe of Mrs Alving's strength, intelligence, and inherent sanity. She is perhaps more nearly akin to the dead mother of Gregers Werle, whose eyes 'were clouded at times', who had also married a man full of the joy of life and had been destroyed in the contest with it. These three studies, in different proportions, different media, and different focusses, in fact illuminate each other; in each case the husband – Captain Alving, Haakon Werle, or Halvard Solness – brought to the union a native joy in life, while the wife brought a sense of duty and convention that wrecked her own life and destroyed or maimed her husband's. It is small wonder then that the meeting of Hilde Wangel and Aline Solness, in the latest of the three plays, is charged with explosive force and danger. If Hilde had met Mrs Alving she would have found her own hope and faith confirmed by the older woman's logically built philosophy, but she meets instead the wife of Halvard Solness, a pitiful victim of her own neuroses and her husband's boisterous genius. (And one cannot repress a suspicion that Aline Solness would have made an excellent wife for Alfred Allmers; she would have brought no disconcerting passion to the union and would have believed to the end in the great, solid book on 'Human Responsibility').

What Ibsen chooses to tell us of her suggests a low-spirited and timid nature ready, even in youth, to cross the border into morbidity.* She loved her dolls long after she was married; she loved the old house and the garden, the pictures (so like those on the walls of Rosmersholm), the old dresses handed down for generations, the old trinkets and jewels. It is very doubtful whether she loved Solness when she married him; all we know is that she loved the dolls. The sudden loss of home and children at once served to throw her back still further into obstinate conservatism; she became the very embodiment of 'duty', its voluntary and determined victim. If all had gone well, the joy in Halvard's nature might have saved her not only from her temperament and training but from the strain of his own ruthless vitality. (For he, in his turn, would have done better to marry Rita's 'gold and green forests' and Rita's temperament to boot.) But all did not go well with Aline Solness and there was nothing in Halvard's impercipient and, later, propitiatory kindliness to protect her from the shock of her loss and from the daily strain of his vitality. Even the privacy that had consoled her went, for the people in the new little houses could look in on her all day and, unlike her sunny, successful husband, she could not live in public. And so she remains, at the time of the play, a solitary, black-clad figure, moving silently from one act of duty to another, but never emancipating herself, as Mrs Alving did, by examining, understanding, judging, or condemning. The three characters at the centre of the play are bound together by ideas, principles, deceptions, and self-deceptions, in a deep-rooted conflict, to the destruction of their lives and happiness.

Little Eyolf stands a little apart from the other three plays; there are unusual features in its subject-matter and character grouping and it has sometimes puzzled its readers. But it is closely akin to the others in structure and ideas and the character of Alfred Allmers, sometimes hard to analyse and yet of profound interest, throws light not only

* For it is clear that at the time of her marriage the idea of duty had already the same kind of hold on her that it had on Mrs Alving in her youth. The dialogue between Hilde and Solness in Act II makes it clear that the children's death was caused not by the fire but by Aline's insistence on her duty and her refusal to acknowledge this truth is revealed in the dialogue between her and Hilde in Act III.

upon those that surround him in the play but upon some of his pre-decessors. Some hints of this reach us through the temporary re-grouping at the beginning of Act II, when Borghejm and Rita are drawn together and Asta and Alfred resume their old relationship. This is a natural grouping, according to temperament. The pattern ordained by nature had been destroyed by accidents, such as Asta's and Alfred's illusion about their blood-relationship, without which Alfred's infatuation for Rita would never have carried him into a marriage for gain that involved a betrayal of love only one degree less surely than those of Sigurd and Karsten Bernick before him or Borkman after him.

But the original lie in Alfred's soul goes further back than this and is of a slightly different kind; it is a misconception of his own powers which leads him into self-deception, into 'lies and shams' that destroy Eyolf's life and maim three more. For Alfred Allmers is a man who has overstrained himself by building an image, not, like Solness, of a man possessed of daemonic powers, but of a noble, serious-minded, and responsible human being, and then forcing himself to be that person without reference to what was in him. Fate or accident has helped to send him along this road, first by giving him the adoring and uncritical love of a devoted younger sister and by isolating the two orphans in their joint absorption in his career, and then by dazzling Rita's common sense through her own passion. The common sense reasserts itself, it is true, long before the play begins, but by then the great book on 'Human Responsibility' has established its stranglehold on the House of Allmers. It has become his justification for his marriage, for Rita's gold and her green forests had set him free for his life-work; Asta still believes unhesitatingly and for Little Eyolf whatever his father writes must be 'worth a lot'. Rita's pas-sionate love of life, put calmly aside by Alfred as something that must submit to the law of change, sets up in her an intolerable conflict which ends in possessive jealousy, but Alfred pursues his illusion ruthlessly until just before the opening of the play. Then, but not till then, some stifled misgiving drives him up to the mountains; there the process of self-discovery begins, to be driven onward by the death of Eyolf and only to be resolved by his final capitulation and the acknowledgement that he has failed in his responsibility not only to the human race and to Eyolf, but to his sister and to his wife.

In the interval, during the course of the play, he has revealed some strange and unlovable features which are yet hardly the essentials of the man. He has become an egoist, something of a prig, a sentimentalist with easy surface feelings and with the emotional callousness of a spoilt child or an intellectual half-god. He is blind to the depth of Asta's distress and he exposes Rita's motives with the ruthlessness of a creature itself infallible and flawless.* In all this there is a terrible irony and yet Ibsen convinces us that there is more in him than Alfred himself or any of the others have seen, that this man's journey in the wilderness with Sintram's Companion was a true illumination, that nature did indeed speak to him as to Brand, to Hilde, to John Gabriel, and to Irene and Rubek. Almost he seems to say with Wordsworth, 'The hand of death rests lightly on the man Who has been born and dies among the mountains'. And at the end of the play, when the pompous diction leaves him and the very syntax of his speech rises into simplicity, his grief, his new-won honesty and humility touch our hearts.

Just as he is not, I believe, the noble figure he thinks himself (and has persuaded some of his readers to think him), so he is not contemptible. He may lack tragic stature, but that, in the nature of the case, is of the essence of his tragedy. He is no fool, however deeply he deceives himself. The people who inhabit Ibsen's late tragedies are not fools – unless it be those half-seen minor figures like Foldal in *John Gabriel Borkman*, who are in some measure God's Fools. The major characters, whether revealed as partly lovable or as mainly repellent, are active intelligences; they are worth the pain of making and of breaking. And among them we cannot refuse Allmers his place. There are moments when he terrifies us, when his bland, serene acceptance of another's damnation chills the blood,** but he is not conceived satirically or without pity. He is to be reckoned with.

Yet his very self-deception springs from a fundamental weakness, from a lack of passion and energy which makes him unequal to the world about him and gives him an unconscious craving for shelter

---

* As when he corners her (in Act II) and extracts the confession that love with her is not stronger than death.

** He meets Rita's passionate demands in Act II (p. 260) with a mild indifference that links him at once with the later Einar in *Brand* or with Solveig's father, who placidly assures us that Peer's soul is undoubtedly 'Quite lost'.

and protection. It is not for nothing that Ibsen shows him in the play as a man of normally placid emotions surrounded by passionate natures. Whether these natures are frank and rich like Rita's, quiet and half-hidden like Asta's, overstrained like Eyolf's, warped like the Rat Wife's, or buoyant and radiant like Borghejm's, all five of the people grouped about him in the play are more passionate than he. Yet he, in this less powerful than any of them, must sustain, command, and dominate the group, as at once the master of a great estate and the leader of thought and conduct. The strain is terrible; he bows under responsibilities that Rosmer carried unconsciously and it is natural enough that it is he and not Rosmer who writes a book on responsibility. But he is not in fact capable of holding authority over one of these people on what Peer Gynt would have called the footing of 'personality'. By nature he is mild and reflective, a walker in quiet ways. His feeling for Asta is probably the most natural thing left to him by the time we meet him in the play and we know that so long as he thought she was his sister he could live with her as a sister, contented and undisturbed. Her discovery that they are not brother and sister brings no shock or illumination to him comparable to the distress it brings to her. There is even a moment (though this may be in part defiance) when he refuses to admit that their new knowledge need interfere with their affection. In truth, the other characters all have in common that capacity for intense attachment which he lacks, and sometimes he seems to stand in bewilderment, looking from one to another, like a man listening to a conversation in a language he does not know.

When we go on to *John Gabriel Borkman* we meet again the balance more familiar in Ibsen's late plays, the battle of the strong, where at the centre of the play stand three natures of unflinching determination joined in a conflict more close and pitiless even than that of *Ghosts*. Here again we find the last phase of a tale of retribution for ancient woe and wrong. Gunhild and Ella, who once fought for possession of John Gabriel, now fight for Erhart, his son, and lose him too – to the adversaries they had forgotten to reckon with, youth and life itself. John Gabriel, who had committed the crime never forgiven in Ibsen's plays, pays for his mercenary marriage with the triple loss of wife, son, and the peace of his soul itself. But John Gabriel is of giant's stature and Gunhild is of the stock of the Valkyries; it is not for nothing that echoes of that early saga play, *The Vikings at Helgeland*, run through this, the last of the completed plays. 'Noblest at the close', he reveals, behind the last phase of their strife, the long history of three heroic spirits, embittered, broken with grief or sustained by obsession that is almost vision. In their conflict, and indeed almost incidentally to it, lesser men go down; the thousands that Borkman's speculations had ruined have hardly a thought and Foldal is not the only man run over by someone else's singleness of purpose. Borkman dies on the mountain-side as do his peers, Brand and Rubek; an ice-cold hand grips his heart and they are overwhelmed by avalanches. All three are men whose stature is to be matched not among their fellow-men, but only among the high mountains themselves.

Yet in this play whose colours seem subdued to the gloom of that stately, overheated room where Gunhild Borkman is always cold or to the black or snow-covered mountain up which Borkman climbs to his last vision and his death, where the voices themselves of the three contestants sound with the ring and clangour of rock and metallic ores, there are moments of distant radiance and the chime of silver sledge-bells. The eager youth of Erhart and Fanny Wilton sweeps through and out, leaving the gloom only deeper, the mood only confirmed, the voices, stern or harsh, as articulate, as clearly defined as ever. The helpless figure of Frida is caught up in this flight and vanishes. But Foldal returns. He returns full of delight because his daughter, the only being who understood him, has left him for the glory of the world that he has missed. The sledge that ran over him, hurt his foot, and broke his spectacles turns out to be the very one which carried her, and his joy at the realization of this is pure, like a child's. He hobbles away in the snow carrying the good tidings to his unhappy home, one of God's Fools crossing the action of the play, one of those 'weak things of the world' chosen 'to put down the strong'. The gloom of the night closes down again and John Gabriel turns to the mountain to begin his last journey. But we have recognized the unmistakable quality with which Ibsen sometimes invests certain figures in the late plays, the homely, selfless, slightly foolish figures, like Aunt Juliane Tesman, whose joy no man taketh from them. After this, further illumination of the battle of the strong is needless.

The structure of the play is no less memorable. This alone calls for far more discussion than space will allow, but one or two suggestions may be made. The opening passages of the first act offer one of the most interesting examples that I know of a technique apparently descriptive and yet in fact essentially dramatic; some sixteen pages, and those at the very opening of a play, consisting of conversation between two characters. But the characters are the twin sisters, Ella and Gunhild, and the talk is of their past lives and defines the terms of their lifelong conflict. Our imaginations are in fact focussed upon John Gabriel and upon his son in a mood of nervous tension where, while learning the relations of all four people, we wait for the expected arrival of Erhart. Character, experience, and intention are all revealed and distinguished. Not until the second act does John Gabriel appear, but he has been with us in spirit almost from the beginning. There is no pause between the acts; the music which drives Erhart out at the end of the first is still sounding when the curtain goes up upon the second, introducing Borkman for the second time. The effect of these successive portraits is cumulative; we see him first through the eyes of the two women, who give two radically different interpretations of him, and we are then left face to face with the man, to make yet another for ourselves with the help this time of Foldal. And so when Ella Rentheim meets him nearly half of the play has gone to prepare us for her denunciation and for his resistance.

The dialogue throughout is naked and definite. Gone are the overtones characteristic of *Rosmersholm*, *The Master Builder*, and *Little Eyolf*, in which the characters grope their way in broken sentences to understanding of themselves, each other and the future before them. The three central figures of *John Gabriel Borkman* have no future; they speak already as from the edge of the grave. They have nothing or very little to discover about the past; like Mrs Alving, each has spent the long, lonely years exploring and interpreting it. They meet to denounce, and deliver the judgements of those years and though their readings of their common past are radically different they build no bridges across the gulfs. Only within a moment of his death does John Gabriel half acknowledge the righteous judgement of Ella Rentheim and only after that death do the two twin sisters agree in their reading of their empty lives. To the end there has been no faltering either in purpose or speech; moments of passion or of grief have passed over them all, but except in the revival of Ella's selfless love for Erhart, none of them has changed in purpose or direction. Such tenacity of thought and will finds its natural expression in a language far other than the sensitive, flexible medium of the other late plays. Of the three, only Ella knows that she has less than a year to live; but in fact all, as we have said, speak as if before a black drop scene on a shallow stage that admits of no movement but in one line, of little change of lighting, and of none of the properties of the theatre of the world. But if there is little colour in the dialogue, there is no obscurity and nothing commonplace. The spirits that John Gabriel loved, the spirits of the mines and of the glittering metals hidden in the fjelds, have invaded his spirit and speak in his speech; hard, clear, and definite, ringing and gleaming but immovable, they reveal themselves in the very form of his language. And a like quality has touched, by some rare transference, the minds of the two women. There is neither time nor room for obscurity or evasion in this, perhaps the greatest play that even the Master Builder ever wrote.

Of the specific problems that confront a translator I have mentioned a few in the earlier volume (pp. 19–21) and I have little now to add to what I have said there. The major semantic and syntactical distinctions between any two languages will always be focal points for these problems; other, minor or incidental difficulties may also arise at special points. A translator may even stray into absurdities, being immersed in the language from which he is translating and forgetting comic overtones momentarily associated with an apparently blameless phrase in his own. In the theatre these do not as a rule survive into production. They are greeted with a shout of delight at the first rehearsal and promptly re-adjusted.

The settings in these four plays are more varied than those of the first volume which were uniformly indoor sets. The whole of *Rosmersholm*, it is true, is set indoors and so are the first three acts of *John Gabriel Borkman*. But the last acts of *The Master Builder* and *John Gabriel Borkman* and the second and final acts of *Little Eyolf* are played out of doors. The indoor sets are easily managed, but the outdoor scenes make some demands on the producer. The fourth act of *John Gabriel Borkman* even requires a moving backcloth,* though this

* See on this point John Northam: *Ibsen's Dramatic Method*, p. 206, second footnote.

is not in itself an insuperable difficulty.

Costume, as always, presents a few problems. I think it is better that these plays should be produced in the costumes of their own periods and settings, based for instance on those in the collection of the Folk Museum at Oslo. But most of us, when reading, visualize characters and customs in terms of our own life and I have accordingly turned bonnets into hats, a morning-dress into a house-coat, and evening tea into supper when it seemed necessary to the continuity of the reading. For the same kind of reason 'Rektor' Kroll becomes 'Principal' or even 'Dr' in English; 'Rector' carrying an entirely wrong association in England. Other similar modifications will be evident to the reader. Occasionally, with the producer in mind, I have added a brief note (see 'Notes') to replace the hat, the house-coat, the suit-case by the garment or luggage suitable to the end of last century in Norway. I have confined these notes principally to two plays, as space was limited and this seemed enough to indicate the principles on which I worked.

The text used throughout is again that of the *Samlede Digterverker* of 1930, edited by Didrik Arup Seip.

It only remains to express again my thanks to my predecessors and to other helpers. The debt to William Archer is, as always, beyond estimate; indeed in his translations of the later plays, where the English becomes more and more flexible and dramatic, the number of classical translations increases steadily; again and again one meets in his volumes phrases that one dare not tamper with. To the translators of the Everyman edition, to Charles Archer, and to M. Prozor's standard translation into French I must also acknowledge some debts, as also to Philip Sterling for many suggestions in the rendering of *Little Eyolf*. My friend Sofie Mess again gave me generous help in clearing up problems. Finally I am indebted to Miss M. Cardwell for invaluable work in checking text and references throughout.

UNA ELLIS-FERMOR

ROSMERSHOLM

CHARACTERS

JOHN ROSMER, *owner of Rosmersholm, formerly the parish clergyman*

REBEKKA WEST, *living in Rosmer's house*

KROLL, *Rosmer's brother-in-law and the headmaster of the local school*

ULRIK BRENDEL

PEDER MORTENSGAARD

MRS HELSETH, *housekeeper at Rosmersholm*

The action takes place at Rosmersholm,
an old property near a little town on a fjord
in the west of Norway

ACT ONE

The living-room at Rosmersholm, large, old-fashioned, and comfortable. Downstage against the right-hand wall is a tiled stove dressed with fresh birch-branches and wild flowers. Further back is a door. In the back wall, a folding door to the hall. In the left-hand wall, a window and in front of it a stand with flowers and plants. By the stove is a table with a sofa and easy chairs. All round the walls hang portraits, older or more recent, of clergy, officers, and government officials in uniform. The window stands open and so does the door to the hall and the outer door of the house. Outside can be seen an alley of tall old trees leading up to the house. It is a summer evening and the sun is down.

REBEKKA WEST *is sitting in an easy chair by the window and crocheting a large white woollen shawl, which is nearly finished. Every now and then she peeps out watchfully between the flowers. After a time* MRS HELSETH *comes in from the right.*

MRS HELSETH: Hadn't I better begin to put some of the supper things on the table, Miss?

REBEKKA: Yes; do, please. Mr Rosmer's sure to be in soon.

MRS HELSETH: Isn't there a draught there, Miss, where you're sitting?

REBEKKA: Yes, there is a little. Perhaps you'd better close the window.

[MRS HELSETH *goes across and shuts the door into the hall and then goes to the window.*]

MRS HELSETH [*looking out before she closes it*]: Why, isn't that the master coming over there?

REBEKKA [*quickly*]: Where? [*Gets up.*] Yes, it's he. [*Keeps behind the curtain.*] Stand at the side. Don't let him catch sight of us.

MRS HELSETH [*moving back into the room*]: Just think, Miss — he's beginning to use the mill-path again.

REBEKKA: He went by the mill-path the day before yesterday too. [*She peeps out between the curtain and the window-frame.*] But now we shall see –

MRS HELSETH: Is he going to take the foot-bridge?

REBEKKA: That's just what I want to see. [*A moment later.*] No. He's turning off. Going up and round again today. [*She leaves the window.*] All that way round.

MRS HELSETH: Oh dear, so he is. Of course it must come hard for the master to cross over that bridge. A place where a thing like that's happened, it's –

REBEKKA [*putting her crochet-work together*]: They cling to their dead a long time here at Rosmersholm.

MRS HELSETH: If you ask me, Miss, I think it's the dead that clings to Rosmersholm so long.

REBEKKA [*looking at her*]: The dead?

MRS HELSETH: Yes, I mean it's almost as though they couldn't tear themselves away from them they've left behind.

REBEKKA: What makes you think that?

MRS HELSETH: Well, I'm sure this white horse here wouldn't be seen, if it wasn't for that.

REBEKKA: Oh yes, Mrs Helseth, what is it exactly – this about the white horse?

MRS HELSETH: Oh, it's best not to talk about it. Besides, you don't believe in that sort of thing.

REBEKKA: Do *you* believe in it?

MRS HELSETH [*going across and shutting the window*]: No, I'm not going to give you the chance of makiing fun of me, Miss. [*Looks out.*] Why – isn't that the master over there on the mill-path again?

REBEKKA [*looking out*]: That man there? [*Goes to the window.*] No, that's the Principal!

MRS HELSETH: Why, so it is. It's Dr Kroll.

REBEKKA: Well, that *is* nice, – he's coming over to see us. You see if he isn't.

MRS HELSETH: Straight over the foot-bridge, *he's* coming.

Even though she was his own sister born. Well, I'll go in
and get the supper laid, Miss.

[*She goes out to the right.* REBEKKA *stands a moment at the
window; then she smiles and nods, greeting someone outside.
It is beginning to get dark.*]

REBEKKA [*going across and speaking out through the door on the
right*]: Oh, Mrs Helseth, will you give us something
specially nice for supper please? You know all about what
Dr Kroll likes best.

MRS HELSETH [*outside*]: Yes certainly, Miss. I will.

REBEKKA [*opening the door into the hall*]: Here you are again, at
last! I'm so glad to see you, Dr Kroll.

KROLL [*in the hall, putting down his stick*]: Thanks. I'm not disturbing you, then?

REBEKKA: *You*? How can you!

KROLL [*coming in*]: Always so kind. [*Looking round.*] Rosmer's
up in his room, I suppose?

REBEKKA: No, he's out for a walk. He's been a little longer
than usual. But he's sure to be here in a minute now. [*Indicating the sofa.*] Sit down till he comes, won't you?

KROLL [*putting down his hat*]: Thank you. [*He sits down and
looks round.*] Well, well; how bright and charming you've
made the old room! Flowers everywhere.

REBEKKA: It means a lot to Mr Rosmer to have fresh, growing flowers about.

KROLL: I fancy it does to you, too.

REBEKKA: Yes, I think the smell's so refreshing. But it was a
joy we had to forego till lately.

KROLL [*nodding gravely*]: Poor Beatë couldn't stand the scent.

REBEKKA: Nor the colours either. She used to get so disturbed –

KROLL: Yes, yes, I remember. [*In a more cheerful voice.*] Well,
now, how are things going on out here?

REBEKKA: Oh, everything's going on in its quiet, placid way.
One day very like another. And all of you? Your wife –?

KROLL: Ah, my dear Miss West, don't let's talk about my affairs. In a family there's always something or other going wrong. Especially in times like these we're living in.

REBEKKA [*after a moment's pause, taking an easy chair by the sofa*]: Why is it you haven't been to see us one, single time in the whole of your holidays?

KROLL: Well, one mustn't always be on people's doorsteps –

REBEKKA: If you only knew how we've missed you –

KROLL: And besides, I've been away, you know –

REBEKKA: Yes, for a couple of weeks. You've been going round to political meetings, haven't you?

KROLL [*nodding*]: Yes, what do you say to that? Did you ever think I should turn into a political agitator in my old age? Eh?

REBEKKA [*smiling*]: Well, you've always been a bit of an agitator, Dr Kroll.

KROLL: Yes, yes; just for my own amusement. But in future it will be in real earnest. Do you ever read these radical newspapers?

REBEKKA: My dear Principal, I won't deny that –

KROLL: My dear Miss West, there's no objection to it. Nothing against your doing so.

REBEKKA: No, I don't think there is. I must keep up. Know what's going on.

KROLL: Well, under any circumstances, I shouldn't expect you, as a woman, to take sides actively in the civic dispute – civil war, I might well call it – that's raging here. But I expect you will have read the attacks these gentlemen of 'the people' have been pleased to shower upon me? The infamous abuse they have dared to think they could permit themselves?

REBEKKA: Yes, but I think you've defended yourself pretty effectively.

KROLL: Yes, I have. I must say that. For I've tasted blood now. And they shall realize that I am not the man to take up a cause and – [*Breaking off.*] But come, come. Don't let's start on that this evening. It's a sad and distressing subject.

REBEKKA: No, don't let's, Dr Kroll.

KROLL: You tell me, instead, how you really are getting on at Rosmersholm, now that you're here alone? Since our poor Beaté –?

REBEKKA: I'm really getting on quite well, thank you. Of course the place is very empty in many ways, now she's gone. And naturally we miss her and grieve for her, too. But otherwise –

KROLL: Do you think of staying on here? More or less permanently, I mean?

REBEKKA: My dear Dr Kroll, I don't think about it, one way or the other. I've got so thoroughly used to it now that I almost feel I belong here too.

KROLL: You! I should think you did, indeed!

REBEKKA: And so long as Mr Rosmer thinks I can be of any comfort or use to him – why, yes, I expect I shall probably stay.

KROLL [*looking at her with some emotion*]: You know – there's something fine about this. For a woman to let the whole of her youth slip away, as you're doing, sacrificing herself to other people.

REBEKKA: Why, what should I have had to live for if I hadn't?

KROLL: When you first came here you had that perpetual trouble with your foster father, crippled and exacting –

REBEKKA: Dr West wasn't so exacting when he was up in Finmark; you mustn't think that. It was those dreadful sea journeys that broke him up. But when we'd moved down here – well, yes, there were a couple of hard years then. Until it was all over for him.

KROLL: What about the years that came next? Weren't they harder still for you?

REBEKKA: Oh, you mustn't talk like that! When you think

how fond I was of Beatë –. And how dreadfully she needed care, poor dear, and a sympathetic companion.

KROLL: Thank you for thinking of her so charitably; it does you credit.

REBEKKA [*coming a little nearer*]: My dear Dr Kroll, you say that so kindly and sincerely that I'm sure there's no ill-feeling behind it.

KROLL: Ill-feeling? What do you mean?

REBEKKA: Well, it wouldn't be so very strange, if you did find it painful. To see an outsider like me having everything my own way, here at Rosmersholm.

KROLL: Now, how on earth –!

REBEKKA: But, you see, you don't! [*Holding out her hand.*] Thank you, dear Dr Kroll! *Thank* you!

KROLL: But where on earth could you have got an idea like that?

REBEKKA: I began to get a little worried when you took to coming here so seldom.

KROLL: Then you've certainly been on quite the wrong track, Miss West. Besides – after all, there's been no real change. All those last years of poor Beatë's unhappy life, you were already managing everything here. You and no one else.

REBEKKA: It was more like a kind of regency in Beatë's name.

KROLL: Well, in any case –. You know, Miss West, I for my part shouldn't mind at all if you –. But one mustn't say these things I suppose.

REBEKKA: What things?

KROLL: If it were to end by your taking the empty place –

REBEKKA: I have the place I want, Dr Kroll.

KROLL: In effect, yes; but not in –

REBEKKA [*interrupting him, gravely*]: Oh come, Dr Kroll! How can you sit and joke about a thing like that?

KROLL: Well, yes; our good friend John Rosmer probably feels he's had more than enough of married life. But all the same –

34

REBEKKA: You know, I almost feel like laughing at you.

KROLL: All the same –. Just tell me, Miss West – that is if you will allow me to ask – how old are you, exactly?

REBEKKA: I'm ashamed to admit it, Dr Kroll, but I'm over twenty-nine. I am now getting on for thirty.

KROLL: Ah, yes. And Rosmer – how old is he? Let me see. He's five years younger than I am. Well then, he's just over forty-three. I think it would be very suitable.

REBEKKA [getting up]: Yes; quite. Very suitable indeed. Will you stay to supper with us this evening?

KROLL: Thank you. I did think of staying, because there's something I want to talk over with our good friend. Well now, Miss West – just so that you shan't have any more foolish ideas – I will come out here every now and then as I did in the old days.

REBEKKA: Oh yes, *do* do that! [*Shaking his hands.*] Thank you! *Thank* you! You really are an awfully kind person.

KROLL [*gruffly*]: Oh, am I? Well, that's more than they say at home.

[JOHN ROSMER *comes in by the door on the right.*]

REBEKKA: Mr Rosmer, do you see who's sitting here?

ROSMER: Mrs Helseth told me.

[KROLL *gets up.*]

ROSMER [*pressing his hands; his manner gentle and subdued*]: Welcome to the house again, my dear Kroll. [*Puts his hands on Kroll's shoulders and looks into his eyes.*] You dear, old friend! I was sure things would be all right again between us some day.

KROLL: But my dear fellow, have you had that absurd fancy too – that there was something wrong?

REBEKKA [*to* ROSMER]: Isn't it wonderful to think it *was* all fancy?

ROSMER: Was it really that, Kroll? But then, why did you cut yourself off from us like that?

KROLL [*quietly and seriously*]: Because I didn't want to come here and be a living reminder of those unhappy years and of her – who died in the mill-race.

ROSMER: That was a kindly thought of yours. You are always so considerate. But there was no need whatever to stay away for that reason. Come along, let's sit on the sofa. [*They sit down.*] No, it's really not painful at all for me to think about Beatë. We talk about her every day. We feel as if she was still a part of the house.

KROLL: Do you really?

REBEKKA [*lighting the lamp*]: Yes we do, indeed.

ROSMER: It's perfectly natural. We were both so deeply attached to her. And Rebek – Miss West and I both know in our hearts that we did everything in our power for that poor, unfortunate woman. We've nothing to reproach ourselves with. And so I find there's something sweet and peaceful in thinking of Beatë now.

KROLL: You dear, splendid people! I'm going to come out and see you every day in future.

REBEKKA [*sitting down in an easy chair*]: Good. Now mind you keep your word.

ROSMER [*hesitating a little*]: My dear Kroll – the last thing I should ever have wanted was a break in our relationship. You've always seemed the natural person for me to turn to for advice as long as we've known each other. Ever since I was a student.

KROLL: Well, well. And I value that very highly too. Is there anything particular, now –?

ROSMER: There are all sorts of things I want to talk to you about, very much. To talk frankly and without any reserves.

REBEKKA: Yes, I can understand that, Mr Rosmer. I think it must be such a comfort – between old friends –

KROLL: Well, you can well believe I've even more to talk to you about. Because, as I suppose you know, I'm an active politician now.

36

ROSMER: Yes, you certainly are. Just how did it happen?

KROLL: I had to, you know. Had to, whether I liked it or not. It's impossible to stand by and be an idle spectator any longer. Now that the Radicals have got so shockingly powerful, it's high time, now –. And so I have persuaded our little circle of friends in town to draw closer together. High time too, I say!

REBEKKA [*with a slight smile*]: Isn't it in fact a little late?

KROLL: Undoubtedly it would have been better to have checked the current at an earlier point. But who could really foresee what was coming? Not I, at all events. [*He gets up and walks about the room.*] Well, now I've had my eyes opened all right. For the spirit of revolt has made its way even into the school.

ROSMER: Into the school? Not in your school, surely?

KROLL: It certainly has. In my own school. What do you think? It's come to my knowledge that the boys in the senior class – that's to say some of the boys – have had a secret society going for more than six months and been taking in Mortensgaard's paper.

REBEKKA: What, *The Lighthouse?*

KROLL: Yes. Wholesome diet for the minds of future public servants, isn't it? But the saddest part of the business is that it's the ablest boys in the class who've conspired and hatched this plot against me. It's only the dunces at the bottom of the class that have stood out.

REBEKKA: Do you feel this so keenly, Dr Kroll?

KROLL: Feel it keenly! To see myself checked and thwarted like that in my life's work. [*More quietly.*] But I feel almost like saying that that must take its course. For I've still got to tell you the worst. [*Looking round him.*] Nobody could be listening at the doors, I suppose?

REBEKKA: No, of course not.

KROLL: Well, let me tell you that the dissension and rebellion have made their way into my own household. Into my own peaceful home. They have destroyed the quiet of my family life.

ROSMER [*getting up*]: What! At home, in your own family –?

REBEKKA [*going over to* KROLL]: But, dear Dr Kroll, what's happened?

KROLL: Will you believe it, that my own children –. Well, in fact – it's Laurits that's the ringleader in the conspiracy at school. And Hilda has embroidered a red portfolio to keep *The Lighthouse* in.

ROSMER: I should never have dreamt it. Your family – in your own house –

KROLL: No, who would dream of a thing like that? In my house, where obedience and order have always reigned, where up till now there has only been the one, united purpose.

REBEKKA: How does your wife take all this?

KROLL: Why, that's the most incredible thing of all. She, who all her life – in everything, great or small – has shared my opinions and supported my views – even she tends to side with the children over many things. And now she blames *me* for what has happened. She says I repress the young people. As if it weren't necessary to –! Well, that's the sort of dissension I have going on at home. But naturally I say as little about it as possible. Things like that are best kept quiet. [*Walking about the room.*] Well, well, well, well. [*He stops by the window with his hands behind his back and looks out.*]

REBEKKA [*going over to* ROSMER *and speaking quietly and quickly;* KROLL *does not hear*]: Do it!

ROSMER [*in the same manner*]: Not this evening.

REBEKKA [*as before*]: Yes, now's the time. [*She goes across and arranges the lamp.*]

KROLL [*coming back across the room*]: Well, my dear Rosmer, now you know. You see how the spirit of the times has thrown its shadow over both my private and my professional life. Am I not to fight it – this pernicious, subversive, disruptive spirit of our time – and with all the weapons to hand? Yes, my dear fellow, that's precisely what I'm going to do. And that both in print and on the platform.

ROSMER: Why, do you think you can correct it like that?

KROLL: At any rate, I will defend the state as a citizen should. And I think it's the duty of every patriotic man to do the same, if he's at all concerned for the right. In fact, – that's my main reason for coming out here this evening. –

ROSMER: But my dear fellow, what do you mean –? What can I –?

KROLL: You're going to help your old friends. Do what the rest of us are doing. Take a hand in it, as best you can.

REBEKKA: But Dr Kroll, you know how Mr Rosmer dislikes that kind of thing.

KROLL: He must overcome that dislike now. You don't take your proper share in things, Rosmer. You sit here and shut yourself up with your historical records. Heaven knows, I recognize the importance of genealogy and all it stands for. But unhappily this is no time for that kind of pursuit. You haven't the least notion what the state of affairs is all over the country. Almost every idea's turned upside down. It's going to be a Herculean task to clear away that mass of error.

ROSMER: I'm sure it is. But I'm no good at that kind of work.

REBEKKA: And I think, you know, Mr Rosmer has come to look at life with wider opened eyes than he used to.

KROLL [with a start]: Wider opened eyes?

REBEKKA: Yes, or freer, if you like. More impartial.

KROLL: What does this mean? Rosmer, you could never be so weak as to let yourself be deceived by a mere chance, by the popular leaders' winning a temporary victory!

ROSMER: My dear fellow, you know quite well I'm no judge of politics. But I really think of late years something more like independence has developed in the thinking of individual people.

KROLL: Well! And you take it for granted that that's a good thing! However, you're mightily mistaken, my friend. Just you look into the opinions that are current among these radicals, out here and in town. They're neither more nor less than the wisdom that's proclaimed in *The Lighthouse*.

REBEKKA: True, Mortensgaard has a great influence round here, and over a good many people.

KROLL: Just to think of it! A man with a disgraceful past like that! A fellow who was thrown out of the school he taught in for immoral conduct! And *he* sets himself up as a leader of the people! And makes a success of it. Actually makes a success. And now, I gather, he's going to enlarge his paper. I know from a reliable source that he's looking for a competent assistant.

REBEKKA: I think it's rather odd that you and your friends don't start something in opposition.

KROLL: That's just what we're going to do. We bought *The County News* today. There was no difficulty about the money side of it, but – [*Turning to* ROSMER.] Well, now I come to my real errand here. It's the management, the editorial management, that's giving us trouble, you see. Tell me Rosmer, wouldn't you – for the sake of the good cause – feel called upon to take it over?

ROSMER [*half-horrified*]: I!

REBEKKA: Why, how can you think of such a thing!

KROLL: It's perfectly natural that you should have a horror of public meetings and not want to expose yourself to the treatment one gets there. But an editor's work goes on in the background, or, to be precise –

ROSMER: No, no, my dear man, you must not ask me for this.

KROLL: I should very much like to try my hand at that kind of thing myself. But it would be quite impossible for me. I'm saddled with innumerable commitments already. But you, now, – you're no longer burdened with a profession–.

Of course the rest of us will help you in every way we can.

ROSMER: I can't do it, Kroll. I'm no good at it.

KROLL: No good at it? That's just what you said when your father got you your living.

ROSMER: I was right. That's why I resigned it, too.

KROLL: Well, if you make as good an editor as you did a parson, we shall be quite satisfied.

ROSMER: My dear Kroll, I tell you, once and for all, I'm not doing it.

KROLL: Well, at any rate, you'll let us use your name, won't you?

ROSMER: My name?

KROLL: Yes, the mere name of John Rosmer will be a great help to the paper. The rest of us are reckoned confirmed party men. Indeed, I gather that I myself am denounced as an out-and-out fanatic. So we can't count on our names' getting the paper much of a circulation among the misguided masses. But you, now – you've always kept out of the fight. That gentle, honest nature of yours, your aristocratic habit of thought, your unimpeachable rectitude – they're known and appreciated by everyone round here. And then there's the respect and deference that come from your having once been a clergyman. And most of all, you know, your old and honourable family name!

ROSMER: Oh, the family name –

KROLL [*pointing to the portraits*]: Rosmers of Rosmersholm – clergymen and soldiers. Public men, trusted by their country. True gentlemen, every one of them. A family that has been here for nearly two centuries, the most influential in the district. [*Laying his hand on* ROSMER'S *shoulder.*] Rosmer, you owe it to yourself and the traditions of your race to stand in with us and defend these things – things that have hitherto been held sacred in our community. [*Turning to* REBEKKA.] What do *you* say, Miss West?

REBEKKA [*with quiet, gentle laughter*]: Dear Dr Kroll, it all sounds so ludicrous to me.

KROLL: *What?* Ludicrous?

REBEKKA: Yes. For I must tell you plainly –

ROSMER [*quickly*]: No, no – don't! Not now.

KROLL [*looking from one to the other*]: But my dear friends, what in the world –? [*Breaking off.*] Hm!

[MRS HELSETH *comes in at the door on the right.*]

MRS HELSETH: There's a man out at the back-door. He says he wants to see the master.

ROSMER [*with relief*]: Oh. Well, ask him to come in.

MRS HELSETH: Here? Into the sitting-room?

ROSMER: Yes, yes.

MRS HELSETH: But he doesn't look the kind of person to show into the sitting-room.

REBEKKA: What does he look like, Mrs Helseth?

MRS HELSETH: Well, he isn't much to look at, Miss.

ROSMER: Didn't he tell you his name?

MRS HELSETH: Yes; I think he said it was Hekman or something like that.

ROSMER: I don't know anyone of that name.

MRS HELSETH: And then he said he was called Ulrik too.

ROSMER [*with a start*]: Ulrik-Hetman! Was that it?

MRS HELSETH: Yes, Hetman. That was it.

KROLL: I'm sure I've heard that name before –

REBEKKA: Why, that was the name *he* used to write under, that extraordinary –

ROSMER [*to* KROLL]: It's Ulrik Brendel's pseudonym, you know.

KROLL: That good-for-nothing Ulrik Brendel. Quite right.

REBEKKA: So he's still alive.

ROSMER: I thought he was on tour with a theatre-company.

KROLL: The last I heard of him, he was in the workhouse.

ROSMER: Tell him to come in, Mrs Helseth.

MRS HELSETH: Very well. [*Going out.*]

KROLL: Are you really going to let that fellow into your house?

ROSMER: Why, you know he was once my tutor.

KROLL: I do. And I know he went and crammed your head with revolutionary ideas, so that your father helped him off the premises with his riding-whip.

ROSMER [*with a little bitterness*]: Father remained a commanding officer, even in his own home.

KROLL: Thank him in his grave for that, my dear Rosmer. Oh, well!

[MRS HELSETH *opens the door on the right for* ULRIK BRENDEL *and then goes out again, shutting it after him. He is a handsome man, with grey hair and beard, rather gaunt, but active and vigorous. As for his clothes, he is dressed like a common tramp, his coat threadbare, his shoes falling to pieces, and no shirt to be seen. He wears an old pair of black gloves, and has a grimy soft hat tucked under his arm and a walking-stick in his hand.*]

ULRIK BRENDEL [*uncertain for a moment, then going quickly over to the schoolmaster and holding out his hand*]: Good evening, John!

KROLL: Excuse me –

BRENDEL: Did you ever expect to see me again? And, at that, inside these detested walls?

KROLL: Excuse me – [*Pointing.*] *There* –

BRENDEL [*turning round*]: True. There we have him. John, my boy – you, whom I loved the best of –!

ROSMER [*taking his hand*]: My old teacher.

BRENDEL: In spite of certain memories, I didn't want to pass Rosmersholm without paying it a flying visit.

ROSMER: You are heartily welcome here now. You may be sure of that.

BRENDEL: Ah, and this charming lady –? [*Bowing.*] Mrs Rosmer, of course.

ROSMER: Miss West.

BRENDEL: A near relation, I take it. And the gentleman over there whom I don't know –? A colleague, I can see.

ROSMER: Dr Kroll, our headmaster.

BRENDEL: Kroll? Kroll? Wait a minute. Did you take the philology course in college?

KROLL: Yes, naturally.

BRENDEL: Why, *Donnerwetter*! Then I used to know you, man!

KROLL: Excuse me –

BRENDEL: Weren't you –?

KROLL: Excuse me –

BRENDEL: – one of those champions of virtue that got me chucked out of the debating society?

KROLL: Quite likely. But I disclaim any nearer acquaintance.

BRENDEL: Well, well. *Nach Belieben, herr doktor*. It's all the same to me. Ulrik Brendel is the man he is for all that.

REBEKKA: You're going on into town, Mr Brendel?

BRENDEL: Madam, you have hit upon the truth. From time to time I am obliged to do a stroke of work for my living. I don't do it willingly; but – *enfin* – stern necessity –

ROSMER: But my dear Mr Brendel, won't you let me do something to help you? In one way or another, I'm sure –

BRENDEL: A preposterous suggestion! Do you want to spoil the bond that binds us to each other? Never, John – never!

ROSMER: But what are you thinking of doing in town? You know, it won't be so easy for you –

BRENDEL: Leave that to me, my boy. The die is cast. I, even I who stand here before you, am engaged on a vast campaign. Vaster than all my former enterprises put together. [*To* DR KROLL.] May I be permitted to ask our professor – *unter uns* – is there a fairly decent, respectable, and sizeable public hall in your excellent town?

KROLL: The largest is the hall belonging to the Working Men's Society.

BRENDEL: Has our instructor of youth any official standing in this doubtless most worthy Society?

KROLL: I've nothing whatever to do with it.

REBEKKA [*to* BRENDEL]: You should apply to Peder Mortensgaard.

BRENDEL: *Pardon, Madame* – what kind of idiot is he?

ROSMER: What makes you think he's an idiot?

BRENDEL: Can't I hear at once, from the name, that he belongs to the lower classes?

KROLL: That's an answer I didn't expect.

BRENDEL: But I will conquer my shrinking. There's nothing else for it. When a man stands, as I do, at the turning-point of his life –. It's settled. I will establish contact with this individual – start direct negotiations –

ROSMER: Are you really serious when you say you're at a turning-point?

BRENDEL: Surely *you* know, my boy, that wherever Ulrik Brendel stands, it's always serious. You see, I am now about to put on a new man. To emerge from the modest retirement I have practised till now.

ROSMER: How –?

BRENDEL: To lay hold on life with a strong hand. Move forward. Move upward. We are breathing the atmosphere of a storm-tossed solstice. – I mean to lay my mite upon the altar of emancipation.

KROLL: *You* too –?

BRENDEL [*to all of them*]: Have the people in this part of the world much acquaintance with my various writings?

KROLL: No, I must in truth admit that –

REBEKKA: I've read a good many. My foster father had them.

BRENDEL: Then, dear lady, you have wasted your time. For they're just trash, let me tell you.

REBEKKA: Oh?

BRENDEL: What you have read, yes. My really important works, no man or woman knows. No one – but I myself.

REBEKKA: Why, how's that?

BRENDEL: Because they're not written.

ROSMER: But, my dear Mr Brendel –

BRENDEL: You know, John, I'm a bit of a sybarite. A *Feinschmecker*. Have been all my days. I believe in keeping one's joy to oneself. That way I get twice the pleasure. Twenty times. You see, when golden dreams descended upon me and enfolded me, when new thoughts were born in me, misty, momentous, to lift and bear me aloft on their wings, I shaped them into poems, visions, pictures. In rough outline, as it were – you understand.

ROSMER: Yes, yes.

BRENDEL: Ah, the joy I have known in my time, the ecstasy! The mysterious rapture of creation – in rough outline, so to speak, as I said. Applause, gratitude, fame, and the laurel crown, all these have I gathered in, my full hands trembling with joy. In my secret thoughts drinking my fill of a delight so vast, so intoxicating –!

KROLL: Hm –.

ROSMER: But never written it down?

BRENDEL: Not a word. That dull, mechanical task of writing it down has always roused a sickening aversion in me. And why, moreover, should I prostitute my own ideals, when I could have them to myself, in all their purity? But now they shall be sacrificed. It's true, I feel like a mother giving her young daughters into their husbands' arms. But I will sacrifice them, nevertheless; sacrifice them on the altar of Emancipation. A series of well-planned lectures, all over the country.

REBEKKA [*with vigour*]: That's fine of you, Mr Brendel! You're giving up the most precious thing you possess.

ROSMER: The only thing.

REBEKKA [*looking at* ROSMER *with special meaning*]: How many of us do actually do that? *Dare* to do it?

ROSMER [*returning her look*]: Who knows?

BRENDEL: My hearers are moved. That warms my heart, and steels my will. And with that, I go forward into action. But one thing –. [*To* KROLL.] Can our good schoolmaster tell me whether there is a Temperance Society in town? A Total Abstainers' Society? I'm sure there is.

KROLL: Yes there is; at your service. I am the president.

BRENDEL: Didn't I know it when I saw you! Now it's just possible that I may come to you and sign on for a week.

KROLL: Excuse me. We don't accept weekly members.

BRENDEL: *A la bonheur*, Mr Principal. Ulrik Brendel has never forced himself upon societies of that kind. [*Turning away.*] But I must not protract my visit in this house, rich as it is in memories. I must get on into town and find somewhere suitable to stay. I take it there's a decent hotel to be found there.

REBEKKA: Won't you have something hot to drink before you go?

BRENDEL: What kind of – my dear lady?

REBEKKA: A cup of tea or –

BRENDEL: Many thanks to my generous hostess! But I never like trespassing on private hospitality. [*Waving his hand.*] Good-bye, my good friends! [*Goes towards the door, but turns back.*] Oh, by the way – John, – Reverend Mr Rosmer – will you do a service to your former tutor, for old friendship's sake?

ROSMER: Why, most gladly.

BRENDEL: Good. Well, lend me – just for a day or two – a starched shirt – with cuffs.

ROSMER: No more than that!

BRENDEL: Because, you see, I'm travelling on foot, just at present. My trunk is being sent after me.

ROSMER: Quite. But isn't there anything else, then?

BRENDEL: Yes, I tell you what – perhaps you could spare an old worn-out summer overcoat?

ROSMER: Yes, yes. Of course I can.

BRENDEL: And if there were a pair of presentable boots belonging to the coat –

ROSMER: I'm sure I can manage that too. As soon as you let us know your address, we'll send the things in.

BRENDEL: Not a bit of it! I'm not going to give you all that trouble. I'll take the odds and ends with me.

ROSMER: All right. Come upstairs with me, then.

REBEKKA: No, let me. Mrs Helseth and I will see to it.

BRENDEL: I couldn't possibly let this distinguished lady –!

REBEKKA: Oh, nonsense! Come along, Mr Brendel. [*She goes out to the right.*]

ROSMER [*stopping* BRENDEL]: Tell me, isn't there anything else I could do for you?

BRENDEL: I don't really know of *anything*. Yes, damn it! – now I think of it – John, do you happen to have eight shillings on you?

ROSMER: Let's see. [*Opening his note-case.*] I've got two ten-shilling notes here.

BRENDEL: Oh well, never mind. I can take them. I can always get change in town. Thanks, in the meantime. Remember, it was two tens I had. Good night my own dear boy! Good night, my good sir.

> [*He goes out to the right, where* ROSMER *says good-bye and shuts the door after him.*]

KROLL: Good heavens! And *that's* the Ulrik Brendel people once expected such great things of.

ROSMER [*quietly*]: He has at least had the courage to live his life his own way. I don't think that's such a little thing, after all.

KROLL: What! A life like his! I half believe he could still turn your ideas upside down.

ROSMER: Oh, no. I see my way clear now on all points.

KROLL: I wish I were sure you did, my dear Rosmer; you're so dreadfully susceptible to outside impressions.

ROSMER: Let's sit down. I want to talk to you.

KROLL: Yes; let us. [*They sit down on the sofa.*]

ROSMER [*after a short pause*]: It's pleasant and comfortable here, don't you think?

KROLL: Yes, it's pleasant and comfortable here now – and peaceful. Yes; you've made a home for yourself, Rosmer. And I have lost mine.

ROSMER: My dear man, don't say that. What is divided now will come together again in time.

KROLL: Never. Never. The sting will still be there. It can never be the same as it was.

ROSMER: Look here, now, Kroll. You and I have been close friends now for many and many a year. Do you think our friendship could possibly break down?

KROLL: I know nothing in the world that could come between us. What makes you think of it?

ROSMER: Because you attach such overwhelming importance to our being at one in thought and opinion.

KROLL: Well, yes; but then we two are practically at one. In the great, fundamental questions, at any rate.

ROSMER [*quietly*]: No. Not any longer.

KROLL [*about to jump to his feet*]: What's this!

ROSMER [*holding him down*]: Now, you must stay where you are. *Please*, Kroll.

KROLL: What's all this about? I don't understand you. Tell me plainly!

ROSMER: A new summer has come into my spirit. A new youth into my vision. And that's why I stand *there* now –

KROLL: Where, – where do you stand?

ROSMER: There, where your children stand.

KROLL: You? You! But it's impossible. Where do you stand, do you say?

ROSMER: On the same side as Laurits and Hilda.

KROLL [*his head sinking*]: Apostate. John Rosmer, apostate.

ROSMER: I should have felt so contented – so deeply happy about this, that you call apostasy. But for all that I suffered keenly. Because I knew well enough that it would mean bitter distress for you.

KROLL: Rosmer, – Rosmer! I shall never get over this. [*Looking at him gloomily.*] Oh, to think that even you should want to join them, to help the work of destruction and ruin in this unhappy land.

ROSMER: It's the work of emancipation I want to share in.

KROLL: Yes, I know all about that. That is what it's called, both by seducers and victims. But do you really think there's any emancipation to be expected from the spirit that now bids fair to poison the whole life of our community?

ROSMER: I'm not attracted to the spirit that prevails. Nor to either of the parties. I want to try and get people together from all sides. As many and as closely as I possibly can. I want to live for this one thing and give it all the strength of my life – to build up a true democratic outlook in the country.

KROLL: So you don't think we have a sufficiently democratic outlook! Myself, I think the whole lot of us are in a fair way to be dragged down into the mud, which usually suits only the common people.

ROSMER: That's just why I want to set democracy to its proper work.

KROLL: What work?

ROSMER: To make all the people in the country into noblemen.

KROLL: All the people –!

ROSMER: As many as possible, at any rate.

KROLL: By what means?

ROSMER: By freeing their minds and chastening their desires, I think.

KROLL: You're a dreamer, Rosmer. Are *you* going to free them? Are *you* going to chasten them?

ROSMER: No, my dear fellow, – I only want to try and rouse them to it. As for doing it – that must be their job.

KROLL: And you think they can?

ROSMER: Yes.

KROLL: By their own strength, eh?

ROSMER: Yes, of course by their own strength. There's no other to be had.

KROLL [*getting up*]: Is that the way for a priest to speak?

ROSMER: I'm not a priest any more.

KROLL: Yes, but – the faith of your childhood, then –?

ROSMER: I haven't that any more.

KROLL: You haven't –!

ROSMER [*getting up*]: I've given it up. I *had* to give it up, Kroll.

KROLL [*shaken, but controlled*]: I see. Yes, yes, yes. Of course the one follows from the other. I suppose that was why you left the service of the Church?

ROSMER: Yes. When I was clear about myself, when I was quite sure that it wasn't just a passing temptation, but that it was something I never more could or would get rid of ... then I left.

KROLL: Then it's been at work in you all this time. And we, your friends, haven't had a hint of it. Rosmer, Rosmer, – how could you hide the sad truth from us?

ROSMER: Because I thought it was a thing that only concerned myself. And then I didn't want to give unnecessary pain to you and my other friends. I thought I could manage to live here as I always have, quiet and contented and happy. I wanted to read and soak myself in all the works that had been closed books to me before. To enter with my whole soul into the great world of truth and freedom that has now opened before me.

KROLL: Apostate. Every word bears it out. But then why do you confess it, nevertheless – this secret apostasy of yours? Or why just at this moment?

ROSMER: You've forced me to, yourself, Kroll.

KROLL: I? I have forced you –?

ROSMER: When I heard of your violent behaviour at meetings – when I read about all the bitter speeches you made there – all your vindictive attacks upon those who take the other side – your scornful denunciation of your opponents –. Oh, Kroll – that you, you, could come to that! Then my duty could not be set aside. People are growing evil in this struggle that's going on. There must be peace and joy and conciliation in our minds. That's why I'm coming forward now and confessing openly to what I am. And then I too want to try my strength. Couldn't you meet me in this, Kroll, from your side?

KROLL: Never in this life will I compromise with the forces of destruction in the community.

ROSMER: Then let us at least fight with the weapons of gentlemen – since it seems we must fight.

KROLL: He who is not with me in the vital issues of life, him I no longer know. And I owe him no consideration.

ROSMER: Does that apply to me, too?

KROLL: You have broken with me yourself, Rosmer.

ROSMER: But *is* this a breach?

KROLL: This! It is a breach with all those who hitherto stood by you. Now you must take the consequences.

[REBEKKA WEST *comes in from the right and throws the door wide open.*]

REBEKKA: There we are; now he's on the way to his great sacrifice. And now we can go to supper. Will you come, Principal.

KROLL [*taking his hat*]: Good night, Miss West. I have nothing more to do here.

REBEKKA [*anxiously*]: What is it? [*She shuts the door and comes nearer.*] Have you been talking –?

ROSMER: He knows now.

KROLL: We shan't let you slip through our fingers, Rosmer. We shall make you come back to us again.

ROSMER: I shall never come back any more.

KROLL: We shall see. You're not the man to go on standing alone.

ROSMER: I'm not so completely alone, after all. There are two of us to bear the loneliness here.

KROLL: Ah –! [*A misgiving stirs in him.*] This too! Beatë's words!

ROSMER: Beatë –?

KROLL [*dismissing the thought*]: No, no, – that was base –. Forgive me.

ROSMER: What? Which?

KROLL: Never mind. For shame! Forgive me. Good-bye. [*He goes towards the hall door.*]

ROSMER [*going after him*]: Kroll! It mustn't end like this between us. I'll come and see you to-morrow.

KROLL [*turning in the hall*]: You shan't set foot in my house! [*He takes his stick and goes.*]

[ROSMER *stands a moment in the open doorway; then he shuts it and goes across to the table.*]

ROSMER: It doesn't matter, Rebekka. We shall hold out all right. We two firm friends. You and I.

REBEKKA: What do you suppose he was thinking of when he said, 'For shame'?

ROSMER: Don't worry about it, my dear. He didn't believe what he was thinking, himself. But I'll go and see him to-morrow. Good night.

REBEKKA: Are you going up so early this evening too? After this?

ROSMER: This evening as usual. I feel so relieved, now that it's over. You see I'm quite calm, Rebekka dear. Take it calmly yourself. Good night.

REBEKKA: Good night, dear friend. And sleep well.

[ROSMER *goes out through the hall door; then we hear him going upstairs.* REBEKKA *goes across and pulls a bell-cord by the stove. After a moment* MRS HELSETH *comes in from the right.*]

REBEKKA: You might as well clear the table again, Mrs Helseth. The master won't have anything – and the Principal's gone home.

MRS HELSETH: Is the Principal gone? Why, what was the matter with him?

REBEKKA [*taking up her crochet-work*]: He thought it was blowing up for a bad storm –

MRS HELSETH: That was queer. There's not a scrap of cloud to be seen tonight.

REBEKKA: Let's hope he doesn't meet the white horse. For I'm afraid we're going to hear from some such spirit pretty soon.

MRS HELSETH: May the Lord forgive you, Miss! Don't say such awful things!

REBEKKA: Come, come, come –

MRS HELSETH [*lowering her voice*]: Do you really think, Miss, that someone here's going to – leave us – soon?

REBEKKA: No I certainly don't think that. But there are so many kinds of white horses in this world, Mrs Helseth. Oh, well; good night. I'm going to my room now.

MRS HELSETH: Good night, Miss.

[REBEKKA *goes out to the right with her crochet-work.*]

MRS HELSETH [*turns the lamp down, shaking her head and muttering to herself*]: Bless my soul, – bless my soul. That Miss West. The way she can talk sometimes.

ACT TWO

John Rosmer's work-room. In the left-hand wall is the entrance door. In the background a doorway with hangings drawn back, which leads into the bedroom. A window on the right and in front of it a writing-table covered with books and papers. Bookshelves and cupboards against the walls. Plain furniture. An old-fashioned sofa with a table downstage on the left. JOHN ROSMER, *dressed in an indoor coat, is sitting in a high-backed chair by the writing-table. He is cutting and turning over the leaves of a periodical and dipping into it here and there. Someone knocks at the door on the left.*

ROSMER [*without turning round*]: Come in. [REBEKKA WEST *comes in, dressed in a house-coat.*]

REBEKKA: Good morning.

ROSMER [*checking something in the book*]: Good morning, my dear. Do you want something?

REBEKKA: I only wanted to hear whether you'd slept well.

ROSMER: Oh, I slept well and soundly. No dreams. [*Turning round.*] And you?

REBEKKA: Yes thanks. Towards morning.

ROSMER: I don't think I've felt so light-hearted for a long time as I do now. Yes, it was a very good thing I got it said.

REBEKKA: Yes, you shouldn't have gone so long without speaking.

ROSMER: I can't understand, myself, how I could be so cowardly.

REBEKKA: Well, it wasn't exactly from cowardice –

ROSMER: Oh yes, yes, my dear, – when I look well into it, there was some cowardice there.

REBEKKA: So much the braver, then, for you to get it over. [*She sits down near him in a chair by the writing-table.*] But now I want to tell you something I've done – and you mustn't be angry with me about it.

ROSMER: Angry? My dear, how can you think –?

REBEKKA: Why, because perhaps it was a little officious of me. But –

ROSMER: Well, let me hear about it.

REBEKKA: Yesterday evening, when our friend Ulrik Brendel was just going, I gave him a line or two to take to Mortensgaard.

ROSMER [*rather thoughtfully*]: But, my dear Rebekka –. Well, what did you say, then?

REBEKKA: I said that he would be doing you a service if he took a little notice of the poor man and helped him in any way he could.

ROSMER: My dear, you shouldn't have done that. You've only harmed Brendel by it. Besides, Mortensgaard's a man I very much want to avoid. You know the trouble I had with him once before.

REBEKKA: But don't you think now it would be as well if you got on good terms with him again?

ROSMER: I? With Mortensgaard? Why do you think that?

REBEKKA: Well, because you can't be really secure now, – since this business has come between you and your friends.

ROSMER [*looking at her and shaking his head*]: Did you really think that Kroll or any of the others would want to take revenge? That they could be capable of –?

REBEKKA: In the first heat of passion, my dear –. No one can be sure about it. I think, after the way the Principal took it –

ROSMER: Oh you ought to know him better than that. Kroll is an honourable man, through and through. I'll go into town this afternoon and talk to him. I'll talk to them all together. Oh, you'll see how easily it will go –

[MRS HELSETH *comes in at the door on the left.*]

REBEKKA [*getting up*]: What is it, Mrs Helseth?

MRS HELSETH: Dr Kroll's downstairs in the hall.

ROSMER [*getting up quickly*]: Kroll!

REBEKKA: The Principal! Why, think –!

MRS HELSETH: He's asking if he can come up and talk to the Rector.

ROSMER [*to* REBEKKA]: What did I say? Yes, of course he can. [*He goes to the door and calls down the stairs.*] Come along up, my dear fellow! You're heartily welcome!

[ROSMER *stands and holds the door open.* MRS HELSETH *goes out.* REBEKKA *pulls the curtain to across the doorway. Then she puts one or two things straight.* DR KROLL *comes in with his hat in his hand.*]

ROSMER [*quietly, but moved*]: I knew well enough that it wasn't the last time –

KROLL: I see the business today in quite a different light from yesterday.

ROSMER: Yes, that's it, Kroll! You do, don't you? Now that you've been able to think it over –

KROLL: You completely misunderstand me. [*He puts his hat on the table by the sofa.*] It is essential for me to speak to you alone.

ROSMER: Why mustn't Miss West –?

REBEKKA: No, no, Mr Rosmer, I'll go.

KROLL [*looking pointedly at her*]: And I must beg Miss West's pardon, too, for coming here so early in the day. For disturbing her before she has had time to –

REBEKKA [*starting*]: What is it? Do you find anything unsuitable in my going about at home in a house-coat?

KROLL: God forbid! I haven't the least idea what has become usual and customary at Rosmersholm.

ROSMER: But, Kroll – you're not like yourself today at all!

REBEKKA: If you will excuse me, Principal. [*She goes out to the left.*]

KROLL: With your permission – [*He sits down on the sofa.*]

ROSMER: Yes, my dear fellow, let's sit down peacefully and talk it over. [*He sits down in a chair opposite the Principal.*]

KROLL: I haven't been able to close my eyes since yesterday. I've been lying all night thinking and thinking.

ROSMER: And what do you say, then, today?

KROLL: It's a long story, Rosmer. Let me begin with a kind of introduction. I can tell you a little about Ulrik Brendel.

ROSMER: Has he been to see you?

KROLL: No. He landed himself in a shady public house. In the shadiest society, of course. Drank and stood drinks as long as he had anything. After that he denounced the whole company as a rabble and mob. In which, incidentally, he was perfectly right. But he got himself beaten and was thrown into the gutter.

ROSMER: So he is really incorrigible after all.

KROLL: He'd pawned his coat, too. But that will have been got out for him. Can you guess by whom?

ROSMER: By you yourself, perhaps?

KROLL: No. By this noble-minded Mr Mortensgaard.

ROSMER: Ah, quite.

KROLL: I rather gathered that Mr Brendel's first visit was to the idiot of a plebeian.

ROSMER: It was certainly very fortunate for him.

KROLL: It was, indeed. [*He leans across the table, a little nearer to* ROSMER.] But now we're touching on a matter that for the sake of our old – of our former friendship I ought to warn you about.

ROSMER: My dear fellow, what is *that*?

KROLL: It's this, that here in your house some game or other's going on behind your back.

ROSMER: How can you believe that? Is it Reb – is it Miss West you're suggesting?

KROLL: Precisely. I can understand it well enough on her side. She's been accustomed for such a long time now to be in control here. But all the same –

ROSMER: My dear Kroll, you're quite wrong about this. She and I – we don't hide anything in the world from each other.

KROLL: Has she also admitted to you that she's in correspondence with the editor of *The Lighthouse*?

ROSMER: Oh, you're talking of the couple of lines she gave Ulrik Brendel to take with him.

KROLL: So you've discovered it then. And do you agree to her forming an alliance like this with that scandal-writer, who tries to make a laughing-stock of me, week after week, both for my school teaching and for my public conduct?

ROSMER: My dear man, I'm sure she's never once thought of that side of the matter. And besides, she naturally has full freedom of action, just as I have mine.

KROLL: Really? Well, no doubt it's part of the new direction you have now taken. For where you stand, there Miss West stands too, I suppose?

ROSMER: She does. We two have worked our way forward together in steady friendship.

KROLL [*looking at him and shaking his head slowly*]: Oh you blind, deluded man!

ROSMER: I? How do you make that out?

KROLL: Because I daren't – won't think the worst. No, no – let me finish what I was saying. You really value my friendship, Rosmer? And my respect too? Don't you?

ROSMER: There's no need for me to answer that question.

KROLL: Yes, but there are other things that do need an answer, a full explanation on your side. Will you consent to my holding a kind of enquiry –?

ROSMER: Enquiry?

KROLL: Yes, to my asking you about one or two things it may be distressing for you to remember. You see, this business of your abandoning your religion – oh, well, your emancipation, as you call it – it hangs together with so much else that you for your own sake must explain to me.

ROSMER: My dear fellow, ask whatever you like. I've nothing to hide.

KROLL: Well, tell me then, what do you really think was the primary cause of Beatë's ending her own life?

ROSMER: Can you have any doubt about it? Or, rather, can one ask the reasons for what a person does who is unhappy, ill, and not responsible?

KROLL: Are you certain that Beatë was so completely irresponsible? The doctors at any rate thought it might not be a foregone conclusion.

ROSMER: If the doctors had sometimes seen her in the state I so often saw her in, night and day, they wouldn't have doubted then.

KROLL: I didn't doubt either at that time.

ROSMER: Of course not, I'm afraid it was impossible to doubt, you know. I've told you about that uncontrollable, fierce passion of hers – that she insisted I should meet. Oh, the horror she filled me with! And then, in her last years, her groundless and consuming passion of self-reproach.

KROLL: Yes, when she had realized that she would be childless all her life.

ROSMER: Well, just think of it yourself. Such constant, hideous agony of mind over something that wasn't in any way her fault! Was she really to be considered accountable?

KROLL: Hm. Can you remember whether you had any books in the house at that time that dealt with the purpose of marriage? According to our modern, advanced views?

ROSMER: I remember Miss West lent me a book of that kind. For she inherited the doctor's library, as you know. But, my dear Kroll, surely you don't think we were so careless as to let that poor invalid come across things of that kind? I can assure you, most emphatically, that we're not to blame. It was her own mental disturbance that drove her so desperately astray.

KROLL: One thing, in any case, I can now tell you. And that

is that poor Beatë, in her misery and obsession, put an end to her own life so that you should be able to live happily – to live freely, in your own way.

ROSMER [*half-starting from his chair*]: What do you mean by that?

KROLL: Now you're to listen to me quietly, Rosmer. Because now I can speak of it. In the last year of her life she came to see me twice, to pour out her dread and her despair.

ROSMER: About this?

KROLL: No. The first time she came and insisted that you were on the road to apostasy. That you were going to break with your father's faith.

ROSMER [*hotly*]: That's impossible, Kroll, what you're saying! Quite impossible! You must be mistaken about this.

KROLL: Why?

ROSMER: Why, because as long as Beatë was alive, I was still in doubt and in conflict with myself. And that fight I fought out alone and in complete silence. I don't believe Rebekka once –

KROLL: Rebekka?

ROSMER: Well, then, Miss West. I call her Rebekka for convenience.

KROLL: I've noticed it.

ROSMER: So it's quite incomprehensible, how Beatë could get hold of the idea. And why didn't she talk to me myself about it? And that she never did. Not a single word.

KROLL: Poor thing – she begged and implored me to speak to you.

ROSMER: And why didn't you do it, then?

KROLL: Could I doubt for a moment, at that time, that she was out of her mind? Such an accusation against a man like you! And then she came again, about a month later. Then she seemed to be quieter in her mind. But as she was going, she said, 'Now they can soon expect the white horse at Rosmersholm.'

ROSMER: Oh, yes. The white horse – she talked of it so often.

KROLL: And when I tried to turn her away from depressing thoughts, she only answered, 'I haven't much time left. For now John must marry Rebekka at once.'

ROSMER [*almost speechless*]: *What* did you say? I, marry –!

KROLL: That was a Thursday afternoon. On the Saturday evening she threw herself down from the bridge into the mill-race.

ROSMER: And you never warned us –!

KROLL: You know yourself how often she hinted that she was going to die quite soon.

ROSMER: I know it well. But all the same – you *should* have warned us!

KROLL: I thought of that too. But it was too late then.

ROSMER: But then why didn't you, later on –? Why have you kept quiet about all this?

KROLL: What good would it have done to come here and distress and harrow your feelings still more? I took the whole thing as just empty, wild fantasies. Until yesterday evening.

ROSMER: And now you don't any longer?

KROLL: Didn't Beatë see quite clearly when she said you were going to lapse from the faith of your childhood?

ROSMER [*looking fixedly ahead of him*]: Yes; that I don't understand. To me it's the most incomprehensible thing in the whole world.

KROLL: Incomprehensible or not, it's so. And now I ask you, Rosmer – how much truth is there in her other accusation? In the last, I mean.

ROSMER: Accusation? Was *that* an accusation?

KROLL: Perhaps you didn't notice how the words went. She was to die, she said. Why? Well?

ROSMER: Why, so that I could marry Rebekka –

KROLL: The words didn't go quite like that. Beatë expressed herself differently. She said, 'I haven't much time left. For now John must marry Rebekka at once.'

ROSMER [*looking at him for a moment and then getting up*]: Now I understand you, Kroll.

KROLL: Well then? What answer have you?

ROSMER [*still quiet and controlled*]: To something so unheard-of? The only proper answer would be to point to the door.

KROLL [*getting up*]: Very well.

ROSMER [*standing before him*]: Now listen. For more than a year – ever since Beatë died – Rebekka West and I have lived alone here at Rosmersholm. All that time you've known what Beatë accused us of. But never for an instant have I noticed that you objected to Rebekka and me living together here.

KROLL: I didn't know till yesterday evening that it was a man without religion and a – an emancipated woman, who were leading this life together.

ROSMER: Oh! So you don't believe that purity of mind is to be found among the free thinkers and the emancipated? You don't think they can have the instinct for morality in them, as a natural desire?

KROLL: I don't build much on the kind of morality that isn't rooted in the faith of the Church.

ROSMER: And you let this apply to Rebekka and me too? To Rebekka's and my relationship?

KROLL: I can't abandon my opinion for the sake of you two – that there's no really wide gulf between free thought and – hm.

ROSMER: And what –?

KROLL: – and free love, since you insist on knowing.

ROSMER [*gravely*]: And you're not ashamed to say that to me! You, who have known me from my earliest childhood upwards.

KROLL: Precisely for that reason. I know how easily you let yourself be influenced by the people you're surrounded with. And this Rebekka of yours – oh, very well, Miss West – we don't actually know very much about her. Put simply, Rosmer, I'm not giving you up. As for you – you must try to save yourself in time.

ROSMER: Save myself? How –?

[MRS HELSETH *peeps in through the door on the left.*]

ROSMER: What do you want?

MRS HELSETH: I was going to ask Miss West to come down.

ROSMER: Miss West isn't up here.

MRS HELSETH: Isn't she? [*Looking round her.*] That's funny. [*Goes out.*]

ROSMER: You said –?

KROLL: Listen. Whatever went on here secretly while Beatë was alive – and whatever is still going on here – I'm not going to enquire too closely about that. Of course you were very unhappy in your marriage. And that may well, in a way, help to excuse you.

ROSMER: Ah, how little you know me, when it comes to it!

KROLL: Don't interrupt me. This is what I want to say: that if this living with Miss West is to go on, it's absolutely essential that you should conceal the change of mind – the sad disloyalty – that she has led you into. Let me speak! Let me speak! I say, however wrong you may be, in heaven's name think and believe and hold what opinions you like, on any subject on earth – but just keep your opinions to yourself. This is an entirely personal matter. It's not in the least necessary to broadcast a thing like that over the whole countryside.

ROSMER: It is necessary for me to withdraw from a false and ambiguous position.

KROLL: But you have a duty to the traditions of your race, Rosmer! Remember that! Since time out of mind Rosmersholm has been like a stronghold of order and discipline – of consideration and respect for all that is honoured and acknowledged by the best of our community. The whole neighbourhood has taken its stamp from Rosmersholm. It will give rise to a disastrous, an irreparable confusion, once it is rumoured that you yourself have broken with what I will call the ideal of the House of Rosmer.

ROSMER: My dear Kroll, I can't see the thing like that. I think it's an imperative duty for me to bring a little light and joy here, where the race of Rosmer has created gloom and oppressiveness all this long, long time.

KROLL [*looking sternly at him*]: Yes, that would be a deed worthy of the man with whom the race dies out. Leave that sort of thing alone, Rosmer. It's not fit work for you. You're made for the life of a quiet scholar.

ROSMER: Yes, perhaps that's true. But now I too want to join in the battle of life.

KROLL: The battle of life – do you know what that will be for you? It'll be a fight to the death with all your friends.

ROSMER [*quietly*]: They probably aren't all of them as fanatical as you.

KROLL: You're an innocent creature, Rosmer. A creature of no experience. You don't realize the violent storm that will break over you.

[MRS HELSETH *peeps in at the door on the left.*]

MRS HELSETH: Miss West wanted me to ask something.

ROSMER: What is it?

MRS HELSETH: There's somebody downstairs who'd like to have a word with the master.

ROSMER: Is it the same gentleman as was here yesterday?

MRS HELSETH: No, it's this Mortensgaard.

ROSMER: Mortensgaard!

KROLL: Aha! So we've got as far as that! That far, already!

ROSMER: What does he want with me? Why didn't you let him go again?

MRS HELSETH: Miss West said I was to ask if he could come up.

ROSMER: Tell him that there's someone –

KROLL [*to* MRS HELSETH]: Let him come up, please. [MRS HELSETH *goes out.*]

KROLL [*taking his hat*]: I relinquish the field – for the time being. But the main battle isn't joined yet.

ROSMER: As true as I'm alive, Kroll, I've nothing to do with Mortensgaard.

KROLL: I don't believe you any more. Not on any point. I shan't believe you in future in any circumstances. Now it's a matter of war to the knife. But we'll see if we can't make you harmless.

ROSMER: Oh, Kroll, how deep – how low you have sunk now!

KROLL: I? And that from a man such as you! Remember Beatë.

ROSMER: Have you come back to that again?

KROLL: No. You must solve the mystery of the mill-race according to your own conscience – if you still have anything of that kind about you.

[PEDER MORTENSGAARD *comes quietly and unobtrusively in by the door on the left. He is a small, slight man with thin reddish hair and beard.*]

KROLL [*with a glance of hatred*]: Ah yes, here is *The Lighthouse*. Shining at Rosmersholm. [*Buttoning his coat.*] Yes, then I cannot be in doubt what course I shall steer.

MORTENSGAARD [*conciliatory*]: *The Lighthouse* shall always be kept shining to guide the Principal home.

KROLL: Yes; you have shown your good-will for a long time. There is, indeed, it is true, a commandment which says that we shall not bear false witness against our neighbour –

MORTENSGAARD: The Principal need not instruct me in the commandments.

KROLL: Not even in the seventh?

ROSMER: Kroll!

MORTENSGAARD: And if there is need, then the Rector is the proper person.

KROLL [*with veiled scorn*]: The Rector? Yes, the Reverend Mr Rosmer is unquestionably the proper man in this case. Good hunting to you, gentlemen! [*He goes out and slams the door behind him.*]

ROSMER [*speaking to himself and still looking towards the door*]: Well, well. There it is then. [*Turning.*] Will you tell me, Mr Mortensgaard, what brings you out here to me?

MORTENSGAARD: It was really Miss West I was looking for. I thought I ought to thank her for the kind letter I had from her yesterday.

ROSMER: I know she wrote to you. Were you able to speak to her?

MORTENSGAARD: Yes, a little. [*With a slight smile.*] I hear that the point of view has changed, one way and another, out here at Rosmersholm.

ROSMER: My point of view has changed in a good many ways. I can almost say – in all.

MORTENSGAARD: She said that – Miss West. That's why she thought I'd better come up and have a word with you, sir, about this.

ROSMER: About what, Mr Mortensgaard?

MORTENSGAARD: May I have leave to report in *The Lighthouse* that you've arrived at other views – and that you support the liberal and progressive cause?

ROSMER: That you certainly may. More than that – I ask you to report it.

MORTENSGAARD: Then it shall be there first thing to-morrow. It will be a great and momentous piece of news, that the Reverend Mr Rosmer of Rosmersholm considers that he can fight for the cause of enlightenment in *this* sense also.

ROSMER: I don't quite understand you.

MORTENSGAARD: I mean to say, it gives our party a strong moral backing every time we win a serious, Christian supporter.

ROSMER [*with some surprise*]: Then you don't know –? Hasn't Miss West told you that too?

MORTENSGAARD: What, sir? The lady was very busy.

She said I'd better come up and hear the rest from you yourself.

ROSMER: Well, then, I will tell you that I have freed myself entirely. In every way. I now have no connexion whatever with the teachings of the Church. In future those matters don't concern me in the least.

MORTENSGAARD [looking at him in bewilderment]: Well – if the moon fell out of the sky, I couldn't be more –! The Rector himself renouncing –!

ROSMER: Yes, I now stand where you yourself have long stood. You can make that known too in *The Lighthouse* tomorrow.

MORTENSGAARD: That too? No, my dear Rector. Pardon me – but it's not advisable to touch on that side of the matter.

ROSMER: Not touch on this?

MORTENSGAARD: Not at first, I think.

ROSMER: But I don't understand.

MORTENSGAARD: Well, because you see, sir –. I don't suppose you're quite so familiar with all the circumstances as I am. But if you've come over now to the liberal party – and if you want, as Miss West said, to take part in this movement – well, no doubt you're doing it with the intention of being as useful, both to the party and to the movement, as you possibly can.

ROSMER: Yes, I sincerely want to.

MORTENSGAARD: Quite. But then I must just tell you, sir, if you come forward openly with this business of your giving up the Church, you'll tie your own hands right away.

ROSMER: Do you think so?

MORTENSGAARD: Yes, you may be sure there won't be much you can do then; not here in these parts. And besides, we've quite enough free-thinkers on hand, sir. I nearly said, we've all too many of those gentry. What the party wants is the Christian element – something everybody has to respect. That's what we're so dreadfully short of. And so it's wisest for you to keep quiet about all those things that don't concern the public. You see, that's what I mean.

ROSMER: Ah, yes. That is, you can't risk associating yourself with me if I openly admit my loss of faith.

MORTENSGAARD [*shaking his head*]: I wouldn't like to, sir. I've made it a rule, of late, never to support anything or anybody that wants to quarrel with the Church.

ROSMER: Have you yourself, then, returned of late to the Church?

MORTENSGAARD: That's a different thing.

ROSMER: Ah yes; so that's it. Yes, now I understand you.

MORTENSGAARD: Mr Rosmer, – you ought to remember that I – I especially haven't a really free hand.

ROSMER: What hinders you, then?

MORTENSGAARD: What hinders me is that I'm a marked man.

ROSMER: Ah – yes.

MORTENSGAARD: A marked man, sir. You in particular ought to remember that. For it was you first and foremost who had the brand set on me.

ROSMER: If I had stood then where I stand now, I should have treated your misdeed more tenderly.

MORTENSGAARD: I think so too. But it's too late now. You've branded me once and for all. Branded me for my whole life. Well, I suppose you don't realize altogether what a thing like that involves. But now you may soon come to feel the pinch yourself, Mr Rosmer.

ROSMER: I?

MORTENSGAARD: Yes. For surely you don't think Dr Kroll and his lot are going to forgive you for a breach like yours? And it's said that *The County News* is going to be quite merciless now. It may well be that you'll become a marked man, too.

ROSMER: I feel invulnerable on all personal grounds, Mr

Mortensgaard. My behaviour offers nothing to lay hold of.

MORTENSGAARD [*with a sly smile*]: That's a pretty big claim, Mr Rosmer.

ROSMER: Very likely. But I have the right to make so great a claim.

MORTENSGAARD: Even if you examined your conduct as thoroughly as you once examined mine?

ROSMER: You say that rather oddly. What is it you're suggesting? Is there anything specific?

MORTENSGAARD: Yes, there's *one* specific matter. Just one single thing. But that could be ugly enough if malicious opponents got news of it.

ROSMER: Will you please let me hear what this matter may be.

MORTENSGAARD: Can't you guess that yourself, sir?

ROSMER: No, not at all. Not in any way.

MORTENSGAARD: Oh well, I shall have to come across with it, then. I have in my possession a curious letter that was written here at Rosmersholm.

ROSMER: Miss West's letter, do you mean? Is that so curious?

MORTENSGAARD: No, that letter's not curious. But I once got another letter from the house here.

ROSMER: Also from Miss West?

MORTENSGAARD: No, Mr Rosmer.

ROSMER: Well, from whom, then? From whom?

MORTENSGAARD: From the late Mrs Rosmer.

ROSMER: From my wife! Did *you* have a letter from my wife?

MORTENSGAARD: Yes, I did.

ROSMER: When?

MORTENSGAARD: It was in Mrs Rosmer's latter days. It would be about eighteen months ago now. And it's that letter that's so curious.

ROSMER: You know, no doubt, that my wife was of unsound mind at that time.

MORTENSGAARD: Yes, I know there were many people who thought so. But I don't think one could deduce anything of the kind from the letter. When I say the letter's curious, I mean it in a different way.

ROSMER: And what in the world did my unhappy wife find to write to you about?

MORTENSGAARD: I have the letter at home. She begins something like this, that she is living in great fear and dread. Because here, in these parts, there are so many wicked people, she writes. And these people are only thinking of doing you harm and damage.

ROSMER: Me?

MORTENSGAARD: Yes, so she says. And then comes the most curious thing of all. Shall I say it, Mr Rosmer?

ROSMER: Yes, of course! Everything. Don't keep anything back.

MORTENSGAARD: The late Mrs Rosmer begs and implores me to be magnanimous. She knows, she says, that it was the Rector who had me dismissed from my teaching post. And so she begs me most earnestly not to take revenge.

ROSMER: How did she think, then, that you could take revenge?

MORTENSGAARD: It says in the letter that if I should come to hear rumours of anything sinful going on at Rosmersholm, I mustn't believe anything of the kind. Because it was only bad people who spread it about to make you unhappy.

ROSMER: It says that in the letter!

MORTENSGAARD: You can read it yourself sir, when you like.

ROSMER: But I don't understand –! What did she imagine, then, the evil rumours were about?

MORTENSGAARD: First, that the Rector should have fallen away from the religion of his childhood. That Mrs Rosmer denied quite definitely – at that time. And next – hm.

ROSMER: Next?

MORTENSGAARD: Well, next she writes – and it's rather confused – that she doesn't know of any sinful relationship at Rosmersholm. That there's never been any wrong done to her. And if rumours of that kind should start, she implores me not to touch on it in *The Lighthouse*.

ROSMER: No name is mentioned?

MORTENSGAARD: No.

ROSMER: Who brought you that letter?

MORTENSGAARD: I've promised not to say that. It was handed in to me one evening at dusk.

ROSMER: If you'd enquired at once, you would have found out that my poor, unhappy wife was not entirely responsible.

MORTENSGAARD: I did enquire, sir. But I must say I didn't get exactly *that* impression.

ROSMER: Didn't you? – But why are you telling me about this old, distracted letter just at this moment?

MORTENSGAARD: In order to advise you to be extremely prudent, Mr Rosmer.

ROSMER: In my life, do you mean?

MORTENSGAARD: Yes. You must remember that in future you're not immune.

ROSMER: You're quite convinced that there's something here to conceal.

MORTENSGAARD: I don't know why a man of emancipated ideas should refrain from living his life as fully as possible. But just be careful, as I said, from now on. If there's a rumour of something or other that goes against people's prejudices, you may be sure the whole liberal cause will suffer for it. Good-bye, Mr Rosmer.

ROSMER: Good-bye.

MORTENSGAARD: So I'll go straight to the printing-house and put the great piece of news in *The Lighthouse*.

ROSMER: Put it all in.

MORTENSGAARD: I'll put in everything that the people need to know. [*He bows and goes.* ROSMER *remains standing at the door while he goes down the stairs. We hear the front-door close.*]

ROSMER [*at the door, calling quietly*]: Rebekka! Re—. Hm. [*Aloud.*] Mrs Helseth – isn't Miss West downstairs?

MRS HELSETH [*heard speaking, down in the hall*]: No, sir, she's not here.

[*The curtain in the background is pulled aside.* REBEKKA *appears in the door-opening.*]

REBEKKA: John!

ROSMER [*turning*]: What! Were you in my bedroom? My dear, what were you doing there?

REBEKKA [*going across to him*]: I was listening.

ROSMER: Oh but, Rebekka, how could you do that!

REBEKKA: Of course I could. He said it so detestably – about my house-coat –

ROSMER: Oh, so you were in there too when Kroll –?

REBEKKA: Yes, I wanted to know what was behind it all with him.

ROSMER: I should have told you all right.

REBEKKA: You wouldn't have told me quite everything. And certainly not in his own words.

ROSMER: Did you hear everything, then?

REBEKKA: Most of it, I think. I had to go down for a moment when Mortensgaard came.

ROSMER: And then you came up again?

REBEKKA: My dear friend, don't be angry about it.

ROSMER: Do whatever you yourself think right and fitting. Of course, you have full freedom. But what do you say, then, Rebekka? Oh, I don't think I've ever needed you so much before.

REBEKKA: Well, you and I were both prepared for what would come some day.

ROSMER: No, no – not for this.

REBEKKA: Not for this?

ROSMER: I could imagine that sooner or later our fine, clear friendship might be misinterpreted and suspected. Not by Kroll. I could never have imagined such a thing of him. But by all these others with the coarse minds and the crude vision. Oh yes, Rebekka, I'd good enough grounds for it, when I so jealously concealed our relationship. It was a dangerous secret.

REBEKKA: Oh, what's the good of worrying about what all these other people think! We know in our own minds that we're not to blame.

ROSMER: I? Not to blame? Yes, I certainly thought that – up till today. But now, – now Rebekka –

REBEKKA: Well, what now?

ROSMER: How am I to explain to myself Beatë's terrible reproach?

REBEKKA [exclaiming]: Oh, don't talk about Beatë! Don't think about Beatë any more. Now that you'd got away from her so well ... from the dead.

ROSMER: Since I came to know all this, it's as though she'd come to life again in some dreadful way.

REBEKKA: Oh, no you mustn't, John! You mustn't!

ROSMER: Yes, I tell you. We must try to get to the bottom of this. How can she have strayed into this sinister delusion?

REBEKKA: Surely you're not beginning yourself to doubt that she was very nearly insane?

ROSMER: Ah, you see – that's just what I can't be quite so sure about any longer. And besides – if it were so –

REBEKKA: If it were so? Well, what then?

ROSMER: I mean, where are we to look for the immediate cause of her sick mind passing over into madness?

REBEKKA: Oh, what good is it your wearing yourself out with worries like these?

ROSMER: I can't do anything else, Rebekka. I can't let go of these nagging doubts, however much I want to.

REBEKKA: Oh but that may be dangerous – to keep on like this, going round and round this one dreary thought.

ROSMER [*walking about, thoughtful and uneasy*]: I must have betrayed myself, in one way or another. She must have noticed how happy I began to feel from the time *you* came to us.

REBEKKA: Yes but, my dear, even supposing it was so –!

ROSMER: You'll find it didn't escape her that we read the same books. That we sought each other out and talked together about all the new ideas. But I don't understand it! For I was so anxious and careful to protect her. When I think back, it seems to me, I did my utmost to keep her from knowing our affairs. Or didn't I, Rebekka?

REBEKKA: Yes, yes, of course you did.

ROSMER: And so did you. And yet nevertheless –! Oh, this is terrible to think of! Here she must have gone about, poor thing, in her diseased affection, always keeping silence, watching us, noticing everything – and misinterpreting everything.

REBEKKA [*clenching her hands*]: Oh, I ought never to have come to Rosmersholm!

ROSMER: Only to think what she suffered in silence! All the evil that she, in her sick mind, must have built up and put together about us! Didn't she ever talk to you about anything that could give you a kind of clue?

REBEKKA [*as though frightened*]: To me! Do you think I'd have stayed here another day if she had?

ROSMER: No, no, that's obvious. Oh, what a fight she must have fought. And fought alone, too, Rebekka. In despair and quite alone. And then, at the end, this tragic, accusing victory – in the mill-race. [*He throws himself down on a chair by the writing-table, props his elbows on the table, and covers his face with his hands.*]

REBEKKA [*approaching him quietly from behind*]: Listen, now,

John. If it was in your power to call Beatë back, to you, to
Rosmersholm, would you do it?

ROSMER: Oh, how do I know what I'd do or not do! I've no
thought for anything but this one thing – which is irrevoc-
able.

REBEKKA: You ought to have begun to live by now, John.
You *had* begun already. You'd freed yourself completely,
on every side. You felt so glad and light-hearted –

ROSMER: Yes, I know. I certainly did. And then comes this
crushing blow.

REBEKKA [*standing behind him with her arms on the back of the
chair*]: How lovely it was when we sat down in the sitting-
room in the twilight. And how we helped each other to
make plans for a new life. You meant to take hold of real
life – the real life of today – as you said. You were to go
from home to home, like a guest who brought freedom.
To win over minds and desires. To make men noble all
around you – in wider and wider circles. Noblemen.

ROSMER: Noblemen and happy.

REBEKKA: Yes – happy.

ROSMER: For it is joy that makes minds noble, Rebekka.

REBEKKA: Don't you think – suffering, too? Great suffering?

ROSMER: Yes. If one can come through it. Above it. Out
above it.

REBEKKA: That's what it is you must do.

ROSMER [*shaking his head gloomily*]: I shall never rise above
this – not entirely. There will always be a lingering doubt.
A question. I shall never come again to delight in the thing
that makes life so wonderful, so beautiful to live.

REBEKKA [*speaking low, over the back of the chair*]: What is it
you mean, John?

ROSMER [*looking up at her*]: Quiet, happy innocence.

REBEKKA [*stepping back*]: Yes. Innocence. [*A short pause.*]

ROSMER [*with his elbow on the table, resting his head on his hand
and looking straight in front of him*]: And the way she managed

to link things up. How systematically she put it together. First she begins to cherish a doubt about the soundness of my faith. How could she get hold of *that* idea then? But she did get hold of it. And then it grew to certainty. And then – yes, then of course it was so easy for her to believe all the rest possible. [*Sitting back in his chair and running his hands through his hair*] Oh, all these wild imaginings! I shall never get rid of them. I'm sure of it. I know it. At any moment they'll come crowding in on me and remind me of the dead.

REBEKKA: Just like the white horse of Rosmersholm.

ROSMER: Yes, like that. Rushing out of the darkness. In the silence.

REBEKKA: And for the sake of this miserable fantasy you'll let go of the real life you were beginning to take hold of.

ROSMER: You're right; it's hard. Hard, Rebekka. But it doesn't rest with me to choose. How could I possibly overcome this!

REBEKKA [*behind the chair*]: By making yourself new ties.

ROSMER [*starting and looking up*]: New ties!

REBEKKA: Yes, new ties with the world outside. Living, working, acting. Not sitting here pondering and brooding over insoluble mysteries.

ROSMER [*getting up*]: New ties? [*He crosses the room, stands by the door and then comes back.*] A question comes to my mind. Haven't you too put that question to yourself, Rebekka?

REBEKKA [*breathing with difficulty*]: Let me ... know ... what it is?

ROSMER: How do you think *our* relationship will shape after today?

REBEKKA: I think our friendship can hold out all right – whatever happens.

ROSMER: Yes, only I didn't mean it quite like that. I was thinking of what brought us together in the first place – what binds us so closely to each other – our common belief in pure comradeship between a man and a woman –

REBEKKA: Yes, yes – what?

ROSMER: I mean that such a relationship – as ours, now – isn't that best suited to a life of still, happy peace –?

REBEKKA: Well?

ROSMER: Only what's opening before me now is a life of battle and unrest and of strong emotions. For I mean to live my life, Rebekka! I won't let myself be struck down by terrifying possibilities. I won't have my way of life dictated to me, either by living men or by – anyone else.

REBEKKA: No, no don't let it be! Be a free man, entirely, John!

ROSMER: But do you realize what I think, then? Don't you know? Don't you see how I can best win freedom from all the haunting, nagging memories – from all the sad things of the past?

REBEKKA: Well?

ROSMER: By setting up against them a new, a living reality.

REBEKKA [groping for the back of the chair]: A living –? What is ... this!

ROSMER [coming nearer]: Rebekka – if I asked you now – will you be my second wife?

REBEKKA [speechless a moment, then crying out with joy]: Your wife! Your –! I!

ROSMER: Good. Let us try it. We two will be one. There must be no place here any longer left empty by the dead.

REBEKKA: I – in Beatë's place –!

ROSMER: Then she'll be out of the story. Right out. For ever and always.

REBEKKA [in a low, trembling voice]: You think so, John?

ROSMER: It must be so! It must! I can't – I won't go through life with a corpse on my back. Help me to throw it off, Rebekka. And let us stifle all reminders in freedom, in delight, in passion. You shall be for me the only wife I have ever had.

REBEKKA [*controlled*]: Don't ever bring this up again. I shall never be your wife.

ROSMER: What! Never! Oh, don't you think you could come to love me? Isn't there actually a touch of love in our friendship already?

REBEKKA [*stopping her ears as if in terror*]: Don't talk in that way, John! Don't say anything like that!

ROSMER [*seizing her by the arm*]: Yes, yes there *is* a growing possibility in our relationship. Ah, I can see it in you that you feel the same. Don't you, Rebekka?

REBEKKA [*firm and composed again*]: Listen, now. I tell you this – if you go on with this, I shall go away from Ros-mersholm.

ROSMER: Go away! You! You can't do that. It's impossible.

REBEKKA: It's even more impossible that I can be your wife. Never in this world can I be that.

ROSMER [*looking at her in surprise*]: You say 'can'. And you say it so strangely. Why can't you?

REBEKKA [*clasping both his hands*]: My dear friend, for your own sake and for mine too, don't ask why. [*Letting him go.*] There it is, John. [*She goes towards the door on the left.*]

ROSMER: For the future, I have no other question than the one – 'Why?'

REBEKKA [*turning and looking at him*]: Then it is ended.

ROSMER: Between you and me?

REBEKKA: Yes.

ROSMER: It will never be ended between us two. You will never go away from Rosmersholm.

REBEKKA [*with her hand on the latch of the door*]: No, I pro-bably won't do that. But if you ask me again – then it is ended nevertheless.

ROSMER: Ended nevertheless? How –?

REBEKKA: Yes; because then I go the way Beatë went. Now you know it John.

ROSMER: Rebekka –!

REBEKKA [*at the door, nodding slowly*]: Now you know it. [*She goes.*]

ROSMER [*gazing like a lost soul towards the closed door and speaking to himself*]: What – is – this?

ACT THREE

The living-room at Rosmersholm. The window and the door to the hall are open. The morning sun is shining outside. REBEKKA WEST, *dressed as in the first act, is standing by the window watering and arranging the flowers. Her crochet-work is lying in the easy chair.* MRS HELSETH *is going round with a feather-broom in her hand, dusting the furniture.*

REBEKKA [*after a moment's silence*]: It's strange the Rector's staying upstairs so long today.

MRS HELSETH: Oh, he often does that. But I expect he'll soon be down now.

REBEKKA: Have you seen anything of him?

MRS HELSETH: Only a glimpse. When I went up with the coffee, he was in his bedroom dressing.

REBEKKA: I was asking because he wasn't very well yesterday.

MRS HELSETH: No, he didn't look it. And I'm wondering if there isn't something wrong between him and his brother-in-law.

REBEKKA: What do you think it could be?

MRS HELSETH: I can't think. Perhaps it's this Mortensgaard has set the two of them against each other.

REBEKKA: That's quite possible. Do you know this Peder Mortensgaard at all?

MRS HELSETH: No, indeed. How can you think so, Miss? A creature like him!

REBEKKA: Do you mean because he publishes that unpleasant newspaper?

MRS HELSETH: Oh, it's not only for *that*. Surely you've heard, Miss, that he had a child by a married woman whose husband had run away?

REBEKKA: I've heard people say so. But it was a long time before I came here.

MRS HELSETH: Yes, indeed, he was quite young then. And she ought to have had better sense than him. All for marrying her, he was, too. But he couldn't manage it. And he certainly suffered for it, pretty badly. But, my word, he's got on his feet since then, has Mortensgaard. There's plenty of people run after *that* man.

REBEKKA: Most of the poorer people turn to him first when there's anything wrong.

MRS HELSETH: Oh, there might be some besides the poor folk, too.

REBEKKA [*glancing covertly at her*]: Really?

MRS HELSETH [*by the sofa, dusting and rubbing vigorously*]: It might be the people one would least expect it of, Miss.

REBEKKA [*arranging the flowers*]: Oh, that's surely just something you imagine, Mrs Helseth. Because *you* can't know a thing like that for certain.

MRS HELSETH: So you think I can't know, Miss? Oh yes, indeed, I can. Because, if I must come out with it – well, I myself once went to Mortensgaard with a letter.

REBEKKA [*turning*]: No, – *did* you?

MRS HELSETH: Yes, I certainly did. And that letter was written at Rosmersholm, too.

REBEKKA: Really, Mrs Helseth?

MRS HELSETH: Yes, 'pon my word it was. And fine paper it was written on. And fine red sealing-wax there was outside it, too.

REBEKKA: And *you* were commissioned to go with it? Well, my dear Mrs Helseth, then it's not difficult to guess who it was from.

MRS HELSETH: Oh, isn't it?

REBEKKA: Of course it was something that poor Mrs Rosmer, when she was an invalid –

MRS HELSETH: It's you that says that, Miss, and not me.

REBEKKA: But what was in the letter, then? No of course – you can't know that.

MRS HELSETH: Hm. I might happen to know it, for all that.

REBEKKA: Did she tell you what she was writing about?

MRS HELSETH: No, she didn't exactly do that. But when that man Mortensgaard had read it, he set to work, asking me such questions about this and that, that I could guess all right what was in it.

REBEKKA: What do you think was in it, then? Oh dear, kind Mrs Helseth, do tell me!

MRS HELSETH: Ah no, Miss. Not for anything in the world.

REBEKKA: Oh, you can tell it to me. We are two such good friends.

MRS HELSETH: Heaven forbid I should say anything to you about *that*, Miss. I can't say more than it was something dreadful they'd gone and made the poor, sick lady believe.

REBEKKA: Who had made her believe it?

MRS HELSETH: Wicked people, Miss West. Wicked people.

REBEKKA: Wicked –?

MRS HELSETH: Yes, I say it again. Downright wicked people, they must have been.

REBEKKA: And who ever do you think it could be?

MRS HELSETH: Oh, I know all right what I think. But heaven forbid *I* should say anything. To be sure there's a certain lady in town - hm!

REBEKKA: I can see that you mean Mrs Kroll.

MRS HELSETH: Yes, she's a terror, she is. She's always been a bit high and mighty with me. And she's never been too fond of you.

REBEKKA: Do you think Mrs Rosmer was in her right mind when she wrote that letter to Mortensgaard?

MRS HELSETH: It's so queer about the mind, Miss. I don't think, you know, she was right off her head.

REBEKKA: But she seemed to go all to pieces when she

realized she couldn't have any children. It was *then* that the madness broke out.

MRS HELSETH: Yes, that came very hard on her, poor lady.

REBEKKA [*taking her crochet-work and sitting on the chair by the window*]: But otherwise, don't you agree that at bottom that was good for the Rector, Mrs Helseth?

MRS HELSETH: What, Miss?

REBEKKA: That there were no children here? Don't you?

MRS HELSETH: Hm. I don't rightly know what to say about that.

REBEKKA: Oh yes, believe me. It was the best thing for him. Mr Rosmer oughtn't to have to put up with crying children.

MRS HELSETH: Children don't cry at Rosmersholm, Miss.

REBEKKA [*looking at her*]: They don't cry?

MRS HELSETH: In this house children have never been used to cry, as long as folk can remember.

REBEKKA: Why, that's strange.

MRS HELSETH: Yes, isn't it? But it runs in the family. And there's another strange thing, too. When they grow up they never laugh. Never laugh, as long as they live.

REBEKKA: But that would be extraordinary –

MRS HELSETH: Have you, Miss, ever heard or seen the Rector laugh – one single time?

REBEKKA: No – when I come to think of it, I almost believe you're right. But it seems to me people don't on the whole laugh much in this district.

MRS HELSETH: They don't. It began at Rosmersholm, they say. And so, I suppose, it's just spread, like any other kind of infection.

REBEKKA: You're a wise woman, you know, Mrs Helseth.

MRS HELSETH: Ah, don't you sit there making fun of me, Miss. [*Listens.*] Tck, tck! – there's the Rector coming down. He doesn't like to see brooms in here.

[*She goes out by the door on the right.* JOHN ROSMER, *with stick and hat in hand, comes in from the hall.*]

ROSMER: Good morning, Rebekka.

REBEKKA: Good morning, my dear. [*After a moment, going on crocheting.*] Are you going out?

ROSMER: Yes.

REBEKKA: The weather's so lovely.

ROSMER: You didn't come up to see me this morning.

REBEKKA: No – I didn't. Not today.

ROSMER: Won't you do it in future, either?

REBEKKA: Oh my dear, I don't know yet.

ROSMER: Has anything come for me?

REBEKKA: *The County News* has come.

ROSMER: *The County News* –!

REBEKKA: It's on the table.

ROSMER [*putting down his hat and stick*]: Is there anything –?

REBEKKA: Yes.

ROSMER: And yet you didn't send it up –

REBEKKA: You'll read it soon enough.

ROSMER: I see. [*Takes the paper and reads it standing by the table.*] What! 'cannot warn strongly enough against the spineless deserters' – [*Looking at her.*] They call me a deserter, Rebekka.

REBEKKA: No name is mentioned.

ROSMER: It's all the same. [*Going on reading.*] 'Secret traitors to the good cause' – 'Judases who boldly acknowledge their apostasy as soon as they think the opportune and – most profitable moment has come.' 'Unscrupulous outrage upon their venerable ancestors' reputations' – 'in the expectation that men in power at the moment will not fail to produce a suitable reward.' [*Lays the paper on the table.*] And they write that about me. They, who have known me so long and so well. This, that they don't believe in themselves. This, that they know there isn't a word of truth in – nevertheless, they write it.

REBEKKA: There's more yet.

ROSMER [*taking up the paper again*]: – 'excuse of inexperienced judgement' – 'perverse influence – perhaps extended also to matters that we will not for the moment make the subject of public comment or animadversion.' [*Looking at her.*] What is this?

REBEKKA: They're pointing at me, you realize.

ROSMER [*putting down the paper*]: Rebekka – this is the behaviour of dishonourable men.

REBEKKA: Yes, I don't think there's much to choose between them and Mortensgaard.

ROSMER [*walking about the room*]: This *must* be put right. Everything that's decent in people will be lost if this is allowed to go on. But it shan't be. Oh how glad – how glad I should feel, if I could bring a little light into all this gloom and horror.

REBEKKA [*getting up*]: Yes, that's true, isn't it? There you have something great and noble to live for!

ROSMER: Just think, if I could rouse them to self-knowledge! Bring them to repent and be ashamed of themselves. Make them draw together in tolerance – in love, Rebekka.

REBEKKA: Yes, just put all your strength into that and you'll see – you'll win!

ROSMER: I think it must be possible to. Oh what a joy it would be then to live! No more embittered strife. Only friendly rivalry. Every eye fixed on the same goal. All wills, all minds reaching forward – upward – each in the way his own nature prompts. Happiness for all – created through all. [*Reaches the window and looks out. Starts and says gloomily.*] Ah! Not through me.

REBEKKA: Not –? Not through you?

ROSMER: And not *for* me either.

REBEKKA: Oh, John, don't let doubts like that come into your mind.

ROSMER: Happiness, Rebekka dear, happiness – that is first and foremost the quiet, glad, secure sense of innocence.

REBEKKA [*gazing in front of her*]: Yes. This business of guilt –

ROSMER: Ah, that's a thing you can't possibly judge of. But I –

REBEKKA: You least of all!

ROSMER [*pointing out of the window*]: The mill-race.

REBEKKA: Oh, John –!

[MRS HELSETH *looks in at the door on the right.*]

MRS HELSETH: Miss West!

REBEKKA: Later on, later on. Not now.

MRS HELSETH: Only a word, Miss.

[*Rebekka goes across to the door.* MRS HELSETH *explains something to her. They stand a moment whispering together.* MRS HELSETH *nods and goes.*]

ROSMER [*uneasily*]: Was it anything for me?

REBEKKA: No, it was only to do with the house. Now you ought to go out in the fresh air, John dear. Go for a good long walk, that's what you ought to do.

ROSMER [*taking his hat*]: Yes, come along. We'll go together.

REBEKKA: No, my dear, I can't come now. You must go by yourself. But shake off all these gloomy thoughts. Promise me you will.

ROSMER: I shall never get them shaken off – I'm afraid.

REBEKKA: Oh, how can anything so groundless take such a hold of you –!

ROSMER: Unfortunately it's not altogether so groundless, you know. I lay thinking over it the whole night. Perhaps Beatë saw the truth after all.

REBEKKA: In what – do you think?

ROSMER: Saw the truth when she thought I loved you, Rebekka.

REBEKKA: Saw the truth in *that*!

ROSMER [*putting his hat down on the table*]: I keep struggling with the question whether we two weren't deceiving ourselves all the time, when we called our relation friendship.

REBEKKA: Do you mean, perhaps, that it could just as well be called –?

ROSMER: – love. Yes, my dear, that's what I mean. Already

87

while Beatë was alive, it was you I gave all my thoughts to. It was you alone that I longed for. It was with you that I felt that quiet, glad, happiness without passion. When we think it over clearly, Rebekka – well, our life together began like the sweet, hidden love of two children. Without desire and without dreams. Didn't you feel it in the same way too? Tell me?

REBEKKA [*fighting with herself*]: Oh – I don't know how to answer you.

ROSMER: And it's this inward life, in each other and for each other, that we've taken for friendship. No, my dear, our relationship has been a spiritual marriage. Perhaps from the very first days. That's why there's guilt on my side. I had no right to it – no right for Beatë's sake.

REBEKKA: No right to live in happiness? Do you believe that, John?

ROSMER: She looked at our friendship through the eyes of *her* love. Judged our friendship after the nature of her love. Of course. Beatë couldn't judge otherwise than she did.

REBEKKA: But how can you reproach yourself for Beatë's delusion!

ROSMER: For love of me – in *her* way – she went into the mill-race. That fact stands firm, Rebekka. I can never get past that.

REBEKKA: Oh, don't think of anything but the great, glorious task you've pledged your life to!

ROSMER [*shaking his head*]: That can never be carried through, my dear. Not by me. Not after what I now know.

REBEKKA: Why not by you?

ROSMER: Because victory is never won for a cause that has its root in guilt.

REBEKKA [*in protest*]: Oh, all these are the doubts that are bred in your race, the fears of your race, the scruples of your race. They say around here that the dead come again as swift, white horses. I think all this is something of that kind.

ROSMER: Let it be whatever it likes. What difference does it make, when I can't get away from it? And you can believe me, Rebekka. It is as I say. The cause that's to win through to lasting victory – it must be upheld by a glad and innocent man.

REBEKKA: Is gladness so essential for *you*, John?

ROSMER: Gladness? Yes, my dear – it is.

REBEKKA: For you, who can never laugh?

ROSMER: Yes. In spite of that. Believe me, I have a great capacity for gladness.

REBEKKA: Now you must go, my dear. A long way – a really long way. Do you hear? See, there's your hat. And there's your stick.

ROSMER [*taking them both*]: Thanks. And you aren't coming with me?

REBEKKA: No, no; I can't now.

ROSMER: Very well. You'll be with me all the same.

[*He goes out through the door to the hall. After a moment* REBEKKA *peeps out under cover of the open door. Then she goes over to the door on the right.*]

REBEKKA [*opening the door and speaking under her voice*]: All right, Mrs Helseth. You can let him in now. [*She goes across towards the window.*]

[*A little while after* DR KROLL *comes in from the right. He bows to her silently and formally, keeping his hat in his hand.*]

KROLL: He is gone, then?

REBEKKA: Yes.

KROLL: Does he usually go for long?

REBEKKA: Yes. But today he's so erratic. And if you don't want to meet him –

KROLL: No, no. It's you I want to talk to. And quite alone.

REBEKKA: Then we'd better not waste time. Sit down, Principal.

[*She sits down in the easy chair by the window.* DR KROLL *sits on a chair beside her.*]

KROLL: Miss West – you can hardly realize, how deeply and keenly it goes to my heart – this change that has taken place in John Rosmer.

REBEKKA: We were prepared for it to be like that – at first.

KROLL: Only at first?

REBEKKA: Mr Rosmer had a firm hope that sooner or later you would join him.

KROLL: I!

REBEKKA: Both you and all his other friends.

KROLL: Yes, there you are! That shows how weak his judgement is when it comes to people and human affairs.

REBEKKA: However, – since he now feels it a necessity to free himself on all sides –

KROLL: Yes, but you know, it's precisely *that* that I don't believe.

REBEKKA: What do you believe, then?

KROLL: I think it's *you* who are at the back of the whole thing.

REBEKKA: You got that from your wife, Dr Kroll.

KROLL: It doesn't make any difference whom I have it from. But it's certain that I feel a strong doubt – an extremely strong doubt, I say – when I think over and weigh up the whole of your conduct ever since you came here.

REBEKKA [*looking at him*]: I seem to remember there was a time when you felt an extremely strong *confidence* in me, my dear Principal. A warm confidence, I might almost say.

KROLL [*in a low voice*]: Whom could you not bewitch when you set your mind to it?

REBEKKA: I set my mind to –!

KROLL: Yes, you did. I am not so foolish any longer as to imagine there was any feeling in the game. You simply wanted to get yourself an entry to Rosmersholm. Establish yourself firmly here. It was that I was to help you with. I see it now.

REBEKKA: So you've quite forgotten that it was Beatë who begged and besought me to move out here.

KROLL: Yes, when you'd bewitched her too. For can that really be called friendship – what she came to feel for you? It turned to adoration – idolatry. Degenerated into –what shall I call it? – into a kind of passionate infatuation. Yes, that's the right word.

REBEKKA: You must please remember your sister's condition. As for me, I don't think I can be called highly-strung in any way.

KROLL: No, that you certainly aren't. But that makes you all the more dangerous to the people you want to get control over. It's so easy for you to do things deliberately and with precise calculation – just because you have a cold heart.

REBEKKA: Cold? Are you so sure of that?

KROLL: I'm quite sure of it now. Else you couldn't have gone on here year after year, following out your purpose so inflexibly. Well, well. You've got what you wanted. You've got him and everything else in your power. But in order to carry all this through, you haven't scrupled to make him miserable.

REBEKKA: It's not true. It isn't I. It's you yourself who've made him miserable.

KROLL: I have!

REBEKKA: Yes, when you led him on to imagine that he was to blame for the terrible end Beatë came to.

KROLL: So it laid such a deep hold on him, then?

REBEKKA: You can well imagine it. A mind as sensitive as his –

KROLL: I assumed that a so-called 'emancipated' man knew how to overcome all his scruples. But there we are, then! Oh, well – as a matter of fact, it was pretty much what I expected. The descendant of the men who are looking down on us here – he won't succeed in breaking away from his heritage, that has come down inviolate from generation to generation.

REBEKKA [*looking thoughtfully down*]: John Rosmer has his roots very deep in his race. That's certainly true.

KROLL: Yes, and you should have made allowances for that, if you had any sympathy for him. But you probably couldn't make that kind of allowance. The point you start from is after all as far asunder as the poles from his.

REBEKKA: What point do you mean?

KROLL: I mean the starting-point in your beginnings. In your parentage, Miss West.

REBEKKA: I see. Yes, it's quite true – I came from very poor surroundings. But at the same time –

KROLL: It's not the position or standing I'm talking of. I'm thinking of the moral starting-point.

REBEKKA: *Starting-point?* For what?

KROLL: For your coming into existence at all.

REBEKKA: What's this you're saying!

KROLL: I'm only saying it because it explains the whole of your conduct.

REBEKKA: I don't understand this. I must have the facts clear!

KROLL: I certainly thought you had the facts. Otherwise it would be odd for you to have let yourself be adopted by Dr West –

REBEKKA [*getting up*]: Oh, that's it. Now I understand.

KROLL: – to have taken his name. Your mother's name was Gamvik.

REBEKKA [*crossing the room away*]: My father's name was Gamvik, Principal.

KROLL: Your mother's work must have brought her regularly into contact with the local doctor.

REBEKKA: That's quite true.

KROLL: And then he takes you to live with him – as soon as your mother was dead. He treats you harshly. And yet you stay with him. You know that he will never leave you a penny. In fact you only got a caseful of books. And yet you stick to him. Put up with him. Care for him to the last.

REBEKKA [*over by the table, looking scornfully at him*]: And that I did all this – you deduce from that that there was something immoral, something criminal about my birth!

KROLL: What you did for him I explain in terms of an unconscious filial instinct. As for the rest of it, I regard the whole of your conduct as the outcome of your parentage.

REBEKKA [*passionately*]: But there's not a true word in anything you're saying! And I can prove it. Because Dr West hadn't come to Finmark when I was born.

KROLL: I'm sorry, Miss West. He came up there the year before. I've found that out.

REBEKKA: You're wrong, I say! You're absolutely wrong!

KROLL: You said here the day before yesterday that you were twenty-nine. Getting on for thirty.

REBEKKA: Really? Did I say that?

KROLL: Yes, you did. And from that I can calculate –

REBEKKA: Stop! There's no point in calculating. For I may just as well tell you at once: I am a year older than I give myself out to be.

KROLL [*smiling, incredulous*]: Really? That's something new. How did it happen?

REBEKKA: When I got to twenty-five, it seemed to me that I was getting much too old – unmarried, as I was. And so I decided to tell a lie and get rid of a year.

KROLL: You? An emancipated woman. Do you cherish prejudices about the age for marriage?

REBEKKA: Yes, it was silly – and ridiculous too. But there's always something or other that clings to one and one can't get rid of. That's how we are.

KROLL: Possibly. But the calculation may be right all the same. For Dr West was up there on a flying visit the year before he was appointed.

REBEKKA [*breaking out*]: It's not true!

KROLL: Isn't it true?

REBEKKA: No. Because my mother never spoke of it.

KROLL: So she didn't?

REBEKKA: No. Never. Nor Dr West either. Not a word.

KROLL: Might that not be because both of them had some reason to skip a year? Just as *you* have, Miss West? Perhaps it's a family characteristic.

REBEKKA [*walking about, clenching and wringing her hands*]: It's impossible. It's only something you want to make me think. It's not true for a moment, all this. Can't be true! Not for a moment!

KROLL [*getting up*]: But, my dear Miss West – why in the name of heaven are you so upset? You make me quite alarmed. What am I to believe or think –!

REBEKKA: Nothing. You're not to believe or think anything.

KROLL: Then you must certainly explain to me how it is you take this business – this possibility – so much to heart.

REBEKKA [*controlling herself*]: It's really quite obvious, Dr Kroll. I've no desire to be looked on here as an illegitimate child.

KROLL: Very well. Yes, let us content ourselves with that explanation – for the time being. But in that case you've retained a certain – prejudice – on that point also.

REBEKKA: Yes, I suppose I have.

KROLL: Well, I think the same thing has happened with most of what you term your emancipation. You've read up for yourself a whole lot of new ideas and opinions. You've acquired knowledge of a sort about researches in various fields – researches which seem to overturn a certain amount of what has hitherto been accepted among us as incontrovertible and unassailable. But all this has remained mere information for you, Miss West. Acquired knowledge. It hasn't got into your blood.

REBEKKA [*thoughtfully*]: It may be that you're right.

KROLL: Yes, just examine yourself and you'll see! And if that's how matters stand with you, then I think we can tell what it has come to with John Rosmer. It's pure, sheer madness – it's plunging headlong into ruin – for *him* to want to come forward openly and acknowledge himself an apostate! Just think – he, with that sensitive mind of his! Imagine *him* disowned – persecuted by the group he has hitherto been part of. Exposed to pitiless attack from the best people in the place. Never in this life will he be the man to stand up to that.

REBEKKA: He *must* stand up to it. It's too late now for him to draw back.

KROLL: Not at all too late. Not by any means. What has happened can be kept quiet, or at least it can be explained away as an aberration, purely temporary, though admittedly regrettable. But *one* step is absolutely necessary.

REBEKKA: And what is that?

KROLL: You must get him to legalize the position, Miss West.

REBEKKA: The position he stands in to me?

KROLL: Yes. You must see to it that he does that.

REBEKKA: You simply can't get rid of the idea, then, that our relationship needs legalizing, as you call it?

KROLL: I don't wish to go into the matter itself more closely. But I certainly think I've observed that the point at which it comes easiest to break with all so-called prejudices, is in – hm.

REBEKKA: Is in the relationship between a man and a woman, you mean?

KROLL: Yes, to speak plainly, I think it is.

REBEKKA [*walking across the room and looking out through the window*]: I nearly said – if only you were right, Dr Kroll.

KROLL: What do you mean by that? You say it so strangely.

REBEKKA: Oh never mind! Don't let's talk about the thing any more. Ah – there he comes.

KROLL: Already! I'll go, then.

REBEKKA [*going across to him*]: No – stay here. Because now you're going to hear something.

KROLL: Not now. I don't think I can bear to see him.

REBEKKA: I beg you – stay. Do. Or you'll regret it afterwards. It's the last time I'll ask you for anything.

KROLL [*looking at her with surprise and putting down his hat*]: Very well, Miss West. As you wish.

> [*There is a moment's silence. Then* JOHN ROSMER *comes in from the hall.*]

ROSMER [*sees* KROLL *and stops in the doorway*]: What! Are *you* here!

REBEKKA: He would much rather not have met you, John.

KROLL [*involuntarily*]: John!

REBEKKA: Yes, Principal. John and I – we use each other's Christian names. The relationship between us has brought that about.

KROLL: Was it *that* that you promised I was to hear?

REBEKKA: Both that and – a little more.

ROSMER [*coming nearer*]: What is the object of your visit here today?

KROLL: I wanted to try once more to stop you and win you back.

ROSMER [*pointing to the newspaper*]: After what's printed there?

KROLL: I didn't write it.

ROSMER: Did you make any attempt to keep it out?

KROLL: That would have been unjustifiable behaviour to the cause I serve. And besides, it wasn't in my power.

REBEKKA [*tearing up the newspaper, crumpling the pieces together and throwing them into the stove*]: That's it. Now it's out of sight. So let it be out of mind too. For there won't be anything more of that kind, John.

KROLL: Ah, I wish you could really manage that.

REBEKKA: Come, my friends, let's sit down. All three of us. Then I'll tell you everything.

ROSMER [*sitting down, without thinking*]: What ever is it that's come over you, Rebekka? This unnatural calm. What ever is it?

REBEKKA: The calm of a decision reached. [*She sits down.*] Sit down too, Principal.

[DR KROLL *takes a seat on the sofa.*]

ROSMER: Of decision, you say. What decision?

REBEKKA: I will give you again what you need to live your life. You shall get back your happy innocence, my dear friend.

ROSMER: But what *is* all this?

REBEKKA: I'm just going to explain. That's all that's needed.

ROSMER: Well?

REBEKKA: When I came down here from Finmark – with Dr West – it seemed as though a great, new, wide world opened before me. The doctor had taught me rather erratically. All the odds and ends I knew about life at that time. [*Battling and barely audible.*] And so –

KROLL: And so?

ROSMER: But, Rebekka – I know this well enough.

REBEKKA [*controlling herself*]: Yes, yes – you're quite right, really. You know it only too well.

KROLL [*looking at her fixedly*]: It's perhaps best for me to go.

REBEKKA: No, my dear Principal, you must stay there. [*To* ROSMER.] Yes, and so *that* was it, you see. I wanted to take part in the new age that was dawning. Take part in all the new thoughts. Dr Kroll told me one day that Ulrik Brendel had had a great influence over you at one time while you were still a boy. I thought it might be possible for me to take this up again.

ROSMER: Did you come here with a hidden design?

REBEKKA: I wanted us two to go forward together towards freedom. Always forward. Always further on. But then there was this gloomy insurmountable barrier between you and full, complete freedom.

ROSMER: What barrier do you mean?

REBEKKA: I mean this, John, that you could only grow up into freedom in the bright sunshine. And here you were instead, ailing and drooping in the gloom of a marriage like that.

ROSMER: Never until today have you talked to me about my marriage in *that* way.

REBEKKA: No, I didn't dare to, because I should have frightened you.

KROLL [*nodding to* ROSMER]: Do you hear that!

REBEKKA [*going on*]: But I saw well enough where the way of escape lay for you. The only escape. And so I took action.

ROSMER: What action is it you're referring to?

KROLL: Do you mean to say that –!

REBEKKA: Yes, John. [*Getting up.*] Stay where you are. You too, Dr Kroll. But now it must come out. It wasn't you, John. You're innocent. It was I who drew – who ended by drawing Beatë out into the devious ways –

ROSMER [*jumping up*]: Rebekka!

KROLL [*getting up from the sofa*]: – the devious ways!

REBEKKA: Into the ways – that led to the mill-race. Now you know it, both of you.

ROSMER [*as though stunned*]: But I don't understand. What's she standing there saying? I don't understand a word.

KROLL: Yes, Rosmer. I'm beginning to understand.

ROSMER: But what did you do, then? What was there you could say to her? There was nothing. Nothing at all!

REBEKKA: She got to know that you meant to free yourself from all the old prejudices.

ROSMER: Yes, but I didn't at that time.

REBEKKA: I knew you would soon come to it.

KROLL [*nodding to* ROSMER]: Aha!

ROSMER: Well, then? What else? Now I want to know the rest as well.

REBEKKA: Some time after that – I begged and besought her to let me go away from Rosmersholm.

ROSMER: Why did you want to go away – then?

REBEKKA: I didn't want to go. I wanted to stay here, where I was. But I said to her that it was much best for us all – for me to go away in time. I gave her to understand that if I stayed here any longer – it might – it might be – that something might happen.

ROSMER: So this is what you said and did.

REBEKKA: Yes, John.

ROSMER: It was *this*, that you called taking action.

REBEKKA [*in a broken voice*]: I called it that; yes.

ROSMER [*after a moment*]: Have you now confessed everything, Rebekka?

REBEKKA: Yes.

KROLL: Not everything.

REBEKKA [*looking at him in terror*]: What more should there be?

KROLL: Didn't you in the end give Beatë to understand that it was necessary – not just that it was best, but that it was necessary – for your sake and Rosmer's, that you should go away somewhere else – as soon as possible? Well?

REBEKKA [*low and indistinctly*]: Perhaps I said something of the kind too.

ROSMER [*sinking into the easy chair by the window*]: And this web of lies and deceit she went on believing – the poor sick creature! Believing so absolutely! So immovably! [*Looking up at* REBEKKA.] And she never turned to me. Never a word! Oh, Rebekka – I see it in your face – *you* advised her not to!

REBEKKA: She had got it fixed in her mind that she – as a childless wife – had no right to be here. And so she imagined that it was her duty to you to make way.

ROSMER: And you – you did nothing to turn her away from this obsession?

REBEKKA: No.

KROLL: Perhaps you strengthened her in it? Answer me! Didn't you?

REBEKKA: That's how she understood me, I suppose.

ROSMER: Yes, yes. And she bowed to your will in everything. And so she made way. [*Springing up.*] How could – how could you carry through this desperate game!

REBEKKA: I thought there were two lives here to choose between, John.

KROLL [*firmly and masterfully*]: *You* had no right to make such a choice!

REBEKKA [*passionately*]: But do you think I set about doing it with cool and cunning composure! I wasn't the same person then as I am now that I'm telling you this. Besides, I believe there are two different sorts of will at work in one person. I wanted Beatë gone. In one way or another. But I never believed that it would happen, all the same. With every step forward that I risked and ventured on, I felt something like a cry within me: No further, now! Not a step further! And yet I *couldn't* let it be. I *had* to risk a tiny fraction more. Only a single one. And then one more – and always one more. And so it happened. That's the way that kind of thing goes.

[*There is a short silence.*]

ROSMER [*to* REBEKKA]: And how do you think things will go with *you* in the future? After this?

REBEKKA: With me – things must go as they can. It doesn't matter very much.

KROLL: Not one word that implies remorse. Perhaps you don't feel any?

REBEKKA [*putting the matter coldly aside*]: You must excuse me, Principal; that's a matter that doesn't concern anyone else. I must settle that with myself.

KROLL [*to* ROSMER]: And this is the woman you're sharing your roof with. On a footing of trust. [*Looking round at the portraits.*] Ah, those who are gone – if they could only see!

ROSMER: Are you going in to town?

KROLL [*taking his hat*]: Yes. The sooner the better.

ROSMER [*taking his hat likewise*]: Then I'll go with you.

KROLL: You will! Yes, I was sure we hadn't quite lost you.

ROSMER: Come along then, Kroll. Come along then.

> [*They both go out through the hall without looking at* REBEKKA. *After a moment* REBEKKA *goes cautiously across to the window and peeps out between the flowers.*]

REBEKKA [*speaking half-aloud to herself*]: Not across the bridge today either. Going up and round. Never over the mill-race. Never. [*Moving away from the window.*] Well, well, then. [*She goes across and pulls the bell-rope. A moment after* MRS HELSETH *comes in from the right.*]

MRS HELSETH: What is it, Miss?

REBEKKA: Mrs Helseth, I wonder if you'd have my trunk brought down from the attic.

MRS HELSETH: Your trunk?

REBEKKA: Yes, you know it; the brown seal-skin trunk.

MRS HELSETH: Very well. But bless us – are you going to make a journey, Miss?

REBEKKA: Yes, I'm going to make a journey now, Mrs Helseth.

MRS HELSETH: And all of a sudden, like this?

REBEKKA: As soon as I've got packed.

MRS HELSETH: Well, I've never heard the like of it! But you'll be coming back again soon, Miss, I suppose?

REBEKKA: I'm never coming back again.

MRS HELSETH: Never! But, good gracious, how ever shall we get on here at Rosmersholm, when Miss West isn't here any longer? Everything had just got so nice and comfortable for the poor Rector.

REBEKKA: Yes, but I've been frightened today, Mrs Helseth.

MRS HELSETH: Frightened! Good lord – but why?

REBEKKA: Because I think I've seen something like a glimpse of white horses.

MRS HELSETH: Of white horses! In broad daylight?

REBEKKA: Oh they're out all right, early and late – the white horses of Rosmersholm. [*With a change of manner.*] Well – so it's the trunk, then, Mrs Helseth.

MRS HELSETH: Very well. The trunk.

[*They both go out to the right.*]

ACT FOUR

The living-room at Rosmersholm. It is late in the evening. The lamp, with a shade over it, is alight on the table. REBEKKA WEST *is standing by the table and packing some odds and ends into a travelling-bag. Her coat, hat, and the white, crocheted woollen shawl are lying over the back of the sofa.* MRS HELSETH *comes in from the right.*

MRS HELSETH [*speaking in a subdued voice and reserved manner*]: Well, all the things are taken out now, Miss. They're in the kitchen passage.

REBEKKA: Good. The coachman's been told?

MRS HELSETH: Yes. He asks what time he's to be here with the carriage.

REBEKKA: I think about eleven o'clock. The boat goes at midnight.

MRS HELSETH [*hesitating a little*]: But what about the Rector? Suppose he hasn't come home by then?

REBEKKA: I shall go just the same. If I don't see him, you can say I'll write to him. A long letter. Say that.

MRS HELSETH: Yes, I suppose that will do – to write. But, poor Miss West – I do feel you ought to try and have one more talk with him.

REBEKKA: Perhaps. Or on the other hand, perhaps not.

MRS HELSETH: Deary me – that I should live to see this! I'd never have thought it.

REBEKKA: Why, what did you think, Mrs Helseth?

MRS HELSETH: Well, I certainly thought Mr Rosmer was more of a man than that.

REBEKKA: More of a man?

MRS HELSETH: Yes, that's what *I* say.

REBEKKA: But my dear Mrs Helseth, what do you mean by that?

MRS HELSETH: I mean what's true and right, Miss. He shouldn't get out of it in this way, that he shouldn't.

REBEKKA [*looking at her*]: Now look here, Mrs Helseth. Tell me, honest and straight – why do you think I'm going away?

MRS HELSETH: Lord bless us, I suppose it's necessary, Miss. Well, well, well! But I really don't think the Rector's done the right thing. Mortensgaard, he had some excuse. Because she'd her husband still living. So *those* two couldn't get married, however much they wanted to. But as for the Rector, he – hm!

REBEKKA [*with a faint smile*]: Could you really have thought such a thing about me and Mr Rosmer?

MRS HELSETH: Never in the world. Well, I mean – not before today.

REBEKKA: But today, then –?

MRS HELSETH: Oh, well – after all the dreadful things they say there is in the papers about the Rector, why –

REBEKKA: Ah!

MRS HELSETH: What I mean is, a man that can go over to Mortensgaard's religon, upon my word, one can believe anything of *him*.

REBEKKA: Ah, yes; perhaps that's so. But how about me, then? What do you say about me?

MRS HELSETH: Bless you, Miss – I don't think there's so much to say against you. It's not so easy for a woman on her own to stand out, I expect. After all, we're all human, Miss West.

REBEKKA: That's a true word, Mrs Helseth. We're all human. What are you listening to?

MRS HELSETH [*in a low voice*]: Goodness gracious! I think he's coming this minute.

REBEKKA [*starting*]: So in spite of everything –! [*Firmly.*] Oh, well. All right.

[JOHN ROSMER *comes in from the hall.*]

ROSMER [*seeing the travelling things, turns to* REBEKKA *with a question*]: What does this mean?

REBEKKA: I'm going away.

ROSMER: At once?

REBEKKA: Yes. [*To* MRS HELSETH.] Eleven o'clock then.

MRS HELSETH: Very well, Miss. [*She goes out to the right.*]

ROSMER [*after a short pause*]: Where are you going to, Rebekka?

REBEKKA: To the north by the boat.

ROSMER: To the north? What are you going to the north for?

REBEKKA: That's where I came from.

ROSMER: But you haven't anything to take you up there now.

REBEKKA: I haven't down here either.

ROSMER: What do you expect to do with yourself?

REBEKKA: I don't know. I just want to make an end of it.

ROSMER: Make an end of it?

REBEKKA: Rosmersholm has broken me.

ROSMER [*his interest aroused*]: What do you say?

REBEKKA: Broken me to pieces. I'd such courage when I came here and such a strong will. Now I've submitted to an alien law. I don't believe I shall ever dare to tackle anything again.

ROSMER: Why not? What is this law that you say you've –?

REBEKKA: My dear, don't let's talk about that now. What happened with you and the Principal?

ROSMER: We've made peace.

REBEKKA: I see. So it came to that.

ROSMER: He got the whole of our old circle together at his house. They made it quite clear to me that the task of ennobling men's minds – it's not my work at all. And besides, it's a hopeless business, anyway, you know. I'm going to let it alone.

REBEKKA: Yes, well – perhaps it's best so.

ROSMER: *That's* what you say now, is it? Is *that* your opinion now?

REBEKKA: I've come to that opinion. In the last day or two.

ROSMER: You're lying, Rebekka.

REBEKKA: Lying –?

ROSMER: Yes, you're lying. You've never believed in me. Never did you believe that I was the man to lead the cause to victory.

REBEKKA: I believed that we two together would win in the end.

ROSMER: That's not true. You believed that you had it in you to achieve something great in life. That you could use me to further your ends. That I could serve your purposes. *That's* what you've believed.

REBEKKA: Listen, now, John –

ROSMER [*seating himself wearily on the sofa*]: Oh, let it be! I see the whole thing now, to the bottom. I've been like a glove in your hands.

REBEKKA: Listen, now, John. Let's talk this over. It'll be the last time. [*Seating herself in a chair near the sofa.*] I did think I would write to you about the whole thing – when I'd got back to the north again. But it'll be best for you to hear it at once.

ROSMER: Have you still more to confess?

REBEKKA: I still have the main thing.

ROSMER: What 'main' thing?

REBEKKA: The thing you've never guessed. The thing that gives light and shade to everything else.

ROSMER [*shaking his head*]: I don't understand a word of this.

REBEKKA: It's quite true that at one time I did play my cards to win an entry to Rosmersholm. I thought I should succeed in making my way here. Either by one means or another, you understand.

ROSMER: You succeeded in carrying it through, too – what you wanted.

REBEKKA: I think I could have carried it through, whatever it had been – in those days. For then I still had that free, fearless will of mine. I didn't recognize any claims. Or any reason for turning aside. But then came the beginning of that thing that has broken my will in me – and made me a miserable coward for the rest of my life.

ROSMER: What came? Talk so that I can understand you.

REBEKKA: There came over me ... this wild, uncontrollable passion ... Oh, John –!

ROSMER: Passion? You –! For what?

REBEKKA: For you.

ROSMER [*springing up*]: What is this!

REBEKKA [*checking him*]: Sit still, my dear. I'll tell you more about it.

ROSMER: And you mean to say that you have loved me ... in this way!

REBEKKA: I thought it could be called loving – in those days. I thought it was love. But it wasn't. It was what I have told you. It was a wild, uncontrollable passion.

ROSMER [*with difficulty*]: Rebekka, is it really you yourself – you – you – sitting here and telling me all this!

REBEKKA: Yes, what do you suppose, John?

ROSMER: Because of this – so it was under the influence of this that you ... *took action*, as you call it.

REBEKKA: It came over me like a storm at sea. It was like one of those storms we can get up north in the winter. It takes hold of you – and sweeps you along with it, you know, – as long as it lasts. No thought of standing against it.

ROSMER: And so it carried the unhappy Beatë out into the mill-race.

REBEKKA: Yes. For it was like a battle for life at that time between Beatë and me.

ROSMER: You were certainly the strongest at Rosmersholm. Stronger than both Beatë and me together.

REBEKKA: I knew you well enough to know – there was no way out for you until you were set free in your surroundings – and in your soul.

ROSMER: But I don't understand you, Rebekka. You, yourself, your whole conduct is a riddle I can't solve. I'm free now – both in my soul and my surroundings. You're standing now right in front of the goal you'd set yourself from the first. And yet – !

REBEKKA: I've never stood further from the goal than now.

ROSMER: – and yet, I say, when I asked you yesterday, begged you to be my wife – then you cried out, as though you were terrified, that it could never be.

REBEKKA: I cried out in despair, my dear.

ROSMER: Why?

REBEKKA: Because Rosmersholm has broken my nerve. I've had my will sapped here and crushed, my own, fearless will. The time is past for me when I dared to tackle whatever turned up. I've lost the power to act, John.

ROSMER: Tell me how it's happened.

REBEKKA: It's happened through sharing my life with you.

ROSMER: But how? How?

REBEKKA: When I was alone with you here – and when you had become yourself –

ROSMER: Yes, well?

REBEKKA: – for you never were entirely yourself as long as Beatë lived –

ROSMER: You're right there, unhappily.

REBEKKA: But when I came to live with you here, in stillness, in solitude, when you told me all your thoughts without reserve, every mood you felt however tender and exquisite, then the great change happened. Bit by bit, you see. Almost imperceptible; but yet overpowering in the end. Right to the depths of my soul.

ROSMER: Why, what *is* all this, Rebekka?

REBEKKA: All the rest, this ugly passion, this delirium of the senses, went from me, far, far away. All these desires that had been roused sank quietly down into silence. Peace of mind came down over me – like the stillness on the mountain-cliffs at home under the midnight sun.

ROSMER: Tell me some more about it. Everything you can describe.

REBEKKA: There isn't much more, my dear. Only this, that then love began in me. The great, selfless love that is content with sharing life in the way we've done.

ROSMER: Oh, if only I'd guessed the least bit of all this!

REBEKKA: It's best as it is. Yesterday, when you asked me if I would be your wife, I cried out in joy –

ROSMER: Yes, you did, Rebekka, didn't you? I thought I'd understood it.

REBEKKA: For a moment, yes. Forgetting myself. It was my old, resilient will trying to get free again. But now at last it has no more power – no more.

ROSMER: How do you explain what's happened to you?

REBEKKA: It's the Rosmers' view of life –or at least *your* view of life – that has infected my will.

ROSMER: Infected?

REBEKKA: And made it sick. Subjected it to laws that meant nothing to me before. You – the life shared with you –has made my mind nobler –

ROSMER: Oh, if I really dared to believe that!

REBEKKA: You can believe it confidently. The Rosmer view of life does ennoble. But [*Shaking her head.*] – but – but –

ROSMER: But? Well?

REBEKKA: – but it kills joy, my dear.

ROSMER: Do you think that, Rebekka?

REBEKKA: For me, at least.

ROSMER: Yes, but are you so sure of that? If I asked you again, now –? Begged you –

REBEKKA: Ah, my dear, don't ever talk about this again. It's an impossibility. Yes, because there's something you must know, John – that I have a ... past behind me.

ROSMER: Something more than you've told me?

REBEKKA: Yes. Something else and something more.

ROSMER [*with a faint smile*]: Isn't it odd, Rebekka? You

know, an idea of that kind has crossed my mind from time to time.

REBEKKA: Has it! And even so –? All the same –?

ROSMER: I never believed it. I only played with it – just in my thoughts, you know.

REBEKKA: If you want me to, I'll tell you all about it, at once.

ROSMER [*putting it aside*]: No, no! I don't want to know a word. Whatever it is – I can put it out of my mind.

REBEKKA: But I can't.

ROSMER: Oh, Rebekka –

REBEKKA: Yes, you see, *that's* the dreadful thing, that now, when all the happiness of life is offered me with full hands – I'm changed, so that my own past bars my way.

ROSMER: Your past is dead, Rebekka. It has no more hold on you, no relation to you – not as you are *now*.

REBEKKA: Ah, my dear, that's only talk, you know. What about innocence then? Where am I to get that?

ROSMER [*sadly*]: Yes, yes – innocence.

REBEKKA: Innocence, yes. From that come joy and gladness. For it was that faith you wanted to awaken in all these glad and noble men that were to be –

ROSMER: Oh, don't remind me of *that*. It was only a half-formed dream, Rebekka. A thoughtless impulse that I don't believe in any more myself. People don't lend themselves to ennobling from without, you know.

REBEKKA [*in a low voice*]: Not through tranquil love, do you think?

ROSMER [*thoughtfully*]: Yes; *that* of course would be the great thing. The most glorious, almost, in the whole of life, I think. If it were so. [*Moving restlessly.*] But how am I to clear up that problem? Get to the bottom of it?

REBEKKA: Don't you believe me, John?

ROSMER: Ah, Rebekka, how *can* I believe in you completely? You, who've been living here covering up and hiding all these things! Now you come out with this new business. If there's any scheme behind it, tell me so straight out. If there's something or other you want to gain by it. I'll only too gladly do everything I can for you.

REBEKKA [*wringing her hands*]: Oh, this murdering doubt! John – John!

ROSMER: Yes, it's terrible, my dear, isn't it? But I can't help it. I shall never be able to free myself from the doubt. Never know for certain that I have your love, whole and un-flawed.

REBEKKA: But isn't there anything in the depth of your mind that assures you that a change has come over me? And that the change has come through you – through you alone?

ROSMER: Ah, my dear, I don't believe any longer in my power to change people. I don't believe in myself in any way any more. I don't believe in myself or in you.

REBEKKA [*looking gloomily at him*]: Then how are you to live your life?

ROSMER: That's what I don't know myself. I can't imagine. I don't see that I *can* live it out. And I don't know, what's more, of anything in the world it would be worth while to live for.

REBEKKA: Oh, life – it has a way of renewing itself. Let us hold fast to it, my dear. We come to the end of it soon enough.

ROSMER [*springing up restlessly*]: Then give me my faith again! Faith in *you*, Rebekka! Faith in your love! Proof! I want proof!

REBEKKA: Proof? How can I give you proof?

ROSMER: You *must*! [*Crossing the room.*] I can't bear this desolation – this terrible emptiness – this – this –

[*There is a loud knocking at the hall door.*]

REBEKKA [*jumping up from her chair*]: Ah, listen to that!

[*The door opens.* ULRIK BRENDEL *comes in. He has on a*

*white shirt, a black coat, and good boots worn outside his
trousers. For the rest he is dressed as in his earlier appearance.
He looks distressed.*]

ROSMER: Oh, it's you, Mr Brendel!

BRENDEL: John, my boy, hail – and farewell!

ROSMER: Where are you going so late?

BRENDEL: Downhill.

ROSMER: How –?

BRENDEL: I'm going home, my beloved pupil. I've grown
homesick for the great nothingness.

ROSMER: Something has happened to you, Mr Brendel.
What is it?

BRENDEL: So you notice the change? Yes, you well may.
When I last entered this hall, then I stood before you a
wealthy man with a well-filled pocket.

ROSMER: Really! I don't quite understand –

BRENDEL: But as you see me this night, I am a deposed
monarch amid the ashes of my burnt-down castle.

ROSMER: If there's anything *I* can help you with –

BRENDEL: You have kept your child's heart, John. Can you
make me a loan?

ROSMER: Yes, yes, most gladly!

BRENDEL: Can you spare an ideal or two?

ROSMER: What do you say?

BRENDEL: One or two cast-off ideals. It'll be doing a good
deed. Because I'm cleaned out now, my dear boy. Down
and out.

REBEKKA: Didn't you manage to give your lecture?

BRENDEL: No, my fair lady. What do you think? Just as
I'm standing ready to empty out the horn of plenty, I make
the uncomfortable discovery that I'm bankrupt.

REBEKKA: But what about all your unwritten works?

BRENDEL: For five and twenty years I've sat like a miser on
his locked money-chest. And then yesterday, when I open
it to take out the treasure – there's nothing there. The teeth

of time had ground it to dust. There was nothing whatever in the whole thing.

ROSMER: But are you quite sure of that?

BRENDEL: There's no room for doubt, my boy. The President has convinced me of that.

ROSMER: The President?

BRENDEL: Well, then, His Excellency. *Ganz nach Belieben.*

ROSMER: Yes, but whom do you mean?

BRENDEL: Peder Mortensgaard, of course.

ROSMER: What!

BRENDEL [*with an air of secrecy*]: Sh! Sh! Sh! Peder Mortensgaard is lord and master of the future. Never have I stood in a more imposing presence. Peder Mortensgaard has in him the strength of omnipotence. He can do whatever he wants.

ROSMER: Oh, don't believe that!

BRENDEL: Yes, my boy! For Peder Mortensgaard never wants to do more than he can. Peder Mortensgaard is capable of living his life without ideals. And *that*, you see, that's the great secret of action and victory. It is the sum of all worldly wisdom. *Basta!*

ROSMER [*quietly*]: Now I see that you are going away poorer than you came.

BRENDEL: Very well. Then take example by your old teacher. Strike out everything that he printed upon your mind. Don't build your castle on shifting sand. And look ahead and see where you're going before you build on this charming creature who's making your life here so sweet.

REBEKKA: Do you mean me?

BRENDEL: Yes, my enchanting mermaid.

REBEKKA: Why should I not be fit to build on?

BRENDEL [*coming a step nearer*]: I've heard that my former pupil has a life-work to carry to victory.

REBEKKA: And so –?

BRENDEL: Victory is assured him. But – notice – upon *one* unavoidable condition.

REBEKKA: What condition?

BRENDEL [*taking her gently by the wrist*]: That the woman who loves him goes gladly out into the kitchen and chops off her delicate pink-and-white little finger, here, just *here* at the middle joint. Furthermore, that the aforesaid loving woman, just as gladly, cuts off her incomparably shaped left ear. [*Lets her go and turns to* ROSMER.] Farewell, my victorious John!

ROSMER: Are you going now? In the dark night?

BRENDEL: The dark night is best. Peace be with you both. [*He goes.*]

[*There is a moment of silence in the room.*]

REBEKKA [*breathing hard*]: Oh, how close and stuffy it is here! [*She goes across to the window, opens it, and stands there.*]

ROSMER [*sitting down in the easy chair over by the stove*]: There's nothing for it, Rebekka, after all. I see that. You must go.

REBEKKA: Yes, I don't see any choice.

ROSMER: Let's make the most of the last hour. Come over here and sit by me.

REBEKKA [*going across and sitting down on the sofa*]: What do you want, John?

ROSMER: First, I want to tell you *this*, you needn't have any anxiety about your future.

REBEKKA [*smiling*]: Hm. *My* future.

ROSMER: I've foreseen all the possibilities. A long time ago. Whatever happens, you are provided for.

REBEKKA: That too, my dear?

ROSMER: You might have been sure of that yourself.

REBEKKA: It's many a long day since I thought about anything of that kind.

ROSMER: Yes, yes. Of course you thought things would never be otherwise than as they were between us.

REBEKKA: Yes, I thought so.

ROSMER: So did I. But now if I were to go –

REBEKKA: Oh, John – you'll live longer than I shall.

ROSMER: It's in my power to dispose of this miserable life myself.

REBEKKA: What do you mean! You're never thinking of –

ROSMER: Do you think it would be so strange? After the wretched, pitiful defeat I've suffered! I, who meant to carry my life's work to victory – and here I've run away from it, even before the fight had really begun!

REBEKKA: Take the battle up again, John! Only try – and you'll see, you'll win. You'll ennoble hundreds, you'll ennoble thousands of minds. Just try!

ROSMER: Ah, Rebekka – I, who no longer believe in my own life's work.

REBEKKA: But your work has already had its proof. *One* person you have at any rate ennobled. Me, as long as I live.

ROSMER: Yes. If I dared believe you in that.

REBEKKA [*wringing her hands*]: Oh, but John – don't you know of anything, anything that could make you believe it?

ROSMER [*starting, as if in dread*]: Don't go into that! No further, Rebekka! Not one word more!

REBEKKA: Oh yes, it's just that we must go into. Do you know of anything that could destroy your doubt? Because *I* don't know of anything in the world.

ROSMER: It's best for you not to know it. Best for us both.

REBEKKA: No, no, no – I've no patience with that! If you know anything that can acquit me in your eyes, then I demand as my right that you tell me.

ROSMER [*as though driven, against his will*]: Well, let us see, then. You say that you are filled with a great love. That your soul is ennobled through me. Is that so? Have you reckoned right, my dear? Shall we check your account? Shall we?

REBEKKA: I'm ready to.

ROSMER: Whenever it may be?

REBEKKA: Whenever you like. The sooner the better.

ROSMER: Then let me see, Rebekka ... whether you ... for my sake ... this very night – [*Breaking off.*] Oh no, no, no!

REBEKKA: Yes, John. Yes. Say it and you shall see.

ROSMER: Have you the courage to ... are you willing to ... gladly, as Ulrik Brendel said ... for my sake, now, this night ... gladly ... to go the same way ... that Beatë went?

REBEKKA [*getting up slowly from the sofa, speaking almost inaudibly*]: John –!

ROSMER: Yes, my dear. That's the question I shall never be able to get rid of, when you are gone. Every hour of the day I shall come back to the same thing. Oh I seem to see you before me as clear as life. You are standing out on the foot-bridge. Out in the middle. Now you are leaning out over the railing! You turn giddy as you are drawn towards the mill–race down below! No. You draw back. You dare not do – what *she* dared.

REBEKKA: But suppose I did have the courage? And the glad will? What then?

ROSMER: Then I should have to believe you. Then I should have faith again in my life's work. Faith in my power to ennoble men's minds. Faith in the power of men's minds to be ennobled.

REBEKKA [*taking her shawl slowly, throwing it over her head, and speaking with self-control*]: You shall have your faith again.

ROSMER: Have you the courage and the will – for that, Rebekka?

REBEKKA: You will be able to judge of that to-morrow – or later – when they fetch me up.

ROSMER [*holding his head*]: There is a fascinating horror in this –!

REBEKKA: For I don't want to stay lying down there. No longer than need be. They must see that they find me.

ROSMER [*jumping up*]: But all this – it's madness. Go – or stay! I will believe you on your bare word, this time too.

REBEKKA: Just words, John. No more cowardice or running away, you know. How can you believe me on my bare word after today?

ROSMER: But I don't want to see your defeat, Rebekka.

REBEKKA: There won't be any defeat.

ROSMER: There will. You'll never have the spirit to go Beatë's way.

REBEKKA: Don't you think so?

ROSMER: Never. You're not like Beatë. You are not subject to the power of a perverted view of life.

REBEKKA: But I am subject now to the Rosmers' view of life. Where I have sinned, it is right I should expiate.

ROSMER [looking fixedly at her]: Is *that* where you stand?

REBEKKA: Yes.

ROSMER [resolved]: Very well. Then so am *I* subject to our unfettered view of life, Rebekka. There is no judge over us. And therefore we must see to it that we judge ourselves.

REBEKKA [misunderstanding him]: That too. That too. My going will save the best in you.

ROSMER: Oh, there's nothing left to save in me.

REBEKKA: There is. But I – after this I should only be like a sea-troll, who hangs on and holds back the ship you're to sail forward in. I must go overboard. Or am I to go about the world limping along with a crippled life? Brooding and brooding over the happiness my past has thrown away? I must get out of the game, John.

ROSMER: If you go, I go with you.

REBEKKA [smiling almost imperceptibly she looks at him and says more gently]: Yes, come with me, my dear and witness to –

ROSMER: I said, I go with you.

REBEKKA: To the bridge, yes. You never dare to go out on it, you know.

ROSMER: Have you noticed that?

REBEKKA [sadly and brokenly]: Yes. That was what made my love hopeless.

ROSMER: Rebekka – now I lay my hand on your head. [*Doing as he says.*] And I take you for my true and lawful wife.

REBEKKA [*taking both his hands and bowing her head against his breast*]: Thank you, John. [*Letting him go.*] And now I'm going – gladly.

ROSMER: Man and wife should go together.

REBEKKA: Only to the bridge, John.

ROSMER: Out on it too. As far as you go – so far I go with you. For now I dare.

REBEKKA: Do you know, beyond doubt, that this way is best for you?

ROSMER: I know it is the only way.

REBEKKA: Suppose you were deceiving yourself? Suppose it was only a delusion? One of these white horses of Rosmersholm.

ROSMER: It might be. For we never escape them – we of this House.

REBEKKA: Then stay, John!

ROSMER: The husband must go with his wife, as the wife with her husband.

REBEKKA: Yes, but tell me this first. Is it you that go with me, or is it I that go with you?

ROSMER: We shall never search that to the bottom.

REBEKKA: I should like to know, though.

ROSMER: We two go with each other, Rebekka. I with you and you with me.

REBEKKA: I almost believe that too.

ROSMER: For now are we two *one*.

REBEKKA: Yes. Now we are *one*. Come. We will go gladly. [*They go out hand in hand through the hall and are seen to turn to the left. The door stands open after them. The room is empty for a moment. Then* MRS HELSETH *opens the door on the right.*]

MRS HELSETH: Miss, the carriage is – [*Looks round her.*] Not here? Out together at this time? Well, now – I must say that's –! Hm! [*Goes out into the hall, looks round, and comes in again.*] Not on the garden seat. Well, well. [*Goes to the window and looks out.*] Good gracious! That white thing there –! Yes, upon my soul, they're both standing on the foot-bridge. God forgive the sinful creatures! If they're not putting their arms round each other! [*Screaming loudly.*] Ah! Over the bridge – both of them! Out into the mill-race. Help! Help! [*Her knees giving way, she holds herself up, trembling, by the back of the chair and can scarcely get the words out.*] No. No help here. The dead mistress has taken them.

THE MASTER BUILDER

CHARACTERS

HALVARD SOLNESS, *the master builder*

ALINE SOLNESS, *his wife*

DR HERDAL, *the family doctor*

KNUT BROVIK, *formerly an architect; now an assistant in Solness's firm*

RAGNAR BROVIK, *his son, a draughtsman*

KAJA FOSLI, *his niece, a book-keeper*

HILDE WANGEL

Some ladies and a crowd in the street

The events take place at Solness's house

ACT ONE

A plainly furnished work-room in Solness's house. Folding doors in the wall to the left lead out to the hall. On the right is a door to the inner rooms of the house. In the back wall is an open door to the drawing-office. Downstage to the left a desk with books, papers, and writing materials. Upstage from the door is a stove. In the right-hand corner is a sofa with a table and a few chairs. On the table a jug of water and a glass. A smaller table with a rocking-chair and an arm-chair is in the foreground to the right. There are shaded lamps burning on the table in the drawing-office, on the table in the corner, and on the desk.

Inside, in the drawing-office, sit KNUT BROVIK *and his son* RAGNAR *busy with plans and calculations. At the desk in the work-room* KAJA FOSLI *stands writing in the ledger.* KNUT BROVIK *is a shrunken old man with white hair and beard. He is dressed in a somewhat worn but well-cared-for black coat. He wears glasses and a white stock which has grown slightly yellow.* RAGNAR BROVIK *is in his thirties, well-dressed, fair-haired, with a slight stoop.* KAJA FOSLI *is a slenderly built girl a little over twenty, neatly dressed, but with a delicate look. She has a green shade over her eyes. All three work for a time in silence.*

KNUT BROVIK [*getting up suddenly from the drawing-table, as if in distress, and breathing heavily and with difficulty as he comes forward into the doorway*]: No, I can't go on much longer!

KAJA [*going over to him*]: You're feeling pretty bad this evening, aren't you, Uncle?

BROVIK: Oh I seem to get worse every day.

RAGNAR [*who has got up, coming nearer*]: You'd much better go home, Father. And try and get a little sleep –

BROVIK [*impatiently*]: Go to bed, I suppose? Do you want me to be suffocated outright?

KAJA: Well, go for a little walk, then.

RAGNAR: Yes, do. I'll go with you.

BROVIK [*angrily*]: I won't go before he comes! Tonight I'm going to speak straight out to – [*With suppressed bitterness.*] – to him – the chief.

KAJA [*alarmed*]: Oh no, Uncle – do let that wait!

RAGNAR: Yes, better wait, Father!

BROVIK [*drawing his breath with difficulty*]: Ha – ha –! I haven't time to wait very long, I haven't.

KAJA [*listening*]: Hush! I can hear him coming up the stairs! [*They all go back to their work again. There is a short silence.* HALVARD SOLNESS, *the master builder, comes in through the hall door. He is a man getting on in years, strong and vigorous, with close-cut curling hair, dark moustache, and dark, thick eyebrows. He wears a grey-green buttoned jacket with a high collar and broad revers. On his head he has a soft grey felt hat and under his arm one or two folders.*]

SOLNESS [*by the door, pointing towards the drawing-office and asking in a whisper*]: Are they gone?

KAJA [*softly, shaking her head*]: No. [*She takes off her eye-shade.*] [SOLNESS *goes across the room, throws his hat on a chair, puts the folders down on the sofa table, and comes back towards the desk.* KAJA *goes on writing uninterruptedly, but seems nervous and ill at ease.*]

SOLNESS [*out loud*]: What is it you're entering up, Miss Fosli?

KAJA [*with a start*]: Oh, it's only something that –

SOLNESS: Let me look at it. [*He bends over her, as though he were looking at the ledger and whispers.*] Kaja?

KAJA [*softly as she writes*]: Yes?

SOLNESS: Why do you always take that shade off when I come in?

KAJA [*as before*]: Oh because I look so ugly with it on.

SOLNESS [*smiling*]: Don't you want to, then, Kaja?

KAJA [*half glancing up at him*]: Not for anything in the world. Not in *your* eyes.

SOLNESS [*stroking her hair gently*]: Poor, poor little Kaja –

KAJA [*bending her head down*]: Hush, they can hear you!

> [SOLNESS *strolls across the room to the right, turns, and stands by the door to the drawing-office.*]

SOLNESS: Has anyone been here for me?

RAGNAR [*getting up*]: Yes, the young people who want to build the villa out at Løvstrand.

SOLNESS [*muttering*]: Oh, those two? Well, they must wait. I'm not quite clear in my mind about the plans yet.

RAGNAR [*coming nearer and speaking with hesitation*]: They were so anxious to have the designs soon.

SOLNESS [*as before*]: Oh lord, yes! That's what they all want!

BROVIK [*looking up*]: They say they're simply longing to move into a place of their own.

SOLNESS: Oh yes; oh yes. We know *that*! And so they make do with whatever comes along. Get themselves something or other to live in. Any kind of roof over their heads. But not a home. No thank you! If that's what they want let them go to someone else. Tell them that, when they come again.

BROVIK [*pushing his spectacles up on his forehead and looking at him in surprise*]: To someone else? Would you let the commission go?

SOLNESS [*impatiently*]: Yes, yes, damn it! If it comes to that –. Better that than start building without knowing where you are. [*Breaking out.*] And I don't know much about these people yet!

BROVIK: The people are respectable enough. Ragnar knows them. He's a friend of the family. Very respectable people.

SOLNESS: Oh, respectable – respectable! That's not what I mean at all. Good lord – don't you understand me either? [*Angrily.*] I won't have anything to do with these strangers.

Let them go to whomever they like, as far as I'm concerned!

BROVIK [*getting up*]: Do you really mean that – seriously?

SOLNESS [*surlily*]: Yes, I do. For once in a while. [*He comes across the room.*]

[BROVIK *exchanges a glance with* RAGNAR, *who makes a warning gesture.* BROVIK *then comes into the front room.*]

BROVIK: May I have a word or two with you?

SOLNESS: Certainly.

BROVIK [*to* KAJA]: Go in there for a moment, my dear.

KAJA [*uneasily*]: Oh, but Uncle –

BROVIK: Do as I tell you, my child. And shut the door after you. [KAJA *goes, with some hesitation, into the drawing-office, glancing anxiously and imploringly at* SOLNESS, *and shuts the door.* BROVIK *lowers his voice a little.*] I don't want the poor children to know how bad things are with me.

SOLNESS: Yes, you look very shaky nowadays.

BROVIK: It'll soon be all up with me. My strength is giving out – from day to day.

SOLNESS: Sit down a moment.

BROVIK: Thank you, – may I?

SOLNESS [*pulling the arm-chair forward for him*]: Here. Please do. Well?

BROVIK [*who has sat down with difficulty*]: Well, it's this business about Ragnar. That's what's weighing on me most. What's going to become of him?

SOLNESS: Your son will stay on here with me, of course, just as long as he wants to.

BROVIK: But that's just what he doesn't want. He doesn't feel he can, any longer.

SOLNESS: Well, he's pretty well paid, I should have thought. But if he wants more, I wouldn't mind –

BROVIK: No, no! It's not that at all. [*Impatiently.*] But he must have a chance too of working for himself some day!

SOLNESS [*without looking at him*]: Do you think Ragnar has the necessary ability for that?

BROVIK: No, you see, that's the dreadful part of it. I've begun to have doubts about the lad. For you've never said so much as – as an encouraging word about him. And yet I can't help feeling it must be there. He must *have* ability.

SOLNESS: Yes, but he hasn't learnt anything – not thoroughly. Except draughtsmanship, of course.

BROVIK [*looking at him with secret hatred and speaking huskily*]: *You* hadn't learnt much about the business either, when you were in my office. But you made your way all right. [*Breathing with difficulty*.] And got on. And took the wind out of my sails and – and a good many other people's.

SOLNESS: Well, you see – it worked out like that for *me*.

BROVIK: You're right. Everything worked out for you. But you can't have the heart to let me go to my grave – without seeing what Ragnar's worth. And then I should so like to see them married too – before I go.

SOLNESS [*sharply*]: Is it she who wants it?

BROVIK: Not Kaja so much. But Ragnar's talking about it every day. [*Imploring*.] You *must* – you must help him to some independent work now! I *must* see something the boy has done. Do you hear?

SOLNESS [*irritably*]: But, damn it all, I can't get commissions from the moon for him!

BROVIK: He can get a good commission this minute. A big piece of work.

SOLNESS [*surprised and uneasy*]: *He* can?

BROVIK: If you'd give your consent.

SOLNESS: What kind of work is it?

BROVIK [*with a little hesitation*]: He can get the villa out at Løvstrand.

SOLNESS: *That*! But I'm going to build that myself!

BROVIK: Oh, you're not very keen on that.

SOLNESS [*flaring up*]: Not keen! I! Who's daring to say that?

BROVIK: You said so yourself just now.

SOLNESS: Oh, don't listen to what I – *say*. Can Ragnar get the commission for the villa?

BROVIK: Yes. You see he knows the family. And then – just for the fun of it – he's made drawings and estimates and everything –

SOLNESS: And these drawings, are they pleased with them? The people who are going to live there?

BROVIK: Yes, if you would just look through them and approve them –

SOLNESS: Then they would let Ragnar build their home for them?

BROVIK: They liked it immensely, what he proposed. They thought it was completely new, they said.

SOLNESS: Ah! *New*! Not the sort of old-fashioned stuff *I'm* accustomed to build!

BROVIK: They thought it was different.

SOLNESS [*with suppressed bitterness*]: So it was Ragnar they came to see – while I was out!

BROVIK: They came to call on you. And to ask whether you would be willing to retire –

SOLNESS [*flaring up*]: Retire! I!

BROVIK: If you found that Ragnar's drawings –

SOLNESS: I! Retire in favour of your son!

BROVIK: Retire from the contract, they meant.

SOLNESS: Oh, it comes to the same thing. [*With a bitter laugh.*] So that's it! Halvard Solness, – he's to begin retiring now! Make room for younger men. For the youngest of all, perhaps! Just make room! Room! Room!

BROVIK: Good gracious, surely there's room here for more than one single –

SOLNESS: Oh no, there isn't so very much room to spare. Anyhow, *that* doesn't matter. I'll never retire! Never give way for anyone! Never of my own accord! Never in this world will I do *that*!

BROVIK [*getting up with difficulty*]: Am I to die then without certainty? Without any joy? Without faith and confidence in Ragnar? Without having seen a single piece of his work? Am I to?

SOLNESS [*turning half aside and muttering*]: Hm, – don't ask any more now.

BROVIK: Yes, answer my question. Am I to die in such absolute poverty?

SOLNESS [*seeming to battle with himself and finally speaking in a low but firm voice*]: You must die as best you can.

BROVIK: Then so be it. [*He goes up across the room.*]

SOLNESS [*following him, half desperately*]: Don't you understand, I *can't* do anything else? I'm what I am. And I can't make myself anything else.

BROVIK: No, no, – I suppose you can't. [*He staggers and stops beside the sofa table.*] Could I have a glass of water?

SOLNESS: Of course. [*He fills and hands him a glass.*]

BROVIK: Thank you. [*He drinks and puts the glass down.*]
[*Solness goes across and opens the door to the drawing-office.*]

SOLNESS: Ragnar. You must come and take your father home.
[RAGNAR *gets up quickly. He and* KAJA *come in to the work-room.*]

RAGNAR: What is it, Father?

BROVIK: Take my arm. And we'll go.

RAGNAR: All right. Put your things on too, Kaja.

SOLNESS: Miss Fosli must stay. Just for a moment. I have a letter to write.

BROVIK [*looking at* SOLNESS]: Good night. Sleep well – if you can.

SOLNESS: Good night.
[BROVIK *and* RAGNAR *go out by the door to the hall.* KAJA *goes across to the desk.* SOLNESS *stands with bowed head near the arm-chair on the right.*]

KAJA [*uncertainly*]: *Is* there a letter –?

SOLNESS [*shortly*]: No, of course there isn't. [*Looking sternly at her.*] Kaja!

KAJA [*anxiously, in a low voice*]: Yes?

SOLNESS [*pointing commandingly with his finger towards the floor*]: Come over here! At once!

KAJA [*hesitating*]: Yes.

SOLNESS [*as before*]: Nearer!

KAJA [*obeying*]: What do you want me for?

SOLNESS [*looking at her for a moment*]: Is it you I have to thank for all this?

KAJA: No, no, don't think that!

SOLNESS: But getting married – that's what you're planning.

KAJA [*softly*]: Ragnar and I have been engaged four – five years, and so –

SOLNESS: And so you think it should come to an end. Isn't that it?

KAJA: Ragnar and Uncle say that I must. And so I'll have to give in, I suppose.

SOLNESS [*more gently*]: Kaja, aren't you, really, rather fond of Ragnar, too?

KAJA: I was very fond of Ragnar once. Before I came here to you.

SOLNESS: But not any longer? Not at all?

KAJA [*passionately, clasping her hands and holding them out towards him*]: Oh, you *know* there's only one person I'm fond of now! Not anyone else in the whole world! I never shall be fond of anyone else!

SOLNESS: Yes, that's what you say. And yet you're going away from me. Leaving me here alone with it all.

KAJA: But couldn't I stay with you, even if Ragnar –?

SOLNESS [*putting it aside*]: No, no, that wouldn't do at all. I Ragnar goes off and sets up in business on his own account, he'll need you himself.

KAJA [*wringing her hands*]: Oh, I don't see *how* I can leave you! It feels absolutely impossible!

SOLNESS: Then see to it that you cure Ragnar of these stupid fancies. Marry him as much as you like – [*Changing his tone.*] Well, well. What I mean is, get him to stay in his good position here with me. For then I can keep you too, Kaja dear.

KAJA: Oh yes, how lovely that would be, if it could be managed.

SOLNESS [*taking her head in both his hands and whispering*]: Because I can't do without you, you see. I must have you with me here every single day.

KAJA [*carried away*]: Oh God! Oh God!

SOLNESS [*kissing her hair*]: Kaja – Kaja!

KAJA [*sinking down before him*]: Oh, how good you are to me! How unspeakably good you are!

SOLNESS [*violently*]: Get up! Get up for goodness sake! I think I hear someone!

[*He helps her up. She staggers across to the desk.* MRS SOLNESS *comes in at the door on the right. She looks thin and worn with grief, but has traces of former beauty. She has fair ringlets. Her dress, of unrelieved black, is in good taste. She speaks rather slowly and with a mournful voice.*]

MRS SOLNESS [*at the door*]: Halvard!

SOLNESS [*turning round*]: Oh, are you there, my dear –?

MRS SOLNESS [*with a glance at* KAJA]: I've come at an inconvenient moment, I'm afraid.

SOLNESS: Not at all. Miss Fosli has only a short letter to write.

MRS SOLNESS: Yes, so I see.

SOLNESS: What was it you wanted, Aline?

MRS SOLNESS: I only wanted to say that Dr Herdal is in the study. Won't you come in too, Halvard?

SOLNESS [*looking at her suspiciously*]: Hm. Does the doctor specially want to talk to me?

MRS SOLNESS: No, not specially. He came to visit me. And he just wanted to say a word to you at the same time.

SOLNESS [*with a quiet laugh*]: I can well believe it. Well, you must ask him to wait a moment.

MRS SOLNESS: Then you'll come in and see him presently?

SOLNESS: Perhaps. Presently – presently, my dear. In a little while.

MRS SOLNESS [*with another glance at* KAJA]: Now, don't you forget, Halvard. [*She goes away and shuts the door behind her.*]

KAJA [*in a low voice*]: Oh dear, oh dear – I'm sure Mrs Solness thinks something dreadful about me!

SOLNESS: Oh, not a bit. At any rate, not more than usual. But all the same you'd better go now, Kaja.

KAJA: Yes, yes, I *must* go now.

SOLNESS [*sternly*]: And get this other business settled for me. Do you hear?

KAJA: Oh, if it only depended on *me*, then –

SOLNESS: I insist on its being settled, I tell you. And that by to-morrow at latest!

KAJA [*in great distress*]: If it can't be done any other way, I'll willingly break it off with him.

SOLNESS [*flaring up*]: Break it off! Have you gone mad! Do you mean to break it off?

KAJA [*desperately*]: Yes, I'd rather. Because I *must*, – I *must* stay here with you. I *can't* go away from you. It's utterly – utterly impossible!

SOLNESS [*breaking out*]: But, damn it all! What about Ragnar? Why Ragnar's the very person I –

KAJA [*looking at him with terrified eyes*]: Is it mostly for Ragnar's sake that – that you –?

SOLNESS [*controlling himself*]: Oh no, of course not! You don't understand at all. [*Gently and quietly.*] Naturally it's you I want. You, first and foremost, Kaja. But that's just why you must make Ragnar keep his job too. Well, well – go home now.

KAJA: Very well. Good night.

SOLNESS: Good night. [*Just as she is going.*] Oh, wait a minute! Are Ragnar's drawings in there?

KAJA: Yes, I didn't see him take them with him.

SOLNESS: Go in then and find them for me. I might perhaps give a look at them after all.

KAJA [*joyfully*]: Oh yes, *do* do that!

SOLNESS: For your sake, Kaja dear. Well, let me have them at once, will you.

[KAJA *goes quickly into the drawing-office, searches anxiously in the table-drawer, finds a portfolio, and brings it.*]

KAJA: Here are all the drawings.

SOLNESS: Good. Put them over there on the table.

KAJA [*putting down the portfolio*]: Good night then. [*Entreating.*] And *do* think kindly of me.

SOLNESS: Oh, I always do that. Good night, dear little Kaja. [*Glancing to the right.*] Go now!

[MRS SOLNESS *and* DR HERDAL *come in at the door on the right. He is a stout elderly man with a round, good-tempered face. He is clean shaven, has thin fair hair, and wears gold-rimmed spectacles.*]

MRS SOLNESS [*still by the door*]: Halvard, I can't keep the doctor any longer.

SOLNESS: Well, come in then.

MRS SOLNESS [*to* KAJA, *who is turning down the lamp on the desk*]: Finished the letter already, Miss Fosli?

KAJA [*embarrassed*]: The letter –?

SOLNESS: Yes, it was quite a short one.

MRS SOLNESS: It must have been very short indeed.

SOLNESS: You may go, Miss Fosli. And come in good time to-morrow morning.

KAJA: I certainly will. Good night, Mrs Solness. [*She goes out through the door to the hall.*]

MRS SOLNESS: It must be a boon for you, Halvard, to have managed to get this girl.

SOLNESS: Yes indeed. She's useful in all sorts of ways.

MRS SOLNESS: She looks it.

DR HERDAL: Clever at book-keeping too?

SOLNESS: Well – she's had a certain amount of practice these last two years. And then she's so good-tempered and willing about everything.

MRS SOLNESS: Yes, that must be a great blessing –

SOLNESS: It certainly is. Especially when one isn't spoilt much in that way.

MRS SOLNESS [*with gentle reproach*]: Can *you* say that, Halvard?

SOLNESS: No, no, my dear Aline. I beg your pardon.

MRS SOLNESS: There's no need. Well, Doctor, so then you'll come back again later on and have supper with us?

DR HERDAL: As soon as I've seen that patient, I'll come along.

MRS SOLNESS: Thank you. [*She goes out by the door on the right.*]

SOLNESS: Are you in a hurry, Doctor?

DR HERDAL: No, not at all.

SOLNESS: May I talk to you, for a moment?

DR HERDAL: Yes, by all means.

SOLNESS: Then let's sit down. [*He invites the doctor to sit in the rocking-chair and takes the arm-chair himself. Looking searchingly at him.*] Tell me, – did you notice anything about Aline?

DR HERDAL: Now, when she was in here, do you mean?

SOLNESS: Yes. To *me*. Did you notice anything?

DR HERDAL [*smiling*]: Well, bless me – one couldn't very well help noticing that your wife, – hm –.

SOLNESS: Well?

DR HERDAL: That your wife isn't very fond of this Miss Fosli.

SOLNESS: Nothing else? I've noticed that myself.

DR HERDAL: And that's not really so very surprising.

SOLNESS: What isn't?

DR HERDAL: That she doesn't exactly like your having another woman here with you, all day long.

SOLNESS: No, no, you may be right. And Aline too. But this business – there's nothing else to be done about it.

DR HERDAL: Couldn't you get yourself a clerk?

SOLNESS: The first one who turned up? No, thank you. That wouldn't suit me.

DR HERDAL: But if your wife –? As ill as she is –. If she can't bear to see it?

SOLNESS: Well, she'll just have to – I almost said. I *must* keep Kaja Fosli. I can't do with anyone but her.

DR HERDAL: No one else?

SOLNESS [*shortly*]: No, no one else.

DR HERDAL [*pulling his chair nearer*]: Now listen to me, my dear Mr Solness. Will you let me ask you a question in confidence?

SOLNESS: Yes, do.

DR HERDAL: Women, you see – they've a deuced keen instinct – about some things.

SOLNESS: They have. That's perfectly true. But –?

DR HERDAL: Well. Now listen. If your wife can't bear this Kaja Fosli at any price –?

SOLNESS: Well, what about it?

DR HERDAL: Hasn't she any kind of – any ground at all for this instinctive dislike?

SOLNESS [*looking at him and getting up*]: Ah!

DR HERDAL: Don't take me the wrong way. But *hasn't* she?

SOLNESS [*shortly and firmly*]: No.

DR HERDAL: Absolutely no ground?

SOLNESS: No other ground than her own suspiciousness.

DR HERDAL: I know you've known a good many women in your life.

SOLNESS: Yes, I have.

DR HERDAL: And been quite fond of some of them.

SOLNESS: Oh yes, that too.

DR HERDAL: But in this business with Miss Fosli –? There's nothing of that kind involved?

SOLNESS: No, not in the least – on *my* side.

DR HERDAL: But on hers?

SOLNESS: I don't think you've any business to ask about that, Doctor.

DR HERDAL: It was the question of your wife's instinct, that started us.

SOLNESS: It was, yes. And as far as that goes –. [*Dropping his voice.*] Aline's instinct, as you call it, – it's already proved itself, to a certain extent.

DR HERDAL: Well – there we are!

SOLNESS [*sitting down*]: Dr Herdal, – I'm going to tell you a queer story. If you care to listen to it.

DR HERDAL: I like listening to queer stories.

SOLNESS: Very well, then. You remember, I expect, that I took Knut Brovik and his son into my service – when things had gone to pieces with the old man.

DR HERDAL: I remember something about it, yes.

SOLNESS: For you see they're really a clever pair of fellows, those two. They have ability, each in his own way. But then the son chose to go and get engaged. And then, of course, he wanted to get married – and to begin to build on his own. That's the way they all think, these young people.

DR HERDAL [*laughing*]: Yes, they've a tiresome habit of wanting to get married.

SOLNESS: Yes. But of course that didn't suit me. For I needed Ragnar myself. And the old man too. He's extraordinarily clever at calculating stresses and cubic content – and all that wretched stuff, you know.

DR HERDAL: Ah well, that's all part of the job, I suppose.

SOLNESS: Yes, it is. But Ragnar, – he must and would begin on his own account. There was no arguing with him.

DR HERDAL: Yet he's stayed with you all the same.

SOLNESS: Yes, now I'll tell you. One day this Kaja Fosli came in to see them on some errand. Hadn't ever been here before. And when I saw how infatuated those two were with each other, the idea struck me: if I could get her here in the office, then perhaps Ragnar would stay too.

DR HERDAL: That was a reasonable enough idea.

SOLNESS: Yes, but I didn't drop a hint at the time, not a word about that. I just stood and looked at her – and wished with all my heart that I had her here. Then I talked in a friendly way to her, – about one thing and another. And then she went away.

DR HERDAL: Well, then?

SOLNESS: But the next day, getting on in the evening, when old Brovik and Ragnar had gone home, she came here to me again and behaved as though I'd made some arrangement with her.

DR HERDAL: An arrangement? What about?

SOLNESS: About the very thing I'd had in my mind. But I hadn't said a single word about it.

DR HERDAL: That was very odd.

SOLNESS: Yes, wasn't it? And now she wanted to know what she was to do here. Whether she might begin at once, the next morning. And so on.

DR HERDAL: Don't you think she did it so as to be with her fiancé?

SOLNESS: That occurred to me, too, in the first place. But no, it wasn't that. She seemed to drift right away from him – as soon as she'd come here to me.

DR HERDAL: Drifted over to you, then?

SOLNESS: Yes. Absolutely. I can see that she's conscious of me when I look at her from behind. She trembles and shivers if I just come near her. What do you think of *that*?

DR HERDAL: Hm – that can be explained all right.

SOLNESS: Well, but what about the other thing? The fact that she thought I had said to her what I'd only wished for and wanted – in silence. Inwardly. To myself. What do you say about that? Can you explain a thing like that, Dr Herdal?

DR HERDAL: No, I won't tackle that.

SOLNESS: That's what I thought at first. And that's why I've never wanted to talk about it before. But it's a cursed nuisance for me in the long run, you know. Here I have to go on day after day pretending I –. And it's treating her badly, poor girl. [*Vigorously.*] But I *can't* do anything else! For if she runs off – then off goes Ragnar too.

DR HERDAL: And you haven't told your wife the truth about this?

SOLNESS: No.

DR HERDAL: Why on earth don't you?

SOLNESS [*looking fixedly at him and speaking in a low voice*]: Because I feel there's, as it were – a kind of salutary self-torture in letting Aline do me an injustice.

DR HERDAL [*shaking his head*]: I don't understand a single, blessed word of this.

SOLNESS: Why, you see – because it's as it were a small payment on a boundless, immeasurable debt –

DR HERDAL: To your wife?

SOLNESS: Yes. And that always gives one's mind a little ease. One can breathe more freely for a time, you understand.

DR HERDAL: No, I'm dashed if I understand a word –

SOLNESS [*breaking off and getting up again*]: Well, well, well, – don't let's talk about it any more, then. [*He wanders across the room, comes back, and stands beside the table. He looks at the doctor with a sly smile.*] I suppose you think you've fairly got me going now, Doctor?

DR HERDAL [*rather sharply*]: Got you going? I still don't understand a particle of this, Mr Solness.

SOLNESS: Oh, say it straight out! I've noticed it, you see, quite clearly!

DR HERDAL: *What* have you noticed?

SOLNESS [*quietly and slowly*]: That you're keeping an eye on me on the quiet.

DR HERDAL: *I* am! Why on earth should I do *that*?

SOLNESS: Because you think I'm –. [*Flaring up.*] Damn it all! You think the same thing about me that Aline does.

DR HERDAL: And what does she think about you, then?

SOLNESS [*regaining his control*]: She's begun to think that I'm – so to speak – that I'm ill.

DR HERDAL: Ill! You! She's never said a single word to me about it. What could be the matter with you, my dear fellow?

SOLNESS [*leaning over the back of the chair and whispering*]: Aline's decided that I'm mad. *That's* what she thinks.

DR HERDAL [*getting up*]: But, my dear, good Mr Solness –!

SOLNESS: Yes, upon my soul! That's how it is. And she's made you believe it too! Oh, I can assure you, Doctor,– I can see it in your face, quite all right. I don't let myself be caught so easily, let me tell you.

DR HERDAL [*looking at him in amazement*]: Never, Mr Solness – never has a thought of the kind come into my head.

SOLNESS [*with a doubting smile*]: Is that so? Really not?

DR HERDAL: No, never! Nor into your wife's, either, I am sure. I'm pretty certain I could swear to that.

SOLNESS: Ah well, you'd better not do that. For in one sense, you see, she might perhaps have some ground, after all, for thinking such a thing.

DR HERDAL: Well, now I really must say –!

SOLNESS [*breaking off, with a sweep of the hand*]: All right, my dear Doctor, – don't let's go into this any further. It's best for each of us to keep his own opinion. [*Changing to a tone of quiet amusement.*] But listen, Doctor – hm –.

DR HERDAL: Yes?

SOLNESS: If you don't think, now, that I'm – ill in any way – or crazy – or mad or anything of that kind –

DR HERDAL: What do you mean?

SOLNESS: Then I presume you imagine I'm a very happy man?

DR HERDAL: Would it be only imagining?

SOLNESS [*laughing*]: No, no, – it's obvious! Heaven forbid! Just think, – to be Solness, the master builder! Halvard Solness! Something to be thankful for!

DR HERDAL: Yes, I must say it seems to me you've had luck on your side to a quite incredible degree.

SOLNESS [*concealing a melancholy smile*]: So I have. Can't complain of that.

DR HERDAL: First that ugly old robber-fortress burnt down for you. And that was certainly a great piece of luck.

SOLNESS [*seriously*]: It was Aline's family home that was burnt. Remember that.

DR HERDAL: Yes, it must have been a great grief for her.

SOLNESS: She's never got over it to this very day. Not in all these twelve or thirteen years.

DR HERDAL: What followed afterwards, that must have been the worst blow for her.

SOLNESS: The two things together.

DR HERDAL: But you, you yourself, you got on in the world through it. You began as a poor boy from the country – and now, here you are, the first man in your profession. Yes indeed, Mr Solness, you've certainly had luck on your side.

SOLNESS [*looking at him with embarrassment*]: Yes, but it's just that that I'm so dreadfully afraid of.

DR HERDAL: Afraid? Because you've luck on your side?

SOLNESS: It makes me so afraid – all the time – so afraid. For some day the luck must turn, you see.

DR HERDAL: Oh, nonsense! What should make it turn?

SOLNESS [*firm and sure*]: It'll come from the younger generation.

DR HERDAL: Bosh! Younger generation! You're not exactly obsolete yourself, I should hope! Oh, no, – you're more firmly established now, I should say, than you've ever been.

SOLNESS: The luck will turn. I can feel it. I can feel it getting near. One or other of them will start saying: Stand back for *me*! And then all the others will come storming after, threatening and shouting: Make room! Make room! Make room! Yes, you can be sure of it, Doctor. Some day the younger generation will come knocking on my door –

DR HERDAL [*laughing*]: Well, good gracious, what about it?

SOLNESS: What about it? Why, then it's all up with Solness the master builder. [*There is a knock on the door on the left. He starts.*] What's that? Did you hear anything?

DR HERDAL: It's someone knocking.

SOLNESS [*loudly*]: Come in!

> [HILDE WANGEL *comes in by the door to the hall. She is of middle height, agile, and slenderly built. Slightly tanned by the sun. Dressed for a walking tour with a shortened skirt, an open sailor's collar, and a small sailor hat on her head. She has a rucksack on her back, a plaid in a strap, and a long alpenstock.*]

HILDE WANGEL [*going across with happy, dancing eyes to* SOLNESS]: Good evening!

SOLNESS [*looking uncertainly at her*]: Good evening –

HILDE [*laughing*]: I don't believe you recognize me!

SOLNESS: No, I must say that – just at the moment –

DR HERDAL [*going up to her*]: But *I* recognize you, young lady –

HILDE [*delighted*]: Well, if it isn't you, who –!

DR HERDAL: Yes of course it's me. [*To* SOLNESS.] We met up in one of the mountain-huts this summer. [*To* HILDE.] What became of the other ladies?

HILDE: Oh they took the road to the west.

DR HERDAL: They didn't much like our making all that noise in the evening.

HILDE: No, I don't think they did.

DR HERDAL [*shaking his finger at her*]: And we must admit, too, that you flirted a little with us.

HILDE: That was more amusing than sitting and knitting socks with all those old women.

DR HERDAL [*laughing*]: I quite agree with you about that!

SOLNESS: Have you come to town this evening?

HILDE: Yes, I've just arrived.

DR HERDAL: Quite alone, Miss Wangel?

HILDE: Oh, yes!

SOLNESS: Wangel? Is your name Wangel?

HILDE [*looking at him with amusement and surprise*]: Yes, of course it is.

SOLNESS: Then I expect you're a daughter of the local doctor up at Lysanger?

HILDE [*as before*]: Yes, who else's daughter should I be?

SOLNESS: Oh, then we've met each other up there. The summer I was there building a tower on the old church.

HILDE [*more seriously*]: Yes, of course it was then.

SOLNESS: Well, that's a long time ago.

HILDE [*looking steadily at him*]: It's exactly ten years ago.

SOLNESS: And at that time you were only a child, I imagine.

HILDE [*casually*]: About twelve or thirteen, anyway.

DR HERDAL: Is this the first time you've been here in town, Miss Wangel?

HILDE: Yes, it is indeed.

SOLNESS: And I suppose you don't know anyone here?

HILDE: No one but you. And your wife, of course.

SOLNESS: So you know *her* too?

HILDE: Only a little. We were both at the same mountain Hydro for a few days.

SOLNESS: Oh, up *there*.

HILDE: She said I might come and see her if I ever came to town. [*Smiling.*] Though there was no need for her to do that.

SOLNESS: Odd that she never said anything about it –

[HILDE *puts down her stick by the stove, takes off her ruck-sack, and puts it and the plaid on the sofa.* DR HERDAL *tries to be helpful.* SOLNESS *stands and looks at her.*]

HILDE [*going over to him*]: Well, now I'm going to ask if I may stay here tonight.

SOLNESS: I'm sure that can be managed.

HILDE: Because I haven't any other clothes, except these I'm wearing. Oh, and a set of underclothes in the rucksack. But they must be washed. For they're very grubby.

SOLNESS: Oh well, that can be seen to. Now, I'll just tell my wife –

DR HERDAL: Then I'll go and see my patient in the meantime.

SOLNESS: Yes, do. And come back again afterwards.

DR HERDAL [*merrily, with a glance at* HILDE]: Yes, you can count on that all right! [*Laughing.*] You made a true prophecy, after all, Mr Solness!

SOLNESS: How did I?

DR HERDAL: The younger generation *did* come and knock at your door.

SOLNESS [*cheerfully*]: Ah well, that was in quite a different way.

DR HERDAL: It certainly was. Undeniably! [*He goes out by the door to the hall.* SOLNESS *opens the door on the right and speaks into the side room.*]

SOLNESS: Aline! Would you mind coming in here. Here's a Miss Wangel whom you know.

MRS SOLNESS [*coming to the door*]: Who is it, do you say? [*Seeing* HILDE.] Oh, is it *you*, Miss Wangel? [*Coming nearer and holding out her hand.*] So you did come to town, after all.

SOLNESS: Miss Wangel has just arrived. And she's asking if she may stay the night here.

MRS SOLNESS: Here with us? Yes, by all means.

SOLNESS: So as to get her clothes put in order a little, you know.

MRS SOLNESS: I'll do the best I can for you. That's no more than my duty. Your luggage is coming later, I suppose?

HILDE: I haven't any luggage.

MRS SOLNESS: Oh well, that will be all right, I hope. But now you must make yourself at home with my husband for the moment. And I'll see about getting a room made comfortable for you.

SOLNESS: Can't we use one of the nurseries? They're quite ready now.

MRS SOLNESS: Oh yes. We've more than enough room *there*. [*To* HILDE.] Just sit down and rest a little.

[*She goes out to the right.* HILDE, *with her hands behind her back, saunters about the room and looks at one thing and another.* SOLNESS *stands down by the table, also with his hands behind his back, and follows her with his eyes.*]

HILDE [*stopping and looking at him*]: Have you got several nurseries?

SOLNESS: There are three nurseries in the house.

HILDE: That's a lot. So I suppose you've a good many children?

SOLNESS: No. We've no children. But now *you* can be our child for the present.

HILDE: For tonight, yes. I shan't cry. I'm going to try and sleep like a log.

SOLNESS: Yes, you must be very tired, I expect.

HILDE: Oh, no! But all the same –. It's simply lovely to lie and dream.

SOLNESS: Do you often dream at night?

HILDE: Oh, yes! Nearly always.

SOLNESS: What do you dream about most?

HILDE: I shan't tell you that this evening. Another time – perhaps. [*She saunters across the room again, stops by the desk, and turns over a few of the books and papers.*]

SOLNESS [*going up to her*]: Is there anything you're looking for?

HILDE: No, I'm just looking at all these things. [*Turning round.*] Perhaps I oughtn't to?

SOLNESS: Yes, do.

HILDE: Is it you who writes in that big ledger?

SOLNESS: No, it's my book-keeper.

HILDE: A woman?

SOLNESS [*smiling*]: Yes of course.

HILDE: Someone you have here in your office?

SOLNESS: Yes.

HILDE: Is she married?

SOLNESS: No, she's single.

HILDE: I see.

SOLNESS: But I think she's getting married quite soon.

HILDE: Well, that's nice for *her*.

SOLNESS: But not quite so nice for *me*. For then I'll have no one to help me.

HILDE: Can't you find yourself another one who's as good?

SOLNESS: Perhaps you'd stay here and – and write in the ledger?

HILDE [*measuring him with her eyes*]: Yes, you can see me doing it! No thank you – we're not having anything of that kind. [*She wanders across the room again and sits down in the rocking-chair.* SOLNESS *goes to the table too.* HILDE *goes on where she left off.*] Because there must be lots of things to do here beside that. [*She looks at him with a smile.*] Don't you think so too?

SOLNESS: That's quite true. First of all, I suppose, you'll go round the shops and really smarten yourself up.

HILDE [*gaily*]: No, I rather think I'll let that alone!

SOLNESS: Really?

HILDE: Yes, because I've got through all my money, you see.

SOLNESS [*laughing*]: Neither luggage nor money then!

HILDE: Not a bit of either. But dash it all – it doesn't matter now.

SOLNESS: Now, I really like you for that!

HILDE: Only for *that*?

SOLNESS: For that and other things. [*Sitting in the arm-chair.*] Is your father still alive?

HILDE: Yes. Father's alive.

SOLNESS: And now perhaps you're thinking of studying here?

HILDE: No, that didn't occur to me.

SOLNESS: But you're going to stay some time here, I suppose?

HILDE: Depends how things work out. [*She sits a moment looking at him, half seriously, half with a suppressed smile. Then she takes off her hat and puts it down in front of her on the table.*] Mr Solness?

SOLNESS: Yes?

HILDE: Are you a very forgetful person?

SOLNESS: Forgetful? No, not so far as I know.

HILDE: But aren't you going to talk to me at all about what happened up there?

SOLNESS [*surprised for a moment*]: Up at Lysanger? [*Casually.*] Well, I don't think there's much to talk about in that.

HILDE [*looking reproachfully at him*]: How can you sit there and say a thing like that?

SOLNESS: Well, *you* talk to *me* about it then.

HILDE: When the tower was finished, we had a great celebration in the town.

SOLNESS: Yes, I shan't forget that day so easily.

HILDE [*smiling*]: You won't? That's nice – from you!

SOLNESS: Nice?

HILDE: There was music in the churchyard. And many, many hundreds of people. We schoolgirls were dressed in white. And we all had flags.

SOLNESS: Ah yes, those flags – I remember them all right!

HILDE: Then you climbed straight up the scaffolding. Right up to the very top. And you had a great wreath with you. And you hung that wreath away up on the weather-cock.

SOLNESS [*briefly, cutting her short*]: I used to do that in those days. It's an old custom.

HILDE: It was so wonderfully exciting to stand down below and look up at you. Suppose he were to over-balance! He – the master builder himself!

SOLNESS [*as if turning the subject aside*]: Yes, yes, yes, that could quite well have happened, too. For one of those little devils in white – she carried on and screamed up at me so –

HILDE [*her eyes dancing with delight*]: 'Hurrah for Mr Solness, the master builder!' Yes!

SOLNESS: – and flapped and waved her flag so that I – that I was nearly giddy with the sight of it.

HILDE [*more quietly, seriously*]: That little devil – that was *me*.

SOLNESS [*fastening his eyes steadily on her*]: I'm sure of that now. It *must* have been you.

HILDE [*full of life again*]: Because it was so terribly exciting and lovely. I couldn't have believed there was a master builder in the whole world who could build such a tremendously high tower. And then, that you stood up there yourself, at the very top! Your real, live self! And that you weren't the least bit giddy. *That* was the very most – it kind of made one giddy to think of it.

SOLNESS: How did you know for certain, that I wasn't –

HILDE [*pushing the idea aside*]: Oh, come now! Nonsense! I knew it inside myself. Because if you had been you couldn't have stood up there and sung.

SOLNESS [*looking at her in amazement*]: Sung? Did *I* sing?

HILDE: Yes, you certainly did.

SOLNESS [*shaking his head*]: I've never sung a note in my life.

HILDE: Oh yes, you sang that time. It sounded like harps in the air.

SOLNESS [*thoughtfully*]: This is very odd – all this.

HILDE [*silent for a moment, looks at him and says with lowered voice*]: But then – afterwards – then came the *real* thing.

SOLNESS: The real thing?

HILDE [*her eyes dancing and eager*]: Yes, surely I haven't got to remind you of *that*?

SOLNESS: Well yes, remind me of *that* a little too.

HILDE: Don't you remember that there was a great dinner for you at the club?

SOLNESS: Ah, yes. That must have been the same afternoon. Because I left the next morning.

HILDE: And you were invited to our house for supper after the club.

SOLNESS: That's quite right, Miss Wangel. Wonderful, how well you've kept all these little things in your head.

HILDE: Little things! Well, *that's* good! I suppose it was a little thing, too, that I was alone in the room when you arrived?

SOLNESS: *Were* you alone?

HILDE [*without answering him*]: You didn't call me a little devil that time.

SOLNESS: No, I don't suppose I did.

HILDE: You said I was lovely in my white dress. And that I looked like a little princess.

SOLNESS: I expect you did, Miss Wangel. And then, too, – I was feeling so light and free that day –

HILDE: And then you said that when I was grown-up I should be *your* princess.

SOLNESS [*laughing a little*]: Well, well, – did I say that too?

HILDE: Yes, you did. And when I asked how long I was to wait, you said that you would come again in ten years' time – like a troll – and carry me away. To Spain, or somewhere like that. And *there* you promised you'd buy a kingdom for me.

SOLNESS [*as before*]: Well, after a good dinner one doesn't count the shillings. But did I really say all that?

HILDE [*laughing quietly*]: Yes. And you said what the kingdom was to be called, too.

SOLNESS: Well? What was it?

HILDE: It was to be called the kingdom of Orangia, you said.

SOLNESS: Well, that was an appetizing name.

HILDE: No, I didn't like it a bit. For it was as if you were trying to make fun of me.

SOLNESS: But I'm sure that wasn't what I meant.

HILDE: No, I shouldn't think it was. Considering what you did next, –

SOLNESS: What in the world did I do next?

HILDE: Yes, that's just what I was waiting for – for you to have forgotten that too! I should have thought one couldn't help remembering a thing like that.

SOLNESS: Yes, well, just start me going and then perhaps – Well?

HILDE [*looking steadily at him*]: You came and kissed me, Mr Solness.

SOLNESS [*with open mouth, getting up from his chair*]: *Did* I?

HILDE: Oh yes, you did. You took me in both arms and bent me over backward and kissed me. Many, many times.

SOLNESS: Why, my dear Miss Wangel –!

HILDE [*getting up*]: You're never going to deny it?

SOLNESS: Yes I certainly *am* going to deny it!

HILDE [*looking scornfully at him*]: Very well.

[*She turns and goes slowly across to the stove and remains standing close beside it, motionless, with her back turned and her hands behind her. There is a short pause.*]

SOLNESS [*going cautiously up behind her*]: Miss Wangel –? [HILDE *is silent and does not move.*] Don't stand there like a statue. All this, that you said, it must be something you've dreamt. [*He puts his hand on her arm.*] Now listen – [HILDE *makes an impatient movement with her arm.* SOLNESS *speaks as though an idea had occurred suddenly to him.*] Unless –! Wait a moment –! There's something here that goes deeper, you'll find. [HILDE *does not move.* SOLNESS *speaks quietly but emphatically.*] I must have *thought* all this. I must have *willed* it. Have *wished* for it. Have *wanted* it. And so –. Wouldn't that be the explanation? [HILDE *is still silent.* SOLNESS *speaks impatiently.*] Oh very well, damn it all, – then I *did* it, I suppose!

HILDE [*turning her head a little, but not looking at him*]: Then you admit it now?

SOLNESS: Yes. Anything you like.

HILDE: That you put your arms round me?

149

SOLNESS: Oh, yes!

HILDE: And bent me over backward?

SOLNESS: A long way back.

HILDE: And kissed me?

SOLNESS: Yes, I did.

HILDE: Many times?

SOLNESS: As many as ever you like.

HILDE [*turning suddenly towards him, with the dancing and happy expression in her eyes again*]: There, you see; I managed to get it out of you in the end!

SOLNESS [*with a faint smile*]: Yes, only think – that I could forget a thing like that.

HILDE [*a little sulky again, moving away from him*]: Oh, you have kissed so many people in your time, I expect.

SOLNESS: No, you mustn't think *that* of me. [HILDE *sits down in the arm-chair.* SOLNESS *stands leaning against the rocking-chair and looks closely at her.*] Miss Wangel?

HILDE: Yes?

SOLNESS: How *was* it now? What happened next – to us two?

HILDE: Nothing more happened. You know that quite well. Because then the other visitors came in and so –! Bah!

SOLNESS: Yes, of course! The others came in. To think I could forget *that*, too.

HILDE: Oh, you haven't really forgotten anything. Only felt a bit ashamed. One doesn't forget things like that, I'm sure.

SOLNESS: No, one wouldn't think so.

HILDE [*looking at him, full of life again*]: Unless perhaps you've forgotten what day it was, too?

SOLNESS: What day –?

HILDE: Yes, what day did you hang the wreath up on the tower? Well? Tell me at once!

SOLNESS: Hm, – upon my soul, I've forgotten the actual day. I only know it was ten years ago. Somewhen in autumn.

HILDE [*nodding her head slowly several times*]: It was ten years ago. On the nineteenth of September.

SOLNESS: Ah, yes, it would have been just about then. You see, you remember that too! [*Stopping.*] But wait a minute – ! Yes, – today's the nineteenth of September.

HILDE: Yes, it is. And the ten years are up. And you didn't come – as you'd promised me.

SOLNESS: Promised you? Threatened you, I suppose you mean?

HILDE: I don't think there was anything threatening in *that*.

SOLNESS: Well, made fun of you a little.

HILDE: Was that all you wanted? To make fun of me?

SOLNESS: Well, to have a little joke with you then! Heaven knows, I don't remember. But it must have been something of that kind. For you were only a child then.

HILDE: Oh, perhaps I wasn't quite such a child as that, either. Not such a silly little thing as you think.

SOLNESS [*looking searchingly at her*]: Did you really and seriously think I should come back?

HILDE [*concealing a half-jesting smile*]: Yes, indeed! I did expect *that* of you.

SOLNESS: That I should come to your home and take you away with me?

HILDE: Just like a troll, yes.

SOLNESS: And make you a princess?

HILDE: You promised me that.

SOLNESS: And give you a kingdom, too?

HILDE [*looking up at the ceiling*]: Why not? For it didn't have to be just an actual, ordinary kingdom.

SOLNESS: But something else just as good?

HILDE: Yes, at least as good. [*Looking at him for a moment.*] If you could build the highest church tower in the world, I thought you must surely be able to produce a kingdom too, of some sort or other

SOLNESS [*shaking his head*]: I can't really make you out, Miss Wangel.

HILDE: Can't you? It seems so easy to me.

SOLNESS: No, I can't be sure whether you mean all you say. Or whether you're just having a joke –

HILDE [*smiling*]: Making fun of you perhaps? I, too?

SOLNESS: Exactly. Making fun. Of both of us. [*Looking at her.*] Have you known long that I was married?

HILDE: Yes, I've known that all along. Why do you ask *that*?

SOLNESS [*casually*]: Oh, well, it just came into my mind. [*Looking seriously at her and speaking quietly.*] Why have you come?

HILDE: Because I want my kingdom. The time's up now.

SOLNESS [*laughing involuntarily*]: Well, you are an amazing person!

HILDE [*merrily*]: Hand over the kingdom, Mr Solness! [*Tapping with her fingers.*] The kingdom on the table!

SOLNESS [*pushing the rocking-chair nearer and sitting down*]: Seriously now, – why have you come? What do you really want to do here?

HILDE: Well, to begin with I want to go round and look at everything you've built.

SOLNESS: Then you'll have plenty of exercise doing that.

HILDE: Yes, I know you've built a terrible lot.

SOLNESS: I have. Mostly of late years.

HILDE: Many church towers too? Tremendously high ones?

SOLNESS: No. I don't build any more church towers. And no churches either.

HILDE: Why, what do you build now?

SOLNESS: Homes, for human beings.

HILDE [*reflectively*]: Couldn't you put a little – a little church tower, as it were, over those homes too?

SOLNESS [*starting*]: What do you mean by *that*?

HILDE: I mean – something that points – straight up into the free air. With a weather-cock so high that it makes one giddy.

SOLNESS [*pondering a moment*]: It's very odd that you should say that. For that's just what I'd most like to do.

HILDE [*impatiently*]: But why don't you *do* it then?

SOLNESS [*shaking his head*]: No, because the people won't have it.

HILDE: To think they don't want it!

SOLNESS [*more lightly*]: But now I'm building myself a new home. Just across from here.

HILDE: For yourself?

SOLNESS: Yes. It's just about finished. And on that there is a tower.

HILDE: High tower?

SOLNESS: Yes.

HILDE: Very high?

SOLNESS: People will be sure to say it's too high. For a home to be.

HILDE: I'll go out and look at that tower the first thing in the morning.

SOLNESS [*sitting leaning his cheek on his hand and gazing at her*]: Tell me, Miss Wangel, – what's your name? Your Christian name, I mean.

HILDE: My name's Hilde, of course.

SOLNESS [*as before*]: Hilde? Really?

HILDE: Don't you remember *that*? You called me Hilde yourself. That day that you behaved so badly.

SOLNESS: Did I do *that* too?

HILDE: But that time you said 'little Hilde'. And I didn't like that.

SOLNESS: So you didn't like that, Miss Hilde?

HILDE: No. Not at that moment. But – 'Princess Hilde' –. That will sound very well, I think.

SOLNESS: Quite. 'Princess Hilde of – of –.' What *was* it the kingdom was to be called?

HILDE: Oh bosh! I don't want to bother about that stupid kingdom. I want to have quite a different one.

SOLNESS [*has leant back in the chair and goes on looking at her*]: Isn't it strange –? The more I think it over – the more it looks to me as if, all these long years, I've gone on tormenting myself with – hm –

HILDE: With what?

SOLNESS: With trying to find something again – some experience I seemed to have forgotten. But I never had any idea what it could be.

HILDE: You should have tied a knot in your handkerchief, Mr Solness.

SOLNESS: Then I should only have gone and puzzled over what the knot could mean.

HILDE: Oh yes, I suppose there *are* trolls like that in the world, too.

SOLNESS [*getting up slowly*]: It's a very good thing you've come to me now.

HILDE [*with a penetrating look*]: *Is* it good?

SOLNESS: Because I have been so lonely here. And staring at it all quite helplessly. [*Lowering his voice.*] I must tell you – I've begun to be so afraid – so terribly afraid of the younger generation.

HILDE [*with a sniff of contempt*]: Pooh! Is the younger generation anything to be afraid of?

SOLNESS: It certainly is. That's why I've locked and bolted myself in. [*Mysteriously.*] You must know, the younger generation will come here some day, thundering at the door! Break in on me!

HILDE: Then I think you ought to go out and open the door to the younger generation.

SOLNESS: Open the door?

HILDE: Yes. So that the younger generation can come in to you. On friendly terms.

SOLNESS: No, no, no! The younger generation – it's retribution, you see. It comes in the forefront of the change. Under a new banner, as it were.

HILDE [*getting up, looking at him and speaking with a tremulous movement of her mouth*]: Can you use *me* for anything, Mr Solness?

SOLNESS: Yes, that I certainly can! For you come too, it seems to me – under a new banner. So youth against youth –!

[DR HERDAL *comes in by the door to the hall.*]

DR HERDAL: Why, you and Miss Wangel still here?

SOLNESS: Yes. We've had a lot of things to talk about.

HILDE: Both old and new.

DR HERDAL: Really, have you?

HILDE: Oh, it's been such fun. Because Mr Solness – he has an absolutely incredible memory. Every imaginable little thing, he remembers it on the spot.

[MRS SOLNESS *comes in by the door on the right.*]

MRS SOLNESS: There you are, Miss Wangel, the room's ready for you now.

HILDE: Oh, how kind you are to me!

SOLNESS [*to his wife*]: The nursery?

MRS SOLNESS: Yes. The middle one. But first we'd better have something to eat.

SOLNESS [*nodding to* HILDE]: Yes, Hilde shall sleep in the nursery.

MRS SOLNESS [*looking at him*]: Hilde?

SOLNESS: Yes, Miss Wangel's name's Hilde. I knew her when she was a child.

MRS SOLNESS: Oh, *did* you Halvard? Well, come along then. Supper's ready.

[*She takes* DR HERDAL'S *arm and goes out with him on the right.* HILDE *has in the meantime collected her travelling things together.*]

HILDE [*softly and quickly to* SOLNESS]: Is it true, what you said? *Can* you use me for something?

SOLNESS [*taking her things from her*]: You're the very person
I've needed most.

HILDE [*looking at him, her eyes full of joy and wonder, and clasping her hands together*]: But then – oh you great, glorious
world –!

SOLNESS [*breathlessly*]: Well –?

HILDE: Then I *have* my kingdom!

SOLNESS [*involuntarily*]: Hilde –!

HILDE [*again with the tremulous movement of her mouth*]: Almost
– I was going to say. [*She goes out to the right.* SOLNESS
follows her.]

ACT TWO

A pleasantly furnished little sitting-room in Solness's house. In the back wall is a glass door leading out to the veranda and the garden. On the right a corner is cut off by a bay in which there are stands for plants and a large window. A corresponding corner is cut off on the left. In this there is a little door covered with wall-paper. In both the side walls there is an ordinary door. Downstage on the right is a console-table with a large mirror over it. Flowers and plants in profusion. Downstage on the left a sofa with a table and chairs. Further back a bookcase. Out in the room, before the bay, a little table and some chairs. It is early in the morning.

SOLNESS is sitting at the little table with Ragnar Brovik's folder open in front of him. He turns over the drawings and looks closely at some of them. MRS SOLNESS is going silently about with a little watering can, attending to the flowers. She is dressed in black as before. Her hat, outdoor coat, and parasol are lying on a chair by the mirror. SOLNESS follows her with his eyes now and then without her noticing. Neither of them speaks.

KAJA FOSLI comes silently in at the door on the left.

SOLNESS [*turning his head and speaking with casual indifference*]: Oh, is that you?

KAJA: I just wanted to tell you I'd come.

SOLNESS: Yes, yes, that's right. Isn't Ragnar there too?

KAJA: No, not yet. He had to stay a little and wait for the doctor. But he is coming presently to hear –

SOLNESS: How are things with the old man today?

KAJA: Pretty bad. He asks you to excuse him because he has to stay in bed today.

SOLNESS: Of course. Let him, by all means. But you go and do your work.

KAJA: Yes. [*Stopping by the door.*] Do you want to speak to Ragnar when he comes?

SOLNESS: No, – I don't know that I've anything special to say to him.

> [KAJA *goes out again to the left.* SOLNESS *goes on sitting and turning over the drawings.*]

MRS SOLNESS [*over by the plants*]: I wonder if *he* isn't going to die now, too.

SOLNESS [*looking at her*]: He too? Who's the other?

MRS SOLNESS [*without answering*]: Oh, yes; old Mr Brovik – he's going to die too, Halvard, I'm sure. You'll see; he will.

SOLNESS: Aline, dear, oughtn't you to go out for a little walk?

MRS SOLNESS: Yes, I suppose I ought to. [*She goes on attending to the flowers.*]

SOLNESS [*bending over the drawings*]: Is she still asleep?

MRS SOLNESS [*looking at him*]: Is it Miss Wangel you're sitting thinking about?

SOLNESS [*indifferently*]: I just happened to remember her.

MRS SOLNESS: Miss Wangel's been up a long time.

SOLNESS: Oh, *has* she?

MRS SOLNESS: When I went in there she was busy arranging her things. [*She goes in front of the mirror and begins slowly to put her hat on.*]

SOLNESS [*after a short pause*]: So we've found a use for a nursery after all, Aline.

MRS SOLNESS: Yes, we have.

SOLNESS: I think that's better than for them all to stand empty.

MRS SOLNESS: This emptiness is dreadful. You're right there.

SOLNESS [*closing the folder, getting up, and going nearer to her*]: You just see, Aline – in future things will be better with us. Far more comfortable. Life will be easier – especially for *you*.

MRS SOLNESS [*looking at him*]: In future?

SOLNESS: Yes, believe me, Aline –

MRS SOLNESS: Do you mean – because *she's* come here?

SOLNESS [*checking himself*]: I mean, of course – when we've once moved into the new house.

MRS SOLNESS [*taking her outdoor coat*]: Oh, do you think so, Halvard? That it will be better then?

SOLNESS: I can't believe it won't. And surely you think so too?

MRS SOLNESS: I don't think about the new house at all.

SOLNESS [*discouraged*]: That's very bad news for me. Because it's mostly for your sake that I've built it, you know. [*He tries to help her on with her coat.*]

MRS SOLNESS [*moving away from him*]: The fact is you do far too much for my sake.

SOLNESS [*with some vehemence*]: No, no, you really mustn't say that, Aline! I can't bear to hear that kind of thing from you.

MRS SOLNESS: Very well, then I won't say it, Halvard.

SOLNESS: But I still maintain it. You'll see – it'll be very nice for you over there in the new house.

MRS SOLNESS: Oh heavens, – nice for me –!

SOLNESS [*eagerly*]: Yes it will! Yes it will! You can be sure of that, my dear! Because there, you see, – there'll be such a tremendous lot that'll remind you of your own home –

MRS SOLNESS: Of the home that had been Father's and Mother's. And that was all burnt down.

SOLNESS [*in a low voice*]: Yes, yes, my poor Aline. That was a dreadful blow for you.

MRS SOLNESS [*breaking out into lamentation*]: You can build as much as ever you like, Halvard – you'll never manage to build a real home again for *me*!

SOLNESS [*crossing the room*]: Well then, for heaven's sake don't let's talk about it any more.

MRS SOLNESS: We never do talk about it, anyhow. Because you just put it away from you –

SOLNESS [*stopping suddenly and looking at her*]: Do I? And why should I do that? Put it away from me?

MRS SOLNESS: Oh yes, I understand you so well, Halvard. You want to spare me. And excuse me, too. As much as ever you can.

SOLNESS [*with astonishment in his eyes*]: You! Is it you, yourself, you're talking about, Aline?

MRS SOLNESS: Yes, of course it's about myself.

SOLNESS [*involuntarily, to himself*]: *That* too!

MRS SOLNESS: As for the old house, – as for *that*, it happened as it had to happen. Heaven knows, once misfortune had begun – why –

SOLNESS: Yes, you're right. There's no escaping misfortune, as they say.

MRS SOLNESS: But the terrible thing, that the fire brought with it –! *That's* the thing! That, that, that!

SOLNESS [*emphatically*]: Don't think about that, Aline!

MRS SOLNESS: Yes, that's just what I must think about. And talk about it, too, at last. Because I don't think I can bear it any longer. And then, never to have the right to forgive myself –!

SOLNESS [*exclaiming*]: *Yourself* –!

MRS SOLNESS: Yes, for I had duties in two directions. Both to you and to the children. I should have hardened myself. Not let the terror get such a hold on me. Nor my grief because my home was burnt down. [*Wringing her hands.*] Oh, if only I *could* have, Halvard!

SOLNESS [*quietly and moved, going towards her*]: Aline, you must promise me you'll never think these thoughts any more. Promise me that, my dear!

MRS SOLNESS: Oh heavens, – promise! Promise! One can promise anything –

SOLNESS [*clenching his hands and going across the room*]: Oh, it's hopeless, this is! Never a gleam of sunshine! Not so much as a ray of light in the home!

MRS SOLNESS: There's no home here, Halvard.

SOLNESS: No, you may well say it. [*Heavily.*] And God knows whether you aren't right in *that* – that it won't be any better for us in the new house either.

MRS SOLNESS: It never will be. Just as empty. Just as desolate. There as here.

SOLNESS [*angrily*]: But why to goodness have we built it then? Can you tell me that?

MRS SOLNESS: No, you must answer that yourself.

SOLNESS [*glancing suspiciously at her*]: What do you mean by *that*, Aline?

MRS SOLNESS: What do I mean?

SOLNESS: Yes, damn it all –! You said it so queerly. As if you had something at the back of your mind.

MRS SOLNESS: No, I can truly assure you –

SOLNESS [*going nearer*]: Thank you, – I know what I know. And I can see and hear, too, Aline. You may be sure of that!

MRS SOLNESS: But what is all this? What is it?

SOLNESS [*stopping in front of her*]: You don't, for instance, find an insidious, hidden meaning in the most innocent word I speak?

MRS SOLNESS: *I*, you say! *I* do that!

SOLNESS [*laughing*]: Ha, ha, ha! But that's reasonable enough, Aline! When you have to deal with a sick man in the house, then –

MRS SOLNESS [*full of anxiety*]: Sick! Are you *ill*, Halvard?

SOLNESS [*breaking out*]: A half-crazy man, then! A man who's out of his mind! Call me what you like.

MRS SOLNESS [*fumbling for the chair-back and sitting down*]: Halvard, – for God's sake –!

SOLNESS: But you're mistaken, both of you. Both you and the doctor. There's nothing like that the matter with me. [*He walks up and down the room.* MRS SOLNESS *follows him anxiously with her eyes. Then he goes across to her. He speaks quietly*.] In fact there's not a thing in the world wrong with me.

MRS SOLNESS: No, there isn't, is there? But then what's upsetting you so much?

SOLNESS: It's this, that I'm often on the point of sinking under this appalling burden of debt –

MRS SOLNESS: Debt, you say! But you're not in debt to anyone, Halvard!

SOLNESS [*quietly, with emotion*]: Boundlessly in debt to you, – to you, – to you, Aline.

MRS SOLNESS [*getting up slowly*]: What is at the back of all this? You might as well say it at once.

SOLNESS: But there *isn't* anything at the back of it. I've never done you any wrong. Not knowingly and intentionally, anyway. And yet all the same – it feels as if a crushing debt lay on me and weighed me down.

MRS SOLNESS: A debt to me?

SOLNESS: Mostly to you.

MRS SOLNESS: Then you are – ill, after all, Halvard.

SOLNESS [*heavily*]: Maybe so. Or something of the kind. [*Looking towards the door on the right, which is opening.*] Ah! It's getting light now.

> [HILDE WANGEL *comes in. She has made one or two changes in her clothes. The skirt of her dress has been let down.*]

HILDE: Good morning, Mr Solness!

SOLNESS [*nodding*]: Slept well?

HILDE: Oh, beautifully! As if I was in a cradle. Yes, – I lay and stretched myself like – like a princess!

SOLNESS [*smiling a little*]: Quite comfortable, then?

HILDE: I should say so!

SOLNESS: And dreamt too, I suppose?

HILDE: Oh yes. But that was horrid.

SOLNESS: Was it?

HILDE: Yes, because I dreamt I was falling over a terribly

high, steep cliff. Don't you ever dream anything like that yourself?

SOLNESS: Why yes, now and then, –

HILDE: It's very exciting – when one falls and falls –

SOLNESS: It seems to make one's blood run cold.

HILDE: Do you tuck your legs up under you, while it's happening?

SOLNESS: Yes, as high as ever I can.

HILDE: I do that too.

MRS SOLNESS [taking her parasol]: I must go into town, now, Halvard. [To HILDE.] And I'll see about bringing in one or two things that you may find useful.

HILDE [as though about to throw herself on her neck]: Oh, dearest, kindest Mrs Solness! That really is too good of you! Awfully good –

MRS SOLNESS [freeing herself, deprecatingly]: Oh not at all. It's only my duty. And so I'm very glad to do it.

HILDE [hurt and pouting]: All the same, I think I could quite well go out in the streets – I've made my dress quite tidy, now. Or can't I, perhaps?

MRS SOLNESS: To tell the truth, I think people would look at you a little.

HILDE [brushing it aside]: Pooh! Is that all? That'll be rather fun.

SOLNESS [with suppressed ill-temper]: Yes, but people might get the idea that you were mad too, you see.

HILDE: Mad? Are there so many mad people, then, here in town?

SOLNESS [touching his forehead with his finger]: You see one here, at any rate.

HILDE: You, – Mr Solness!

MRS SOLNESS: Oh, come! My dear Halvard!

SOLNESS: Haven't you observed that yet?

HILDE: No, I certainly haven't. [Thinking better of it and laughing a little.] Well, perhaps in one, single thing.

SOLNESS: There, do you hear that, Aline?

MRS SOLNESS: What thing is that, Miss Wangel?

HILDE: No, I won't say.

SOLNESS: Oh yes, do!

HILDE: No thank you, – I'm not as mad as that.

MRS SOLNESS: When you and Miss Wangel are alone, I expect she'll tell you, Halvard.

SOLNESS: Oh, – do you think so?

MRS SOLNESS: Yes, of course. Because you knew her so well in the past. Ever since she was a child – you say. [*She goes out by the door on the left.*]

HILDE [*after a moment*]: Doesn't your wife like me at all?

SOLNESS: Did you think you noticed anything like that?

HILDE: Didn't you notice it yourself?

SOLNESS [*evasively*]: Aline's got so shy with people in these last years.

HILDE: Has she really?

SOLNESS: But if only you could get to know her well –. Because she's so kind – and so good – and so nice, really–

HILDE [*impatiently*]: But if she's like *that* – why did she say that about duty?

SOLNESS: About duty?

HILDE: Yes, she said she would go out and buy something for me. Because it was her *duty*, she said. Oh, I can't bear that horrid, ugly word!

SOLNESS: Why can't you?

HILDE: Because it sounds so cold and sharp and stinging. Duty – duty–duty. Don't you feel that too? That it sort of stings you?

SOLNESS: Hm, – haven't thought about it very much.

HILDE: Yes, it does! And if she's so kind, – as you say she is, – why should she talk like that?

SOLNESS: But, good lord, what should she have said?

HILDE: She could have said that she would do it because she liked me so awfully much. Something of that kind, she could have said. Something that was really warm and affectionate, you know.

SOLNESS [*looking at her*]: Is that how you want it to be?

HILDE: Yes, just like that. [*She walks round the room, stops by the bookcase, and looks at the books.*] You've got a lot of books.

SOLNESS: Yes, I've acquired a few.

HILDE: And do you read all these books?

SOLNESS: I tried to at one time. Do you read much?

HILDE: Not I! Never – any more. I can't see any point in it.

SOLNESS: That's just how it is with me too.

[HILDE *wanders about a little, stops by the small table, opens the folder, and turns over the sheets.*]

HILDE: Is it you who've drawn all this?

SOLNESS: No, it's a young man I have to help me.

HILDE: Someone you've taught yourself?

SOLNESS: Oh yes, I expect he's learnt something from me too.

HILDE [*sitting down*]: So I suppose he's very clever? [*Glancing at a drawing*]. Isn't he?

SOLNESS: Oh, not too bad. For *my* purpose, –

HILDE: Yes, of course! He must be terribly clever.

SOLNESS: Do you think you can see that from the drawings?

HILDE: Oh bosh, – these scrawls! But if he's been trained in *your* office, then –

SOLNESS: Oh, as for *that* –. There are plenty of people here who've learnt from *me*. And haven't come to much for all that.

HILDE [*looking at him and shaking her head*]: Well, if my life depended on it, I couldn't understand how you can be so stupid.

SOLNESS: Stupid? Do you think I'm so very stupid?

HILDE: Yes, I certainly do. If you're content to go training all these people, well –

SOLNESS [*starting*]: Well? And why not?

HILDE [*getting up, half serious and half laughing*]: Oh nonsense,

Mr Solness! What's the good of *that*? No one but you should have the right to build. You should be quite alone. Do it all yourself. Now you know.

SOLNESS [*involuntarily*]: Hilde –!

HILDE: Well?

SOLNESS: How on earth did you get that idea?

HILDE: Do you think it's such a stupid idea of mine – that?

SOLNESS: No, it's not that. But now I'll tell you something.

HILDE: Well?

SOLNESS: Here am I – incessantly – in silence and solitude – turning over that very thought.

HILDE: Well, that's natural enough, it seems to me.

SOLNESS [*looking at her rather watchfully*]: And no doubt you've observed it already?

HILDE: No, I haven't – not at all.

SOLNESS: But just now, – when you said you thought I was – a little – unbalanced? At least in one thing –?

HILDE: Oh, I was thinking of something quite different.

SOLNESS: Different? In what way?

HILDE: Never mind about that, Mr Solness.

SOLNESS [*going across the room*]: Well, well, – as you like. [*Stopping by the bay.*] Come over here and I'll show you something.

HILDE [*going nearer*]: What is it?

SOLNESS: Do you see, – over there in the garden –?

HILDE: Yes?

SOLNESS [*pointing*]: Just above the big stone quarry?

HILDE: That new house, you mean?

SOLNESS: The one that's being built, yes. Practically finished.

HILDE: It has a very high tower, it seems to me.

SOLNESS: The scaffolding's still up.

HILDE: Is it your new house, that?

SOLNESS: Yes.

HILDE: The house you're soon going to move into?

SOLNESS: Yes.

HILDE [*looking at him*]: Are there nurseries in that house too?

SOLNESS: Three, just as there are here.

HILDE: And no child?

SOLNESS: There never will be, either.

HILDE [*with a half smile*]: Well, then, isn't it as I said –?

SOLNESS: That –?

HILDE: That you're – so to speak – a little mad after all?

SOLNESS: Was that what you were thinking about?

HILDE: Yes, about all those empty nurseries, where I slept.

SOLNESS [*lowering his voice*]: We *did* have children, – Aline and I.

HILDE [*looking at him in suspense*]: Did you –?

SOLNESS: Two little boys. They were both the same age.

HILDE: Twins.

SOLNESS: Yes, twins. It's eleven or twelve years ago now.

HILDE [*tentatively*]: And so both of them are –? Then you haven't the twins any longer?

SOLNESS [*with quiet emotion*]: We only kept them about three weeks. Or not quite that. [*Breaking out.*] Oh Hilde, I can't tell you what a comfort it is to me – that you've come! For now at last I've got someone I can talk to!

HILDE: Can't you do that with – with *her*, too?

SOLNESS: Not about this. Not the way I want to and need to. [*Heavily.*] And not about so many other things either.

HILDE [*in a low voice*]: Was that all you meant, when you said you needed me?

SOLNESS: It was that most of all. Yesterday at least. For to-day I'm not so sure any longer – [*Breaking off.*] Come here and let's sit down, Hilde. Sit here on the sofa, – so that you have the garden to look at. [HILDE *sits down in the corner of the sofa.* SOLNESS *pulls a chair nearer.*] Would you like to hear about it?

HILDE: Yes, I shall love it – to sit and listen to you.

SOLNESS [*sitting down*]: Then I'll tell you all about it.

HILDE: Now I've got both the garden and you to look at, Mr Solness. So tell me! Right away!

SOLNESS [*pointing to the bay window*]: Over there on the rise, – where you see the new house –

HILDE: Yes?

SOLNESS: That's where Aline and I lived for the first few years. For up there, in those days, there was an old house that had belonged to her mother. And we inherited it from her. And the whole of the big garden with it.

HILDE: Was there a tower on *that* house too?

SOLNESS: Not a thing of that kind. Seen from the outside, it was a large, ugly, dark wooden box. But pleasant and comfortable enough inside all the same.

HILDE: Did you pull the old place down then?

SOLNESS: No. It was burnt down.

HILDE: The whole of it?

SOLNESS: Yes.

HILDE: Was that a great misfortune for you?

SOLNESS: Depends how you look at it. The fire put me on my feet as a master builder –

HILDE: Well, but –?

SOLNESS: We had just had the two little boys at that time –

HILDE: The poor little twins, yes.

SOLNESS: They started life so strong and healthy. And they grew from day to day, so that one could really see it.

HILDE: Young children grow a lot in the first few days.

SOLNESS: It was the prettiest sight one's eyes could see, Aline lying there with the two of them. But then came the night of the fire –

HILDE [*breathlessly*]: What happened? Tell me! Was anyone burnt in it?

SOLNESS: No; not that. They were all got safely out of the house –

HILDE: Well, but then what –?

SOLNESS: The fright had shaken Aline so dreadfully. The

alarm – getting out of the house – the hurry and rush – and the freezing night air into the bargain –. For they had to be carried out just as they were. Both she and the children.

HILDE: Couldn't they stand it?

SOLNESS: Oh yes, *they* stood it all right. But it turned to a fever with Aline. And that affected her milk. She insisted on feeding them herself. Because it was her duty, she said. And both our little boys, they – [*Clenching his hands.*] they – ah!

HILDE: They didn't get over *that*?

SOLNESS: No, *that* they didn't get over. It was that that took them from us.

HILDE: It must have been terribly hard for you.

SOLNESS: Hard enough for me. But ten times harder for Aline. [*Clenching his hands in silent fury.*] Oh, that such things can be allowed to happen in this world! [*Shortly and firmly.*] From the day I lost them I never wanted to build churches.

HILDE: Perhaps you didn't like building our church tower, either?

SOLNESS: I didn't like it. I know how glad and light-hearted I felt when that tower was finished.

HILDE: *I* know that too.

SOLNESS: And now I shall never build that kind of thing – never any more! Neither churches nor church towers.

HILDE [*nodding slowly*]: Only houses that people can live in.

SOLNESS: Homes for human beings, Hilde.

HILDE: But homes with high towers and spires on them.

SOLNESS: Preferably. [*Changing to a lighter note.*] Yes, you see, – as I said – that fire set me on my feet. As a master builder, that is.

HILDE: Why don't you call yourself an architect like the others?

SOLNESS: I didn't have the proper training for that. What I know, – for the most part I've found it out for myself.

HILDE: But you got on to your feet, all the same.

SOLNESS: Thanks to the fire, yes. I laid out almost the whole of the garden in lots for small houses. And *there* I was able to build exactly as I liked. And *then* things went ahead with me.

HILDE [*looking searchingly at him*]: You certainly must be a very happy man. The way things are with you.

SOLNESS [*gloomily*]: Happy? Do *you* say that too? Like all the others?

HILDE: Yes, for I think you must be. If only you could stop thinking about the two little children, –

SOLNESS [*slowly*]: The two little children – they're not so easy to forget, Hilde.

HILDE [*a little uncertainly*]: Do they still trouble you so much? Such a long, long time afterwards?

SOLNESS [*looking steadily at her, without answering*]: Happy man, you said –

HILDE: Yes, but aren't you that – in other ways?

SOLNESS [*goes on looking at her*]: When I told you all this about the fire – hm –

HILDE: Well?

SOLNESS: Wasn't there a special idea, that you – that you fastened on?

HILDE [*reflecting in vain*]: No. What kind of idea would it be?

SOLNESS [*with quiet emphasis*]: It was simply and solely through that fire that I was given the chance to build homes for human beings. Cosy, comfortable, bright homes; where the father and mother and a whole lot of children could live safely and happily feeling that it's good to be alive in the world. And most of all, to belong to each other – in big things and little.

HILDE [*eagerly*]: Yes, but isn't it a very happy thing for you, that you can make such beautiful homes?

SOLNESS: The price, Hilde. The terrible price I had to pay to get there.

HILDE: But can't you ever get over that?

SOLNESS: No. For in order to build homes for others I had to give up – give up for ever – having a home of my own. I mean a home for a lot of children. And for the father and mother too.

HILDE [*tentatively*]: But *did* you have to? For ever, you say?

SOLNESS [*nodding slowly*]: *That* was the price of the happiness that people are always talking about. [*Breathing heavily.*] That happiness, – hm, – that happiness wasn't to be bought any cheaper, Hilde.

HILDE [*as before*]: But mayn't it come all right after all?

SOLNESS: Never in this world. Never. That's another consequence of the fire. And of Aline's illness afterwards.

HILDE [*looking at him with an unfathomable expression*]: And yet you build all these nurseries.

SOLNESS [*earnestly*]: Haven't you ever noticed, Hilde, that the impossible – it, as it were, fascinates and calls to one?

HILDE [*reflecting*]: The impossible? [*Full of life.*] Why, yes! Have you discovered that too?

SOLNESS: Yes, I have.

HILDE: So there must be – a little bit of the troll in you too?

SOLNESS: Why of the troll?

HILDE: Well, what are you going to call it?

SOLNESS [*getting up*]: Well, well, it may be so. [*Impetuously.*] But how can I help becoming a troll – the way it goes with me all the time, in everything! In everything!

HILDE: What do you mean?

SOLNESS [*with lowered voice and inward emotion*]: Pay attention to what I say to you, Hilde. Everything that I've succeeded in making, building, shaping into beauty and security, into cheerful comfort – into splendour, too – [*Clenching his hands.*] Oh, isn't it terrible, just to think of –!

HILDE: *What* is so terrible?

SOLNESS: That all that, I've got to make good. Pay for it. Not in money. But with human happiness. And not with my own happiness only. But with others' too. Yes, yes, consider *that*, Hilde! That's the price my place as an artist has cost me – and others. And every single day I must go on watching that price paid for me afresh. Over again, and over again, – and always over again!

HILDE [*getting up and looking fixedly at him*]: Now you must be thinking of – of *her*.

SOLNESS: Yes. Chiefly of Aline. Because Aline – she had *her* life-work, too. Just as much as I had mine. [*His voice trembles.*] But her life-work had to be ruined, crushed, all knocked to pieces – so that mine could break its way through to – to something like a great victory. For you must know that Aline – she had her gift for building too.

HILDE: She! For building?

SOLNESS [*shaking his head*]: Not houses and towers and spires – and the sort of thing I work at –

HILDE: Well, but what then?

SOLNESS [*tenderly and with emotion*]: For building up the souls of little children, Hilde. Building up children's souls so that they could grow into balanced, noble, beautiful forms. So that they could rise up into independent, full-grown human souls. That was what Aline had a gift for. And all this – there it lies now. Unused and useless, for ever. And serving no purpose in the world. Just like a heap of ruins after a fire.

HILDE: Yes, but even if it were so –?

SOLNESS: It *is* so! It *is* so! I know it.

HILDE: Well, but in any case you're not to blame.

SOLNESS [*fastening his eyes on her and nodding slowly*]: Well, you see, that – that's the great, the terrible question. *That's* the doubt that gnaws me – night and day.

HILDE: That!

SOLNESS: Yes, suppose now that I *was* to blame. In some way.

HILDE: You! For the fire!

SOLNESS: For the whole thing. For everything. And yet perhaps – quite innocent, all the same.

HILDE [*looking at him with distress*]: Oh, Master Builder, – if you can say a thing like that, then you must be – ill, after all.

SOLNESS: Hm, – I doubt if I shall ever be quite sound at that point.

[RAGNAR BROVIK *cautiously opens the little door in the corner on the left.* HILDE *moves across the room.*]

RAGNAR [*when he sees* HILDE]: Oh –. I beg your pardon, Mr Solness. [*He is about to withdraw.*]

SOLNESS: No, no, please stay. Then it'll be done.

RAGNAR: Oh yes, – if only it could be!

SOLNESS: Things aren't going any better with your father, I hear.

RAGNAR: My father is sinking fast, now. And that's why I do beg of you, – give me a few words of approval on one of the plans! Something that Father can read before he –

SOLNESS [*emphatically*]: You mustn't talk to me any more about these drawings of yours.

RAGNAR: Have you looked at them?

SOLNESS: Yes, – I have.

RAGNAR: And they're no good? And I'm no good either?

SOLNESS [*evasively*]: You stay here with me, Ragnar. You shall have everything your own way. Then you can marry Kaja. Live without any worry. Quite happily maybe. Only don't think of building yourself.

RAGNAR: Well, well, then I must go home and tell Father what you say. Because I promised him I would. *Am* I to tell Father that – before he dies?

SOLNESS [*with a groan*]: Oh, tell him – tell him what you like, as far as I'm concerned. Best not to tell him anything! [*Breaking out.*] I *can't* do anything else, Ragnar!

RAGNAR: May I have the drawings to take with me, then?

SOLNESS: Yes, take them, – just take them! They're lying there on the table.

RAGNAR [*going over to the table*]: Thank you.

HILDE [*laying her hand on the folder*]: No, no, leave them there.

SOLNESS: What for?

HILDE: Because I want to see them too.

SOLNESS: But you *have* – [*To* RAGNAR.] All right, leave them here, then.

RAGNAR: Very well.

SOLNESS: And go straight home to your father.

RAGNAR: Yes, I suppose I'd better.

SOLNESS [*as if in desperation*]: Ragnar, – you *mustn't* ask anything of me that I *can't* do! Listen to me, Ragnar! You *mustn't*!

RAGNAR: No, no. Excuse me. [*He bows and goes out by the door in the corner.*]

    [HILDE *goes across and sits on a chair by the mirror.*]

HILDE [*looking angrily at* SOLNESS]: That was very mean of you.

SOLNESS: Do you think so too?

HILDE: Yes, it was thoroughly mean. And hard and wicked and ugly too.

SOLNESS: Ah, you don't understand how things are with me.

HILDE: All the same –. No, *you* shouldn't be like that.

SOLNESS: You said yourself just now that *I* was the only person who should have the right to build.

HILDE: I can say a thing like that. But *you* mustn't.

SOLNESS: I most of all, surely. So dearly as I've bought my place.

HILDE: Oh yes, – with what you call domestic comfort – and things like that.

SOLNESS: And with my peace of soul into the bargain.

HILDE [*getting up*]: Peace of soul! [*With feeling.*] Yes, yes, you're right! Poor Mr Solness, – you imagine that –

SOLNESS [*with a quiet chuckle*]: Just sit down again, Hilde. And I'll tell you something amusing.

HILDE [*in suspense, sitting down*]: Well?

SOLNESS: It sounds such a ridiculous little thing. For the

whole story turns on nothing more than a crack in a chimney, you see.

HILDE: On nothing but that?

SOLNESS: No; not to begin with.

[*He moves a chair nearer to* HILDE'S *and sits down.*]

HILDE [*impatiently, tapping her knee*]: Well then, the crack in the chimney!

SOLNESS: I'd noticed the split in the flue long, long before the fire. Every time I was up in the loft, I looked to see if it was still there.

HILDE: And it *was*?

SOLNESS: Yes. For no one else knew about it.

HILDE: And you said nothing?

SOLNESS: No, I didn't.

HILDE: Didn't think of having the flue mended, either?

SOLNESS: I thought of it all right, – but never got any further. Every time I meant to do something about it, it was just as if a hand interposed. Not today, I thought. Tomorrow. Nothing ever came of it.

HILDE: But why did you go on putting it off like that?

SOLNESS: Because I was thinking things over. [*Slowly and quietly.*] Through that little, black crack in the chimney I might perhaps make my way up to success – as a builder.

HILDE [*looking straight in front of her*]: That must have been exciting.

SOLNESS: Almost irresistible. Quite irresistible. For at that time the whole thing looked to me so easy and simple. I wanted it to happen somewhen in the winter. A little while before dinner. I was to be out, taking Aline for a drive in the sledge. The people at home were to have made large fires in the stoves –

HILDE: Yes, because it was to be bitterly cold that day?

SOLNESS: Pretty biting – yes. And they wanted to have it really warm and cosy for Aline when she came in.

HILDE: Because I expect she feels the cold very much.

SOLNESS: She does. And so on our way home we were to see the smoke.

HILDE: Only the smoke?

SOLNESS: The smoke first. But when we got to the garden gate, the whole of the old wooden building was to be in a seething mass of flames. That was how I wanted to have it, you see.

HILDE: Oh, why on earth couldn't it have happened like that!

SOLNESS: Yes, you may well say that, Hilde.

HILDE: Well, but listen, now, Mr Solness. Are you so absolutely sure that the fire did come from that little crack in the chimney?

SOLNESS: No, quite the opposite. I'm absolutely certain that the crack in the chimney had nothing whatever to do with the fire.

HILDE: What!

SOLNESS: It was made perfectly clear that the fire broke out in a clothes cupboard in quite a different part of the house.

HILDE: Well, then, what's all this nonsense you're talking about the crack in the chimney?

SOLNESS: May I talk to you a little longer, Hilde?

HILDE: Yes, if you'll talk like a reasonable being –

SOLNESS: I'll try to. [*He moves his chair nearer.*]

HILDE: Out with it, now, Mr Solness.

SOLNESS [*confidentially*]: Don't you believe, too, Hilde, that there are a few, special, chosen people who've been graced with the power and ability to *want* something, *desire* something, *will* something – so insistently and so – so inexorably – that they *must* get it in the end? Don't you believe that?

HILDE [*with an expression in her eyes that is hard to read*]: If that's so, we'll see one day – if *I* belong to these chosen people.

SOLNESS: One doesn't do them *alone*, these great things. Oh no – the servers and ministers, – they must be with us, too, if anything is to be done. But they never come of their own accord. One must call upon them with determination. Inwardly, you know.

HILDE: What are these servers and ministers?

SOLNESS: Oh, we can talk about that another time. Let's keep to this business of the fire for the moment.

HILDE: Don't you think that fire would have come just the same – even if you hadn't wanted it?

SOLNESS: If the house had been old Knut Brovik's, it would never have burnt down so conveniently for *him*. I'm quite sure of that. For he doesn't know how to call upon the servers, nor upon the ministrants either. [*Getting up in restlessness of mind.*] You see, Hilde – it's I who'm to blame, after all, for the two little boys having to pay with their lives. And do you suppose I'm not to blame for that too – that Aline has never been what she should and might have been? And what she most wanted to be.

HILDE: Yes, but if it's only these servers and ministers –?

SOLNESS: Who called on the servers and ministers? *I* did! And so they came and bowed to my will. [*In rising excitement.*] That's what people call having the luck with one. But I'll tell you what that luck feels like. It feels like a great, raw place here on my breast. And the servers and ministers keep on flaying pieces of skin off other people to mend *my* wound! But yet the wound isn't healed. Never, – never! Oh, if you knew how it can burn and smart sometimes.

HILDE [*looking searchingly at him*]: You *are* ill, Master Builder. Very ill, I almost think.

SOLNESS: Say *mad*. For that's what you mean.

HILDE: No, I don't think there's much wrong with your understanding.

SOLNESS: With *what*, then? Out with it!

HILDE: I'm not sure, you know, that you didn't come into the world with a sickly conscience.

SOLNESS: Sickly conscience? What devilment is that?

HILDE: I mean that your conscience is very fragile. As it were, fine-drawn. Can't bear to tackle things. To lift and carry anything heavy.

SOLNESS [*muttering*]: Hm! What should one's conscience be like, then, may I ask?

HILDE: What I should like for you is a conscience – well, thoroughly robust.

SOLNESS: Oh? Robust? Well. Have you a robust conscience, I wonder?

HILDE: Yes, I'm pretty sure I have. I've never noticed that it wasn't.

SOLNESS: I don't suppose it's really been put to any severe test.

HILDE [*with a tremulous movement of the mouth*]: Oh, it wasn't so easy to leave Father; I'm so terribly fond of him.

SOLNESS: Oh come! Just for a month or two –

HILDE: I don't think I'll ever go home again.

SOLNESS: Never? Why did you leave him, then?

HILDE [*half serious, half jesting*]: Now have you forgotten it again – that the ten years are up?

SOLNESS: Nonsense. Was something wrong at home? Eh?

HILDE [*completely serious*]: It was this thing inside me that spurred and drove me here. Fascinated and drew me, too.

SOLNESS [*eagerly*]: Now we've got it! Now we've got it, Hilde! There's a troll in you, too. As there is in me. For it's the troll in one, you see, – it's *that* that calls on the powers outside us. And then we *must* give in – whether we want to or not.

HILDE: I almost think you're right, Master Builder.

SOLNESS [*walking about the room*]: Ah, there are numberless devils about in the world, Hilde, that one doesn't *see*.

HILDE: Devils too?

SOLNESS [*stopping*]: Good devils and bad devils. Fair-haired devils and dark-haired devils. If only you always knew whether it's the fair or the dark that have got hold of you.

[*Walking about.*] Ha, ha! There wouldn't be any problem then.

HILDE [*following him with her eyes*]: Or if one had a thoroughly strong conscience, bursting with health. So that one *dared* to do what one *wanted*.

SOLNESS [*stopping by the console-table*]: I think, you know, that most people are just as feeble as I am over this.

HILDE: Most likely they are.

SOLNESS [*leaning on the table*]: In the sagas –. Have you read any of the old sagas?

HILDE: Oh yes! In the days when I used to read books, I –

SOLNESS: In the sagas there are tales of vikings who sailed to foreign lands and plundered and burnt and killed men –

HILDE: And carried off women –

SOLNESS: – and kept them captive –

HILDE: – took them home with them in their ships –

SOLNESS: – and treated them like – like the worst of trolls.

HILDE [*looking straight before her with half-veiled eyes*]: I think *that* must have been exciting.

SOLNESS [*with a short, deep laugh*]: To carry off women, eh?

HILDE: To *be* carried off.

SOLNESS [*glancing at her*]: Oh, indeed.

HILDE [*as though breaking off the subject*]: But what is it you're driving at with these vikings, Master Builder?

SOLNESS: Why, because those fellows, – *they* had your robust conscience all right! When they got home again they could eat and drink. And they were as happy as children, too. And as for the women! Often they didn't want to leave them at all. Can you understand that, Hilde?

HILDE: I can understand those women perfectly well.

SOLNESS: Aha! Perhaps you could do the same yourself?

HILDE: Why not?

SOLNESS: To live – of your own accord – with a scoundrel like that?

HILDE: If the scoundrel was one I'd got really fond of –

SOLNESS: *Could* you get fond of anyone like that?

HILDE: Good lord, one can't choose whom one gets fond of, you know.

SOLNESS [*looking thoughtfully at her*]: Ah no. It's the troll in one, I expect, that sees to that.

HILDE [*with a half laugh*]: And all these precious devils that you know so well. Both the fair-haired and the dark-haired.

SOLNESS [*warmly and quietly*]: Then I'll hope that the devils will choose carefully for you, Hilde.

HILDE: They *have* chosen for me, already. Once for all.

SOLNESS [*looking earnestly at her*]: Hilde, – you're like a wild bird of the woods.

HILDE: Far from it. I don't hide myself away under bushes.

SOLNESS: No, no. There's rather something of the bird of prey in you.

HILDE: Rather that – perhaps. [*With great energy.*] And why not a bird of prey! Why shouldn't I go hunting, too? Take the prey I have a mind to? If I can only get my claws into it. Do as I like with it.

SOLNESS: Hilde, – do you know what you are?

HILDE: Yes, I'm some strange kind of bird.

SOLNESS: No. You're like dawning day. When I look at you, – it's like looking towards the sunrise.

HILDE: Tell me, Master Builder, – are you sure that you didn't ever call me? Perhaps subconsciously?

SOLNESS [*softly and slowly*]: I almost think I must have.

HILDE: What do you want me *for*?

SOLNESS: You're the younger generation, Hilde.

HILDE [*smiling*]: That younger generation you're so frightened of?

SOLNESS [*nodding slowly*]: And that in my heart I yearn for so sorely.

[HILDE *gets up, goes across to the little table, and takes up Ragnar Brovik's folder.*]

HILDE [*holding out the folder to him*]: Well, now, there were these drawings –

SOLNESS [*shortly, waving it aside*]: Put those things away! I've seen quite enough of them.

HILDE: Yes, but you're to endorse them for him.

SOLNESS: Endorse them! Never in the world!

HILDE: But now, when the poor old man's at the point of death! Can't you give him and his son a little joy before they're parted? And then perhaps he might get the commission for them.

SOLNESS: Yes, that's exactly what he would do. He's made sure of that all right – this clever young man.

HILDE: But, good lord, if he has, can't you tell a white lie, then?

SOLNESS: A lie? [*Furious.*] Hilde, – get away with you and those damn drawings!

HILDE [*withdrawing the folder a little*]: There, there, there, – don't bite me. You talk about trolls. I think you're behaving like a troll yourself. [*Looking about her.*] Where do you keep your pen and ink?

SOLNESS: Don't keep that sort of thing here.

HILDE [*going towards the door*]: But in the office where that girl is –

SOLNESS: Stay where you are, Hilde! I was to tell a lie, you said. Oh, well, I might as well do it for his old father's sake. For I broke him once upon a time. Trod him down.

HILDE: Him too?

SOLNESS: I had to have room for myself. But this Ragnar – he mustn't on any account be allowed to get on his feet.

HILDE: Poor fellow, I don't suppose he will either. If he isn't worth anything, well –

SOLNESS [*coming closer, looking at her and whispering*]: If Ragnar Brovik gets on to his feet, he'll strike me to the ground. Break me – just as I did his father.

HILDE: Break *you*! Is he equal to that?

SOLNESS: Yes, you can depend on it, he *is* equal to it! He's the younger generation, standing ready to knock at my door. And make a final riddance of Solness, the master builder.

HILDE [*looking quietly and reproachfully at him*]: And yet you want to shut him out. For shame, Master Builder!

SOLNESS: It's cost enough in heart's blood, the fight I've fought. And then, I'm afraid the servers and ministers won't obey me any more.

HILDE: Then you'll have to get along by yourself. There's nothing else for it.

SOLNESS: Hopeless, Hilde. The luck will change. A little sooner or a little later. Because retribution is inexorable.

HILDE [*stopping her ears in distress*]: Don't talk like that! Do you want to kill me? Take from me what's more to me than life?

SOLNESS: And what's that?

HILDE: To see you great. See you with a wreath in your hand. High, high up on a church tower. [*Calm again.*] Well, get out your pencil. For I suppose you've got a pencil on you?

SOLNESS [*taking out his pocket-book*]: I've got one here.

HILDE [*putting the folder on the sofa table*]: Good. And now we'll sit down here, both of us, Mr Master-Builder. [SOLNESS *sits down at the table.* HILDE, *behind him, leans over the back of his chair.*] And now we'll write on the drawings. We'll write something really nice and encouraging. For this tiresome Roar – or whatever he's called.

SOLNESS [*writing a few lines, then turning his head and looking up at her*]: Tell me one thing, Hilde.

HILDE: Yes?

SOLNESS: If you've been waiting for me all these ten years –

HILDE: What about it?

SOLNESS: Why didn't you write to me? Then I could have answered you.

HILDE [*quickly*]: No, no, no! That's just what I didn't want.

SOLNESS: Why not?

HILDE: I was afraid it would all be spoilt for me then. But we were going to write on the drawings, Mr Master-Builder.

SOLNESS: So we were.

HILDE [*leaning over him and watching as he writes*]: Very kindly and warmly. Oh, how I hate – how I hate this Roald –

SOLNESS [*writing*]: Haven't you ever really cared for anyone, Hilde?

HILDE [*harshly*]: What do you say?

SOLNESS: Haven't you ever cared for anyone?

HILDE: For anyone else, I suppose you mean?

SOLNESS [*looking up at her*]: For anyone else, yes. Haven't you ever? In these ten years? Never?

HILDE: Well, yes, now and again. When I was really furious with you because you didn't come.

SOLNESS: Then you did take an interest in other people?

HILDE: Just a little. For a week or so. Good lord, Master Builder, surely you know what that sort of thing's like.

SOLNESS: Hilde, – what is it you've come for?

HILDE: Don't waste time talking. That poor old man might go and die in the meantime.

SOLNESS: Answer me, Hilde. What is it you want from me?

HILDE: I want my kingdom.

SOLNESS: Hm – [*He gives a quick glance towards the door on the left and then goes on writing on the drawings.* MRS SOLNESS *comes in at the same moment. She has some parcels with her.*]

MRS SOLNESS: I've brought a few things for you with me, Miss Wangel. The large parcels will be sent out later.

HILDE: Oh, how awfully kind of you!

MRS SOLNESS: Only my plain duty. Nothing else at all.

SOLNESS [*reading through what he has written*]: Aline!

MRS SOLNESS: Yes?

SOLNESS: Did you notice whether she – whether the book-keeper was out there?

MRS SOLNESS: Yes of course *she* was there.

SOLNESS [*putting the drawings into the folder*]: Hm –

MRS SOLNESS: She was standing at the desk, as she always is – when *I* go through the room.

SOLNESS [*getting up*]: I'll give this to her, then. And tell her that –

HILDE [*taking the folder from him*]: Oh no, let me have that pleasure! [*Going towards the door and then turning.*] What's her name?

SOLNESS: Her name's Miss Fosli.

HILDE: Nonsense, that sounds so chilly! Her Christian name, I mean?

SOLNESS: Kaja – I believe.

HILDE [*opening the door and calling out*]: Kaja! Come in here! Hurry up! Mr Solness wants to speak to you.

[KAJA FOSLI *comes into the doorway.*]

KAJA [*looking at him nervously*]: Here I am –?

HILDE [*holding out the folder to her*]: Look here, Kaja! You can take this home. Mr Solness has endorsed it now.

KAJA: Oh, at last!

SOLNESS: Give it to the old man as soon as you can.

KAJA: I'll go straight home with it.

SOLNESS: Yes, do. Then Ragnar may be able to build for himself.

KAJA: Oh, may he come and thank you for everything –?

SOLNESS [*in a hard voice*]: I don't want any thanks! Tell him that from me.

KAJA: Yes, I will –

SOLNESS: And tell him at the same time that I don't need him in future. Nor you either.

KAJA [*in a low and tremulous voice*]: Nor me either?

SOLNESS: You'll have other things to think about now. And to attend to. And that's just as it should be. Well, go along home with the drawings, Miss Fosli. At once! Do you hear!

KAJA [*as before*]: Yes, Mr Solness. [*She goes out.*]

MRS SOLNESS: Heavens, what deceitful eyes she has!

SOLNESS: She! That poor little creature.

MRS SOLNESS: Oh, I see all right what I see, Halvard. – Are you really dismissing them?

SOLNESS: Yes.

MRS SOLNESS: Her as well?

SOLNESS: Wasn't that what you wanted?

MRS SOLNESS: But how can you do without *her* –? Oh well, no doubt you've got someone else in mind, Halvard.

HILDE [*merrily*]: Well, *I'm* no good at any rate at standing by a writing-desk.

SOLNESS: Well, well, well – it'll all settle itself, Aline. Now all you've got to think about is moving into the new home – as soon as you can. We'll put the wreath up this evening – [*Turning to* HILDE.] – high up on the spire of the tower. What do you say to that, Miss Hilde?

HILDE [*gazing at him with dancing eyes*]: It'll be absolutely glorious to see you so high up again.

SOLNESS: Me!

MRS SOLNESS: Good heavens, Miss Wangel, don't imagine such a thing! My husband –! When he always gets so giddy!

HILDE: Giddy! No, that he certainly doesn't!

MRS SOLNESS: Oh but he does, indeed.

HILDE: But I've seen him myself right on the top of a high church tower!

MRS SOLNESS: Yes, I hear people talk about that. But it's utterly impossible –

SOLNESS [*emphatically*]: Impossible, – yes, impossible! But I did stand there all the same!

MRS SOLNESS: Oh, how can you say that, Halvard? Why you can't even bear to go out on the balcony, up here on the second floor. You've always been like that.

SOLNESS: You may perhaps see something different this evening.

MRS SOLNESS [*in dread*]: No, no, no! Please God I shan't ever see that! I'll write to the doctor at once. And I'm sure he'll stop you doing it.

SOLNESS: But Aline –!

MRS SOLNESS: Yes, because you must be ill, Halvard! This can't be anything else! Oh heavens, – oh heavens!

[*She goes quickly out to the right.*]

HILDE [*looking intently at him*]: *Is* it true or isn't it?

SOLNESS: That I can't stand heights?

HILDE: That my master builder *daren't*, – *can't* climb as high as he builds?

SOLNESS: Is that how you look at the thing?

HILDE: Yes.

SOLNESS: I don't believe a corner in me can be safe from you.

HILDE [*looking towards the bay window*]: Up there, then. Right up there –

SOLNESS [*coming nearer*]: You could have the top room of the tower, Hilde. You could live like a princess there.

HILDE [*uncertainly, between jest and earnest*]: Yes, that's what you promised me.

SOLNESS: *Did* I, really?

HILDE: For shame, Mr Master-Builder! You said I was to be a princess. And that I should have a kingdom from you. And then you went and – Well, really!

SOLNESS [*cautiously*]: Are you quite certain that this isn't some kind of dream, – a fancy that's got into your head?

HILDE [*caustically*]: So I suppose you *didn't* do it?

SOLNESS: Don't know, myself. [*In a lower voice.*] But this I do know now, for certain, that I –

HILDE: That you –? Say it at once!

SOLNESS: That I *ought* to have done it.

HILDE [*in a vivid outburst*]: *You've* never felt giddy in your life!

SOLNESS: This evening, then, we'll hang up the wreath – Princess Hilde.

HILDE [*with a shade of bitterness*]: Over your new home, yes.

SOLNESS: Over the new house. That will never be a home for me. [*He goes out through the garden door.*]

HILDE [*looking straight in front of her with a veiled expression and whispering to herself. The only words heard are:*] – terribly exciting –

ACT THREE

A long, broad veranda belonging to Solness's dwelling-house. A part of the house with a door leading out to the veranda is seen on the left and on the right of the veranda is a railing. At the back a flight of steps leads down from the narrow end of the veranda to the garden, which lies lower. Great, old trees in the garden stretch their branches over the veranda and towards the house. On the far right, in among the trees, there can just be seen the lowest part of the new house with scaffolding round the part that has the tower. In the background the garden is bounded by an old wooden fence. Outside the fence is a street with low, dilapidated little houses. The clouds in the evening sky are lit up by the sun.

On the veranda a garden bench stands against the wall of the house and in front of the bench a long table. On the other side of the table are an arm-chair and some stools. All the furniture is of wicker-work.

MRS SOLNESS, wrapped up in a large, white crape shawl, sits resting in the arm-chair and gazing out to the right. After a moment HILDE WANGEL comes up from the garden by the steps. She is dressed as before and has her hat on. In the front of her dress she is wearing a little bunch of small common flowers.

MRS SOLNESS [turning her head a little]: Have you been walking round the garden, Miss Wangel?

HILDE: Yes, I've been looking round down there.

MRS SOLNESS: And found some flowers too, I see.

HILDE: Rather! There are heaps of them. In among the bushes.

MRS SOLNESS: Oh, are there? Still? Well, of course, I hardly ever go there.

HILDE [approaching]: What! Don't you run down into the garden every day, then?

MRS SOLNESS [*with a faint smile*]: I don't 'run' anywhere now. Not any longer.

HILDE: Well, but don't you go down every now and then and have a look at all the lovely things there?

MRS SOLNESS: It's grown so strange to me, all of it. I'm almost afraid to see it again.

HILDE: Your own garden!

MRS SOLNESS: I don't feel it's *mine* any longer.

HILDE: What do you mean –?

MRS SOLNESS: No, no, it *isn't*. It's not like it was in Mother's and Father's time. They've taken such a dreadful lot of the garden away, Miss Wangel. Just think – they've cut it up in lots and built houses for strangers. People I don't know. And *they* can sit and look in at me from their windows.

HILDE [*with a radiant expression*]: Mrs Solness?

MRS SOLNESS: Yes?

HILDE: May I stay here with you for a little?

MRS SOLNESS: Yes, of course, if you like.

[HILDE *moves a stool across to the arm-chair and sits down.*]

HILDE: Ah, – here one can sit and sun oneself like a cat.

MRS SOLNESS [*laying her hand gently on* HILDE'S *neck*]: It's nice of you to want to sit with *me*. I thought you'd go in to my husband.

HILDE: What would I do with him?

MRS SOLNESS: Help him, I thought.

HILDE: No thanks. Besides, he isn't in. He's down there with the workmen. But he looked so fierce that I didn't dare speak to him.

MRS SOLNESS: Oh, he's really so gentle and tender-hearted.

HILDE: *He?*

MRS SOLNESS: You don't know him properly yet, Miss Wangel.

HILDE [*looking affectionately at her*]: Are you glad you're going to move over into the new place?

MRS SOLNESS: I *ought* to be glad, of course. Because it's what Halvard wants –

HILDE: Oh surely not just because of that.

MRS SOLNESS: Yes, indeed, Miss Wangel. Because that's only my duty, to submit to him. But it very often comes so hard, to force one's mind to obedience.

HILDE: Yes, that must come very hard.

MRS SOLNESS: You may be sure it does. When one has so many weaknesses as I have –

HILDE: When one's gone through so much trouble as you have –

MRS SOLNESS: How do you know that?

HILDE: Your husband told me.

MRS SOLNESS: He so seldom talks about those things with me. Yes, I can tell you I've been through more than enough in my life, Miss Wangel.

HILDE [*looking at her sympathetically and nodding slowly*]: Poor Mrs Solness. First you had that fire –

MRS SOLNESS [*with a sigh*]: Yes. Everything of *mine* was burnt.

HILDE: And then came what was worse.

MRS SOLNESS [*looking at her questioningly*]: Worse?

HILDE: The worst of all.

MRS SOLNESS: What do you mean?

HILDE [*softly*]: You lost the two little boys.

MRS SOLNESS: Ah, yes. Them. Well, you see *that* was a different kind of thing. That was the will of the Lord. And one must submit to a thing like that. And give thanks, too.

HILDE: Do you?

MRS SOLNESS: Not always, I'm afraid. I know quite well that it's my duty. But I *can't* do it, all the same.

HILDE: No, no, that's only natural, I think.

MRS SOLNESS: And time and again I have to say to myself, that it was a just punishment for me –

HILDE: Why?

MRS SOLNESS: Because I wasn't steadfast enough in misfortune.

HILDE: But I don't see that –

MRS SOLNESS: Oh no, no, Miss Wangel. Don't talk to me any more about the two little boys. We must only be glad for them. For everything's well with them – all's well, now. No, it's the small losses in life that cut one to the heart. To lose all the things that other people think next to nothing of.

HILDE [*laying her arms on* MRS SOLNESS'S *knee and looking affectionately up at her*]: Dear Mrs Solness – tell me what kind of things?

MRS SOLNESS: As I say. Only little things. All the old portraits on the walls were burnt. And so were all the old silk dresses. They'd been in the family for generations. And all Mother's and Grandmother's lace – that was burnt too. And just think – their jewels, too. [*Heavily*.] And then all the dolls.

HILDE: The dolls?

MRS SOLNESS [*choking with sobs*]: I had nine beautiful dolls.

HILDE: And they were burnt too?

MRS SOLNESS: All of them. Oh it was so hard – so hard for me.

HILDE: Why, had you kept all those dolls put away? Ever since you were little?

MRS SOLNESS: Not put away. The dolls and I had gone on living together all the time.

HILDE: After you were grown-up?

MRS SOLNESS: Yes, long after that.

HILDE: After you were married, too?

MRS SOLNESS: Oh yes. So long as he didn't see it –. But they were all burnt up, poor dears. There was no one who thought of saving *them*. Oh, it's so miserable, to think about. But you mustn't laugh at me, Miss Wangel.

HILDE: I'm not laughing a bit.

MRS SOLNESS: For you know, in a way, there was life in them too. I carried them under my heart. Like small, unborn children.

[DR HERDAL, *with his hat in his hand, comes out through the door and gives a look at* MRS SOLNESS *and* HILDE.]

DR HERDAL: So you're sitting outside, and catching cold, eh, Mrs Solness?

MRS SOLNESS: I think it's nice and warm here today.

DR HERDAL: Oh, well. But is there anything happening here? I got a note from you.

MRS SOLNESS [*getting up*]: Yes, there's something I must talk to you about.

DR HERDAL: All right. Then suppose we go in. [*To* HILDE.] In mountain clothes today too, Miss Wangel?

HILDE [*gaily, getting up*]: *Rather!* In full kit. But I'm not climbing today, to break my neck. We two are going to stay quietly down below and look on, Doctor.

DR HERDAL: What are we to look on at?

MRS SOLNESS [*low and frightened, to* HILDE]: Hush, hush, for heaven's sake! He's coming. Try and make him give up that idea. And do let's be friends, Miss Wangel. Can't we?

HILDE [*throwing her arms impetuously round her neck*]: Oh, if only we could!

MRS SOLNESS [*freeing herself gently*]: There, there, there. There he comes, Doctor. Let me have a word with you.

DR HERDAL: Is it about *him*?

MRS SOLNESS: Yes indeed it is. Come inside.

[*She and the* DOCTOR *go into the house. A moment later* SOLNESS *comes up the steps from the garden. A serious look comes over* HILDE'S *face.*]

SOLNESS [*glancing towards the door of the house, which is closed cautiously from inside*]: Have you noticed, Hilde, that as soon as I come she goes away?

HILDE: I've noticed that as soon as you come you *make* her go away.

SOLNESS: Perhaps I do. But I can't help it. [*Observing her closely.*] Are you cold, Hilde? I think you look cold.

HILDE: I've just come up from a vault.

SOLNESS: What does *that* mean?

HILDE: That I've got a chill in my bones, Mr Solness.

SOLNESS [*slowly*]: I think I understand –

HILDE: What have you come up here for now?

SOLNESS: I caught sight of you from over there.

HILDE: But then you must have seen her too, didn't you?

SOLNESS: I knew she'd go at once if I came.

HILDE: Does it make you very unhappy, that she gets out of your way like this?

SOLNESS: In a way it seems like a relief.

HILDE: That you haven't got her under your eyes?

SOLNESS: Yes.

HILDE: That you don't constantly see how hard she takes all this, about the little boys?

SOLNESS: Yes. Mostly that.

> [HILDE *strolls across the veranda with her hands behind her back, stands still by the railing, and looks out over the garden.*]

SOLNESS [*after a short pause*]: Did you talk to her long?

HILDE [*stands motionless and doesn't answer*].

SOLNESS: Long, I'm asking?

HILDE [*silent, as before*].

SOLNESS: What did she talk about, Hilde?

HILDE [*still silent*].

SOLNESS: Poor Aline! I suppose it was about the little boys.

HILDE [*a nervous shudder runs through her; then she nods quickly once or twice*].

SOLNESS: She'll never get over it. Never get over it, all her life. [*Coming nearer.*] Now you're standing there like a statue again. Just like you stood last night.

HILDE [*turning and looking at him with large, serious eyes*]: I'm going away.

SOLNESS [*sharply*]: Going away!

HILDE: Yes.

SOLNESS: Oh no, I shan't let you do that!

HILDE: What am I to do *here* now?

SOLNESS: Just *be* here, Hilde!

HILDE [*looking him up and down*]: No thank you. It wouldn't stop at that.

SOLNESS [*impetuously*]: So much the better!

HILDE [*angrily*]: I *can't* do any harm to a person I *know*! Not take away something that belongs to her.

SOLNESS: Who's asking you to?

HILDE [*continuing*]: A stranger, yes! Because that's something quite different! Someone I'd never set eyes on. But someone I've come close to –! Oh, no! No! Oh!

SOLNESS: Yes, but I haven't suggested that.

HILDE: Oh, Mr Solness, you know quite well what would happen. So I'm going away.

SOLNESS: And what's to become of *me*, when you're gone? What shall I have to live for then? After that?

HILDE [*with the unfathomable expression in her eyes*]: There's no problem for *you*. You have your duties to her. Live for those duties.

SOLNESS: Too late. These powers – these – these –

HILDE: – devils –

SOLNESS: Yes, devils! And the troll in me too. They've sucked all the life-blood out of her. [*With a laugh of despair.*] They did it to make me happy! Yes, indeed! [*Heavily.*] And now she's dead – for my sake. And I'm living, chained to the dead. [*In desperate misery.*] I – I who can't live without joy.

> [HILDE *goes round the table and sits on the bench with her elbows on the table and her head propped in her hands.*]

HILDE [*sitting and looking at him for a moment*]: What are you going to build next?

SOLNESS [*shaking his head*]: I don't think there'll be much more now.

HILDE: None of those cosy, happy homes, then, for the mother and father? And for lots of children?

SOLNESS: Heaven knows whether people will want that kind of thing in the future.

HILDE: Poor Master Builder! You, who have gone on all these ten years – giving your life up – only for that.

SOLNESS: You may well say so, Hilde.

HILDE [*breaking out*]: Oh, I think it's absolutely stupid, so stupid – all of it!

SOLNESS: All of what?

HILDE: That one daren't reach out for one's own happiness. For one's own life! Just because there's someone standing in the way that one knows!

SOLNESS: Someone that one has no right to put aside.

HILDE: I wonder whether one *hasn't* the right to, really? But all the same –. Oh if one could only go to sleep and get away from the whole business! [*She lays her arms flat down on the table, rests the left side of her head on her hands, and shuts her eyes.*]

SOLNESS [*turning round the arm-chair and sitting down beside the table*]: Did *you* have a cosy, happy home – up there with your father, Hilde?

HILDE [*motionless and answering as if half-asleep*]: I only had a cage.

SOLNESS: And you don't mean to go back into it?

HILDE [*as before*]: The wild bird from the forest never wants to go into the cage.

SOLNESS: Rather range through the free air –

HILDE [*still as before*]: The bird of prey likes ranging best –

SOLNESS [*letting his gaze rest on her*]: If one could only face life like the vikings –

HILDE [*in her normal voice, opening her eyes, but not moving*]: And the rest? Say what *that* was!

SOLNESS: A robust conscience.

[HILDE *sits up on the bench, full of life. Her eyes have again their happy, dancing expression.*]

HILDE [*nodding to him*]: I know what you're going to build next!

SOLNESS: Then you know more than I do, Hilde.

HILDE: Yes, master builders are so stupid, you see.

SOLNESS: And what's it to be, then?

HILDE [*nodding again*]: The castle.

SOLNESS: What castle?

HILDE: *My* castle, of course.

SOLNESS: Do you want a castle now?

HILDE: Don't you owe me a kingdom, may I ask?

SOLNESS: Yes, so you say.

HILDE: Very well. You owe me this kingdom, then. And with a kingdom there goes a castle, I should think.

SOLNESS [*becoming more and more alive*]: Why yes, that's usually so.

HILDE: Good. Then build it for me! At once!

SOLNESS [*laughing*]: At once, this very minute?

HILDE: Yes, of course! For they're up now – the ten years. And I won't go on waiting any longer. So – hand out the castle, Mr Master-Builder!

SOLNESS: It's no light matter to owe you anything, Hilde.

HILDE: You should have thought of that before. Now it's too late. And so – [*Rapping on the table.*] – the castle on the table! It's *my* castle! I want it at *once*!

SOLNESS [*more seriously, leaning nearer, with his arms on the table*]: What did you imagine the castle would be like, Hilde?

[*Her glance veils itself little by little. She gazes as it were into herself.*]

HILDE [*slowly*]: My castle shall stand high up. Very high, it shall stand. And free on every side. So that I can see far, far out.

SOLNESS: And I suppose there's to be a high tower on it?

HILDE: A terribly high tower. And at the very top of the tower there shall be a balcony. And I will stand out on that –

SOLNESS [*clutching his forehead involuntarily*]: How you can like standing at such a giddy height –!

HILDE: Oh, I shall! I'll stand right up there and look down at the others – people who build churches. And homes for the mother and father and lots of children. And you can come up and look at it too.

SOLNESS [*in a low voice*]: Is the master builder to be allowed to come up to the princess?

HILDE: If the master builder wants to.

SOLNESS [*more softly*]: Then I think the master builder will come.

HILDE [*nodding*]: The master builder – he'll come.

SOLNESS: But he'll never build any more, – poor master builder.

HILDE [*full of life*]: Of course he will! We two will do it together. And then we'll build the most beautiful – quite the most beautiful thing to be found in all the world.

SOLNESS [*excited*]: Hilde, – tell me what that is!

HILDE [*looking at him with a smile, shaking her head a little, pursing her lips, and speaking as if to a child*]: Master builders, they're very – very stupid people.

SOLNESS: Oh yes, they're stupid enough. But tell me, now, what it is! This thing that's the most beautiful in the world. And that we two are to build together?

HILDE [*silent for a moment and then speaking with an unfathomable expression in her eyes*]: Castles in the air.

SOLNESS: Castles in the air?

HILDE [*nodding*]: Yes, castles in the air! Do you know what a castle in the air's like?

SOLNESS: It's the most beautiful thing in the world, you say.

HILDE [*getting up impetuously and pushing aside the idea with a gesture*]: Yes, of course! Yes. Castles in the air, they're so easy to hide in. And easy to build, too. [*Looking scornfully at him.*] Especially for master builders that have a – a conscience that can't stand heights.

SOLNESS[*getting up*]: After today we two will build together, Hilde.

HILDE [*with a half-doubtful smile*]: A genuine castle in the air?

SOLNESS: Yes. One with a foundation under it.

[RAGNAR BROVIK *comes out from the house. He carries a large green wreath with flowers and silk ribbons.*]

HILDE [*with an exclamation of joy*]: The wreath! Oh that'll be absolutely glorious!

SOLNESS [*surprised*]: Have *you* come with the wreath, Ragnar?

RAGNAR: I promised the foreman I would.

SOLNESS [*relieved*]: Oh, then I suppose your father's better?

RAGNAR: No.

SOLNESS: Didn't it make him feel better – what I wrote?

RAGNAR: It came too late.

SOLNESS: Too late!

RAGNAR: When she got back with it he was unconscious. He'd had a stroke.

SOLNESS: But go home to him then! Look after your father!

RAGNAR: He doesn't need me any more.

SOLNESS: But surely you ought to be with him.

RAGNAR: *She's* sitting at his bedside.

SOLNESS [*a little uncertain*]: Kaja?

RAGNAR [*looking darkly at him*]: Yes, – Kaja. Yes.

SOLNESS: Go home, Ragnar. Both to him and to her. Let *me* have the wreath.

RAGNAR [*concealing an amused smile*]: You're never going to – yourself –?

SOLNESS: I'll go down with it myself. [*Taking the wreath from him.*] And now, you go home. We don't need you today.

RAGNAR: I know you don't need me in future. But I'll stay today.

SOLNESS: Oh well, stay then, if you really want to.

HILDE [*by the railing*]: Mr Solness, – I'll stand here and watch you.

SOLNESS: Watch me!

HILDE: It's going to be terribly exciting.

SOLNESS [*in a low voice*]: You and I'll talk about that presently, Hilde.

[*He goes down the steps with the wreath and out across the garden.*]

HILDE [*looks after him and then turns round to* RAGNAR]: You might just as well have thanked him, I think.

RAGNAR: Thanked him? I ought to have thanked *him*?

HILDE: Yes, you certainly should!

RAGNAR: I think it's rather *you* I ought to thank.

HILDE: How can you say such a thing?

RAGNAR [*without answering her*]: But you just be careful, Miss Wangel! For you don't know him properly yet.

HILDE [*with spirit*]: Oh, I'm the one who knows him best!

RAGNAR [*laughing bitterly*]: Thank him, who has kept me down year after year! He, who's made my father doubt me. Made me doubt myself –. And all that just so that–!

HILDE [*as though guessing something*]: So that –? Tell me at once!

RAGNAR: So that he should be able to keep her with him.

HILDE [*with a sudden movement towards him*]: The girl at the desk!

RAGNAR: Yes.

HILDE [*threatening, with clenched hands*]: That's not true! You're lying about him!

RAGNAR: *I* wouldn't have believed it either till today – when she said so herself.

HILDE [*as if beside herself*]: *What* did she say? I will know it! At once! At once!

RAGNAR: She said he'd taken hold of her mind – utterly and completely. Taken possession of all her thoughts, for himself alone. She says she can never let him go. That she'll stay here, where *he* is –

HILDE [*with flashing eyes*]: She won't be allowed to!

RAGNAR [*as though feeling his way*]: Who won't allow her?

HILDE [*quickly*]: *He* won't allow her either!

RAGNAR: Oh no, – I understand the whole thing now. In future she would only be – in the way.

HILDE: You don't understand anything – if you can say a thing like that! No, *I'll* tell you why he wanted her.

RAGNAR: Why did he?

HILDE: In order to keep *you*.

RAGNAR: Has he told you that?

HILDE: No, but it *is* that! It *must* be that! [*Wildly.*] I will – I *will* have it be that!

RAGNAR: And as soon as *you* came – then he let her go.

HILDE: *You – you* were the one he let go! What do you think he cares about strange women like that?

RAGNAR [*reflecting*]: Can it have been that – all this time – he was afraid of me?

HILDE: *He* afraid! I don't think you need be as conceited as that.

RAGNAR: Well, he must have seen long ago that I was worth something too. Besides – *afraid* – that's just what he is, you see.

HILDE: *He*! You won't make me believe *that*!

RAGNAR: In his own way, he *is* afraid. He, the great master builder. Taking their life's happiness from other people – just as he's done to my father and to me – he's not afraid of *that*. But a simple thing like climbing up a wretched scaffold – he takes jolly good care not to risk *that*!

HILDE: Ah, you should just have seen him high up – at such a giddy height as I saw him once!

RAGNAR: Did you see that?

HILDE: Yes, I certainly did. So free and proud as he stood and fastened the wreath to the weather-vane of the church!

RAGNAR: I know he risked it *once* in his life. One single time. We younger men have often talked about it. But no power on earth will make him do it again.

HILDE: He'll do it again today!

RAGNAR [*scornfully*]: Yes, you may well believe it!

HILDE: We're going to see it!

RAGNAR: Neither you nor I are going to see that.

HILDE [*violent and uncontrolled*]: I *will* see it! I *will* and I *must* see it!

RAGNAR: But he won't do it. Simply daren't do it. For he's always got this weak spot – the great master builder.

[MRS SOLNESS *comes out from the house on to the veranda.*]

MRS SOLNESS [*looking round her*]: Isn't he here? Where's he gone?

RAGNAR: Mr Solness is down there with the workmen.

HILDE: He went with the wreath.

MRS SOLNESS [*in terror*]: He went with the wreath! Oh heavens! Heavens! Mr Brovik, – you must go down to him! Try to bring him up here.

RAGNAR: Shall I say you want to speak to him, Mrs Solness?

MRS SOLNESS: Oh yes, please do. No, no, – don't say *I* want him for anything! You can say there's someone here. And he must come at once.

RAGNAR: Good. I'll do that, Mrs Solness. [*He goes down by the steps and out through the garden.*]

MRS SOLNESS: Oh Miss Wangel, you can't imagine how anxious I feel about him.

HILDE: But is this anything to be so much afraid about?

MRS SOLNESS: Oh yes, surely you realize that. Suppose he does it, in earnest! Suppose he gets the idea of climbing up the scaffolding!

HILDE [*excited*]: Do you think he will?

MRS SOLNESS: Oh, one never knows what he may take into his head. He might do absolutely anything.

HILDE: Ah, so you think too that he's – well –?

MRS SOLNESS: Oh, I don't know what to think of him any longer. The doctor's told me so many things now. And when I put it all together with one thing and another that I've heard him say –

[DR HERDAL *looks out through the door*.]

DR HERDAL: Isn't he coming soon?

MRS SOLNESS: Yes, I think so. At any rate, a message is gone to him.

DR HERDAL [*nearer*]: But you'll have to go in, I think, Mrs Solness –

MRS SOLNESS: Oh no, no! I want to stay outside and wait for Halvard.

DR HERDAL: Yes, but some ladies have come to see you –

MRS SOLNESS: Oh heavens, that *too*! And just at this moment!

DR HERDAL: They say they really must see the ceremony.

MRS SOLNESS: Very well. Then I must go in to them I suppose. Of course it's my duty.

HILDE: Can't you ask the ladies to go away?

MRS SOLNESS: No, that wouldn't do. Since they've come here, it's my duty to see them. But you stay out here for the present – and be here when he comes.

DR HERDAL: And try to keep him talking as long as possible –

MRS SOLNESS: Yes, do, dear Miss Wangel. Keep as firm a hold on him as ever you can.

HILDE: Wouldn't it be best for you to do that yourself?

MRS SOLNESS: Why, yes, heaven knows, it's *my* duty of course. But when one has duties in so many directions –

DR HERDAL [*looking towards the garden*]: He's coming now!

MRS SOLNESS: To think – I've got to go in!

DR HERDAL [*to* HILDE]: Don't say anything about my being here.

HILDE: All right! I expect I'll find something else to talk to Mr Solness about.

MRS SOLNESS: And whatever you do, keep hold of him. I think *you* can do that best.

[MRS SOLNESS *and* DR HERDAL *go into the house.* HILDE *remains standing on the veranda.* SOLNESS *comes up the steps from the garden.*]

SOLNESS: I hear there's someone here who wants to see me.

HILDE: Oh yes, it's me, Master Builder.

SOLNESS: Oh, it's you, Hilde. I was afraid it would be Aline and the doctor.

HILDE: You're very easily frightened, aren't you?

SOLNESS: You think so?

HILDE: Yes, people say you're afraid of scrambling about – up on scaffolds and things.

SOLNESS: Oh well, that's quite a different thing.

HILDE: But you're afraid of it – you are, aren't you?

SOLNESS: Yes, I am.

HILDE: Afraid you'll fall down and kill yourself?

SOLNESS: No, not that.

HILDE: What, then?

SOLNESS: I'm afraid of retribution, Hilde.

HILDE: Of retribution? [*Shaking her head.*] I can't see that.

SOLNESS: Sit down. And I'll tell you something.

HILDE: Yes, do! At once! [*She sits on a stool by the railing and looks expectantly at him.*]

SOLNESS [*throwing his hat on the table*]: You know, of course, what I first began on was building churches.

HILDE [*nodding*]: I know that all right.

SOLNESS: For you see, I came as a boy from a pious home out in the country. And so of course I thought that this building churches was the finest thing I could choose.

HILDE: Yes, yes.

SOLNESS: And this I can say, that I built those poor little churches with such an honest, warm, sincere devotion that – that –

HILDE: That –? Well?

SOLNESS: Well, that I think he ought to have been pleased with me.

HILDE: *He*? What 'he'?

SOLNESS: He who was to have the churches, of course. He, whom they were to serve with honour and glory.

HILDE: Well, well! But are you sure that – that he wasn't – pleased with you?

SOLNESS [*scornfully*]: *He* pleased with *me*! How can you talk like that, Hilde? He, who gave the troll in me leave to domineer, just as it liked. He who told them to be on hand night and day to serve me – all these – these –

HILDE: Devils –

SOLNESS: Yes, of one kind and another. Oh no, I was made to realize that he wasn't pleased with me. [*Mysteriously.*] You see, that was really why he let the old house burn down.

HILDE: Was that why?

SOLNESS: Yes, don't you see it? He wanted me to have the chance of becoming a real master in my domain – and of building churches to his still greater glory. In the beginning I didn't understand what he was getting at. But all of a sudden it dawned on me.

HILDE: When was that?

SOLNESS: It was when I was building the church tower up in Lysanger.

HILDE: I thought so.

SOLNESS: For you see, Hilde, up there, in that new place, I used to go about musing and turning things over in my mind. Then I saw clearly why he had taken my children from me. It was so that I shouldn't have anything else to attach myself to. Nothing like love or happiness, you understand. I was only to be a master builder. Nothing more. And so all through my life I was to go on building for him. [*Laughing.*] But nothing much came of *that*!

HILDE: What did you do, then?

SOLNESS: First I looked into and tested myself –

HILDE: And then?

SOLNESS: Then I did the *impossible*. *I*, just like *him*.

HILDE: The impossible!

SOLNESS: I'd never before been able to climb up, free and high in the air. But that day I could.

HILDE [*jumping up*]: Yes, yes, you could!

SOLNESS: And when I stood right up on the top there and hung the wreath over the weather-vane, then I said to him: Hear me, now, Thou Almighty! In future I too will be a free master builder. In my own sphere. As Thou in Thine. I will never build churches for Thee again. Only homes for human beings.

HILDE [*with wide, dancing eyes*]: *That* was the song I heard in the air!

SOLNESS: But he found grist for his mill, in the long run.

HILDE: What do you mean by *that*?

SOLNESS [*looking despondently at her*]: This building homes for human beings – it's not worth talking of, Hilde.

HILDE: Is *that* what you say now?

SOLNESS: Yes, because now I see it. Human beings haven't any use for these homes of theirs. Not for being happy in. And I shouldn't have had any use for a home like that either. If I'd had one. [*With a quiet, embittered laugh.*] So that's what it all amounts to, however far I look back. Nothing really built. And nothing sacrificed to get anything built, either. Nothing, nothing – the whole thing, nothing!

HILDE: And you'll never build anything new again?

SOLNESS [*with vigour*]: Oh, yes, I'm just going to begin!

HILDE: What? What? Tell me at once!

SOLNESS: The only thing I think human beings can be happy in – that's what I'll build now.

HILDE [*looking steadily at him*]: Master Builder, – now you mean our castles in the air.

SOLNESS: The castles in the air, yes.

HILDE: I'm afraid you'd turn giddy before we got half-way up.

SOLNESS: Not if I can go hand in hand with you, Hilde.

HILDE [*with a touch of controlled anger*]: Only with me? Won't there be several of us going?

SOLNESS: Who else do you mean?

HILDE: Oh, – her, – that Kaja at the desk. Poor thing, – aren't you going to take her with you too?

SOLNESS: Ah! It was she Aline was talking to you about.

HILDE: *Is* it true, or isn't it?

SOLNESS [*angrily*]: I'm not going to answer you about a thing like that! You've got to trust me, out and out!

HILDE: For ten years I've trusted you utterly – utterly.

SOLNESS: You must go on trusting me!

HILDE: Then let me see you standing free and high up!

SOLNESS [*heavily*]: Oh, Hilde – I can't do things like that every day.

HILDE [*passionately*]: I want you to! I want you to! [*Imploring.*] Only one more time, Master Builder! Do the *impossible* once more!

SOLNESS [*standing and looking searchingly at her*]: *If* I try it, Hilde, I'll stand up there and speak to him as I did last time.

HILDE [*in rising excitement*]: What will you say to him?

SOLNESS: I'll say to him: Hear me, Almighty Lord, – Thou must judge of me as seems good to Thee. But hereafter I will build only the most beautiful thing in the world –

HILDE [*carried away*]: Yes – yes – yes!

SOLNESS: – build it together with a princess, whom I love –

HILDE: Yes, tell him that! tell him that!

SOLNESS: Yes. And then I'll say to him: Now I'll go down and throw my arms round her and kiss her –

HILDE: – many times! Say that!

SOLNESS: – many, many times, I'll say.

HILDE: And then –?

SOLNESS: Then I'll wave my hat – and come down to earth – and do what I told him.

HILDE [*with outstretched arms*]: Now I see you again as I did when there was a song in the air!

SOLNESS [*looking at her with bowed head*]: How did you come to be what you are, Hilde?

HILDE: How did you make me what I am?

SOLNESS [*shortly and firmly*]: The princess shall have her castle.

HILDE [*clapping her hands with joy*]: Oh, Master Builder –! My beautiful, beautiful castle! Our castle in the air!

SOLNESS: With a foundation under it.

[*In the street a number of* PEOPLE *have gathered, who can be seen indistinctly through the trees. The music of wind instruments is heard from a distance behind the new house.* MRS SOLNESS *with a fur collar round her neck,* DR HERDAL *with her white shawl on his arm, and* SOME LADIES *come out on the veranda.* RAGNAR BROVIK *comes up at the same time from the garden.*]

MRS SOLNESS [*to* RAGNAR]: Is there to be a band, too?

RAGNAR: Yes. It's the Builders' Association. [*To* SOLNESS.] I was to say from the foreman that he's ready now to go up with the wreath.

SOLNESS [*taking his hat*]: Good. I'll go down myself.

MRS SOLNESS [*anxiously*]: What are you going to do down there, Halvard?

SOLNESS [*shortly*]: I must be down below with my people.

MRS SOLNESS: Yes, down below. Only down below.

SOLNESS: I always do. In the ordinary way. [*He goes down the steps and out across the garden*].

MRS SOLNESS [*calling after him over the railing*]: But do tell the man to be careful when he goes up! Promise me, Halvard!

DR HERDAL [*to* MRS SOLNESS]: You see I was right? He isn't thinking of that nonsense any more.

MRS SOLNESS: Oh, what a relief! We've had people fall twice. And both of them killed themselves on the spot. [*Turning to* HILDE.] I'm most grateful to you, Miss Wangel, for having kept hold of him so firmly. *I* should never have been able to manage him.

DR HERDAL [*merrily*]: Yes, yes, Miss Wangel. You know how to keep a hold on anyone when you really want to!

[MRS SOLNESS *and* DR HERDAL *go across to the* LADIES, *who are standing nearer the steps and looking out across the garden.* HILDE *remains standing by the railing in the foreground.* RAGNAR *goes across to her.*]

RAGNAR [*with suppressed laughter, half lowering his voice*]: Miss Wangel, – do you see all the young people down on the street?

HILDE: Yes.

RAGNAR: They're my fellow-students, come to look at the master.

HILDE: What do they want to look at him for?

RAGNAR: They want to see him not daring to climb up on his own house.

HILDE: Oh, so that's what those young men want!

RAGNAR [*angrily and scornfully*]: He's kept us down so long. Now we want to see him too, standing meekly down below.

HILDE: You won't see that. Not this time.

RAGNAR [*smiling*]: Really? Where shall we see him then?

HILDE: High, – high up by the vane, you'll see him!

RAGNAR [*laughing*]: He! You may well believe it!

HILDE: He means to go up to the top. And so you'll see him there.

RAGNAR: Oh, he means to, all right. I can quite believe that. But he simply can't. Everything would be going round him long before he got half-way. He'd have to creep down again on hands and knees.

DR HERDAL [*pointing out*]: Look! There goes the foreman up the ladders.

MRS SOLNESS: And of course he has the wreath to carry as well. Oh, if only he'll be careful!

RAGNAR [*staring incredulously and crying out*]: But that *is* –!

HILDE [*with an outbreak of joy*]: It's the master builder himself!

MRS SOLNESS [*screaming in terror*]: Yes, it's Halvard! Oh, great God –! Halvard! Halvard!

DR HERDAL: Hush! Don't scream at him!

MRS SOLNESS [*half beside herself*]: I'll go to him! Get him down again!

DR HERDAL [*holding her*]: Stand quite still, everybody! Not a sound!

HILDE [*motionless, following* SOLNESS *with her eyes*]: He climbs and climbs. Always higher. Always higher! Look! Just look!

RAGNAR [*breathless*]: Now he *must* turn back. There's nothing else for it.

HILDE: He climbs and climbs. He'll soon be up now.

MRS SOLNESS: Oh, I shall die of fright. I can't bear the sight of it.

DR HERDAL: Don't look up at him, then.

HILDE: There he is, standing on the topmost planks! Right up!

DR HERDAL: No one's to move! Do you hear!

HILDE [*exultant, with quiet intensity*]: At last! At last! Now I see him great and free again!

RAGNAR [*almost speechless*]: But this is –

HILDE: That's how I've seen him all these ten years. How secure he stands! Terribly exciting all the same. Look at him! Now he's hanging the wreath on the vane!

RAGNAR: This is like looking at something quite impossible.

HILDE: Yes, it is the *impossible*, that he's doing now! [*With the unfathomable expression in her eyes.*] Can you see anyone else up there with him?

RAGNAR: There's no one else.

HILDE: Oh yes, there's someone he's fighting with.

RAGNAR: You're quite wrong.

HILDE: Don't you hear the song in the air either?

RAGNAR: That must be the wind in the tree-tops.

HILDE: *I* hear a song. A mighty song! [*Crying out in wild jubilation and joy.*] Look, look! Now he's waving his hat! Greeting us down here! Oh, let's send him up a greeting in return! For now, now it's done! [*Snatches the white shawl from the* DOCTOR, *waves it, and shouts upward.*] Hurrah for the master builder!

DR HERDAL: Stop it! Stop it! For God's sake –!

[*The* LADIES *on the veranda wave their handkerchiefs and the cries of 'hurrah' are echoed down in the street. Then they are suddenly silenced and the* CROWD *breaks instead into a shriek of terror. A human body and some planks and poles can be indistinctly seen plunging down in among the trees.*]

MRS SOLNESS AND THE LADIES [*together*]: He's falling! He's falling!

[MRS SOLNESS *staggers, sinks backwards fainting, and is caught in the arms of the* LADIES, *with cries and confusion. The* CROWD *in the street breaks down the fence and streams into the garden.* DR HERDAL *also hurries down there. There is a short silence.*]

HILDE [*staring upward without moving her eyes and speaking as if turned to stone*]: *My* master builder.

RAGNAR [*trembling and supporting himself by the railing*]: He must be smashed to pieces. Dead on the spot.

ONE OF THE LADIES [*as* MRS SOLNESS *is carried into the house*]: Run down for the doctor –

RAGNAR: Can't move a foot –

ANOTHER LADY: Call down to someone then!

RAGNAR [*trying to call*]: How is it? Is he alive?

A VOICE [*down in the garden*]: Mr Solness is dead!

OTHER VOICES [*nearer*]: His whole head is crushed. – He fell straight into the quarry.

HILDE [*turning to* RAGNAR *and saying quietly*]: I can't see him up there now.

RAGNAR: Terrible business. So he couldn't manage it.

HILDE [*as though in a quiet, bewildered triumph*]: But he got right to the top. And I heard harps in the air. [*Swings the shawl up and cries with wild intensity.*] *My – my* master builder!

LITTLE EYOLF

CHARACTERS

ALFRED ALLMERS, *landed proprietor and man of letters,*
formerly a tutor
RITA ALLMERS, *his wife*
EYOLF, *their child; nine years old*
ASTA ALLMERS, *Alfred's younger half-sister*
BORGHEJM, *an engineer*
THE RAT WIFE

The action takes place on ALLMERS' property
near the fjord, some miles from the town

ACT ONE

A pleasant and richly decorated garden-room, full of furniture, flowers, and plants. In the background, open glass doors leading out to a veranda and giving a wide view across the fjord. Wooded heights in the distance. In each of the side walls there is a door, that on the right is a double door and further towards the back. Downstage right is a sofa with scattered cushions and rugs. Chairs and a little table by the sofa-corner. Downstage left is a larger table with arm-chairs round it. On the table stands an open travelling bag. It is early one summer morning and warm, sunny weather.

RITA ALLMERS *is standing at the table with her back to the right-hand door and unpacking the bag. She is a good-looking, fair woman of about thirty, rather tall, and full of vitality. She wears a light-coloured morning dress.*

After a moment ASTA ALLMERS *comes in by the door on the right, wearing a light brown summer suit, with a hat, coat, and parasol and carrying under her arm a fairly large, locked brief-case. She is slim, of medium height, with dark hair and deep, serious eyes. She is twenty-five.*

ASTA [*in the doorway*]: Good morning, Rita dear!

RITA [*turning her head and nodding to her*]: Oh, it's you, Asta! Come from town so early? All the way out here?

ASTA [*putting down her things on a chair near the door*]: Yes, I'd no peace or quiet of mind. I felt I *must* come out today and have a look at little Eyolf. And you as well. [*Putting down the brief-case on the table by the sofa.*] And so I came over on the steamer.

RITA [*smiling at her*]: And I suppose you met some pleasant friend or other on board? Quite by chance, I mean.

ASTA [*placidly*]: No, I didn't meet anyone I knew, at all. [*Noticing the bag.*] Why, Rita – what ever's that?

215

RITA [*going on unpacking*]: Alfred's travelling-bag. Don't you know it?

ASTA [*happily, coming nearer*]: What! Is Alfred back?

RITA: Yes, just imagine, – he came quite unexpectedly on the night-train.

ASTA: Oh, so *that's* what I was feeling! That's what made me come out here! And he hadn't written ahead at all? Not even a postcard?

RITA: Not a single word.

ASTA: And didn't wire either?

RITA: Oh yes, – an hour before he arrived. Quite short and cold. [*Laughing.*] That's just like him, Asta, isn't it?

ASTA: Yes, just. He's so quiet about everything.

RITA: But it was all the nicer for that, when I did get him back.

ASTA: Yes, I'm sure it was.

RITA: A whole fortnight before I expected him!

ASTA: And everything all right with him? Not depressed?

RITA [*shutting the bag with a snap and smiling at her*]: He looked absolutely transfigured when he came in at the door.

ASTA: And not at all tired either?

RITA: Oh yes, I think he was tired, all right. Very tired. But, poor dear, he'd come on foot nearly all the way.

ASTA: And then the air on the high fells – perhaps it's been too keen for him.

RITA: No, I don't think that for a moment. I haven't heard him cough, not once.

ASTA: Well, then, there you are, you see! It was a blessing after all, – the doctor persuading him to make that trip.

RITA: Yes, now that it's over all right, well –. But I can tell you, Asta, it's been a dreadful time for me. I never felt like talking about it. And, besides, you so seldom came out to see me –

ASTA: Yes, that certainly wasn't very nice of me. But –

RITA: Well, well, well. After all, you had the school there in town. [*Smiling.*] And our road-builder – he'd gone away too.

ASTA: Oh, stop that, Rita!

RITA: All right. Never mind about the road-builder. But, oh Asta, how I missed Alfred! The place so empty! So desolate! Ugh! It was as if there'd been a funeral in the house.

ASTA: But, good gracious, – only six or seven weeks –!

RITA: Yes, but you must remember Alfred's never been away from me before. Never so much as a single day and night. Never in all these ten years –

ASTA: No, but that's just why I think it was high time he did get away for a little this year. He should have gone for a walking-tour in the mountains every single summer. That's what he should have done.

RITA [*half smiling*]: Ah yes, it's all very well for you to talk, my dear. If I were as – as sensible as you are, I should have let him loose sooner. Perhaps. But I didn't feel as if I could, Asta! I kept thinking I should never get him back again. Surely you can understand *that* all right?

ASTA: No. But most likely it's because I've no one to lose.

RITA [*with a teasing smile*]: Really no one – no one at all?

ASTA: Not that *I* know of. [*Changing the subject.*] But tell me, Rita – where is Alfred? I suppose he's asleep?

RITA: Not a bit of it. He got up as early as usual today.

ASTA: Oh well then, he wasn't so very tired after all.

RITA: Yes, he was last night. When he got here. But he's had Eyolf in with him now for more than an hour.

ASTA: That poor little white-faced boy! Has he got to start learning and learning again?

RITA [*shrugging her shoulders*]: Alfred insists on it, you know.

ASTA: Yes, but I think you should try to stop it, Rita.

RITA [*a little impatiently*]: No. You know, that's a thing I really can't interfere with. Alfred must know about those things much better than I do. And what do you want Eyolf to do with himself? He can't run about and play – like other children.

ASTA [*firmly*]: I will talk to Alfred about this.

RITA: Yes, my dear; you do it. Oh, there he is.

[ALFRED ALLMERS, *in summer clothes, comes in by the door on the left, leading* EYOLF *by the hand. He is a thin, slightly built man, about thirty-six or thirty-seven years old, mild-eyed, and with thin brown hair and beard. His face wears a serious, thoughtful expression.* EYOLF *has on a suit made like a uniform, with gold frogs and military buttons. He is lame and has a crutch under his left arm, for that leg is paralysed. He is undersized and looks sickly, but has fine, intelligent eyes.*]

ALLMERS [*letting* EYOLF *go, comes happily forward holding out both hands to* ASTA]: Asta! My dearest Asta! You out here! To think of seeing you so soon!

ASTA: I felt I had to –. Welcome home again!

ALLMERS [*shaking her hands*]: Thank you for that!

RITA: Doesn't he look well?

ASTA [*looking steadily at him*]: Splendid! Really splendid! His eyes are so bright! Yes, you must have written a lot while you were away. [*With a joyful exclamation.*] Perhaps the whole book's finished, is it Alfred?

ALLMERS [*shrugging his shoulders*]: The book? Oh, that –

ASTA: Yes, I thought myself you'd find it came easily, once you got away.

ALLMERS: I thought so too. But you know, my dear, it turned out quite differently. The fact is I haven't written a line of the book.

ASTA: You haven't been writing –!

RITA: So that's it! I couldn't think why all the paper in the bag was untouched.

ASTA: But, my dear Alfred, what did you do all that time?

ALLMERS [*smiling*]: Just thought and thought and thought.

RITA [*putting her arm round his shoulders*]: Thought a little, too, about the people at home?

ALLMERS: Yes, you can be sure of that. A great deal. Every single day.

RITA [*letting him go*]: Ah well, then everything's all right.

ASTA: But you haven't written any of the book? And yet you can look so happy and peaceful? You aren't like that as a rule. I mean, not when your work's going badly.

ALLMERS: You're quite right there. Because, you see, I've been so stupid up to now. This business of thinking – the best of you goes into that. What goes down on paper isn't really worth much.

ASTA [*with a cry of protest*]: Not worth much!

RITA [*laughing*]: Why, Alfred, have you gone crazy?

EYOLF [*looking up at him trustingly*]: Oh, but Daddy – what *you* write is worth a lot.

ALLMERS [*smiling and stroking his hair*]: Well, well, if you say so, then – But believe me, there's someone coming presently who will do it better.

EYOLF: Whoever will that be? Oh, do tell us?

ALLMERS: Give him time. He'll come all right and declare himself.

EYOLF: And what will you do then?

ALLMERS [*seriously*]: Then I will go to the hills again –

RITA: Oh Alfred, you ought to be ashamed of yourself!

ALLMERS: – up on the heights and the great waste lands.

EYOLF: Daddy, don't you think I'll soon be strong enough to go with you?

ALLMERS [*keenly touched*]: Oh, well, perhaps you will, my boy.

EYOLF: Because I think it would be so grand if I could climb the hills too.

ASTA [*to change the subject*]: Why, how fine and smart you are today, Eyolf!

EYOLF: Yes, Auntie, don't you think I am?

ASTA: I do. Is it because of Daddy that you've put on these new clothes?

EYOLF: Yes, I asked Mummy to let me. Because I wanted Daddy to see me in them.

ALLMERS [*quietly, to* RITA]: You shouldn't have given him that kind of suit.

RITA [*with lowered voice*]: Yes, but he kept on bothering me. Begged for it so. He gave me no peace.

EYOLF: And I tell you what, Daddy. Mr Borghejm's bought me a bow. And taught me to shoot with it, too.

ALLMERS: Now, that's nice, Eyolf; that's just the thing for you.

EYOLF: And when he comes next time, I'll ask him to teach me to swim, too.

ALLMERS: To swim! But why do you want to do that?

EYOLF: Why, because all the other boys down on the beach, they can all swim. I'm the only one who can't.

ALLMERS [*distressed, putting his arms round him*]: You shall learn whatever you like. Everything you want to.

EYOLF: Oh, do you know what I want most, Daddy?

ALLMERS: What? Tell me.

EYOLF: Most of all I want to learn to be a soldier.

ALLMERS: Oh, Eyolf dear, there are so many other things that are better than that.

EYOLF: Yes, but when I'm grown-up I shall *have* to be a soldier. You know that.

ALLMERS [*clenching his hands*]: Well, well, well. We shall have to see –

ASTA [*sitting down by the table on the left*]: Eyolf! Come over here to me and I'll tell you something.

EYOLF [*going across*]: What is it, Auntie?

ASTA: Just think, Eyolf – I've seen the Rat Wife.

EYOLF: What! You've seen the Rat Wife? Oh, you're only teasing!

ASTA: No, it's true. I saw her yesterday.

EYOLF: Where did you see her?

ASTA: I saw her on the road, just beyond the town.

ALLMERS: I saw her too, somewhere out in the country.

RITA [who is sitting on the sofa]: Then perhaps we shall see her too, Eyolf.

EYOLF: Auntie, don't you think it's odd that she should be called the Rat Wife?

ASTA: People only call her that because she goes round the country driving away all the rats.

ALLMERS: I believe her real name is actually Miss Weir.

EYOLF: Were? That means a wolf, that does.

ALLMERS [patting him on the head]: So you know that, Eyolf, do you?

EYOLF [thoughtfully]: So perhaps it may be true after all, that she's a werewolf in the night. Do you believe it, Daddy?

ALLMERS: Oh no, I don't believe that. But now you should go down and play in the garden for a little.

EYOLF: Hadn't I better take some books with me?

ALLMERS: No, no books in future. Go down on the beach instead, to the other boys.

EYOLF [a little embarrassed]: No, Daddy, I don't want to go down to the boys today.

ALLMERS: Why not?

EYOLF: Oh, because I've got these clothes on.

ALLMERS [frowning]: Do you mean they make fun of – of your nice clothes?

EYOLF [evasively]: No, they don't dare. Because then I should hit them.

ALLMERS: Well, then – what is it?

EYOLF: But they're so horrid, those boys. And then they say I can't ever be a soldier.

ALLMERS [controlling his anger]: Why do they say that, do you think?

EYOLF: I expect they're jealous of me. You see, Daddy,

they're so poor themselves that they have to go about with
bare feet.

ALLMERS [*in a low, bitter voice*]: Oh Rita – it just breaks my
heart, all this!

RITA [*comfortingly, getting up*]: There, there, there!

ALLMERS [*threateningly*]: But those boys, they shall find out
one of these days who's master down there on the beach.

ASTA [*listening*]: There's someone knocking

EYOLF: That'll be Mr Borghejm!

RITA: Come in!

> [THE RAT WIFE *comes softly and silently in by the right-
> hand door. She is a little, thin, shrivelled creature, old and
> grey-haired, with deep, piercing eyes, wearing an old-
> fashioned flowered dress and a black hood and cloak. In her
> hand she has a large red umbrella and looped over her arm
> a black bag.*]

EYOLF [*in a low voice, clutching* ASTA'S *dress*]: Auntie! It must
be her!

THE RAT WIFE [*curtseying by the door*]: My humblest apolo-
gies, but have the lady and gentleman anything that worries
them here in the house?

ALLMERS: We? No, I don't think so.

THE RAT WIFE: Because if they had I should be so glad to help
them get rid of it.

RITA: Yes, we quite understand. But we haven't anything of
that kind.

THE RAT WIFE: That's a great pity. Because I'm just going on
my round now. And goodness knows when I'll be in these
parts again. Oh, I'm so tired!

ALLMERS [*pointing to a chair*]: Yes, you do look tired.

THE RAT WIFE: One should never get tired of doing a kind-
ness to the poor little things, when they're hated and persecuted so bitterly. But it does use up one's strength so.

RITA: Won't you sit down and rest a little?

THE RAT WIFE: Thank you so very much. [*Sitting down on a*

chair between the door and the sofa.] Because I've been out at work all night.

ALLMERS: Oh, have you?

THE RAT WIFE: Yes, over on the islands. [*Chuckling*.] The people sent for me, they did. They hated having to do it. But there was nothing else to be done. They had to make the best of it and bite the sour apple. [*Looking at* EYOLF *and nodding*.] Sour apple, little gentleman. Sour apple.

EYOLF [*involuntarily and rather timidly*]: Why did they have to –?

THE RAT WIFE: What?

EYOLF: To bite it?

THE RAT WIFE: Why, because they'd nothing left to live on. Because of the rats, you see, young gentleman, and because of all the little rats.

RITA: Oh! The poor people! Have they so many of them?

THE RAT WIFE: Yes. It swarmed and teemed with them. [*Laughing, with quiet enjoyment*.] Up on the beds they scribbled and scrabbled the whole night long. Into the milk-tubs they plumped. And all over the floor they whistled and rustled, cross and criss-cross.

EYOLF [*in a low voice, to* ASTA]: I shan't ever go out there, Auntie.

THE RAT WIFE: But then *I* came – and someone with me. And we took them all away with us. The dear, little creatures! We managed them all.

EYOLF [*with a cry*]: Daddy – look, look!

RITA: Good gracious, Eyolf!

ALLMERS: What's the matter?

EYOLF [*pointing*]: There's something moving about in the bag!

RITA [*crying out, as she moves away to the left*]: Oh! Turn her out, Alfred!

THE RAT WIFE [*laughing*]: Ah, gentle lady, you mustn't be afraid of a little fellow like him.

ALLMERS: But what ever is it?

THE RAT WIFE: It's only Mopsemand. [*Loosens the cord of the bag.*] Come up out of the dark, my precious little friend. [*A little dog with a broad, black snout pokes its head up out of the bag.*]

THE RAT WIFE [*nodding and beckoning to* EYOLF]: Come nearer, my little wounded soldier, and don't be afraid. He won't bite. Come here! Come here!

EYOLF [*holding on to* ASTA]: No, I daren't.

THE RAT WIFE: Now, little sir, don't you think he's got a lovely, gentle expression?

EYOLF [*pointing in amazement*]: That thing there!

THE RAT WIFE: Aye, him.

EYOLF [*half to himself, staring fixedly at the dog*]: I think he has the most dreadful ... expression ... I've ever seen.

THE RAT WIFE [*shutting the bag*]: Oh, it'll come. It'll come all right.

EYOLF [*approaching unwillingly, until he has crossed the room, and stroking the bag gently*]: Beautiful – he's beautiful, though.

THE RAT WIFE [*in a warning voice*]: But now he's so tired and weary, poor dear. Tired out, he is. [*Looking at* ALLMERS.] Because you can believe me, sir, it uses up one's strength – that kind of game.

ALLMERS: What kind of game do you mean?

THE RAT WIFE: Casting charms.

ALLMERS: Oh, I suppose it's the dog that casts the charm over the rats?

THE RAT WIFE [*nodding*]: Mopsemand and I. We do it together. And it all goes so smoothly – to look at. He just has a string through his collar. Then I lead him three times round the house. And play on the pipes. And when they hear *that* – then up from the cellars they have to come and down from the lofts and out of the holes – every blessed little creature.

EYOLF: Does he bite them to death then?

THE RAT WIFE: Not a bit of it! No; we go down to the boat, he and I. And they come after us. Both the grown-ups and all their little young ones.

EYOLF [*thrilled*]: And then what – ? Tell me!

THE RAT WIFE: Then we push off from the land. And I scull with an oar and play on the pipes. And Mopsemand, he swims behind. [*With snapping eyes.*] And all those scribbling-scrabbling creatures, they follow and follow us out to the waters of the deep. Aye, for they *have* to.

EYOLF: Why do they *have* to?

THE RAT WIFE: Just because they don't want to. Because they're so horribly afraid of the water – that's why they have to go out into it.

EYOLF: Are they drowned then?

THE RAT WIFE: Every blessed one. [*Lower.*] And then it's as quiet and nice and dark for them as ever they can want – the pretty little things. They sleep down there, such a long, sweet sleep. All of them, that human beings hate and persecute. [*Getting up.*] Aye, once upon a time I didn't need any Mopsemand. I worked my own charms. By myself.

EYOLF: What sorts of things did you charm?

THE RAT WIFE: Men. One most.

EYOLF [*excitedly*]: Oh, tell me who that was!

THE RAT WIFE [*laughing*]: It was my sweetheart, it was, little breaker of hearts.

EYOLF: Where is he now, then?

THE RAT WIFE [*in a hard voice*]: Down below, with all the rats. [*Gently again.*] But now I must be off about my business again. Always on the move. [*To* RITA.] Have the lady and gentleman nothing at all for me to do today? Because, if they had, I could see to it while I'm here.

RITA: No, thank you; I don't think there's anything.

THE RAT WIFE: Ah well, gentle lady, one never knows. If they should find there's anything here gnawing and biting, and scribbling and scrabbling – well, just have us sent for, me and Mopsemand. Farewell, farewell. Many, many farewells.

[*She goes out by the door on the right.*]

EYOLF [*softly, but triumphantly, to* ASTA]: Just think, Auntie! *I've* seen the Rat Wife too!

[RITA *goes out on the veranda and fans herself with her pocket-handkerchief. After a moment* EYOLF *steals out on the right, but no one notices him.*]

ALLMERS [*taking the brief-case from the table by the sofa*]: Asta, is this your brief-case here?

ASTA: Yes. I've got some of the old letters in it.

ALLMERS: Oh yes, the family letters –

ASTA: You know, you asked me to sort them for you while you were away.

ALLMERS [*patting her on the head*]: And you've even found time for that, bless you!

ASTA: Oh yes. I did some of it out here and some of it at home in town.

ALLMERS: Thank you, my dear. And did you find anything much in them?

ASTA [*casually*]: Oh well, you know, one always finds one or two things in old papers like these. [*Lowering her voice; seriously.*] Those in the case there are the letters to Mother.

ALLMERS: Oh, of course, you must keep those yourself.

ASTA [*with an effort*]: No, Alfred, I want you to go through them too. Some day – later on in your life. But I haven't got the key of the case with me today.

ALLMERS: It doesn't matter, Asta dear –. Because, in any case, I'm never going to read your mother's letters.

ASTA [*fastening her eyes on him*]: Then some time – some quiet evening – I'll tell you something about what's in them.

ALLMERS: Yes, that's what you'd better do. But you keep your mother's letters yourself. You haven't so very many mementos of her. [*He hands the brief-case to* ASTA. *She takes it and puts it over on the chair under her coat.*]

[RITA *comes into the room again.*]

RITA: Ugh! I feel as if that dreadful old woman had brought in the smell of a corpse with her.

ALLMERS: Yes, she was rather dreadful, I agree.

RITA: I felt almost ill while she was in the room.

ALLMERS: All the same, I think I can understand the power she talked about; drawing, compelling. The solitude up among the high tops and the great waste lands has something of the same kind.

ASTA [*looking at him observantly*]: What ever is it that has happened to you, Alfred?

ALLMERS [*smiling*]: To me?

ASTA: Yes, something's happened. Almost like a transformation. Rita's noticed it too.

RITA: Yes, I saw it directly you came in. But it's only – something good, isn't it Alfred?

ALLMERS: It *ought* to be good – all to the good. And so it must and shall be.

RITA [*exclaiming*]: You've been through something while you were away. Don't say you haven't. Because I can see by the look of you.

ALLMERS [*shaking his head*]: Nothing at all – not outwardly. But –

RITA [*excitedly*]: But –?

ALLMERS: But inwardly – there's certainly been a minor revolution.

RITA: Good heavens!

ALLMERS [*soothing her and patting her hand*]: Only to the good, Rita, my dear. You can rest assured of that.

RITA [*sitting on the sofa*]: Now you must tell us about this at once. All about it!

ALLMERS [*turning to* ASTA]: Yes, let us sit down too. Then I'll try and tell you. As best I can. [*He sits on the sofa beside* RITA.

ASTA *pulls a chair across and sits near him. There is a moment's pause.*]

RITA [*looking at him expectantly*]: Well, now –?

ALLMERS [*looking straight in front of him*]: When I think back over my life – and my fate – in the last ten or eleven years, why, it almost looks to me like a fairy-tale or a dream. Don't you think so too, Asta?

ASTA: Yes, in many ways, I do.

ALLMERS [*continuing*]: When I think, Asta, what we two were before that ... We two poor, wretched orphans –

RITA [*impatiently*]: Oh, but that's all so long ago.

ALLMERS [*without listening to her*]: And here I am now, comfortable and prosperous. I've been able to follow my calling. Been able to work and study – just as I wanted to. [*Holding out his hand.*] And all this great, incredible good fortune – we owe it to you, my dearest Rita.

RITA [*half joking, half protesting, slaps his hand*]: Now, will you just stop that kind of talk.

ALLMERS: I'm only mentioning that as a sort of introduction.

RITA: Oh, then skip the introduction!

ALLMERS: Rita, you mustn't think it was the doctor's advice that made me go up into the mountains.

ASTA: Wasn't it, Alfred?

RITA: What was it, then, made you go?

ALLMERS: It was because I no longer felt at peace with my work.

RITA: Not at peace! But, my dear, who was disturbing you?

ALLMERS [*shaking his head*]: No one from outside. But I had a feeling that I was actually misusing – or – no, neglecting my best powers. That I was throwing my time away.

ASTA [*wide-eyed*]: When you were sitting writing your book?

ALLMERS [*nodding*]: Because I haven't gifts just for that alone. I must be capable of one or two other things as well.

RITA: Was *that* what you were sitting worrying over?

ALLMERS: Yes. Mostly that.

RITA: And that's why you've been so much at odds with yourself lately. And with the rest of us, too. Yes, because you *were*, Alfred!

ALLMERS [*looking straight in front of him*]: There I sat, bent over my table, writing day after day. Very often half the night too. Writing and writing at that great, solid book on 'Human Responsibility'. Hm!

ASTA [*putting a hand on his arm*]: But, my dear – that book is to be your life-work.

RITA: Yes, that's what you've said often enough.

ALLMERS: That's what I thought. Ever since I began to grow up. [*With warmth in his eyes.*] And then you, my dear Rita, made it possible for me to work at it.

RITA: Don't be silly!

ALLMERS [*smiling at her*]: You, with 'your gold and your green forests' –

RITA [*half laughing and half irritated*]: If you start that nonsense again, I shall hit you.

ASTA [*looking at him with a troubled expression*]: But your book, Alfred?

ALLMERS: It began, as it were, to slip away from me. But the thought of higher duties that laid their claims on me came closer and closer.

RITA [*with shining eyes, seizing his hand*]: Alfred!

ALLMERS: The thought of Eyolf, Rita dear.

RITA [*hurt, and letting go his hand*]: Oh – of Eyolf!

ALLMERS: Poor little Eyolf has taken a deeper and deeper hold of me. After that unhappy fall from the table –. And most of all since we've been sure it's incurable –.

RITA [*earnestly*]: But you do look after him, Alfred, as much as ever you can!

ALLMERS: As a schoolmaster, yes. But not as a father. And it's a father I want to be to Eyolf in future.

RITA [*looking at him and shaking her head*]: I don't think I really understand you.

ALLMERS: I mean that I'm going to try with all my might to make what can't be cured as light and easy for him as possible.

RITA: But, my dear – I don't believe, thank God, he does feel it so deeply.

ASTA [*with emotion*]: Oh yes, Rita, he does.

ALLMERS: Yes, you can be sure he feels it deeply.

RITA [*impatiently*]: But, my dear, what more can you do for him?

ALLMERS: I'm going to try and bring light to all the rich potentialities that are dawning in his child's mind. All the seeds of nobility in him, I want to make them shoot up – to flower and come to fruition. [*He gets up, growing more and more eager.*] And I'll do more than that. I'll help him reconcile his desires with what lies within his reach. Because he isn't doing that now. The whole set of his mind is towards things that, all through his life, will be impossible for him to do. But I'll build up the instinct for happiness in his mind. [*He walks up and down across the floor.* ASTA *and* RITA *follow him with their eyes.*]

RITA: You shouldn't take these things so much to heart, Alfred.

ALLMERS [*stopping beside the table on the left and looking at them*]: Eyolf shall take up my life's work. Provided he wants to. Or else he shall choose something that's entirely his own. Perhaps better that. But in any case I shall put mine aside.

RITA [*getting up*]: But Alfred, my dear, can't you work for yourself as well as for Eyolf?

ALLMERS: No, that I can't do. Impossible. I can't divide myself over this. And that's why I shall give way. Eyolf shall be the crowning achievement of our family. And I will find my new life-work in making him that consummation.

ASTA [*who has got up, crosses over to him*]: All this has cost you a terribly hard battle, Alfred.

ALLMERS: Yes, it has. I should never have conquered myself here at home. Never have subdued myself to renunciation. Never, here at home.

RITA: So was that why you went away this summer?

ALLMERS [*with shining eyes*]: Yes. And so I went up into the everlasting solitude. Saw the sunrise light up the high mountain-tops. Felt myself nearer the stars. Almost in communion with them, and understanding. And then I was able to do it.

ASTA [*looking sadly at him*]: But you will never write any more of the book on 'Human Responsibility'?

ALLMERS: No, never, Asta. I can't divide myself between two tasks, I tell you. But I will carry out my human responsibility – in my life.

RITA [*with a smile*]: Do you really think you can hold to such a high purpose, here at home?

ALLMERS [*taking her hand*]: In partnership with *you*, I can. [*Stretching out his other hand.*] And with you as well, Asta.

RITA [*withdrawing her hand*]: With two, then. So you can divide yourself, after all.

ALLMERS: But my dear Rita –! [RITA *walks away from him and stands in the garden door. Someone knocks lightly and quickly at the door on the right.* BORGHEJM, *the engineer, comes quickly in. He is a young man of about thirty. He has a happy and cheerful expression and an erect carriage.*]

BORGHEJM: Good morning, Mrs Allmers, good morning! [*Stops with pleasure at the sight of* ALLMERS.] Why, what do I see? Home again already, Mr Allmers?

ALLMERS [*shaking his hand*]: Yes, I got back last night.

RITA [*gaily*]: He hadn't permission to stay any longer, Mr Borghejm.

ALLMERS: Well, no, that's not quite true, Rita –

RITA [*coming nearer*]: Yes, it's perfectly true. His leave was up.

BORGHEJM: Do you keep your husband on such a firm rein, then, Mrs Allmers?

RITA: I hold to my rights. And besides, everything has to have an end.

BORGHEJM: Oh, not everything – I hope. – Good morning, Miss Allmers.

ASTA [*with reserve*]: Good morning.

RITA [*looking at BORGHEJM*]: Not everything, you say?

BORGHEJM: Why, I most certainly believe there's at least *something* in this world that has no end.

RITA: Now I suppose you're thinking of love – or something like that.

BORGHEJM [*warmly*]: I am thinking of everything that is lovely.

RITA: And that never comes to an end. Yes, let us think about that and hope for it, all of us.

ALLMERS [*coming across to them*]: You'll soon be finished now with your road-construction out here?

BORGHEJM: I'm finished already. Finished yesterday. It's lasted long enough. But thank heaven *that* did come to an end.

RITA: And you're delighted about it?

BORGHEJM: Yes, I certainly am!

RITA: Well, I must say –

BORGHEJM: What, Mrs Allmers?

RITA: It's not very nice of you, Mr Borghejm.

BORGHEJM: Isn't it? Why not?

RITA: No, because you won't come out to this district very much in future.

BORGHEJM: No, that's true. I hadn't thought of that.

RITA: Oh well, you'll probably come to see us now and again, all the same.

BORGHEJM: No, I'm sorry to say that'll be impossible for me for some time.

ALLMERS: Will it? Why's that?

BORGHEJM: Oh, because I've got a big, new job that I must get on with at once.

ALLMERS: No, have you? [*Clasping his hand.*] I'm delighted at that.

RITA: Congratulations! Congratulations, Mr Borghejm!

BORGHEJM: Hush, hush – I really haven't any business to be talking openly about it yet! But I can't stop myself. It's a great job of road-construction up in the North. With mountains to cross – and the most incredible difficulties to deal with! [*Breaking out.*] Ah, what a great, glorious world it is! And what a wonderful thing – to be a road-builder!

RITA [*smiling and looking jestingly at him*]: Is it just because of the road-construction that you've come here today in such high spirits?

BORGHEJM: No, not because of that only. But because of all the bright and shining prospects that are opening before me.

RITA [*as before*]: Ah yes. Perhaps there is something even lovelier to come?

BORGHEJM [*glancing towards* ASTA]: Who knows! When good fortune once begins, it generally comes like the floods in spring. [*Turning to* ASTA.] Miss Allmers, couldn't you and I go for a little walk together? As we usually do?

ASTA [*hurriedly*]: No, no thank you. Not now. Not today.

BORGHEJM: Oh, do come! Only a little, short walk! I feel I've so much to talk to you about before I go away.

RITA: I suppose *that's* something that you mustn't talk about openly yet?

BORGHEJM: Well, that depends –

RITA: Because you could just as well whisper, you know. [*Half under her breath.*] Asta, you really must go with him.

ASTA: But, Rita dear –

BORGHEJM [*imploring*]: Miss Asta, remember this must be our farewell walk – for a long, long time.

ASTA [*picking up her hat and parasol*]: Oh well, let's go down the garden, then, for a little round.

BORGHEJM: Oh, thank you, thank you!

ALLMERS: And just give an eye to Eyolf at the same time.

BORGHEJM: Why yes, Eyolf, of course! Where's Eyolf gone today? I've got something for him.

ALLMERS: He's down there somewhere, playing.

BORGHEJM: No, really? So he's begun to play now? Usually he only sits indoors and reads.

ALLMERS: That's going to be stopped. He's to turn into a real outdoor boy.

BORGHEJM: There now, that's right! Out into the open air with him, poor kid! Good heavens, one can't do anything better than play in this blessed world. The whole of life seems like playing to me! Come along, Miss Asta!

[BORGHEJM and ASTA go out on the veranda and down through the garden.]

ALLMERS [stands looking after them]: I say, Rita – do you think there's anything between those two?

RITA: I don't know what to say. I used to think so. But Asta's behaved so oddly with me lately – she's been impossible to understand.

ALLMERS: Has she really? While I was away?

RITA: Yes, this last week or two, I think.

ALLMERS: And you don't think she's much interested in him any longer?

RITA: Not seriously. Not whole-heartedly or unreservedly. I don't think so. [Looking searchingly at him.] Would you dislike it if she were?

ALLMERS: Not exactly dislike it. But I must admit it would be a disturbing thought.

RITA: Disturbing?

ALLMERS: Yes, because you must remember I'm responsible for Asta. For her life's happiness.

RITA: Oh, come – responsible! Asta's grown-up, isn't she? She knows how to choose for herself all right, I should have thought.

ALLMERS: Yes, we'll hope she does, Rita.

RITA: I, for my part, don't think there's anything wrong with Borghejm.

ALLMERS: No, my dear, and I don't either. Quite the contrary. But all the same –

RITA [*going on*]: And I should very much like to see a match of it between him and Asta.

ALLMERS [*annoyed*]: Oh, why, precisely?

RITA [*with rising emotion*]: Yes, because then she'd have to go a long way away with him! And so she couldn't ever come out here to us, as she does now.

ALLMERS [*looking at her in amazement*]: What! Do you really want to get rid of Asta?

RITA: Yes, Alfred, yes!

ALLMERS: But why on earth –

RITA [*throwing her arms passionately round his neck*]: Why, because then at last I should have you all to myself! Except – no, not *then* either. Not all to myself! [*Bursting into convulsive sobs.*] Oh, Alfred, Alfred, I *can't* let you go!

ALLMERS [*freeing himself gently*]: But, my dearest Rita, do be sensible!

RITA: I don't care a straw about being sensible. I only care about you! You alone in all the world! [*Throwing herself again on his neck.*] You, you, you!

ALLMERS: Let go, let go – you're choking me.

RITA [*letting him go*]: I wish to heaven I could! [*Looking at him with flashing eyes.*] Oh, if you only knew how I've hated you!

ALLMERS: Hated me –!

RITA: Yes. When you sat in there by yourself. And brooded over your work. Till long, long into the night. [*Wailing.*] So long – so late, Alfred! Oh, how I hated your work.

ALLMERS: But now that's all finished with.

RITA [*laughing bitterly*]: Oh, indeed! Now you are absorbed in something even worse.

ALLMERS [*shocked*]: Worse! Do you call the child something worse?

RITA [*with energy*]: Yes, I do. I do call it worse, for the relationship between us two. Because the child – the child's a live human being into the bargain. [*With growing excitement.*] But I won't stand it, Alfred! I won't stand it, I tell you!

ALLMERS [*looking steadily at her and speaking in a lowered voice*]: There are often times when I'm almost afraid of you, Rita.

RITA [*sombrely*]: I'm often afraid of myself. And that's just why you mustn't rouse the evil in me.

ALLMERS: Oh, but, in heaven's name – do I do that?

RITA: Yes, you do. When you tear to pieces the holiest thing there is between us!

ALLMERS [*earnestly*]: But think, Rita, think. It's your own child, our only child, that we're talking about.

RITA: The child's only half my own. [*With another outburst.*] But *you* shall be mine only! All mine, you shall be! I've the right to claim that from you!

ALLMERS [*shrugging his shoulders*]: Oh, my dear Rita, it's no use claiming things. Everything must be given freely.

RITA [*looking at him in suspense*]: And you mean you can't do that in future?

ALLMERS: No, I can't. I *must* share myself between Eyolf and you.

RITA: But if Eyolf had never been born? What then?

ALLMERS [*evasively*]: Well, that would be another matter. Then I should only have had you to be fond of.

RITA [*in a low, trembling voice*]: Then I could wish I'd never borne him.

ALLMERS [*flaring up*]: Rita! You don't know what you are saying.

RITA [*trembling with emotion*]: I brought him into the world with such unspeakable pain. But I bore it all with joy and gladness for your sake.

ALLMERS [*warmly*]: Oh yes, yes, I know that quite well.

RITA [*firmly*]: But there it must end. I want to live my life. Beside you. All with you. I can't go on just being Eyolf's mother. Only that. Nothing more at all. I *won't*, I tell you! I *can't*! I want to be everything for you! For you, Alfred!

ALLMERS: But that's just what you *are*, Rita. Through our child –

RITA: Oh – soft, sentimental talk! Not a thing more. No, Alfred, that sort of thing's no use to *me*. I was made for bearing the child, but not to be its mother. You must take me as I am, Alfred.

ALLMERS: And you used to be so deeply attached to Eyolf.

RITA: I felt so sorry for him. Because you didn't care what happened to him. Just made him read and work. Hardly ever noticed him.

ALLMERS [*nodding slowly*]: No; I was blind. The time hadn't come for me –

RITA [*looking at him*]: But *now* it's come, all right?

ALLMERS: Yes, now at last. Now I realize that the greatest thing I have to do in this world is to be a true father to Eyolf.

RITA: And to me? What are you going to be to me?

ALLMERS [*gently*]: I will go on being fond of you. With deep and quiet affection. [*He tries to take her hands.*]

RITA [*avoiding him*]: I'm not interested in your quiet affection. I want the whole of you, entirely. And alone! Just as I had you in those first lovely, glorious days. [*Hard and vehement.*] I'm not going to be put off with scraps and leavings, Alfred – never in this world!

ALLMERS [*gently*]: I think there ought to be happiness in abundance here for all three of us, Rita.

RITA [*scornfully*]: Then you're easily satisfied. [*Sitting by the table on the left.*] Now listen.

ALLMERS [*coming nearer*]: Well? What is it?

RITA [*looking up at him with a subdued gleam in her eye*]: When I got your telegram yesterday evening –

ALLMERS: Yes? What about it?

RITA: – then I put on a white dress –

ALLMERS: Yes, I saw you were in white when I came in.

RITA: I'd let down my hair –

ALLMERS: Your cloud of fragrant hair –

RITA: – so that it flowed down over my neck and shoulders –

ALLMERS: I saw it. I saw it. Oh, how lovely you were, Rita!

RITA: There were rose-pink shades over both lamps. And we two alone, we two. The only people awake in the whole house. And there was champagne on the table.

ALLMERS: I didn't drink any.

RITA [*looking bitterly at him*]: No, that's true. [*With a sharp laugh.*] 'You had champagne, but you touched it not' – as the poem says. [*She gets up from the arm-chair and walks across as if she were weary and sits, half lying, on the sofa.*]

ALLMERS [*crosses the room and stops in front of her*]: I was so full of serious thoughts. I had planned to talk to you about our future, Rita. And first and foremost about Eyolf.

RITA [*smiling*]: And so you did, my dear.

ALLMERS: No, I didn't get to it. Because you began to undress.

RITA: Yes, and you talked about Eyolf all the time. Don't you remember? You asked how little Eyolf's digestion was.

ALLMERS [*looking at her reproachfully*]: Rita –!

RITA: And then you lay down in your bed. And slept so beautifully.

ALLMERS [*shaking his head*]: Rita, Rita –!

RITA [*lying back and looking up at him*]: Well? Alfred?

ALLMERS: Yes?

RITA: 'You had champagne, but you touched it not.'

ALLMERS [*in a voice almost hard*]: No. I did not touch it. [*He moves away from her and stands at the garden door.* RITA *lies motionless for a moment with closed eyes.*]

RITA [*springing suddenly up*]: But one thing I will say to you, Alfred.

ALLMERS [*turning round at the door*]: Well?

RITA: You shouldn't feel so safe, my dear.

ALLMERS: Not safe?

RITA: No, you shouldn't be so complacent! Not so sure that you *have* me!

ALLMERS [*coming nearer*]: What do you mean by that?

RITA [*with trembling lips*]: Never, with a thought, have I been unfaithful to you, Alfred! Never for a moment.

ALLMERS: No, Rita, I know that. I, who know you so well.

RITA [*with flashing eyes*]: But if you put me aside –!

ALLMERS: Put you aside! I don't know what you're driving at!

RITA: Ah, you don't know all the things that might be roused up in me, if –

ALLMERS: If –?

RITA: If I should discover some day that you didn't care for me any more. Didn't love me any longer as you used to.

ALLMERS: But, my dearest Rita – the change that comes to all people in the course of the years – that must happen some day in *our* life too. As it does to everybody else.

RITA: Never to me! And I won't hear of any change in you either. I shouldn't be able to bear that, Alfred. I mean to keep you for myself alone.

ALLMERS [*looking at her with distress*]: You have a terribly jealous nature.

RITA: I can't make myself other than I am. [*Threateningly.*] If you share yourself out between me and anyone else –

ALLMERS: Well, what?

RITA: Then I shall revenge myself on you, Alfred!

ALLMERS: What could you revenge yourself with?

RITA: I don't know. Oh, yes, I do know.

ALLMERS: Well?

RITA: I shall go and throw myself away –

ALLMERS: Throw yourself away, do you say!

RITA: Yes, I shall. I shall throw myself straight into the arms of – of the first man who comes along!

ALLMERS [*looking kindly at her and shaking his head*]: That you will never do – my noble, proud, faithful Rita.

RITA [*putting her arms round his neck*]: Ah, you don't know what I might come to, if you – if you didn't want to have any more to do with me.

ALLMERS: No more to do with you, Rita? How can you say such a thing!

RITA [*letting him go, half laughing*]: I might even try to ensnare him – that road-builder who's here.

ALLMERS [*relieved*]: Oh, thank goodness – you're only joking.

RITA: Not a bit. Why not him as well as any other?

ALLMERS: Well, because he seems pretty firmly attached already.

RITA: All the better! For then I should take him away from someone else. That's exactly what Eyolf's done to me.

ALLMERS: Do you mean to say that our little Eyolf has done *that*?

RITA [*pointing her finger at him*]: There, you see! You see! The minute you so much as speak Eyolf's name, you're tender and your voice trembles. [*Threateningly, clenching her hands.*] Oh, I could almost be tempted to wish – oh!

ALLMERS [*looking at her anxiously*]: What could you wish, Rita?

RITA [*moving away from him angrily*]: No, no, no – I won't tell you that! Never!

ALLMERS [*going over nearer to her*]: Rita! I implore you – for your sake and mine – don't let yourself be tempted to anything evil.

> [BORGHEJM *and* ASTA *come up from the garden. They are both controlling strong emotions. They look grave and depressed.* ASTA *remains standing outside on the veranda.* BORGHEJM *comes into the room.*]

BORGHEJM: That's that. Miss Allmers and I have had our last walk together.

RITA [*looking at him with some surprise*]: Oh. And there's no longer journey to follow the walk?

BORGHEJM: Oh yes. For me there is.

RITA: For you alone?

BORGHEJM: Yes, for me alone.

RITA [*looking gloomily at* ALLMERS]: Do you hear, Alfred? [*Turning to* BORGHEJM.] I could wager that it's the Evil Eye that's played you this trick.

BORGHEJM [*looking at her*]: The evil eye?

RITA [*nodding*]: Yes, the evil eye.

BORGHEJM: Do you believe in the evil eye, Mrs Allmers?

RITA: Yes, I have begun to believe in the evil eye. Most of all in the evil eye of a child.

ALLMERS [*shocked, whispering*]: Rita – how can you –!

RITA [*under her breath*]: It's you who are making me evil and ugly, Alfred.

> [*Distant, confused shouts and cries are heard down by the water-side.*]

BORGHEJM [*going to the glass door*]: What ever's that noise –?

ASTA [*at the door*]: Look at all the people running down to the jetty.

ALLMERS: What can it be? [*Glancing out.*] Those young devils, I suppose, at some mischief again.

BORGHEJM [*shouting out from the railing*]: Hi! You lads down there! What's the matter?

> [*Several of them can be heard answering indistinctly and all together.*]

RITA: What are they saying?

BORGHEJM: They say it's a child that's drowned.

ALLMERS: A child drowned?

ASTA [*uneasily*]: A little boy, they say.

ALLMERS: Oh, they can all swim, the lot of them.

RITA [*screaming in terror*]: Where's Eyolf gone?

ALLMERS: Keep calm. Keep calm. Eyolf's in the garden playing.

ASTA: No, he wasn't in the garden.

RITA [*with upraised arms*]: Oh, if only it isn't *him*!

BORGHEJM [*listens and then shouts down*]: Whose child is it, do you say?

> [*Confused voices are heard.* BORGHEJM *and* ASTA *give a stifled cry and dash down through the garden.*]

ALLMERS [*in an agony of dread*]: It isn't Eyolf! It isn't Eyolf, Rita!

RITA [*on the veranda, listening*]: Hush; be quiet. Let me hear what they're saying.

> [RITA *falls back with a piercing cry into the room.*]

ALLMERS [*following her*]: What was it they said?

RITA [*sinking down by the arm-chair on the left*]: They said: 'The crutch is floating.'

ALLMERS [*almost stunned*]: No! No! No!

RITA [*hoarsely*]: Eyolf! Eyolf! Oh, but they *must* save him!

ALLMERS [*half out of his mind*]: They *must*! Such a precious life! Such a precious life!

> [*He rushes down through the garden.*]

ACT TWO

A little, narrow glen in Allmers' forest down by the shore. Tall old trees to the left lean over the place. Down over the hill side in the background there falls a brook, which loses itself among the stones at the edge of the wood. A path winds beside the brook. On the right there stand only scattered trees, between which the fjord can be seen. In the foreground we see the corner of a boat-house with a boat drawn up. Under the old trees on the left stands a table with a bench and a few chairs, all made out of thin birch-trunks. It is a heavy, damp day with driving clouds of mist. ALFRED ALLMERS, dressed as before, is sitting on the bench and resting his arms on the table. His hat is lying before him. He stares in front of him out over the water, motionless and abstracted. After a moment ASTA ALLMERS comes down by the wood-path. She is carrying an open umbrella.

ASTA [*going quietly and timidly across to him*]: You oughtn't to sit down here in this grey weather, Alfred.

ALLMERS [*nods slowly without answering*].

ASTA [*shutting up her umbrella*]: I've been looking for you for such a long time.

ALLMERS [*without any expression*]: Thank you.

ASTA [*bringing over a chair and sitting beside him*]: Have you been sitting down here long? The whole time?

ALLMERS [*does not answer. After a moment he says*]: No, I can't take it in. It seems so utterly impossible.

ASTA [*laying her hand sympathetically on his arm*]: Poor Alfred.

ALLMERS [*gazing at her*]: Is it really true, then, Asta? Or have I gone mad? Or am I only dreaming? Oh, if it was only a dream! Think, how wonderful – if I woke up now!

ASTA: How I wish I really could wake you.

ALLMERS [*looking out over the water*]: How pitiless the fjord looks today. Lies there so heavy and dull. Leaden grey, with a yellow glint, and reflecting the rain-clouds.

ASTA [*begging*]: Oh, Alfred, don't sit and stare out over the fjord!

ALLMERS [*without listening to her*]: On the surface, of course. But down in the depths – *there* runs the strong undertow.

ASTA [*in dread*]: Oh, for God's sake – don't think about the depths!

ALLMERS [*looking gently at her*]: You think he's lying just outside here, don't you? But he isn't, Asta. You mustn't believe that. Because you must remember how swiftly the current runs out here. Right out to sea.

ASTA [*throws herself forward sobbing on the table, with her hands before her face*]: Oh, God! Oh, God!

ALLMERS [*heavily*]: And so little Eyolf has gone so far – far away from the rest of us now.

ASTA [*looking imploringly at him*]: Oh, Alfred, don't say that kind of thing!

ALLMERS: Yes, but you can work it out yourself. You who are so clever. In twenty-eight – twenty-nine hours. Let me see –. Let me see –.

ASTA [*crying out and stopping her ears*]: Alfred!

ALLMERS [*gripping the table hard with his hand*]: But can you see any meaning yourself in a thing like this?

ASTA [*looking at him*]: Like what?

ALLMERS: This thing that has been done to Rita and me.

ASTA: 'Meaning' in it?

ALLMERS [*impatiently*]: Yes, meaning, I say. Because there must *be* a meaning in it. Life, existence, destiny can't surely be so utterly meaningless.

ASTA: Oh Alfred, my dear, who can say anything for certain about these things?

ALLMERS [*laughing bitterly*]: No; you're probably right there. Perhaps the whole thing works by chance, you know. Goes its own way, like a drifting wreck without a rudder.

That may very well be it. At any rate, it almost seems like it.

ASTA [*thoughtfully*]: Supposing it only seems –?

ALLMERS [*angrily*]: Really? Perhaps *you* can unravel it for me? Because *I* can't do it. [*More gently.*] Here is Eyolf, just on the point of entering the life of conscious thought. Full of such infinite possibilities. Rich possibilities, maybe. He was to fill my being with joy and pride. And all that's needed is for a mad old woman to come along and show us a dog in a bag –

ASTA: But we don't know at all how it really happened.

ALLMERS: Oh yes, we do. The boys saw her, all right, rowing out across the fjord. They saw Eyolf standing alone, right out at the end of the jetty. Saw him gaze after her – and seem to turn giddy. [*Brokenly.*] And so he fell forward – and was gone.

ASTA: Yes, yes. But all the same –

ALLMERS: She has dragged him down to the depths. Be sure of that, Asta.

ASTA: But, my dear, why should she?

ALLMERS: Yes, you see – that's the question! Why should she? There's no retribution behind it. Nothing to atone for, I mean. Eyolf never did her any harm. Never shouted after her. Never threw stones at the dog. He'd never even set eyes on her or the dog till yesterday. So there's no retribution. So pointless, the whole thing. So utterly meaningless, Asta. Nevertheless, the world order requires it.

ASTA: Have you talked to Rita about these things?

ALLMERS [*shaking his head*]: I feel as if I can talk to *you* better about this kind of thing. [*Sighs heavily.*] And about everything else, too.

[ASTA *takes her sewing things and a little paper packet out of her pocket.* ALLMERS *sits absently looking on.*]

ALLMERS: What's that you've got there, Asta?

ASTA [*taking his hat*]: A little black band.

ALLMERS: Oh, what's the use of a thing like that?

ASTA: Rita's asked me to do it. May I?

ALLMERS: Oh, yes; I don't mind.

[*She sews the band round the hat.*]

ALLMERS [*sitting looking at her*]: Where's Rita gone?

ASTA: She's walking about up in the garden, I think. Borghejm's with her.

ALLMERS [*a little surprised*]: Oh? Is Borghejm out here again today?

ASTA: Yes. He came out on the midday train.

ALLMERS: I never expected that.

ASTA [*sewing*]: He was very fond of Eyolf.

ALLMERS: Borghejm's a faithful soul, Asta.

ASTA [*with quiet warmth*]: Yes, he's faithful enough. That's certain.

ALLMERS [*fixing his eyes on her*]: You're fond of him, really.

ASTA: Yes, I am.

ALLMERS: But, all the same, you can't make up your mind to –?

ASTA [*interrupting*]: Oh, Alfred dear, don't talk about that!

ALLMERS: Yes, but just tell me why you can't –

ASTA: Oh, no! Please don't. You really mustn't ask me. It's so dreadful for me, you know. There we are. Now the hat's finished.

ALLMERS: Thank you.

ASTA: But there was the left arm too.

ALLMERS: Has *that* got to have a band as well?

ASTA: Yes, it generally does.

ALLMERS: Oh well – do what you think best.

[*She moves nearer and begins to sew.*]

ASTA: Keep your arm still. So that I don't prick you.

ALLMERS [*with a half smile*]: This is like the old days.

ASTA: Yes it is, isn't it?

ALLMERS: In the days when you were a little girl, you used to sit like this and mend my clothes.

ASTA: As best I could, yes.

ALLMERS: The first thing you sewed for me – that was a black band too.

ASTA: Was it?

ALLMERS: Round my college cap. The time Father died.

ASTA: Did I – *then*? Just think, I don't remember that.

ALLMERS: Why, no; you were so little in those days.

ASTA: Yes, I was little then.

ALLMERS: And then two years later – when we lost your mother – you sewed a large arm-band for me again.

ASTA: I thought it was the right thing to do.

ALLMERS [*patting her hand*]: Yes, yes and it *was* the right thing too, Asta. And then when we were left alone in the world, we two –. Have you finished already?

ASTA: Yes. [*She puts her sewing things together.*] That was a happy time for us Alfred, when all's said. We two alone.

ALLMERS: Yes, it was. Hard as we worked.

ASTA: *You* worked.

ALLMERS [*more alive*]: Oh you too, you worked as much in your way. [*Smiles.*] You, my dear, faithful – Eyolf.

ASTA: Oh! you mustn't remind me of that stupid trick with the name.

ALLMERS: Well, if you'd been a boy, you'd have been called Eyolf.

ASTA: Yes, *if* I had. But then when you'd become a student –. [*Smiles involuntarily.*] Fancy your being so childish even then.

ALLMERS: Was it *me* that was childish?

ASTA: Yes, when I remember it now, I think it really was. Because you were ashamed of not having any brother. Only a sister.

ALLMERS: No, that was you, you know. *You* were ashamed.

ASTA: Well, yes, perhaps I was too, a little. And then I felt rather sorry for you –

247

ALLMERS: Yes, you did. And so you looked out the old clothes I'd had as a boy –

ASTA: Your best Sunday suit, yes. Can you remember the blue blouse and the shorts?

ALLMERS [*with his eyes resting on her*]: How well I remember you when you used to put them on and wear them.

ASTA: Yes, but I only did that when we were at home alone.

ALLMERS: And how serious and proud of ourselves we were then, Asta. And I always called you Eyolf.

ASTA: But, Alfred, you've never told Rita all this, have you?

ALLMERS: Why yes, I believe I did tell her once.

ASTA: Oh but, Alfred, how could you do that?

ALLMERS: Well, you see, one tells one's wife everything – more or less.

ASTA: Yes, I suppose one does.

ALLMERS [*as if awakening, putting his hand to his forehead and jumping up*]: Oh – how can I sit here and –!

ASTA [*getting up and looking at him with distress*]: What's the matter?

ALLMERS: He almost slipped away from me. He went right out of my mind.

ASTA: Eyolf!

ALLMERS: Here was I living in memories. And he wasn't part of them.

ASTA: Oh yes, Alfred, little Eyolf was at the back of it just the same.

ALLMERS: He wasn't. He slipped out of my mind. Out of my thoughts. I didn't see him before me for a moment, while we were sitting and talking. Forgot him completely all that time.

ASTA: Oh, but you must have a little rest from your grief.

ALLMERS: No, no, no! That's just what I mustn't do! I've no business to do that. No right to. And no heart for it, either. [*He walks away to the right, deeply disturbed.*] I have only one

248

thing to do – to think of him out there, where he lies and drifts deep down.

ASTA [*following him and taking fast hold of him*]: Alfred, Alfred! Don't go to the fjord!

ALLMERS: I *must* go out to him! Let me go, Asta! I'll get the boat.

ASTA [*crying out*]: Don't go to the fjord, I tell you!

ALLMERS [*giving in*]: No, no. I won't. Let me be.

ASTA [*leading him across to the table*]: You must give your thoughts a rest, Alfred. Come here and sit down.

ALLMERS [*going to sit on the bench*]: All right. As you like.

ASTA: No, you shan't sit *there*.

ALLMERS: Yes, let me.

ASTA: No; don't. You'll only sit and look out there. [*Pushes him down on to a chair facing away from the right-hand side.*] There you are. Now you're all right. [*Sits down herself on the bench.*] And so we'll go on talking a little.

ALLMERS [*sighing audibly*]: It did me good to deaden the loss and the grief for a moment.

ASTA: You must do that, Alfred.

ALLMERS: But don't you think it's terribly unfeeling and weak of me, that I can do that?

ASTA: Not a bit. It's quite impossible to keep going over and over the same thing.

ALLMERS: Yes, it's impossible for me. Before you came down to me, I was sitting here, tormenting myself beyond words in that rending, gnawing grief –

ASTA: Yes?

ALLMERS: And, would you believe it, Asta –? Hm –

ASTA: Well?

ALLMERS: In the midst of my misery I caught myself wondering what we should have for lunch today.

ASTA [*soothingly*]: Well, well, so long as there's any relief in it, why –

ALLMERS: Yes, do you know, it seemed to me there *was* a

kind of relief in it. [*Holds out his hand to her across the table.*] What a blessing it is that I've got you, Asta. I'm so glad of that. Glad, glad – in the midst of the grief.

ASTA [*looking earnestly at him*]: First and foremost you must be glad that you have Rita.

ALLMERS: Yes, of course; that goes without saying. But Rita and I don't belong to the same family. It's not like having a sister.

ASTA [*intently*]: Do you think that, Alfred?

ALLMERS: Yes, *our* family is something apart. [*Half jokingly.*] Now, we've always had names beginning with vowels. Do you remember how often we used to talk about that? And all our relations – they're all equally poor. And we all have the same kind of eyes.

ASTA: Do you think I have too –?

ALLMERS: No, *you* take after your mother altogether. Not a bit like the rest of us. Not even like Father. But all the same –

ASTA: All the same –?

ALLMERS: Well, I believe that, all the same, living together has shaped us two after each other's likeness. In the mind, I mean.

ASTA [*much moved*]: Oh, you mustn't ever say that, Alfred. It's only I, who have taken your impression. And it's to you that I owe everything – everything good in the world.

ALLMERS [*shaking his head*]: You don't owe me anything, Asta. Just the opposite –

ASTA: I owe you everything. You must realize that yourself. No sacrifice has been too great for you –

ALLMERS [*interrupting*]: What! Sacrifice! Don't say things like that. I have only been fond of you, Asta. Ever since you were a small child. [*After a brief pause.*] And then, too, I always thought I had so much wrong to put right again.

ASTA [*amazed*]: Wrong! *You?*

ALLMERS: Not exactly on my own account. But –

ASTA [*breathless*]: But –?

ALLMERS: On Father's.

ASTA [*half starting from the bench*]: On – Father's! [*Sitting down again.*] What do you mean by that, Alfred?

ALLMERS: Father was never really nice to you.

ASTA [*impetuously*]: Oh, don't say that!

ALLMERS: Yes, because it's true. He wasn't fond of you. Not quite as he should have been.

ASTA [*evasively*]: Well, perhaps not quite in the way he was of you. But that was understandable.

ALLMERS [*continuing*]: And he was often hard to your mother, too. At any rate in the last years.

ASTA [*gently*]: Mother was so much, much younger than he. Remember that.

ALLMERS: Do you think they didn't get on well together?

ASTA: Perhaps they didn't.

ALLMERS: Yes, but all the same –. Father, who was otherwise so gentle and kind-hearted –. So friendly to everybody –.

ASTA [*quietly*]: Mother wasn't always quite what she should have been, either.

ALLMERS: Your mother wasn't?

ASTA: Perhaps not always.

ALLMERS: To Father, do you mean?

ASTA: Yes.

ALLMERS: I never noticed that.

ASTA [*getting up, fighting against tears*]: Oh, Alfred dear – let them be at peace – those who are gone. [*She goes across to the right.*]

ALLMERS [*standing up*]: Yes, let them be at peace. [*Wringing his hands.*] But those who are gone – they don't leave us in peace, Asta. Neither day nor night.

ASTA [*looking affectionately at him*]: But in time it will all feel less bitter, Alfred.

ALLMERS [*looking helplessly at her*]: Yes, don't you think so too? But how I'm to get through these first, dreadful days – [*Huskily.*] No, that I can't see.

ASTA [*laying her hands on his shoulders, pleading with him*]: Go up to Rita. Oh, I do beg you to –

ALLMERS [*withdrawing in excitement*]: No, no, no – don't talk to me about *that*! For I can't, I tell you. [*More calmly.*] Let me stay here with you.

ASTA: Yes, I won't leave you.

ALLMERS [*taking her hand and holding it fast*]: Thank you for that! [*Looking out for a moment over the fjord.*] Where is my little Eyolf gone now? [*Smiling sadly at her.*] Can you tell me *that* – you, my big, clever Eyolf? [*Shaking his head.*] No one in this whole world can tell me that. I only know the one, terrible fact, that I haven't got him any more.

ASTA [*looking up to the left and drawing back her hand*]: They're coming now.

[MRS ALLMERS *and* BORGHEJM *enter, coming down the path through the wood, she in front and he following. She is dressed in dark clothes, with a black veil over her head. He has an umbrella under his arm.*]

ALLMERS [*going to meet her*]: How do you feel, Rita?

RITA [*passing him by*]: Oh, don't ask me.

ALLMERS: What have you come here for?

RITA: Only to look for you. What are you doing?

ALLMERS: Nothing. Asta came down to me.

RITA: Yes, but before Asta came? You have been away from me all the morning.

ALLMERS: I've been sitting here and looking out over the water.

RITA: Oh – how can you!

ALLMERS [*impatiently*]: I'm best alone now!

RITA [*wandering restlessly about*]: And then sitting still! In one and the same place!

ALLMERS: But I've nothing in the world to do anywhere else.

RITA: *I* can't bear to stay anywhere. Least of all here – **with** the fjord almost beside one.

ALLMERS: That's just it – the fjord is so near.

RITA [*to* BORGHEJM]: Don't you think he ought to come up with the rest of us?

BORGHEJM [*to* ALLMERS]: I believe it would be better for you.

ALLMERS: No, no – let me stay where I am.

RITA: Then I'll stay with you, Alfred.

ALLMERS: Very well, you stay, then. You stay too, Asta.

ASTA [*whispering to* BORGHEJM]: Let them be alone.

BORGHEJM [*with a glance of understanding*]: Miss Allmers, shall we go on a little way – along the shore? For the very last time?

ASTA [*picking up her umbrella*]: Yes, come along. Let's go on a little further.

[ASTA *and* BORGHEJM *go out together behind the boat-house.* ALLMERS *walks about for a little and then sits down on a stone under the trees in the foreground to the left.*]

RITA [*coming nearer and standing in front of him, her hands hanging folded before her*]: Can you take it in, Alfred, the thought that we've lost Eyolf?

ALLMERS [*looking drearily at the ground*]: We've got to get used to the thought.

RITA: I can't. I can't. And then this terrible sight that will be with me all through my life.

ALLMERS [*looking up*]: What sight? What have you seen?

RITA: I haven't seen anything myself. Only heard them describe it. Oh –!

ALLMERS: You'd better tell me at once.

RITA: I took Borghejm down with me to the jetty –

ALLMERS: What did you want there?

RITA: To ask the boys how it had happened.

ALLMERS: We know that well enough.

RITA: We found out some more

ALLMERS: Well?

RITA: It's not true, what they said, that he was carried right away at once.

ALLMERS: Do they say *that* now?

RITA: Yes, they say they saw him lying down at the bottom. Deep down in the clear water.

ALLMERS [*grinding his teeth*]: And they didn't save him!

RITA: They probably couldn't.

ALLMERS: They could swim. All of them. Did they say how he was lying when they saw him?

RITA: Yes. They said he was lying on his back. And with wide open eyes.

ALLMERS: Open eyes. But quite still?

RITA: Yes, quite still. And then something came and carried him away out. They called it an undertow.

ALLMERS [*nodding slowly*]: So *that* was the last they saw of him.

RITA [*choked with tears*]: Yes.

ALLMERS [*in a toneless voice*]: And never – never will anyone see him again.

RITA [*wailing*]: Day and night he will be before me, as he lay down there.

ALLMERS: With the wide open eyes.

RITA [*shuddering*]: Yes, with the wide open eyes. I see them! I see them before me.

ALLMERS [*getting up slowly, looking at her quietly, but with menace*]: Were they evil, those eyes, Rita?

RITA [*turning pale*]: Evil –!

ALLMERS [*going close up to her*]: Were they evil eyes that stared up? Down there, from the deep?

RITA [*shrinking back*]: Alfred –!

ALLMERS [*following*]: Answer me that! Were they the evil eyes of a child?

RITA [*screaming*]: Alfred! Alfred!

ALLMERS: Now we have it – the very thing you wanted, Rita.

RITA: I? What did *I* want?

ALLMERS: That Eyolf was not here.

RITA: Never in the world did I want that! That Eyolf didn't stand between us two – that was what I wanted.

ALLMERS: Well – in future he won't do that any more.

RITA [*in a low voice, staring in front of her*]: Most of all, perhaps, in future. [*Starting.*] Oh, that terrible sight!

ALLMERS [*nodding*]: The evil eyes of a child. Yes.

RITA [*in terror, shrinking back*]: Leave me alone, Alfred! I'm afraid of you! I've never seen you like this before.

ALLMERS [*looking hard and coldly at her*]: Grief makes people evil and ugly.

RITA [*afraid, but yet defiant*]: I feel that's so, myself.

[ALLMERS *goes over to the right and looks out over the fjord.* RITA *sits down by the table. There is a short pause.*]

ALLMERS [*turning his head towards her*]: You've never really loved him. Never!

RITA [*cold and controlled*]: Eyolf would never really let me take him to my heart.

ALLMERS: Because you didn't want to.

RITA: Oh yes, I did. I wanted to very much. But someone stood in the way. Right from the beginning.

ALLMERS [*turning completely round*]: *I* stood in the way, do you mean?

RITA: Oh no. Not from the beginning.

ALLMERS [*going nearer*]: Who, then?

RITA: His aunt.

ALLMERS: Asta?

RITA: Yes. Asta stood and barred the way for me.

ALLMERS: Can you say that, Rita?

RITA: Yes. Asta – she took him to her heart. From the time it happened – that dreadful fall.

ALLMERS: If she did that she did it out of love.

RITA [*angrily*]: Exactly! I can't bear to share a thing with anyone else! Not when it's love!

ALLMERS: We two should have shared him between us in love.

RITA [*looking at him with scorn*]: We? Oh, you've never had any real love for him either, not really.

ALLMERS [*looking at her in surprise*]: *I* haven't –!

RITA: No, you haven't. At first you were so wrapped up in that book – on responsibility.

ALLMERS [*firmly*]: Yes, I was. But it was that very thing, you know, that I sacrificed for Eyolf's sake.

RITA: Not for love of him.

ALLMERS: Why, then, do you suppose?

RITA: Because you were getting consumed with mistrust of yourself. Because you'd begun to doubt whether you *had* any great task in the world to live for.

ALLMERS [*searchingly*]: Did you notice anything like that in me?

RITA: Oh, yes. By degrees. And so you had to have something new to satisfy you. I suppose *I* was no longer enough for you.

ALLMERS: That's the law of change, Rita.

RITA: That was why you wanted to make a wonder-child of poor little Eyolf.

ALLMERS: I didn't want to. I wanted to make a happy creature of him. That was all I wanted.

RITA: But not for love of him. Look into yourself. [*With embarrassment in her expression.*] And examine all that lies beneath it – and behind.

ALLMERS [*avoiding her eyes*]: There's something you don't want to admit.

RITA: You too.

ALLMERS [*looking thoughtfully at her*]: If it is what you think, then we two have never really possessed our own child.

RITA: No. Not fully, in love.

ALLMERS: And yet here we are, grieving so bitterly over him.

RITA [*bitterly*]: Yes, isn't it odd to think of? Here we are, grieving like this, over a strange little boy.

ALLMERS [*protesting*]: Oh, don't call him strange!

RITA [*shaking her head miserably*]: We never won the child, Alfred. I didn't. Nor did you.

ALLMERS [*wringing his hands*]: And now it's too late! Too late!

RITA: And so utterly desolate – everything.

ALLMERS [*flaring up suddenly*]: You're the guilty one here!

RITA [*getting up*]: *I*!

ALLMERS: Yes, *you*! It's your fault that he became – what he was. It's your fault that he couldn't save himself in the water.

RITA [*in protest*]: Alfred, you shan't lay the blame on me!

ALLMERS [*more and more nearly beside himself*]: Oh yes, I do. It was you who left that tiny child lying on the table to look after himself.

RITA: He was lying so comfortably on the pillows. And sleeping so soundly. And you had promised to look after the child.

ALLMERS: Yes, I had. [*Dropping his voice.*] But then you came, you, you – and drew me to you.

RITA [*looking defiantly at him*]: Say rather that you forgot the child and everything else.

ALLMERS [*in suppressed fury*]: Yes, that's true. [*In a lower voice.*] I forgot the child – in your arms!

RITA [*outraged*]: Alfred! Alfred, that's abominable of you!

ALLMERS [*quietly, clenching his fists against her*]: In that moment you condemned little Eyolf to death.

RITA [*wildly*]: So did you! You, too! If that's true.

ALLMERS: Oh yes – call me to account too, if you want to. We've sinned, both of us. And so there *was* retribution in Eyolf's death after all.

RITA: Retribution?

ALLMERS [*more controlled*]: Yes. A judgement on you and me. Here we are now, where we deserve to be. We let ourselves shrink from him while he was alive, in secret, craven remorse. Couldn't bear to see it – the thing he had to drag about –

RITA [*in a low voice*]: The crutch.

ALLMERS: Yes, that. And this thing that we're now calling grief and bereavement – it's the gnawing of conscience, Rita. Nothing else.

RITA [*looking at him helplessly*]: I think this is going to drive us to despair – to madness, both of us. Because we can never – never put it right again.

ALLMERS [*controlled by a quieter mood*]: I dreamt about Eyolf last night. I thought I saw him coming up from the jetty. He could jump, like other boys. And so nothing had happened to him. Neither the one nor the other ... I thought the heart-breaking truth was only a dream after all. Oh, how I thanked and blessed – [*Checking himself.*] Hm –

RITA [*looking at him*]: Whom?

ALLMERS [*evasively*]: Whom –?

RITA: Yes; whom did you thank and bless?

ALLMERS [*avoiding her question*]: I was lying dreaming, you know –

RITA: Someone whom you don't believe in yourself?

ALLMERS: It came over me like that, all the same. I was asleep, of course –

RITA [*reproachfully*]: You shouldn't have taken away my faith, Alfred.

ALLMERS: Would it have been right of me, if I'd let you go through life on empty fancies?

RITA: It would have been better for me. For then I should have had something to hold on to. Now I don't know where I am.

ALLMERS [*looking keenly at her*]: If you had your choice, now –. If you could follow Eyolf down there, where he is now –?

RITA: Yes? What then?

ALLMERS: If you were quite certain that you would find him again, know him, understand him –?

RITA: Yes, yes; what then?

ALLMERS: Would you then, of your own free will, make the leap across to him? Go away of your own free will from everything here? Take your leave of the whole life of the earth? Would you do that, Rita?

RITA [*in a low voice*]: Now, at once?

ALLMERS: Yes; now; today. This very hour. Answer that. Would you?

RITA [*hesitant*]: Oh, I don't know, Alfred. No; I believe I'd want to stay here for a time with you.

ALLMERS: For my sake?

RITA: Yes, only for your sake.

ALLMERS: But then afterwards? Would you then –? Answer!

RITA: Oh, how can I answer a thing like that? No, I couldn't go away from you. Never! Never!

ALLMERS: But now, if I went to Eyolf? And if you had the fullest conviction that you would meet both him and me there. Would you come over to us then?

RITA: I should want to. Oh, so much! So much! But –

ALLMERS: Well?

RITA [*moaning softly*]: I couldn't do it – I feel I couldn't. No, no; I couldn't possibly do it. Not for all the glory of heaven!

ALLMERS: Nor could I.

RITA: No, that's true, Alfred, isn't it? You couldn't do it either, could you?

ALLMERS: No. For it's here, in the life of the earth, we living creatures belong and are at home.

RITA: Yes, here's the kind of happiness we understand.

ALLMERS [*gloomily*]: Oh, happiness – happiness, my dear –

RITA: I suppose you mean that happiness – we shall never find it again. [*Looking questioningly at him.*] But supposing –? [*Passionately.*] No, no; I daren't say that! Nor even think it.

ALLMERS: Yes, say it. Say it, Rita.

RITA [*hesitating*]: Couldn't we try to –? Wouldn't it be possible for us to forget him?

ALLMERS: Forget Eyolf...

RITA: Forget the remorse and the misery, I mean.

ALLMERS: Would you want to do that?

RITA: Yes. If only it could be done. [*Breaking out.*] Because all this – there'll come a time when I shan't be able to bear it! Oh, can't we find anything that will help us to forget?

ALLMERS [*shaking his head*]: Why, what could it be?

RITA: Couldn't we try travelling – far away?

ALLMERS: Away from home? You, who are never really well anywhere else but here.

RITA: Well, then, what about having a lot of people in? Keeping open house. Throwing ourselves into something that might deaden and dull –

ALLMERS: That sort of life's no good to me. No. I'd do better to try and take up my work again.

RITA [*bitterly*]: Your work? The thing that's so often stood like a barrier between us?

ALLMERS [*slowly, looking sternly at her*]: There must always be a barrier between us two in future.

RITA: Why must there –?

ALLMERS: Who knows whether the wide open eyes of a child aren't watching us night and day?

RITA [*low, shuddering*]: Alfred – that's a terrible thought to have!

ALLMERS: Our love has been like a consuming fire. Now it must be quenched –

RITA [*going towards him*]: Quenched!

ALLMERS [*in a hard voice*]: It is quenched – in one of us.

RITA [*as if turned to stone*]: And you dare say that to me!

ALLMERS [*more gently*]: It's dead, Rita. But in what I feel for you now, in our common guilt and longing to atone – in that I think I see a kind of resurrection –

RITA [*violently*]: Oh, I'm not interested in resurrections!

ALLMERS: Rita!

RITA: I'm a warm-blooded human animal, myself! I don't go round drowsing – with fish-blood in my veins. [*Wringing her hands.*] And to be shut in for a life-time – in remorse and misery! Shut in with someone who's no longer mine, mine, mine.

ALLMERS: It had to end like this, Rita, some day.

RITA: Had to end like this! What began between us as passion so eagerly shared!

ALLMERS: I did not share your passion from the first.

RITA: What did you feel for me, then, at the very beginning?

ALLMERS: Dread.

RITA: That I can understand. But how did I win you, then, after all?

ALLMERS [*quietly*]: You were so irresistibly beautiful, Rita.

RITA [*looking searchingly at him*]: And so it was only that? Tell me, Alfred! Only that?

ALLMERS [*mastering himself*]: No; there was something else besides.

RITA [*breaking out*]: I can guess what that something was! It was 'the gold and the green forests', as you call it. Wasn't it, Alfred?

ALLMERS: Yes.

RITA [*looking at him, deeply reproachful*]: How could – how could you!

ALLMERS: I had Asta to think of.

RITA [*angrily*]: Asta, yes! [*Bitterly.*] And so it was Asta, in fact, who brought us two together.

ALLMERS: She knew nothing about it. She doesn't even suspect it, to this very day.

RITA [*putting it aside*]: It was Asta, all the same. [*Smiling with a contemptuous glance sideways.*] Or no, – it was little Eyolf. Little Eyolf, you know.

ALLMERS: Eyolf –?

RITA: Yes. Usedn't you to call her Eyolf? I think you said so once – in a secret moment. [*Going nearer.*] Do you remember it, Alfred, that irresistibly beautiful moment?

ALLMERS [*shrinking back as if in horror*]: I don't remember anything! I won't remember!

RITA [*following him*]: It was in that hour – that your other little Eyolf was crippled.

ALLMERS [*in a toneless voice, supporting himself by the table*]: Retribution.

RITA [*threatening*]: Yes, retribution.

> [ASTA *and* BORGHEJM *come back by the boat-house. She is carrying some water-lilies in her hand.*]

RITA [*controlled*]: Well, Asta, have you and Mr Borghejm managed to talk things over thoroughly?

ASTA: Yes. More or less. [*She puts down her umbrella and lays the flowers on a chair.*]

BORGHEJM: Miss Allmers has been very reticent on our walk.

RITA: Really? Has she? Well, Alfred and I've managed to talk things over enough to –

ASTA [*looking breathlessly at both of them*]: What's this?

RITA: – to last for the rest of our lives, I should say. [*Breaking off.*] But come along, now, let's go up, all four of us. We must have people about us in future. Alfred and I can't get along alone.

ALLMERS: Yes, just go ahead, you two. [*Turning.*] But I must have a word with you first, Asta.

RITA [*looking at him*]: Must you? Oh well, you come with me then, Mr Borghejm.

> [RITA *and* BORGHEJM *go up the wood-path.*]

ASTA [*anxiously*]: Alfred, what's the matter?

ALLMERS [*gloomily*]: The fact is, I can't hold out any longer here.

ASTA: Here! With Rita, do you mean?

ALLMERS: Yes. Rita and I can't go on living together.

ASTA [*shaking him by the arm*]: But, Alfred – don't say anything so dreadful!

ALLMERS: It's true, what I say. We are making one another evil and ugly.

ASTA [*sharply distressed*]: Oh, I never – never dreamt of anything like this!

ALLMERS: It didn't occur to me either until today.

ASTA: And now you want –! Yes, what is it you really want, Alfred?

ALLMERS: I want to get away from everything here. Far away from all of it.

ASTA: And stand quite alone in the world?

ALLMERS [*nodding*]: Just as before, yes.

ASTA: But you're not made for standing alone!

ALLMERS: Oh yes I am. I was before, at any rate.

ASTA: Before – yes. But then you had me with you.

ALLMERS [*trying to take her hand*]: Yes. And it's you, Asta, that I want to come home to again.

ASTA [*avoiding him*]: To me! No, no, Alfred! That's utterly impossible.

ALLMERS [*looking sadly at her*]: So Borghejm does stand in the way after all?

ASTA [*earnestly*]: No, no; he doesn't! You're wrong there!

ALLMERS: Good. Then I'll come to you – my dear, dear sister. I *must* come back to you. Home to you, to be purified and restored after my life with –

ASTA [*shocked*]: Alfred, that's a sin against Rita!

ALLMERS: I *have* sinned against her. But not in this. Oh, just think of it, Asta! What was our life like together, yours and mine? Wasn't it like one long, high holy day from first to last?

ASTA: Yes, it was, Alfred. But a time like that can't be lived over again.

ALLMERS [*bitterly*]: Do you mean that marriage has ruined me so completely?

ASTA [*peaceably*]: No, I don't mean that.

ALLMERS: Well, then, we two will live our old life over again.

ASTA [*decidedly*]: We can't do that, Alfred.

ALLMERS: Yes, we can. A brother's and sister's love –

ASTA [*breathless*]: Yes, what?

ALLMERS: That relation is the only one that's not subject to the law of change.

ASTA [*in a low voice, trembling*]: But if that relation were not –

ALLMERS: Not?

ASTA: – not *our* relation?

ALLMERS [*looking at her with amazement*]: Not ours? My dear, what do you mean by that?

ASTA: It's best for me to tell you at once, Alfred.

ALLMERS: Yes, yes, tell me!

ASTA: The letters to my mother –. Those in the brief-case –

ALLMERS: Yes, well?

ASTA: You must take them and read them – when I'm gone.

ALLMERS: Why must I?

ASTA [*battling with herself*]: Why, because then you'll see that –

ALLMERS: Well?

ASTA: – that I've no right to have – your father's name.

ALLMERS [*falling back*]: Asta! What's this you're saying!

ASTA: Read the letters. Then you'll see. And understand. And perhaps forgive – my mother, too.

ALLMERS [*clasping his head*]: I can't take this in. Can't get hold of the idea. You, Asta, – then you're not –

ASTA: You're not my brother, Alfred.

ALLMERS [*looking at her quickly, half defiant*]: Well, but what's really changed in our relation? Nothing, really.

ASTA [*shaking her head*]: Everything's changed, Alfred. Our relationship isn't a brother's and sister's.

ALLMERS: Well, no. But just as sacred for all that. Always will be as sacred.

ASTA: Don't forget, – it's subject to the law of change, – as you said a moment ago.

ALLMERS [*looking searchingly at her*]: Do you mean by that, that –?

ASTA [*quietly, deeply moved*]: Not another word. Dear, dear Alfred. [*She takes the flowers from the chair.*] Do you see these water-lilies?

ALLMERS [*nodding slowly*]: They're the kind that stretch up, from deep down at the bottom.

ASTA: I picked them in the tarn. Just where it flows out into the fjord. [*Holding them out.*] Will you have them, Alfred?

ALLMERS [*taking them*]: Thank you.

ASTA [*her eyes full of tears*]: They are like a last greeting to you from – from little Eyolf.

ALLMERS [*looking at her*]: From Eyolf who is out there? Or from you?

ASTA [*quietly*]: From us both. [*Picking up the umbrella.*] Now come up with me to Rita. [*She goes up the wood-path.*]

ALLMERS [*taking his hat from the table and whispering sadly*]: Asta. Eyolf. Little Eyolf –! [*He follows her up the path.*]

ACT THREE

A high crag overgrown with copsewood in Allmers' grounds. A steep precipice with a railing in the background and a flight of steps leading down on the left. A wide prospect over the fjord, which lies far below. A flagstaff with halyard but no flag stands beside the railing. In the foreground on the right is a summer-house, covered with climbing plants and wild vines. A bench out in front of it. It is late in the summer evening with a clear sky. Twilight is coming on. ASTA is sitting on the bench with her hands in her lap. She is wearing her coat and hat, has her parasol beside her and a little haversack on a strap over her shoulder. BORGHEJM comes up from the back on the left. He too has a haversack over his shoulder. Under his arm he is carrying a rolled-up flag.

BORGHEJM [*catching sight of* ASTA]: Oh, so you're up here?

ASTA: I was looking out there for the last time.

BORGHEJM: So it was just as well I had a look up here too.

ASTA: Have you been looking for me?

BORGHEJM: Yes, I have. I very much wanted to say good-bye to you – for the present. Not for the last time, I hope.

ASTA [*with a subdued smile*]: You're indefatigable, aren't you?

BORGHEJM: A road-builder has to be.

ASTA: Did you see anything of Alfred? Or Rita?

BORGHEJM: Yes, I saw them both.

ASTA: Together?

BORGHEJM: No. Each in a different place.

ASTA: What are you going to do with the flag?

BORGHEJM: Mrs Allmers asked me to come and run it up.

ASTA: Run up the flag now?

BORGHEJM: At half-mast. It's to fly there night and day, she said.

ASTA [*sighing*]: Poor Rita. And poor Alfred.

BORGHEJM [*busy with the flag*]: Have you the heart to go away from them? I'm asking because I see you're dressed for travelling.

ASTA [*in a low voice*]: I *must* go.

BORGHEJM: Oh well, if you *must*, then –

ASTA: And of course you go tonight, too.

BORGHEJM: I must too. I'm taking the train. Are you doing that?

ASTA: No. I'm going in by the steamer.

BORGHEJM [*glancing at her*]: Each his own way, then.

ASTA: Yes. [*She sits and watches while he hoists the flag to half-mast. When he has finished he goes across to her.*]

BORGHEJM: Miss Asta, – you can't imagine how sad I am about little Eyolf.

ASTA [*looking up at him*]: Yes, I'm sure you are.

BORGHEJM: And it's so hard for me. Because it doesn't really come naturally to me to be sad.

ASTA [*turning her eyes to the flag*]: It will pass over in time – all of it. All our sorrows.

BORGHEJM: All? Do you believe that?

ASTA: Like stormy weather. When once you get a long way away, then –

BORGHEJM: It'll have to be a *very* long way away.

ASTA: And then you've got this great, new piece of road work, too.

BORGHEJM: But no one to help me with it.

ASTA: Oh yes, of course you have.

BORGHEJM [*shaking his head*]: No one. No one to share the joy with. Because it's the joy that matters most.

ASTA: Not the effort and the trouble?

BORGHEJM: Pooh! One can always get through that sort of thing alone.

ASTA: But joy – that must be shared with someone, you mean?

BORGHEJM: Yes, what fun would there be otherwise in having the joy?

ASTA: Ah, well, – there may be something in that.

BORGHEJM: Oh, naturally one can make shift for a time to feel glad inside oneself. But it doesn't work for long. No; joy, there must be two for that.

ASTA: Always just two? Never more? Never several?

BORGHEJM: Ah, but – that's a different kind of thing. Miss Asta, can't you really bring yourself, after all, to share happiness and joy and – and effort and trouble with *one* person, – with *one* single person only?

ASTA: I've tried it – once.

BORGHEJM: Have you!

ASTA: Yes, all that time that my brother – that Alfred and I lived together.

BORGHEJM: Oh, with your brother, yes. That's something quite different. I think that's better described as peace than happiness.

ASTA: It was lovely all the same.

BORGHEJM: Now, look – even *that* seems lovely to you. But just think, – if he hadn't been your brother!

ASTA [*on the point of getting up, but remains sitting*]: Then of course we should never have lived together. For I was a child then. And he not much more.

BORGHEJM [*after a moment*]: *Was* it so lovely, that time?

ASTA: Yes, believe me, it was.

BORGHEJM: Did anything really gay and happy come your way in those days?

ASTA: Oh yes, lots of things. A tremendous lot.

BORGHEJM: Tell me a bit about it, Miss Asta.

ASTA: Only small things, really...

BORGHEJM: Such as –? Well?

ASTA: Such as the time when Alfred had taken his examination. And had come out so well. And then when he got a post, from time to time, in some school or other. Or when he sat writing an article. And read it out to me. And later on got it printed in a paper.

BORGHEJM: Yes, I quite believe it must have been a pleasant, peaceful life. A brother and sister sharing their happiness. [*Shaking his head.*] I can't see how your brother could let you go, Asta!

ASTA [*suppressing her emotion*]: Alfred got married, you see.

BORGHEJM: Wasn't that hard on you?

ASTA: Oh yes, at first. I felt I'd lost him completely all at once.

BORGHEJM: Well, luckily you hadn't done that.

ASTA: No.

BORGHEJM: But, all the same – how could he do it! Marry, I mean – when he could have kept you all to himself.

ASTA [*looking straight in front of her*]: He was subject to the law of change, I suppose.

BORGHEJM: The law of change?

ASTA: Alfred calls it that.

BORGHEJM: Pooh, – a stupid sort of law, that must be! I don't believe in that law for a moment.

ASTA [*getting up*]: You may come to believe in it in time.

BORGHEJM: Never while I live! [*Earnestly.*] But look here, Miss Asta! Do be reasonable – for once in a while. In this business, I mean –

ASTA [*interrupting*]: Oh no, no, – *don't* let us start on that again!

BORGHEJM [*continuing as before*]: Yes, Asta – I can't possibly let you go so easily. Your brother's got everything arranged now the way he likes best. He's living his life quite contentedly without you. Doesn't miss you at all. And then there's the – the thing that at one stroke alters your whole position out here –

ASTA [*starting*]: What do you mean by that?

BORGHEJM: The child's gone. What else?

ASTA [*recovering herself*]: Little Eyolf's gone; yes.

BORGHEJM: And so what more have you really to do here?

You haven't got the poor little boy to look after any longer. No duties, no work here of any kind –

ASTA: Oh, please, Mr Borghejm – don't make it so hard for me!

BORGHEJM: Why, I should have to be a fool, not to try my utmost. One of these days I shall leave town. Shan't be able to meet you there. Perhaps not be able to see you again for a long, long time. And who knows what may happen in the meanwhile?

ASTA [*smiling seriously*]: Are you afraid of the law of change, after all?

BORGHEJM: No; that I am *not*! [*Laughs bitterly.*] And there's nothing to change, either. Not with you, I mean. For you don't care much about me, I can see.

ASTA: You know very well I do.

BORGHEJM: Yes, but not *enough*, by a long way. Not in the way I want. [*More excitedly.*] Good lord, Asta – Miss Asta– this is crazy of you! Absolutely mad! Somewhere in the next few days, perhaps, all life's happiness may be lying waiting for us. And we're to let it lie! Aren't we going to regret that, Asta?

ASTA [*quietly*]: I don't know. But we have to let them lie, just the same – all the radiant possibilities.

BORGHEJM [*controlling himself and looking at her*]: I'm to build my roads alone, then?

ASTA [*warmly*]: Oh, if only I could share that with you! Help you with the work. Share the joy with you –

BORGHEJM: Would you do it – if you could?

ASTA: Yes. I would.

BORGHEJM: But you can't?

ASTA [*looking down*]: Would you be satisfied with half of me?

BORGHEJM: No. I must have you whole and entire.

ASTA [*looking at him and speaking quietly*]: Then I can't.

BORGHEJM: Good-bye, then, Miss Asta. [*He is about to go.*

ALLMERS *comes up the height in the background from the left.*
BORGHEJM *stops.*]

ALLMERS [*at the top of the steps, speaking quietly and pointing*]:
Is Rita in there in the summer-house?

BORGHEJM: No; there's no one here but Miss Asta. [ALL-
MERS *comes nearer.*]

ASTA [*going towards him*]: Shall I go down and look for her?
Bring her up here, perhaps?

ALLMERS [*putting the suggestion aside*]: No, no, no. Let it
be. [*To* BORGHEJM.] Is it you who've hoisted the flag
there?

BORGHEJM: Yes. Mrs Allmers asked me to. That's why I
came up here.

ALLMERS: And you go tonight, don't you?

BORGHEJM: Yes. Tonight I'm going for certain.

ALLMERS [*with a glance towards* ASTA]: And have secured a
good travelling companion, I expect.

BORGHEJM [*shaking his head*]: I'm travelling alone.

ALLMERS [*surprised*]: Alone!

BORGHEJM: Quite alone.

ALLMERS [*absently*]: Really?

BORGHEJM: And shall remain alone, too.

ALLMERS: There's something terrible in being alone. It seems
to chill me right through –

ASTA: Oh but, Alfred, you're not alone!

ALLMERS: There can be something terrible in *that* too,
Asta.

ASTA [*sick at heart*]: Oh, don't talk like that! Don't think like
that!

ALLMERS [*without listening to her*]: But since you're not travelling with –? Since there's nothing that ties you? Why
won't you stay out here with me – and with Rita?

ASTA [*uneasily*]: No, I can't do that. I simply must go into
town now.

ALLMERS: But only into town, Asta. You hear!

ASTA: Yes.

ALLMERS: And you're to promise me you'll come out here again quite soon.

ASTA [*quickly*]: No, no; I can't promise you that, as yet.

ALLMERS: All right. As you like. So we'll meet in town, then.

ASTA [*imploring*]: But, Alfred, you *must* stay at home with Rita now!

ALLMERS [*turns to* BORGHEJM, *without answering*]: It might be best for you not to have any travelling companion after all.

BORGHEJM [*protesting*]: Oh, how can you say a thing like that!

ALLMERS: Yes, because you can never tell whom you may happen to meet afterwards. On the way.

ASTA [*involuntarily*]: Alfred!

ALLMERS: The right companion for the journey. When it is too late. Too late.

ASTA [*low and tremulously*]: Alfred! Alfred!

BORGHEJM [*looking from one to the other*]: What does this mean? I don't understand –

[RITA *comes up from the left at the back.*]

RITA [*with a cry of distress*]: Oh, don't all go away from me!

ASTA [*going to meet her*]: You said you'd rather be alone –

RITA: Yes, but I daren't. It's beginning to get so dark and ugly. I feel as if there were wide open eyes looking at me.

ASTA [*softly and with sympathy*]: And even if there were, Rita? You shouldn't be afraid of those eyes.

RITA: How can you say that! Not afraid!

ALLMERS [*earnestly*]: Asta, I implore you – by everything on earth – stay here – with Rita!

RITA: Yes! And with Alfred too! Do! Do, Asta!

ASTA [*fighting*]: Oh, I want to, more than I can say –

RITA: Well, do it, then! For Alfred and I *can't* live through the grief and the loss alone.

ALLMERS [*sombrely*]: Say rather – through the remorse and the torment.

RITA: Oh, whatever you want to call it – we can't bear it alone, the two of us. Oh, Asta, I do beg and beseech you! Stay here and help us! Take Eyolf's place for us –

ASTA [*shrinking*]: Eyolf's –!

RITA: Yes, won't she be welcome to, Alfred?

ALLMERS: If she will and can.

RITA: You used to call her your little Eyolf before. [*Seizing her hand*.] In future you shall be *our* Eyolf, Asta! Eyolf, just as you were before.

ALLMERS [*with controlled passion*]: Stay – and share our life, Asta. With Rita. With me. With me – your brother!

ASTA [*having reached her decision, withdrawing her hand*]: No. I can't. [*Turning to* BORGHEJM.] Mr Borghejm, what time does the steamer go?

BORGHEJM: Immediately.

ASTA: Then I must go on board. Will you come with me?

BORGHEJM [*with a suppressed outburst of joy*]: Will I? Yes, yes, yes!

ASTA: Come along, then.

RITA [*slowly*]: Ah, that's it. Well, then you can't stay with us.

ASTA [*throwing herself on her neck*]: Thank you for everything, Rita! [*Crossing over and seizing* ALFRED'S *hand*.] Alfred, – good-bye! A thousand, thousand good-byes!

ALLMERS [*low and eagerly*]: What is this, Asta? It looks like flight.

ASTA [*in quiet anguish*]: Yes, Alfred. It is a flight.

ALLMERS: A flight – from *me*!

ASTA [*whispering*]: A flight from you – and from myself.

ALLMERS [*shrinking back*]: Ah –!

> [ASTA *goes quickly down the path in the background.* BORGHEJM *waves his hat and follows her.* RITA *leans against the entrance to the summer-house.* ALLMERS, *in great mental agitation, goes over to the railing and stands there, looking down. A pause.*]

ALLMERS [*turning and speaking with hard-won control*]: Here comes the steamer. Look there Rita.

RITA: I daren't look at it.

ALLMERS: You daren't?

RITA: No. Because it has a red eye. And a green one, too. Great glowing eyes.

ALLMERS: Why, that's only the lights, you know.

RITA: In future they will be eyes. For me. They gaze and gaze out of the gloom. And into the gloom too.

ALLMERS: Now it's come alongside.

RITA: Where is it putting in tonight, then?

ALLMERS [*nearer*]: At the jetty, as usual, my dear –

RITA [*standing erect*]: How *can* it put in *there*!

ALLMERS: It must.

RITA: But it was *there* that Eyolf –! How *can* those people put in there!

ALLMERS: Yes, life is pitiless, Rita.

RITA: Human beings are heartless. They've no thought. Either for the living or for the dead.

ALLMERS: You're quite right. Life goes on its way. Exactly as if nothing in the world had happened.

RITA [*looking straight in front of her*]: It's rather that nothing *has* happened. Not for the others. Only for us two.

ALLMERS [*his grief awaking*]: Yes, Rita, – it was so useless, your bearing him in pain and tears. Because now he's gone again – and left no trace behind him.

RITA: Only the crutch was saved.

ALLMERS [*angrily*]: Be quiet! Don't let me hear that word!

RITA [*lamenting*]: Oh, I can't bear the thought, that we haven't got him any more.

ALLMERS [*coldly and bitterly*]: You could do without him perfectly well, while you had him. You didn't set eyes on him for half a day at a time.

RITA: No, because then I knew that I could see him any moment I wanted to.

ALLMERS: Yes, that's just how we've gone on, throwing away the short time we had with little Eyolf.

RITA [*listening, in anguish*]: Do you hear, Alfred! Now it's ringing again!

ALLMERS [*looking out*]: It's the steamer, that's ringing. They're just putting out.

RITA: Oh, it's not *that* bell I mean. I've heard it all day ringing in my ears. Now it's ringing again!

ALLMERS [*going across to her*]: You're mistaken, Rita.

RITA: No, I hear it so clearly. It sounds like the passing-bell. Slow. Slow. And always the same words.

ALLMERS: Words? What words?

RITA [*nodding, in time*]: 'The crutch – is float – ing. The crutch – is float – ing.' Oh, surely you must be able to hear it too.

ALLMERS [*shaking his head*]: I don't hear anything. And there isn't anything, either.

RITA: Oh, yes, you can say what you like. I hear it so clearly.

ALLMERS [*looking out over the railing*]: They're on board now, Rita. The boat's crossing now to the town.

RITA: To think you can't hear it! 'The crutch – is float – ing. The crutch – is float – ing.'

ALLMERS [*going across*]: You're not to stand listening for something that doesn't exist. I'm telling you that Asta and Borghejm are on board now. On their way already. Asta is gone.

RITA [*looking timidly at him*]: So I suppose you will soon be gone too, Alfred?

ALLMERS [*quickly*]: What do you mean by *that*?

RITA: That you'll follow your sister.

ALLMERS: Has Asta said anything?

RITA: No. But you said yourself it was for Asta's sake that – that we two came together.

ALLMERS: Yes, but you, you yourself held me. By our life together.

RITA: Oh, but I'm not—not so – irresistibly beautiful for you any more.

ALLMERS: The law of change could perhaps hold us together, nevertheless.

RITA [nodding slowly]: There is a change going on in me now. I find it agonizing.

ALLMERS: Agonizing?

RITA: Yes, for there's something like birth in that too.

ALLMERS: It is that. Or a resurrection. Passing on to higher life.

RITA [looking despondently before her]: Yes, – with the loss of all, all life's happiness.

ALLMERS: That loss, that is precisely the gain.

RITA [angrily]: Oh, words! Good lord, we're creatures of earth, after all.

ALLMERS: We have some kinship with sea and heavens too, Rita.

RITA: You, perhaps. Not I.

ALLMERS: Oh yes. You, more than you realize yourself.

RITA [coming a step nearer]: Listen, Alfred – couldn't you think of taking up your work again?

ALLMERS: The work you used to hate?

RITA: I'm more easily satisfied now. I'm willing to share you with the book.

ALLMERS: Why?

RITA: Simply to keep you here with me. Just near at hand.

ALLMERS: Oh, I can help you so little, Rita.

RITA: But perhaps I could help you.

ALLMERS: With my work, do you mean?

RITA: No. To live your life.

ALLMERS [shaking his head]: I don't think I've any life to live.

RITA: Well, to bear your life, then.

ALLMERS [looking sombrely before him]: I believe it would be best for both of us if we parted.

RITA [*looking searchingly at him*]: Where would you go, then? Maybe to Asta, after all?

ALLMERS: No. Never to Asta again.

RITA: Where, then?

ALLMERS: Up to the solitude.

RITA: Up among the hills? Is *that* what you mean?

ALLMERS: Yes.

RITA: But this is mere fantasy, Alfred! You couldn't live up there.

ALLMERS: I'm drawn to them, nevertheless.

RITA: Why? Tell me why!

ALLMERS: Sit down. And I'll tell you something.

RITA: Something that happened to you up there?

ALLMERS: Yes.

RITA: And that you didn't tell Asta and me?

ALLMERS: Yes.

RITA: Ah, you're so quiet about everything. You shouldn't be.

ALLMERS: Sit down there. And I'll tell you about it.

RITA: Yes, yes – you tell me! [*She sits on the bench by the summer-house.*]

ALLMERS: I was alone up there. In the middle of the high fells. And I came to a great, desolate mountain lake. And that lake I had to cross. But I couldn't do it. For there was no boat and no people.

RITA: Well? And so?

ALLMERS: So I struck out on my own into a side valley. For there I thought I should come out above the fells and among the mountain-tops. And down again to the other side of the lake.

RITA: Oh, Alfred! So I suppose you lost your bearings!

ALLMERS: Yes; I made a mistake in the direction. For there was no road or path. And I walked the whole day. And the whole of the next night, too. And in the end I didn't think I should ever get back to human beings again.

RITA: Not home to us? Ah then, I'm sure, your thoughts came back here.

ALLMERS: No, – they didn't.

RITA: Didn't?

ALLMERS: No. It was so strange. It seemed as though you and Eyolf had gone far, far away from me. And so had Asta, too.

RITA: But what did you think about, then?

ALLMERS: I didn't think. I went on, dragging myself along the precipices – and enjoyed the peace and well-being of the presence of death.

RITA [jumping up]: Oh, don't use words like that about something so horrible!

ALLMERS: That was how I felt. No fear at all. It seemed as though death and I were going along like two good travelling companions. It was so reasonable – the whole thing seemed so simple at the time. People in my family don't usually live to be old –

RITA: Oh, don't talk about things like that, Alfred! For you came out of it all right in the end.

ALLMERS: Yes; all of a sudden I was through. On the other side of the lake.

RITA: It was a night of terror for you, Alfred. But now it's over, you won't admit it to yourself.

ALLMERS: That night lifted me to the heights of resolution. And that's how it was I turned and came straight home. To Eyolf.

RITA [softly]: Too late.

ALLMERS: Yes. And then – my companion came and took him. And then there *was* horror in him. In everything. In all the things – that nevertheless we dare not leave. We're so earthbound, Rita, both of us.

RITA [with a glimmer of joy]: Yes, aren't we? You, too! [Coming nearer.] Oh, let's live our life together as long as we can!

ALLMERS [*shrugging his shoulders*]: Live our life, yes! And have nothing to fill life with. All desolation and emptiness. As far as I can see.

RITA [*in misery*]: Oh, sooner or later you will leave me, Alfred! I feel it! And I can see it in you, too! You'll leave me!

ALLMERS: With my travelling companion, do you mean?

RITA: No, what I mean's worse than that. You'll leave me of your own free will. For you think it's only here, with me, that you've nothing to live for. Answer me! Isn't that what you think?

ALLMERS [*looking steadily at her*]: And suppose I did think so – ?

[*A noise and brawling as if of anger; fierce voices are heard from far below.* ALLMERS *goes to the railing.*]

RITA: What ever is it? [*Exclaiming.*] Ah, you'll see, they've found him!

ALLMERS: He'll never be found.

RITA: But what is it, then?

ALLMERS [*coming back*]: Only a fight – as usual.

RITA: Down on the shore?

ALLMERS: Yes. That whole settlement on the shore ought to go. Now the men have come home. Drunk, as they always are. Knocking the children about. Listen to the boys screaming. The women are yelling for help for them –

RITA: Well, shouldn't we send someone down to help them?

ALLMERS [*hard and angry*]: Help them, who didn't help Eyolf? No, let them go – just as they let Eyolf go!

RITA: Oh, you mustn't talk like that, Alfred! Mustn't think like that!

ALLMERS: I can't think anyhow else. All those old hovels ought to be torn down!

RITA: And what will become of all those poor people?

ALLMERS: They must go somewhere else.

RITA: And the children?

ALLMERS: Won't it be much the same, where they come to an end?

RITA [quiet and reproachful]: You're forcing yourself to be hard, Alfred.

ALLMERS [excited]: I've a right to be hard, in future! It's my duty, too!

RITA: Your duty!

ALLMERS: My duty to Eyolf. He mustn't go unavenged. That's what it comes to, Rita! As I tell you. Think the thing over. Have the whole place down there levelled to the ground – when I'm gone.

RITA [looking searchingly at him]: When you're gone?

ALLMERS: Yes, for then you'll have something at any rate to fill your life with. And that you must have.

RITA [firmly and clearly]: You're right, there. I must. But can you guess what I'm going to do – when you're gone?

ALLMERS: Why, what is it?

RITA [slowly, with decision]: As soon as you've left me, I shall go down to the shore and bring all those poor, outcast children up here with me to our place. All the wretched little boys –

ALLMERS: What will you do with them here?

RITA: I will make them my own.

ALLMERS: You will?

RITA: Yes, I will. From the day you go, they shall be here, all of them – as if they were my own.

ALLMERS [shocked]: In our little Eyolf's place!

RITA: Yes, in our little Eyolf's place. They shall have Eyolf's rooms to live in. They shall have his books to read. His toys to play with. They shall take turns at sitting in his chair at table.

ALLMERS: All this sounds like absolute madness! I don't know a person in the world less fitted for a thing like that than you.

RITA: Then I must educate myself for it. Teach myself. Train myself.

ALLMERS: If this is in real earnest – everything you're saying – then there must have been a change in you.

RITA: Yes. There has, Alfred. You've seen to that. You have made an empty place in me. And I must try to fill it up with something. Something that could seem like love.

ALLMERS [standing thoughtful for a moment, then looking at her]: As a matter of fact, we haven't done much for those poor people down there.

RITA: We've done nothing for them.

ALLMERS: Hardly ever thought about them.

RITA: Never thought about them in sympathy.

ALLMERS: We, who had 'the gold and the green forests' –

RITA: Our hands were closed against them. And our hearts closed, too.

ALLMERS [nodding]: So perhaps it's natural enough, after all, that they didn't risk their lives to save little Eyolf.

RITA [softly]: Think, Alfred. Are you so sure that – that we would have dared that ourselves?

ALLMERS [uneasily, refusing the idea]: Don't ever doubt that, Rita!

RITA: Ah, we're creatures of this earth, my dear.

ALLMERS: What exactly do you think you'll do for all these outcast children?

RITA: Try my best, I suppose, to see if I can make their paths in life kindlier – and nobler.

ALLMERS: If you can do that, then Eyolf was not born in vain.

RITA: And not taken from us in vain either.

ALLMERS [looking steadily at her]: Be clear about one thing, Rita. It's not love that is driving you to this.

RITA: No, it's not. At least, not yet.

ALLMERS: Well, what is it then exactly?

RITA [*half avoiding the question*]: You have so often talked to Asta about human responsibility –

ALLMERS: About the book you hated.

RITA: I still hate that book. But I sat and listened when you talked. And now I will try to go on myself. In *my* way.

ALLMERS [*shaking his head*]: It's not for the sake of the book that wasn't finished –

RITA: No, I have another reason too.

ALLMERS: What, then?

RITA [*softly, smiling sadly*]: I want to make my peace, you see, with the wide open eyes.

ALLMERS [*deeply impressed, fixing his eyes on her*]: Perhaps I could join you? And help you, Rita?

RITA: Would you?

ALLMERS: Yes – if I only knew that I could.

RITA [*hesitating*]: But then you'd have to stay here.

ALLMERS [*softly*]: Let's see if it wouldn't work.

RITA [*almost inaudibly*]: Let us, Alfred.

> [*They are both silent. Then* ALLMERS *goes over to the flagstaff and hoists the flag to the top.* RITA *stands by the summer-house and looks quietly at him.*]

ALLMERS [*coming back again*]: There will be a hard day's work before us, Rita.

RITA: You'll see – the peace of the sabbath will rest upon us from time to time.

ALLMERS [*quietly, touched*]: And we shall know then, perhaps, that the spirits are with us.

RITA [*whispering*]: Spirits?

ALLMERS [*as before*]: Yes. They will be beside us perhaps – those whom we have lost.

RITA [*nodding slowly*]: Our little Eyolf. And your big Eyolf, too.

ALLMERS [*gazing ahead*]: It may be that, once or twice on life's way, we shall see a glimpse of them.

RITA: Where shall we look, Alfred –?

ALLMERS [*fastening his eyes on her*]: Up.

RITA [*nodding her agreement*]: Yes, yes. Up.

ALLMERS: Up, – to the mountain-tops. To the stars. And to the great stillness.

RITA [*holding out her hand to him*]: Thanks.

JOHN GABRIEL BORKMAN

CHARACTERS

JOHN GABRIEL BORKMAN, *formerly a bank director*
GUNHILD BORKMAN, *his wife*
ERHART BORKMAN, *their son; a student*
MISS ELLA RENTHEIM, *Mrs Borkman's twin sister*
MRS WILTON
VILHELM FOLDAL, *clerk in a government office*
FRIDA FOLDAL, *his daughter*
MRS BORKMAN'S MAID

The action takes place one winter evening
on the Rentheim family estate outside
the capital

ACT ONE

MRS BORKMAN'S *living-room, furnished with old-fashioned, faded grandeur. An open sliding door leads into a garden-room with windows and a glass door in the background. Through it we look out to the garden where a snow-storm is driving in the dusk. In the right-hand wall is a door leading in from the hall. Further forward is a large, old, iron stove with a fire in it. On the left, towards the back is a single, smaller door. Downstage on the same side is a window, covered with thick curtains. Between the window and the door is a sofa upholstered in horse-hair, with a table in front of it covered with a cloth. On the table is a lighted lamp with a shade. By the stove is a high-backed arm-chair.*

MRS BORKMAN *is sitting on the sofa with her crochet-work. She is an elderly woman of cold, distinguished appearance, her carriage stiff and her expression rigid; her thick hair is strongly marked with grey and she has fine, transparent hands. She wears a thick, dark silk dress which has once upon a time been handsome but is now rather shabby and worn, and has a woollen shawl over her shoulders.*

She sits for a time erect and unmoving at her crocheting. Then the sound of bells is heard from a sledge driving by outside.

MRS BORKMAN [*listening; her eyes light up with pleasure and she whispers involuntarily*]: Erhart! At last! [*She gets up and looks out between the curtains. She seems disappointed and sits down again on the sofa at her work.*]

> [*After a moment the* MAID *comes in from the hall with a visiting-card on a little tray.*]

MRS BORKMAN [*quickly*]: Has Mr Erhart come after all?

THE MAID: No, ma'am. But there's a lady out here –

MRS BORKMAN [*putting her crochet aside*]: Oh, Mrs Wilton, I expect –

THE MAID [*coming nearer*]: No, it's a *strange* lady –

287

MRS BORKMAN [*reaching for the card*]: Let me see – [*She reads it, gets up quickly and looks intently at the maid.*] Are you sure this is for me?

THE MAID: Yes, that's what I understood – it was for madam.

MRS BORKMAN: Did she ask to speak to Mrs Borkman?

THE MAID: Yes, she did.

MRS BORKMAN [*shortly, with decision*]: Very well. Then say that I'm at home.

[*The MAID opens the door for the stranger and goes out herself. MISS ELLA RENTHEIM comes into the room. She is like her sister in appearance, but there is more of suffering than of hardness in the expression of her face. It still shows signs of great beauty and character in her earlier years. Her heavy hair is brushed back in natural waves from her forehead and is pure silver-white. She is dressed in black velvet with a hat and fur-lined cloak of the same stuff. The two sisters stand a moment in silence and look searchingly at each other. Each of them is evidently waiting for the other to speak first.*]

ELLA RENTHEIM [*who has remained near the door*]: Well, you look surprised to see me, Gunhild.

MRS BORKMAN [*standing erect and motionless between the sofa and the table and resting her finger-tips on the cloth*]: Haven't you come to the wrong place? The estate manager lives in the side wing, you know.

ELLA RENTHEIM: It isn't the manager I want to talk to today.

MRS BORKMAN: Is it me, then, that you want?

ELLA RENTHEIM: Yes. I must speak to you for a moment.

MRS BORKMAN [*coming forward into the room*]: Well, sit down then.

ELLA RENTHEIM: Thank you. I can quite well stand for the moment.

MRS BORKMAN: Just as you like. But at least undo your cloak.

ELLA RENTHEIM [*undoing her cloak*]: Yes, it's very warm here.

MRS BORKMAN: I am always cold.

ELLA RENTHEIM [*standing a moment and looking at her, her arms resting on the back of the arm-chair*]: Well – Gunhild, it'll soon be eight years since we last saw each other.

MRS BORKMAN [*coldly*]: Since we spoke to each other, at any rate.

ELLA RENTHEIM: To be exact, since we spoke to each other; yes. Because you've probably seen me from time to time, when I had to make my yearly visit to the estate manager.

MRS BORKMAN: Once or twice, I believe.

ELLA RENTHEIM: And I've seen a glimpse of you now and then. In the window there.

MRS BORKMAN: It must have been through the curtains. You have good eyes, of course. [*Hard and cuttingly.*] But the last time we *spoke* to each other – it was in here, in this room of mine –

ELLA RENTHEIM [*turning it aside*]: Yes, yes, I know that, Gunhild!

MRS BORKMAN: The week before he – before he came out.

ELLA RENTHEIM [*moving away to the back*]: Oh, don't talk about *that*!

MRS BORKMAN [*firmly, but in a low voice*]: It was the week before he – the bank director was released.

ELLA RENTHEIM [*coming forward*]: Oh yes, yes, yes! I'm not forgetting that time. But it's too terrible to think about! Only to go back to it for a single moment – oh!

MRS BORKMAN [*heavily*]: And yet one's thoughts never manage to dwell on anything else. [*Passionately, striking her hands together.*] No, I can't understand it. I never shall! I can't see why such a thing as that – why something so dreadful can fall upon one, single family! And, to think, – *our* family! A family as distinguished as ours! Think of it, that it should overtake just *that* one!

ELLA RENTHEIM: Oh, Gunhild, there were many, many more than *our* family – that the blow fell on.

MRS BORKMAN: Presumably; but I don't mind so much about all those others. For it was only a matter of some money, or some papers, with them. But for *us* -! For me! And then for Erhart! A child, as he was then! [*With mounting excitement.*] The shame that came on us two, who were innocent! The dishonour! The hideous, terrible dishonour! And then, completely ruined as well!

ELLA RENTHEIM [*tentatively*]: Tell me, Gunhild - how does he take it?

MRS BORKMAN: Erhart, do you mean?

ELLA RENTHEIM: No - he himself. How does he take it?

MRS BORKMAN [*with a gesture of contempt*]: Do you suppose I ask about that?

ELLA RENTHEIM: Ask? You surely don't need to ask -?

MRS BORKMAN [*looking at her in amazement*]: But surely you don't suppose I have anything to do with him? That I ever meet him? See anything of him?

ELLA RENTHEIM: Not even that?

MRS BORKMAN [*in the same tone*]: *He*, who was under lock and key for five years! [*Hiding her face in her hands.*] Oh, such a crushing humiliation! [*With gathering anger.*] And then to think what the name of John Gabriel Borkman stood for in the old days! No, no, no - never see him again! Never!

ELLA RENTHEIM [*looking at her for a moment*]: You have a hard heart, Gunhild.

MRS BORKMAN: For *him*, yes.

ELLA RENTHEIM: Still, he is your husband.

MRS BORKMAN: Didn't he say in court that it was *I* who began his ruin? That I spent so much money -?

ELLA RENTHEIM [*cautiously*]: But *wasn't* there some truth in that?

MRS BORKMAN: But wasn't it he himself who wanted me to? Everything had to be so senselessly extravagant -

ELLA RENTHEIM: I know that well enough. But that's just

290

why you should have stood out against it. And you certainly didn't.

MRS BORKMAN: Did I know that it wasn't his own – the money he gave me to squander? And that he squandered himself, too. Ten times more than I did!

ELLA RENTHEIM [*quietly*]: Well, I suppose his position called for it. For a great part of it, anyhow.

MRS BORKMAN [*scornfully*]: Yes, the excuse always was that we must 'keep up an appearance'. And he kept up an appearance all right – with a vengeance! Drove a four-in-hand – as if he were a king. Had people bowing and scraping to him, like a king. [*Laughing.*] And they called him by his Christian name too – all over the country – just as if he were the king himself. 'John Gabriel', 'John Gabriel'. They all knew what a great man 'John Gabriel' was!

ELLA RENTHEIM [*warmly and emphatically*]: He *was* a great man in those days, too.

MRS BORKMAN: Yes, it certainly looked like it. But never, not by a single word, did he let me know how his affairs really stood. Never a hint as to where he got his means from.

ELLA RENTHEIM: No, no – the others had no idea of that either.

MRS BORKMAN: It didn't matter about the others. But he was bound in duty to tell the truth to *me*. And he never did! He only lied – lied to me absolutely –

ELLA RENTHEIM [*interrupting*]: That he certainly didn't, Gunhild! He may have concealed it. But he certainly didn't lie.

MRS BORKMAN: Oh well, call it what you like. It comes to just the same thing. Anyhow, it fell to ruins. Everything. All that glory came to an end.

ELLA RENTHEIM [*to herself*]: Yes, everything fell to ruins – for him – and for others.

MRS BORKMAN [*drawing herself up and speaking threateningly*]:

But I tell you this, Ella – I'm not giving up yet. I shall find a way to raise myself up again. You may be sure of that!

ELLA RENTHEIM [*anxiously*]: Raise yourself up? What do you mean by that?

MRS BORKMAN: Raise up my name and honour and position! Raise up my whole ruined life, that's what I mean! I have someone behind me, let me tell you. Someone who shall wash clean all that – that *he* has blackened.

ELLA RENTHEIM: Gunhild! Gunhild!

MRS BORKMAN [*with mounting passion*]: There's an avenger living, I tell you. One who shall make up to me for all his father's crimes.

ELLA RENTHEIM: Erhart, I suppose.

MRS BORKMAN: Yes, Erhart – my splendid son! He will be able to raise up the family, the house, the name. Everything that *can* be raised up. And perhaps more besides.

ELLA RENTHEIM: And in what way do you expect this to be done?

MRS BORKMAN: That must come as it can. I don't know *how* it will come. But I know that it *will* and it *shall* come some day. [*Looking at her with a question.*] Why, – Ella – isn't it actually what you've been thinking too, ever since he was a child?

ELLA RENTHEIM: No, I can't quite say that.

MRS BORKMAN: Isn't it? Then why did you take charge of him? At that time when the storm broke loose over – over this house.

ELLA RENTHEIM: You couldn't do it yourself at that time, Gunhild.

MRS BORKMAN: No. I couldn't do it. As for his father, the law relieved him of his responsibility, where he was ... so well guarded ...

ELLA RENTHEIM [*outraged*]: Oh, to think that you can say such things! *You*!

MRS BORKMAN [*with a venomous expression*]: And that *you*

could bring yourself to take charge of a – a child of John Gabriel. Exactly as if the child was your own. Take him from *me* – and go home with him. And keep him in your home year after year. Till the boy was nearly grown-up. [*Looking mistrustingly at her.*] Just why did you do that, Ella? Why did you keep him?

ELLA RENTHEIM: I got to be so fond of him –

MRS BORKMAN: More than I – his mother!

ELLA RENTHEIM [*avoiding the subject*]: I don't know about that. And then Erhart was rather delicate as a growing boy –

MRS BORKMAN: Erhart – delicate!

ELLA RENTHEIM: Yes, I think so. At that time, at any rate. And then the air's so much milder out there on the west coast than it is here, you know.

MRS BORKMAN [*with a bitter smile*]: Hm. Is that it? [*Breaking off.*] Yes, you certainly have done a great deal for Erhart, I know. [*Changing her tone.*] Well, of course, you have the means to. [*Smiling.*] You were so fortunate you see, Ella. You got back everything that was yours.

ELLA RENTHEIM [*hurt*]: I took no steps about that, I can assure you. I had no idea – till long, long after – that the papers that were in my account at the bank – that they were saved –

MRS BORKMAN: Well, well, I don't understand that kind of thing. I only say that you were fortunate. [*Looking at her, with a question.*] But since you did, of your own accord, undertake to bring up Erhart for me –? What was your purpose, then, in doing that?

ELLA RENTHEIM [*looking at her*]: My purpose –?

MRS BORKMAN: Yes, of course you must have had a purpose. What did you want to do with him? To make of him, I mean?

ELLA RENTHEIM [*slowly*]: I wanted to smooth the way for Erhart and let him be happy here on earth.

MRS BORKMAN [*scornfully*]: Pooh! People in our situation have something more to do than think of happiness.

ELLA RENTHEIM: What – what do you mean?

MRS BORKMAN [*looking firmly and earnestly at her*]: Erhart has first and foremost to see to it that his brilliance is recognized far and wide, so that no one in the country sees a trace, any longer, of the shadow his father cast upon me – and upon my son.

ELLA RENTHEIM [*searchingly*]: Tell me, Gunhild, is that what Erhart *himself* asks of life –?

MRS BORKMAN [*in surprise*]: Well, we'll hope so!

ELLA RENTHEIM: – or isn't it rather what *you* ask of him?

MRS BORKMAN [*shortly*]: Erhart and I always ask the same things of ourselves.

ELLA RENTHEIM [*sadly and slowly*]: You're so sure of your boy after all, Gunhild.

MRS BORKMAN [*with veiled triumph*]: Yes, God be thanked, I am. You may be certain of that.

ELLA RENTHEIM: Then it seems to me you must really count yourself happy after all. In spite of all the rest.

MRS BORKMAN: I do, too. As far as *that* goes. But then, every minute, you see, all these other things come rushing down upon me like a storm.

ELLA RENTHEIM [*with a change of voice*]: Tell me, and you may as well do it straight away –. For it was really *that* I came to see you about –

MRS BORKMAN: What?

ELLA RENTHEIM: Something I think I must talk to you about ... Tell me. Erhart isn't living out here with – with the rest of you.

MRS BORKMAN [*in a hard voice*]: Erhart can't live out here with me. He has to live in town.

ELLA RENTHEIM: That's what he wrote me.

MRS BORKMAN: He must, for the sake of his studies. But he comes out to see me for a little while every evening.

ELLA RENTHEIM: Well, I wonder if I could see him, then? And talk to him at once?

MRS BORKMAN: He hasn't come yet. But I'm expecting him every minute.

ELLA RENTHEIM: Yes, Gunhild, he must have come. I can hear him walking about upstairs.

MRS BORKMAN [*with a rapid glance*]: Up in the gallery?

ELLA RENTHEIM: Yes. I've heard him up there ever since I came.

MRS BORKMAN [*turning her eyes away from Ella*]: That's not he, Ella.

ELLA RENTHEIM [*with surprise*]: *Isn't* that Erhart? [*Guessing.*] Who is it then?

MRS BORKMAN: The director.

ELLA RENTHEIM [*softly, controlling her distress*]: John Gabriel Borkman!

MRS BORKMAN: He walks up and down like that; to and fro. From morning till night. Day in, day out.

ELLA RENTHEIM: It's true, I've heard rumours of it –

MRS BORKMAN: I can believe it. No doubt there are rumours about us out here.

ELLA RENTHEIM: Erhart has spoken of it. In his letters. That his father generally kept to himself – up there. And you to yourself, down here.

MRS BORKMAN: Yes, it's been like that, Ella. Ever since they let him out. And sent him home to me. Through all those eight long years.

ELLA RENTHEIM: But I've never believed it could really be true. That it could be possible –

MRS BORKMAN [*nodding*]: It is true. And can never be anyhow else.

ELLA RENTHEIM [*looking at her*]: This must be a terrible life, Gunhild.

MRS BORKMAN: More than terrible, Ella. Hardly to be borne much longer.

ELLA RENTHEIM: I can understand that.

MRS BORKMAN: Always hearing his step up there. Right

from early morning till far into the night. And so clearly as it sounds down here.

ELLA RENTHEIM: Yes, it's odd how clear it is here.

MRS BORKMAN: Many a time it comes over me that I have a sick wolf pacing his cage up there in the gallery. As though it were right over my head. [*Listens and whispers.*] Just listen, now! Listen! To and fro – the wolf going to and fro.

ELLA RENTHEIM [*tentatively*]: Couldn't anything else be done, Gunhild?

MRS BORKMAN [*dismissing the question*]: He has never made any move about it.

ELLA RENTHEIM: But couldn't you make the first move?

MRS BORKMAN [*flaring up*]: I! After all the injury he has done me! No, thank you. I'd rather let the wolf go on pacing round up there.

ELLA RENTHEIM: It's too warm for me here. May I take my things off, after all?

MRS BORKMAN: Yes, I asked you to before –

[ELLA RENTHEIM *puts down her cloak and hat on a chair near the entrance door.*]

ELLA RENTHEIM: Don't you ever happen to meet him outside the house?

MRS BORKMAN [*laughing bitterly*]: In society, do you mean?

ELLA RENTHEIM: I mean when he goes out for fresh air. On the paths in the wood, or –

MRS BORKMAN: The director never goes out.

ELLA RENTHEIM: Not sometimes in the dusk?

MRS BORKMAN: Never.

ELLA RENTHEIM [*moved*]: He can't bring himself to it?

MRS BORKMAN: Apparently he can't. He has his big mountain cape and his hat hanging in the cupboard. In the hall, you know –

ELLA RENTHEIM [*to herself*]: The cupboard we used to play in when we were small –

MRS BORKMAN [*nodding*]: And now and again, late in the

evening, I can hear him come down to put his things on and go out. But instead he stops half-way down the stairs – and turns back. And then he goes up again to the gallery.

ELLA RENTHEIM [*quietly*]: Don't any of his old friends go up there and see him?

MRS BORKMAN: He *has* no old friends.

ELLA RENTHEIM: But he had so many – once.

MRS BORKMAN: Hm. He took a sure way of getting rid of them. He was a dear friend to his friends, was John Gabriel.

ELLA RENTHEIM: Ah yes; you're right there, Gunhild.

MRS BORKMAN [*angrily*]: All the same, I must say it's petty, low, mean, contemptible to set so much store by any small loss they may have suffered through him. After all, it was only a money loss. Nothing more.

ELLA RENTHEIM [*without answering*]: So he lives up there all alone. Absolutely by himself.

MRS BORKMAN: Yes, pretty nearly. It's true, I hear that an old copying clerk or someone like that goes up to see him now and again.

ELLA RENTHEIM: Oh, yes. That's probably a man called Foldal. I know those two were friends as young men.

MRS BORKMAN: Yes, they were, I believe. But I don't know anything about him. He never came into our circle of acquaintances. In the days when we *had* one –

ELLA RENTHEIM: But *now* he does come to see him?

MRS BORKMAN: Yes, he's not above that. But it goes without saying that he only comes when it's dark.

ELLA RENTHEIM: This Foldal – he was one of the people who lost something when the bank failed.

MRS BORKMAN [*casually*]: Yes, I think I do remember that he lost some money too. But it was no doubt quite inconsiderable.

ELLA RENTHEIM [*with slight emphasis*]: It was all he possessed.

MRS BORKMAN [*smiling*]: Why, good gracious, what *he*

possessed – it must really have been negligible, you know. Nothing to speak of.

ELLA RENTHEIM: It certainly *wasn't* spoken of at the trial – not by Foldal.

MRS BORKMAN: And besides, I can assure you that Erhart has made a very fair return for the trifling sum.

ELLA RENTHEIM [*surprised*]: Erhart has! How has Erhart managed to do that?

MRS BORKMAN: He's taken up Foldal's youngest daughter. And educated her – so that perhaps she'll be able to make her way and support herself some day. That's much more, you realize, than the father could have done for her.

ELLA RENTHEIM: Yes, the father's pretty badly off, I should think.

MRS BORKMAN: And then Erhart's arranged for her to learn music. She's got on so well already that she can go up to – to him upstairs, in the gallery – and play to him.

ELLA RENTHEIM: So he's still fond of music?

MRS BORKMAN: Oh yes, I suppose he is. Of course he has the piano that you sent out here – when he was expected back –

ELLA RENTHEIM: And she plays to him on that?

MRS BORKMAN: Yes, every now and then. In the evenings. Erhart saw to that too.

ELLA RENTHEIM: But does the poor girl have to come all that long way out here? And then home to town again?

MRS BORKMAN: No, she doesn't need to do that. Erhart has arranged for her to stay with a lady who lives quite near here. It's a Mrs Wilton –

ELLA RENTHEIM [*interested*]: Mrs Wilton!

MRS BORKMAN: A very rich woman. Someone you don't know.

ELLA RENTHEIM: I've heard the name. Mrs Fanny Wilton, I think –

MRS BORKMAN: Yes, quite right.

ELLA RENTHEIM: Erhart has written about her several times. Does she live out here now?

MRS BORKMAN: Yes, she's taken a small house here. She moved out from town some time ago.

ELLA RENTHEIM [hesitating a little]: People say she's divorced from her husband.

MRS BORKMAN: Her husband's been dead several years.

ELLA RENTHEIM: Yes, but they were divorced –. He divorced her.

MRS BORKMAN: He left her, that's what he did. The fault certainly wasn't hers.

ELLA RENTHEIM: Do you know her at all well, Gunhild?

MRS BORKMAN: Oh yes, fairly well. She lives quite close at hand. So she looks in to see me every now and then.

ELLA RENTHEIM: And you like her all right?

MRS BORKMAN: She's so extremely intelligent. Remarkably acute in her judgements.

ELLA RENTHEIM: In her judgements about people, you mean?

MRS BORKMAN: Yes, principally about people. Erhart, now; she's studied him carefully. Right through and through – to his very soul. And so she worships him – quite naturally.

ELLA RENTHEIM [with some subtlety]: So perhaps she knows Erhart even better than she knows you?

MRS BORKMAN: Yes, Erhart used to meet her very often in town. Before she came out here.

ELLA RENTHEIM [incautiously]: And yet she moved out from town?

MRS BORKMAN [taken aback and looking sharply at her]: Yet! What do you mean by that?

ELLA RENTHEIM [evasively]: Oh, well, – I don't know.

MRS BORKMAN: You said it in such a curious way. There was something you meant by it, Ella!

ELLA RENTHEIM [looking her straight in the eyes]: Yes, there was, too, Gunhild. There *was* something I meant by it.

MRS BORKMAN: Very well, then, say it straight out!

ELLA RENTHEIM: First I want to say this; I think I too have a kind of right in Erhart. Or do you perhaps think I haven't?

MRS BORKMAN [*looking across the room*]: Of course. After the money you've spent on him, well –

ELLA RENTHEIM: Oh not for that, Gunhild. But because I'm fond of him –

MRS BORKMAN [*smiling scornfully*]: Of *my* son? Can you be? You? In spite of everything?

ELLA RENTHEIM: Yes, I can. In spite of everything. And I am. I'm fond of Erhart. As fond as I possibly *can* be of anyone – nowadays. At my age.

MRS BORKMAN: Oh very well then, never mind. But –

ELLA RENTHEIM: And so, you see, I get anxious directly I see anything that threatens him.

MRS BORKMAN: Threatens Erhart! Why, *what* threatens him? Or *who* threatens him?

ELLA RENTHEIM: In the first place, *you* do, – in your way –

MRS BORKMAN [*vehemently*]: I!

ELLA RENTHEIM: And then this Mrs Wilton too – I'm afraid of her.

MRS BORKMAN [*looking at her speechless for a moment*]: And you can believe a thing like that about Erhart! About my own son! *He*, who has his great mission to carry out!

ELLA RENTHEIM [*disregarding it*]: Oh, his mission!

MRS BORKMAN [*indignantly*]: How dare you say that so contemptuously!

ELLA RENTHEIM: Do you think that a young man, at Erhart's age – healthy and high-spirited – do you think he's going to sacrifice himself for – for such a thing as a 'mission'!

MRS BORKMAN [*firm and determined*]: Erhart will! That I know for certain.

ELLA RENTHEIM [*shaking her head*]: You neither know it nor believe it, Gunhild.

MRS BORKMAN: Not believe it!

ELLA RENTHEIM: It's only a dream of yours. Because if you hadn't that to cling to you feel you'd fall into utter despair.

MRS BORKMAN: Yes, I certainly should despair. [*Angrily.*] And perhaps *that's* what you'd rather see, Ella!

ELLA RENTHEIM [*lifting her head*]: Yes, I'd rather see that – if you can't save yourself except by sacrificing Erhart.

MRS BORKMAN [*threateningly*]: You want to come between *us*! Between mother and son! *You*!

ELLA RENTHEIM: I want to free him from your control, your power – your dominance.

MRS BORKMAN [*triumphantly*]: You can't do that any more! You had him tied to you – all that time – till he was fifteen. But now I've won him back, you see!

ELLA RENTHEIM: Then I'll win him back from you! [*Huskily; almost in a whisper.*] We two, we have fought to the death for a man before this, Gunhild!

MRS BORKMAN [*looking at her exultantly*]: Yes, and I won the victory.

ELLA RENTHEIM [*smiling contemptuously*]: Do you still think you won anything by that victory?

MRS BORKMAN [*gloomily*]: No; you're certainly right in that.

ELLA RENTHEIM: You won't win anything by it this time either.

MRS BORKMAN: Not win anything, by keeping a mother's control over Erhart!

ELLA RENTHEIM: No, because it's only *control* over him that you want.

MRS BORKMAN: And *you*, then?

ELLA RENTHEIM [*warmly*]: I want his affection – his soul – his whole heart –!

MRS BORKMAN [*passionately*]: You won't ever get that again in this world!

ELLA RENTHEIM [*looking at her*]: Have you ... seen to that?

MRS BORKMAN [*smiling*]: Yes, I've taken that into my hands. Couldn't you tell from his letters?

ELLA RENTHEIM [*nodding slowly*]: Yes. I could hear you speaking in his letters lately.

MRS BORKMAN [*provocatively*]: I used those eight years, you see – while I had him under my eye.

ELLA RENTHEIM [*controlling herself*]: What did you say to Erhart about me? Is it anything you can tell me?

MRS BORKMAN: Oh yes, certainly.

ELLA RENTHEIM: Then do so, please.

MRS BORKMAN: I only told him what's true.

ELLA RENTHEIM: Well?

MRS BORKMAN: I impressed upon him continually that he must please remember that it was you we had to thank for it that we can live in the way we do. That we *can* live at all.

ELLA RENTHEIM: Nothing more than that?

MRS BORKMAN: Oh, a thing like that rankles, you know. I feel that myself.

ELLA RENTHEIM: But that's only more or less what Erhart knew already.

MRS BORKMAN: When he came home to me, he imagined that you did it all from goodness of heart. [*Looking spitefully at her.*] Now he doesn't believe that any longer, Ella.

ELLA RENTHEIM: Then what does he believe now?

MRS BORKMAN: He believes what's true. I asked him how he explained to himself that Aunt Ella never came out here to see us –

ELLA RENTHEIM [*interrupting*]: He knew why before!

MRS BORKMAN: He knows it better now. You'd led him to believe that it was to spare me – and him up there in the gallery –

ELLA RENTHEIM: And so it was.

MRS BORKMAN: Erhart doesn't believe any of that now.

ELLA RENTHEIM: Then what have you made him believe about me?

MRS BORKMAN: He believes, as is true, that you're ashamed of us – despise us. And don't you? Didn't you once plan to get him right away from me? You think, Ella. You'll remember all right.

ELLA RENTHEIM [*putting it aside*]: That was during the worst of the scandal. While the case was in court. I'm not thinking of that any longer.

MRS BORKMAN: It wouldn't help you if you were. For what would become of his mission, then! Oh no, thank you! It's *me* Erhart needs, not *you*. And so he's as good as dead for you! And you for him!

ELLA RENTHEIM [*cold and resolved*]: We shall see. Because now I'm going to stay out here.

MRS BORKMAN [*staring at her*]: Here at the house?

ELLA RENTHEIM: Yes, here.

MRS BORKMAN: Here – with us? The whole night?

ELLA RENTHEIM: I'm going to stay here all the rest of my life, if necessary.

MRS BORKMAN [*collecting herself*]: Very well, Ella – of course, the place is yours.

ELLA RENTHEIM: Oh, don't be absurd!

MRS BORKMAN: The whole of it is yours. The chair I'm sitting on is yours. The bed I lie on, tossing sleeplessly, – that belongs to you. The food we eat, we get it from you.

ELLA RENTHEIM: That can't be arranged any other way. John Gabriel can't hold any property of his own. Because someone would come at once and take it away from him.

MRS BORKMAN: I know that quite well. We must put up with living on your pity and charity.

ELLA RENTHEIM [*coldly*]: I can't prevent your looking at it in that way, Gunhild.

MRS BORKMAN: No, you can't. When do you want us to move?

ELLA RENTHEIM [*looking at her*]: To move?

MRS BORKMAN [*excitedly*]: Yes, you surely don't imagine I'm going to go on living under the same roof as you? No, I'd rather go into the workhouse or out on the roads!

ELLA RENTHEIM: Very well. Then let me take Erhart with me –

MRS BORKMAN: Erhart! My own son! My child!

ELLA RENTHEIM: Yes. For then I'll go straight home again.

MRS BORKMAN [*after a moment's reflection, firmly*]: Erhart shall choose between us himself.

ELLA RENTHEIM [*looking at her with doubt and uncertainty*]: *He* choose? Why – dare you do that, Gunhild?

MRS BORKMAN [*with a hard laugh*]: Do I dare! Let my boy choose between his mother and you! Yes, I certainly dare.

ELLA RENTHEIM [*listening*]: Is somebody coming? I think I hear –

MRS BORKMAN: Then I expect it's Erhart –

[*There is a quick knock on the door leading to the hall, which is opened immediately afterwards.* MRS WILTON *comes in in evening dress and with an outdoor coat on. The* MAID *follows her, having had no time to announce her and looking bewildered. The door is left standing half open.* MRS WILTON *is a strikingly handsome woman in the thirties, full of vitality. She has wide, red, smiling lips, dancing eyes, and thick, dark hair.*]

MRS WILTON: Good evening, my dear Mrs Borkman!

MRS BORKMAN [*rather drily*]: Good evening, Mrs Wilton. [*To the* MAID, *pointing to the garden-room.*] Take out the lamp in there and light it.

[*The* MAID *takes the lamp and goes out with it.*]

MRS WILTON [*seeing* ELLA RENTHEIM]: Oh, I beg your pardon – you've got visitors –

MRS BORKMAN: Only my sister who's come over here –

[ERHART BORKMAN *flings open the half closed hall door and rushes in. He is a young man with bright, merry eyes. Very well dressed. His moustache is just beginning to show.*]

ERHART BORKMAN [*standing on the threshold, radiant with happiness*]: What's this! Has Aunt Ella come? [*Going across to her and seizing her hands.*] Aunt Ella, Aunt Ella! Why, is it possible? *You* here!

ELLA RENTHEIM [*throwing her arms round his neck*]: Erhart! My dear, precious boy! Why, how tall you've grown! Oh, how lovely it is to see you again!

MRS BORKMAN [*sharply*]: What does this mean, Erhart? Were you out in the hall hiding yourself?

MRS WILTON [*quickly*]: Erhart – Mr Borkman came with me.

MRS BORKMAN [*measuring him with her eyes*]: I see, Erhart. You don't come to your mother first?

ERHART: I just had to go in to Mrs Wilton's for a moment – to fetch little Frida.

MRS BORKMAN: Is that Miss Foldal with you too?

MRS WILTON: Yes, we have her waiting outside in the hall.

ERHART [*calling out through the door*]: Just go up, Frida.

[*There is a pause.* ELLA RENTHEIM *watches* ERHART. *He seems embarrassed and rather impatient; his face takes on a strained and colder expression. The* MAID *brings the lighted lamp into the garden-room, goes out again, and shuts the door behind her.*]

MRS BORKMAN [*with forced politeness*]: Well, Mrs Wilton, if you would care to stay for the evening, then –

MRS WILTON: No, thank you very much indeed, my dear Mrs Borkman. I really can't do that. We have another invitation. We're going down to Mr Hinkel's.

MRS BORKMAN [*looking at her*]: 'We'? What do you mean by 'we'?

MRS WILTON [*laughing*]: Well, I really only mean myself. But I was asked by the ladies of the house to bring Mr Borkman with me – if I should happen to see him.

MRS BORKMAN: And you did happen to, as I see.

MRS WILTON: Yes, luckily. As he was so kind as to look in on me – to fetch little Frida.

MRS BORKMAN [*drily*]: My dear Erhart, I didn't realize that you knew that family – these Hinkels.

ERHART [*irritated*]: No, I don't actually know them. [*He goes on a little impatiently.*] You know perfectly well yourself, Mother, what people I know and don't know.

MRS WILTON: Oh, that's nothing! One soon gets to know people in that house! Lively, merry, hospitable people. The house is full of young women.

MRS BORKMAN [*with emphasis*]: If I know my son aright, Mrs Wilton, that is not precisely the sort of society for him.

MRS WILTON: But good gracious, my dear Mrs Borkman, after all he's young too!

MRS BORKMAN: Yes, fortunately he is young. It wouldn't be much use if he weren't.

ERHART [*hiding his impatience*]: All right, Mother – it goes without saying I shan't go down to these Hinkels tonight. I'll stay here, of course, with you and Aunt Ella.

MRS BORKMAN: I was sure of that, my dear Erhart.

ELLA RENTHEIM: No, Erhart – you certainly mustn't stay away, for my sake, –

ERHART: Why yes, of course, my dear Aunt; I wouldn't think of anything else. [*He looks uncertainly at* MRS WILTON.] But how shall we explain it? Will it really be all right? Because you've said 'yes' – for me.

MRS WILTON [*good-humouredly*]: Oh nonsense! Why shouldn't it be all right? When I arrive down there, in those bright, festive rooms – alone and forlorn (just think of it!) – why, I shall say 'no' – for you.

ERHART [*slowly*]: Well, if you really think it will be all right, then –

MRS WILTON [*brushing it lightly aside*]: I've many a time said yes and no – for myself. How could you leave your aunt now, when she's just this minute arrived? Come, come, Mr Erhart – would that be behaving like a son?

MRS BORKMAN [*displeased*]: Like a son?

MRS WILTON: Well, like an adopted son, then, Mrs Borkman.

MRS BORKMAN: Yes, you may well add that.

MRS WILTON: Oh, I think myself one has more to thank a good foster mother for than one's own real mother.

MRS BORKMAN: Has that been your experience?

MRS WILTON: Well, unhappily – I knew very little about my mother. But if *I'd* had such a good foster mother too – perhaps I shouldn't have been so – so badly behaved as people say I am. [*She turns to* ERHART.] Yes, my young friend, so you're to stay quietly at home with your mother and your aunt and have tea! [*To the* LADIES.] Good-bye, good-bye, dear Mrs Borkman! Good-bye, Miss Rentheim!

[*The* LADIES *bow silently. She goes towards the door.*]

ERHART [*following her*]: Shan't I come with you a little way?

MRS WILTON [*at the door, with a gesture of refusal*]: You shan't come a step with me. I'm perfectly used to going about alone. [*She stops in the doorway, looks at him and nods.*] But I tell you, Mr Borkman – you be careful, now!

ERHART: Why am I to be careful?

MRS WILTON [*gaily*]: Why, because, as I go down the road – alone and forlorn, as I said – I shall try and cast a spell on you.

ERHART [*laughing*]: Oh, that! You're going to try *that* again.

MRS WILTON [*half in earnest*]: Yes, now take care. As I go down the hill, I will say in my own mind – right from my innermost will – I'll say, 'Mr Erhart Borkman, get your hat at once!'

MRS BORKMAN: And then he'll get it, you think?

MRS WILTON [*laughing*]: Yes, indeed; he'll seize his hat at once. And then I'll say, 'Put your overcoat on nicely, Erhart Borkman! And your goloshes! Don't forget the goloshes whatever you do! And then follow me. Obediently, obediently, obediently!'

ERHART [*with forced gaiety*]: Yes, you can be sure of that.

MRS WILTON [*raising her forefinger*]: Obediently! Obediently! Good night!

[*She laughs, nods to the* LADIES, *and shuts the door after her.*]

MRS BORKMAN: Does she really practise tricks of that kind?

ERHART: Oh, not a bit of it! How can you believe that? It's only a kind of joke. [*Changing the subject.*] But don't let's talk about Mrs Wilton now. [*He makes* ELLA RENTHEIM *sit in the arm-chair by the stove and stands looking at her for a moment.*] Well, to think you've made this long journey, Aunt Ella! And now, in the winter!

ELLA RENTHEIM: I had to, in the end, Erhart.

ERHART: Did you? Why was that?

ELLA RENTHEIM: I had to come in sometime to consult the doctors.

ERHART: Well, that's a good thing!

ELLA RENTHEIM [*smiling*]: Do you think it's such a good thing?

ERHART: I mean, that you made up your mind at last.

MRS BORKMAN [*coldly, from the sofa*]: Are you ill, Ella?

ELLA RENTHEIM [*looking hardly at her*]: You know quite well that I'm ill.

MRS BORKMAN: Oh yes, more or less ailing, as you've been for some years –

ERHART: I kept telling you when I was with you that you ought to see a doctor.

ELLA RENTHEIM: Well, out there in my part of the world there's no one I've any real confidence in. Besides, it didn't seem so bad then.

ERHART: Why, are you worse, now, Aunt?

ELLA RENTHEIM: Yes, my dear. It's grown rather worse now.

ERHART: Oh, but surely not dangerously?

ELLA RENTHEIM: Well that depends how you look at it.

ERHART [*energetically*]: Well then I tell you what, Aunt Ella, – you mustn't go home again yet awhile.

ELLA RENTHEIM: No, and I certainly shan't.

ERHART: You must stay here in town. Because here you've got all the best doctors to choose from.

ELLA RENTHEIM: Yes, that was my idea when I left home.

ERHART: And you must see that you find yourself a really good place to stay – a cosy, quiet sort of boarding-house.

ELLA RENTHEIM: I went to the old one this morning, where I've stayed before.

ERHART: Oh yes, you're really comfortable there.

ELLA RENTHEIM: Yes, but I shan't go on staying there, after all.

ERHART: Shan't you? But why not?

ELLA RENTHEIM: No, I decided not to when I'd come out here.

ERHART [in astonishment]: Really? You decided not to –?

MRS BORKMAN [without looking up from her crocheting]: Your aunt will stay here in her house, Erhart.

ERHART [looking from one to the other of them]: Here! With us! With us! Is it true, Aunt Ella?

ELLA RENTHEIM: Yes, I have decided on that now.

MRS BORKMAN [as before]: The whole place belongs to your aunt, you know.

ELLA RENTHEIM: So I'll stay out here, Erhart. At first. For the present. I'll make my own arrangements. Over there in the manager's wing –

ERHART: That's a good idea. There are always spare rooms over there. [Suddenly full of life.] But look here, Aunt – aren't you awfully tired after your journey?

ELLA RENTHEIM: Yes, I am rather tired.

ERHART: Well then, I think you ought to go to bed really early.

ELLA RENTHEIM [looking at him with a smile]: That's what I'm going to do.

ERHART [eagerly]: Because then, you see, we could have a much better talk to-morrow – or some other day. About everything. All sorts of things. You and Mother and I. Wouldn't that be better, Aunt Ella?

MRS BORKMAN [passionately, as she gets up from the sofa]: Erhart, I can see by your face that you're going to leave me!

ERHART [starting]: What do you mean by that?

MRS BORKMAN: You're going down to – to the Hinkels'!

ERHART [*involuntarily*]: Oh, that! [*Collecting himself.*] Well, you don't think I should sit here and keep Aunt Ella up till all hours? She's ill, Mother. Remember that.

MRS BORKMAN: You're going down to the Hinkels, Erhart!

ERHART [*impatiently*]: Well, but good gracious, Mother! – I don't think I can very well get out of it. What do *you* say, Aunt?

ELLA RENTHEIM: Decide for yourself, Erhart. That's best.

MRS BORKMAN [*turning threateningly to her*]: You want to take him away from me!

ELLA RENTHEIM [*getting up*]: Yes, if I only could, Gunhild! [*Music is heard from above.*]

ERHART [*writhing, as if in pain*]: Oh, I can't stand this! [*Looking round him.*] Where'd I put my hat? [*To* ELLA.] Do you know that tune she's playing up there in the gallery?

ELLA RENTHEIM: No. What is it?

ERHART: It's the *Danse Macabre*. The Dance of Death. Don't you know the Dance of Death, Aunt?

ELLA RENTHEIM [*smiling sadly*]: Not yet, Erhart.

ERHART [*to* MRS BORKMAN]: Mother – I do beg of you – please let me go!

MRS BORKMAN [*looking hardly at him*]: From your mother? So that's what you want?

ERHART: Of course I'll come out here again – perhaps tomorrow!

MRS BORKMAN [*with passionate excitement*]: You want to leave me! You want to be with those strangers! With – with –. No, I won't so much as think of it!

ERHART: There are all those bright lights down there. And young, happy faces. And there's music there, Mother!

MRS BORKMAN [*pointing up towards the ceiling*]: There's music up there too, Erhart.

ERHART: Yes, it's the music *there* – that's what's driving me out of the house.

ELLA RENTHEIM: Do you grudge your father a moment's escape from himself?

ERHART: Of course I don't. I'm only too glad for him to have it. So long as I don't have to listen to it myself.

MRS BORKMAN [*looking commandingly at him*]: Be strong, Erhart! Strong, my boy! Never forget that you have your great mission!

ERHART: Oh, Mother – don't start talking like that! I'm not made for a missionary. Good night, my dear Aunt! Good night, Mother! [*He goes hurriedly out through the hall.*]

MRS BORKMAN [*after a short silence*]: You've got him back again quickly enough, Ella, after all.

ELLA RENTHEIM: If I only dared believe it.

MRS BORKMAN: But you won't manage to keep him long, you'll find.

ELLA RENTHEIM: Because of you, you mean?

MRS BORKMAN: Because of me or – because of her, that other woman.

ELLA RENTHEIM: Better her than you, then.

MRS BORKMAN [*nodding slowly*]: I can understand that. I say the same. Better her than you.

ELLA RENTHEIM: Whatever were to become of him in the end –

MRS BORKMAN: It comes to much the same thing, I think.

ELLA RENTHEIM [*taking her outdoor coat over her arm*]: For the first time in our lives we two twin sisters are agreed. Good night, Gunhild.

[*She goes out through the hall. The music sounds more loudly from the gallery above.*]

MRS BORKMAN [*stands still for a moment; then starts, shrinks together and whispers involuntarily*]: The wolf is howling again. The sick wolf. [*She stands still for a moment, then throws herself down on the floor, writhing and crying in a grief-stricken whisper.*] Erhart! Erhart – be true to me! Oh, come home and help your mother! I can't bear this life any longer!

ACT TWO

The gallery upstairs, formerly the reception-room in the Rentheims' house. The walls are covered with old, woven tapestries, representing hunting-scenes, shepherds, and shepherdesses, all in dim, faded colours. In the left-hand wall is a sliding door and further downstage a piano. In the left-hand corner of the back wall is a tapestried door without a frame. Against the middle of the right-hand wall is a large, carved-oak writing-table with several books and papers. Further downstage on the same side is a sofa with a table and chairs. The furniture is arranged in the stiff style of the Empire. There are lighted lamps on the writing-desk and on the table.

JOHN GABRIEL BORKMAN *is standing beside the piano with his hands behind his back, listening to* FRIDA FOLDAL, *who is sitting playing the last bars of the* Danse Macabre. BORKMAN *is a solid, strongly-built man of middle height in his late sixties. He has a distinguished appearance, a finely-cut profile, penetrating eyes, and curling, silver-grey hair and beard. He is dressed in a black suit, not quite up to date, and wears a white cravat.* FRIDA FOLDAL *is a pretty, pale girl of fifteen with a rather tired, strained look, cheaply dressed in light-coloured clothes. The music is played to the end. There is silence.*

BORKMAN: Can you guess where I first heard music like this?
FRIDA [*looking up at him*]: No, Mr Borkman?
BORKMAN: It was down in the mines.
FRIDA [*not understanding*]: Oh? Down in the mines?
BORKMAN: I'm a miner's son, you know. Or perhaps you didn't know that?
FRIDA: No, Mr Borkman.
BORKMAN: A miner's son. And my father took me down the mines with him sometimes. Down there the metal sings.
FRIDA: Does it? Sings?

BORKMAN [*nodding*]: When it's loosened. The blows of the hammer that loosen it – they're the midnight bell striking to set it free. And so the metal sings – for joy – in its own way.

FRIDA: Why does it do that, Mr Borkman?

BORKMAN: It wants to come up into the light of day and serve mankind. [*He walks to and fro across the gallery, always with his hands behind his back.*]

FRIDA [*sitting waiting for a moment, then looking at her watch and getting up*]: I'm sorry, Mr Borkman – but I'm afraid I really must go.

BORKMAN [*stopping in front of her*]: Are you going already?

FRIDA [*putting her music into its case*]: Yes, I really must. [*Obviously embarrassed.*] Because I'm engaged somewhere this evening.

BORKMAN: Somewhere where there's a party?

FRIDA: Yes.

BORKMAN: And you're going to play to the guests?

FRIDA [*biting her lip*]: No – I'm only to play for the dancing.

BORKMAN: Only for the dancing?

FRIDA: Yes; they're going to dance after dinner.

BORKMAN [*standing and looking at her*]: Do you like playing for dancing? From house to house like this?

FRIDA [*putting on her outdoor coat*]: Yes, when I can get an engagement, I –. Of course, there's always a little to be made by it.

BORKMAN [*persisting*]: Is *that* what you think of most when you're sitting, playing dance-music?

FRIDA: No; I'm mostly thinking how hard it is that I can't join in and dance myself.

BORKMAN [*nodding*]: That was exactly what I wanted to know. [*Walking restlessly about the room.*] Yes. Yes. Yes. *That*, not being able to join in oneself, that's hardest of all. [*Stopping.*] But then there's one compensation for you, Frida.

FRIDA [*looking at him questioningly*]: Whatever is that, Mr Borkman?

BORKMAN: It's this, that you've ten times more music in you than all the dancers put together.

FRIDA [*smiles deprecatingly*]: Oh that's by no means so certain.

BORKMAN [*holding up his forefinger admonishingly*]: Now, never be so foolish as to doubt yourself!

FRIDA: But, good gracious, even when nobody knows about it?

BORKMAN: So long as you yourself know about it, that's enough. Where is it you're to play this evening?

FRIDA: Over at Mr Hinkel's, the lawyer's.

BORKMAN [*suddenly looking severely at her*]: Hinkel's, you say?

FRIDA: Yes.

BORKMAN [*with a sarcastic smile*]: Do people call at that man's house? Can *he* get people to visit him?

FRIDA: Yes, a tremendous lot of people go there, from what Mrs Wilton says.

BORKMAN [*angrily*]: But what kind of people? Can you tell me that?

FRIDA [*a little anxiously*]: No, I don't really know that. Well, that's to say I know young Mr Borkman's to be there this evening.

BORKMAN [*taken aback*]: Erhart! My son?

FRIDA: Yes, he'll be there.

BORKMAN: How do you know that?

FRIDA: He said so himself. An hour ago.

BORKMAN: Is he out here today, then?

FRIDA: Yes, he's been at Mrs Wilton's all the afternoon.

BORKMAN [*searchingly*]: Do you know whether he was in here too? Whether he was in talking to anyone downstairs, I mean?

FRIDA: Yes, he went in to Mrs Borkman for a little while.

BORKMAN [*bitterly*]: Ah yes – I might have known it.

FRIDA: But there was a strange lady with her too, I think.

BORKMAN: Oh? Was there? Oh well, I suppose people come in to see Mrs Borkman now and again.

FRIDA: Shall I tell Mr Erhart, if I meet him later, that he's to come up here and see *you* as well?

BORKMAN [*gruffly*]: You're to say nothing! I absolutely forbid it! People who want to come up and see *me*, can come of their own accord. I don't ask anyone.

FRIDA: Oh very well, then I won't say anything. Good night, Mr Borkman.

BORKMAN [*walking about and muttering*]: Good night.

FRIDA: I wonder if I might run down the winding stair? It's quicker.

BORKMAN: Oh, lord yes. – Run down any staircase you like as far as I'm concerned. Good night to you!

FRIDA: Good night, Mr Borkman. [*She goes out through the little tapestry door in the background to the left.*]

> [BORKMAN, *wrapt in thought, goes across to the piano; he is going to close it, but lets it be. He looks round him at all the emptiness and turns to pacing up and down across the room, from the corner by the piano to the right-hand corner at the back – to and fro continually, nervous and restless. At last he goes over to the writing-table, listens in the direction of the sliding door, picks up a hand-mirror quickly, looks at himself in it and straightens his cravat. There is a knock at the sliding door.* BORKMAN *hears it, looks quickly in that direction, but remains silent. After a moment, there is another knock; louder this time.*]

BORKMAN [*standing by the writing-table with his left hand resting on the table top and his right hand thrust into the breast of his coat*]: Come in!

> [VILHELM FOLDAL *comes cautiously into the room. He is a bowed, worn-out man with mild blue eyes and long, thin grey hair coming down over his coat-collar. He has a case*

*under his arm, a soft felt hat in his hand and wears large
horn spectacles which he pushes up on his forehead.]*

BORKMAN [*changing his attitude and looking at the visitor with a
half-disappointed, half-pleased expression*]: Oh, it's only you?

FOLDAL: Good evening to you, John Gabriel. Why, yes, it's
me.

BORKMAN [*with a stern look*]: Incidentally, I think you're
rather late getting here.

FOLDAL: Well, it's not such a very short distance, you know.
Especially for anyone who's doing it on foot.

BORKMAN: But why *do* you always walk, Vilhelm? You've
got the tram right by you.

FOLDAL: It's healthier to walk. And then it's the tuppence
saved, too. Well, has Frida been up here lately, playing to
you?

BORKMAN: She went just this minute. Didn't you meet her
outside?

FOLDAL: No, I haven't seen anything of her for a long time.
Not since she came to live with this Mrs Wilton.

BORKMAN [*sitting on the sofa and indicating a chair with a gesture
of his hand*]: You may sit down too, Vilhelm.

FOLDAL [*sitting down on the edge of the chair*]: Many thanks.
[*Looking at him unhappily.*] Oh, you can't think how lonely
I feel since Frida left home.

BORKMAN: Oh come – you've plenty more.

FOLDAL: Yes, lord knows I have. No less than five of them.
But Frida was the only one who as it were understood me a
little. [*Shaking his head sadly.*] The others don't understand
me at all.

BORKMAN [*gloomily, looking straight ahead and drumming on the
table*]: No, that's the trouble. *That's* the curse that we out-
standing people, we men of destiny have to endure. The
common herd, all those average people – they don't understand us, Vilhelm.

FOLDAL [*resigned*]: One could do without understanding.

With a little patience one can always go on waiting for that a little longer. [*In a voice choked with tears.*] But there's something that's more bitter, you know.

BORKMAN [*vehemently*]: There's nothing more bitter than that!

FOLDAL: Yes, there is, John Gabriel. I've just had·a scene at home – before I came out here.

BORKMAN: Have you? Why was that?

FOLDAL [*breaking out*]: My people at home – they despise me.

BORKMAN [*starting*]: Despise –!

FOLDAL [*wiping his eyes*]: I've noticed it a long time. But to-day it came out openly.

BORKMAN [*after a moment's silence*]: I'm afraid you made a bad choice when you married.

FOLDAL: There practically wasn't any choice for me. And besides – one does want to marry, when one begins to get on in years. And I was so low, so down on my luck at that time–

BORKMAN [*springing up in anger*]: Is this a reference to me? A reproach –?

FOLDAL [*nervously*]: No, for heaven's sake, John Gabriel –!

BORKMAN: Yes it is; you're thinking about all that misfortune that fell upon the bank –!

FOLDAL [*soothingly*]: But I don't blame *you* for that! Heaven knows I don't –!

BORKMAN [*muttering, as he sits down again*]: Well, that's just as well.

FOLDAL: And besides you mustn't think it's my wife I'm complaining of. She hasn't much education, poor thing, that's true. But she's a good sort, all the same. No, it's the children, you see –

BORKMAN: I might have known it.

FOLDAL: Because the children – they've more culture. And so they expect more of life.

BORKMAN [*looking sympathetically at him*]: And so the young people despise you, Vilhelm?

FOLDAL [*shrugging his shoulders*]: I haven't made much of a career, you see. One must admit that –

BORKMAN [*coming nearer and laying his hand on his arm*]: Don't they know, then, that you wrote a tragedy in your youth?

FOLDAL: Yes, of course they know *that*. But it doesn't seem to make much impression on them.

BORKMAN: Then they lack judgement, my friend. Because your tragedy is good. I'm absolutely certain of that.

FOLDAL [*brightening up*]: Yes, don't you think there are some good things in it, John Gabriel? Heavens! If only I could get it produced – [*He begins eagerly to open the case and turn over the papers in it.*] Look! Now I'll show you something I've altered –

BORKMAN: Have you got it with you?

FOLDAL: Yes, I brought it along. It's such a long time now, since I read it to you. And so I thought perhaps it would distract you to hear an act or two.

BORKMAN [*waving it aside and getting up*]: No, no, let's leave it till another time.

FOLDAL: All right; as you like. [BORKMAN *paces to and fro across the room.* FOLDAL *puts the manuscript away again.*]

BORKMAN [*coming to a stand in front of him*]: You're right in what you said just now, that you haven't made anything of your career. But I promise you *this*, Vilhelm, that once the hour of rehabilitation strikes for me –

FOLDAL [*beginning to get up*]: Oh, thank you –!

BORKMAN [*with a gesture of his hand*]: Stay where you are, please. [*In rising excitement.*] When the hour of rehabilitation strikes for me – when they realize that they cannot do without me – when they come up here to me in this room and humble themselves and beseech me to take the reins of the bank again –! The new bank that they've founded – and can't manage –. [*He stands by the writing-table as he did before and strikes his breast.*] *Here* I will stand and confront them! And it shall be known all over the land what conditions

John Gabriel lays down for – [*He stops suddenly and looks at* FOLDAL.] You look at me so doubtfully! Can it be that you don't believe they'll come? That they *must, must, must* come to me some day? Don't you believe that?

FOLDAL: Yes, heaven knows I do, John Gabriel.

BORKMAN [*sitting down again on the sofa*]: I firmly believe it. I *know* it – with unshakeable conviction – that they'll come. If I hadn't had that conviction, I should have put a bullet through my head long ago.

FOLDAL [*anxiously*]: Oh no, not for the world –!

BORKMAN [*exultantly*]: But they'll come! They'll come all right! You watch! Any day, any moment, I can expect them here. And you see I hold myself prepared to confront them.

FOLDAL [*with a sigh*]: If only they'd come quickly.

BORKMAN [*uneasily*]: Yes, my friend, time passes; the years pass; life – ah no – I daren't think of that! [*Looking at him.*] Do you know what I sometimes feel like?

FOLDAL: What?

BORKMAN: I feel like a Napoleon who was maimed in his first battle.

FOLDAL [*laying his hand on the case*]: I know that feeling too.

BORKMAN: Oh well, that's something on a smaller scale.

FOLDAL [*quietly*]: My little realm of poetry is very precious to *me* John Gabriel.

BORKMAN [*excitedly*]: Yes, but *I*, who could have made millions! All the mines I should have controlled! New workings stretching out endlessly! Waterfalls! Quarries! Trade routes and shipping lines over the whole wide world! All this, – I should have created it all, alone!

FOLDAL: Yes, I know that well enough. There wasn't a thing you shrank from.

BORKMAN [*clenching his hands*]: And now I must sit here like a wounded grouse and watch the others get in ahead of me – and take it from me, bit by bit!

FOLDAL: That's how it is with *me* too, you know.

BORKMAN [*without taking any notice of him*]: To think of it. I'd practically reached the goal. If I'd just had eight days' leeway to turn round in. All the deposits would have been restored. All the securities I had made bold use of would have been back in their places as before. Those enormous stock companies were within a hair's breadth of being set up. Not a single person would have lost a farthing –

FOLDAL: Heavens, yes! On the very verge, as you were –!

BORKMAN [*with suppressed rage*]: And then the betrayal came upon me! At the very moment of achievement. Do you know what I regard as the most infamous crime a man can commit?

FOLDAL: No, tell me.

BORKMAN: It's not murder. Not robbery or housebreaking. Not even perjury. For those sorts of things, they're done as a rule to people one hates or is indifferent to and who don't count.

FOLDAL: But the most infamous thing, John Gabriel?

BORKMAN [*with emphasis*]: The most infamous is a friend's abuse of a friend's trust.

FOLDAL [*rather doubtfully*]: Yes, but you know –

BORKMAN [*flaring up*]: What's that you're going to say? I can see it in your face. But it doesn't apply. The people who had their securities in the bank, they would have had everything back. Every single penny! No, my friend. The most shameful thing a man can do, is to misuse a friend's letters – to expose to the whole world what was entrusted to him alone, only between themselves, like a whisper in an empty, dark, locked room. The man who can use such means is poisoned and infected through and through with the morals of a master criminal. And I had a friend like that. And it was he who destroyed me.

FOLDAL: I can guess whom you mean.

BORKMAN: There wasn't a corner in all my affairs that I

hesitated to lay open before him. And then when the moment came, he turned the weapons against me that I myself had put in his hands.

FOLDAL: I've never been able to understand why he –. Well, there certainly were rumours of all sorts at the time.

BORKMAN: What were there rumours about? Tell me. I don't know anything. Because I went straight into – into seclusion. What did people hint at, Vilhelm?

FOLDAL: You were to have gone into the Cabinet, they said.

BORKMAN: It was offered me. But I refused.

FOLDAL: So you didn't stand in his way?

BORKMAN: Oh no; it wasn't for that he betrayed me.

FOLDAL: Well, *then* I don't really understand –

BORKMAN: I may as well tell you, Vilhelm.

FOLDAL: Well?

BORKMAN: It was – something to do with a woman, you see.

FOLDAL: To do with a woman? Why but, John Gabriel –?

BORKMAN [*breaking off*]: Oh well, well. We won't talk any more about these old, foolish stories. Well, neither he nor I got into the Cabinet.

FOLDAL: But he got very high up in the world.

BORKMAN: And I sank into the abyss.

FOLDAL: Ah, it's a terrible tragedy –

BORKMAN [*nodding to him*]: Nearly as terrible as *yours*, I think, when one considers it.

FOLDAL [*trustingly*]: Yes, at least as terrible.

BORKMAN [*laughing quietly*]: But looked at from another side, it's really a kind of comedy, too.

FOLDAL: A comedy? All this?

BORKMAN: Yes, the way it seems to be turning out. For I must tell you –

FOLDAL: Well?

BORKMAN: Of course, you didn't meet Frida when you came.

FOLDAL: No.

BORKMAN: While we two are sitting here, she's sitting playing for a dance, down at the house of the man who betrayed and ruined me.

FOLDAL: I'd no idea of that.

BORKMAN: Yes, she took her music and went from here to – to the mansion.

FOLDAL [*apologetically*]: Well, well, the poor child –

BORKMAN: And can you guess whom she's playing for – among others?

FOLDAL: Who?

BORKMAN: For my son, mark you.

FOLDAL: What!

BORKMAN: Yes, what do you think of that, Vilhelm? My son is down there tonight in the ranks of the dancers. So isn't it a comedy, as I said?

FOLDAL: Yes, but then of course he doesn't know anything.

BORKMAN: What doesn't he know?

FOLDAL: Of course he doesn't know how *he* – this man – well –

BORKMAN: You needn't mind saying the name. I can quite well bear it now.

FOLDAL: I'm sure your son doesn't know the circumstances, John Gabriel.

BORKMAN [*gloomily, sitting and drumming on the table*]: He knows it, my friend, as surely as I sit here.

FOLDAL: But can you believe, if he did, he'd want to visit at that house?

BORKMAN [*shaking his head*]: My son probably doesn't look at things in the same way as I do. I dare be sworn he takes the part of my enemies. He no doubt thinks, like them, that Hinkel only did his accursed duty when he went and betrayed me.

FOLDAL: But, my dear man, who could have made him see the thing in that light?

BORKMAN: Who? Do you forget who brought him up?

First his aunt – from the time he was six or seven years old. And ever since – his mother!

FOLDAL: I think you're doing them wrong in this.

BORKMAN [*flaring up*]: I never do anybody wrong! The two of them have set him against me, I tell you!

FOLDAL [*gently*]: Well, yes; I suppose they have.

BORKMAN [*indignantly*]: Oh, these women! They pervert and corrupt life for us! Ruin the whole of our destiny, our march to victory!

FOLDAL: Not all of them, you know!

BORKMAN: No? Name me a single one who's worth anything!

FOLDAL: Well, that's the trouble. The few I know aren't worth much.

BORKMAN [*snorting contemptuously*]: Well, what good is it then? That such women exist – if one doesn't know them!

FOLDAL [*warmly*]: Yes, John Gabriel, it is some good, all the same. It's such a sweet and blessed thing to think of, that somewhere or other around us, far away – *there* the true woman is to be found.

BORKMAN [*moving impatiently on the sofa*]: Oh, stop talking this poetical nonsense.

FOLDAL [*looking at him, deeply hurt*]: Do you call my most sacred belief poetical nonsense?

BORKMAN [*hardly*]: Yes, I do. It's this that's to blame for your never having got on in the world. If you'd only get rid of all this, I could still help you on to your feet – help you to get on.

FOLDAL [*seething inwardly*]: Oh, you can't do that.

BORKMAN: I *can*, when I once get into power again.

FOLDAL: But that's such a terribly long way off.

BORKMAN [*angrily*]: I suppose you think that time will never come? Answer me!

FOLDAL: I don't know how to answer you.

BORKMAN [*getting up, cold and dignified, with a gesture of his hand towards the door*]: Then I have no longer any use for you.

FOLDAL [*jumping up from the chair*]: No use –!

BORKMAN: If you don't believe that my fortune will change –

FOLDAL: But I can't believe against all reason! You'd have to be cleared by law –

BORKMAN: Go on! Go on!

FOLDAL: It's true, I didn't take my examination. But I did read that much law in my time –

BORKMAN [*quickly*]: Impossible, you mean?

FOLDAL: There's no precedent for such a thing.

BORKMAN: It's not necessary for exceptional men.

FOLDAL: The law takes no account of such distinctions.

BORKMAN [*hard and decisively*]: You're no poet, Vilhelm.

FOLDAL [*clasping his hands involuntarily*]: Do you say that in all earnest?

BORKMAN [*dismissing the question without answering it*]: We're only wasting time on each other. It's best for you not to come again.

FOLDAL: Do you want me to leave you, then?

BORKMAN [*without looking at him*]: I've no use for you any longer.

FOLDAL [*gently, taking up his case*]: No, no, no; I suppose not.

BORKMAN: Here you've been, lying to me the whole time.

FOLDAL [*shaking his head*]: Never lying, John Gabriel.

BORKMAN: Haven't you sat here, putting hope and faith and trust into me with your lies?

FOLDAL: They weren't lies, as long as *you* believed in *my* vocation. As long as you believed in me, so long I believed in you.

BORKMAN: Then we've been deluding each other mutually. And perhaps deluding ourselves – both of us.

FOLDAL: But isn't that at bottom what friendship is, John Gabriel?

BORKMAN [*with a bitter smile*]: Yes, to delude – that's friendship. You're right there. I've had that experience once before.

FOLDAL [*looking at him*]: No poet. And you could say that to me so harshly.

BORKMAN [*his voice a little gentler*]: Well, I'm no authority in that field.

FOLDAL: Perhaps more than you realize.

BORKMAN: I?

FOLDAL [*quietly*]: Yes, my friend. Because I've had my doubts myself now and again, you must know. That terrible doubt – that I've ruined my life for the sake of a fantasy.

BORKMAN: If you doubt yourself, then you're losing your footing.

FOLDAL: That's why it was such a comfort to me to come here and lean on you, who did believe in me. [*Taking up his hat.*] But now you're like a stranger to me.

BORKMAN: And you to me.

FOLDAL: Good night, John Gabriel.

BORKMAN: Good night, Vilhelm.

[FOLDAL *goes out to the left.* BORKMAN *stands a moment gazing at the closed door; makes a movement as if he would call* FOLDAL *back but thinks better of it and begins to go up and down across the floor with his hands behind his back. Then he stops beside the sofa table and turns out the lamp. It becomes half dark in the gallery. After a little, someone knocks on the tapestry door at the back on the left.*]

BORKMAN [*beside the table, starts, turns, and asks in a loud voice*]: Who is it who's knocking? [*There is no answer. Then another knock comes.*]

BORKMAN [*still standing there*]: Who *is* it? Come in!

[ELLA RENTHEIM, *with a light in her hand, appears in the doorway. She is dressed as before in a black dress with a cloak thrown loosely over her shoulders.*]

BORKMAN [*gazing at her*]: Who are *you*? What do you want with me?

ELLA RENTHEIM [*shutting the door behind her and coming nearer*]: It's me, John Gabriel. [*She puts down the light on the piano and remains standing there.*]

BORKMAN [*standing as if thunder-struck, gazing fixedly at her and whispering under his voice*]: Is it – is it Ella? Is it Ella Rentheim?

ELLA RENTHEIM: Yes. It's 'your' Ella – as you called me in the old days. Once. Many, many years ago.

BORKMAN [*as before*]: Yes, it's you, Ella – I see that now.

ELLA RENTHEIM: Do you know me again?

BORKMAN: Yes, now I begin to –

ELLA RENTHEIM: Yes, the years have been hard on me, John Gabriel, and it's autumn now. Don't you think so?

BORKMAN [*with constraint*]: You are rather changed. At least, at first glance –

ELLA RENTHEIM: I have no dark curls hanging down my back now. Those curls you once loved so to twist round your fingers.

BORKMAN [*quickly*]: That's it! I see it now, Ella. You've done your hair differently.

ELLA RENTHEIM [*with a sad smile*]: Quite right. It's the hair that makes the difference.

BORKMAN [*changing the subject*]: I'd no idea that you were in this part of the country.

ELLA RENTHEIM: I've only just come.

BORKMAN: Why have you made the journey over here – now, in winter?

ELLA RENTHEIM: You shall hear about that.

BORKMAN: Is it anything you want *me* for?

ELLA RENTHEIM: You among others. But if we're going to talk about *that*, I must begin a long way back.

BORKMAN: You must be tired.

ELLA RENTHEIM: Yes, I am tired.

BORKMAN: Won't you sit down? *There*, on the sofa.

ELLA RENTHEIM: Yes, thanks. I'd better sit down.

> [*She goes over to the right and sits in the sofa-corner nearest the front of the stage.* BORKMAN *stands by the table with his hands behind his back and looks at her. There is a short silence.*]

ELLA RENTHEIM: It's a very long time since we two met face to face, John Gabriel.

BORKMAN [*gloomily*]: A long, long time. All that terrible business lies between.

ELLA RENTHEIM: A whole life-time lies between. A wasted life-time.

BORKMAN [*looking keenly at her*]: Wasted!

ELLA RENTHEIM: Yes, indeed. Wasted. For both of us.

BORKMAN [*in a cold, matter-of-fact tone*]: I don't regard my life as wasted yet.

ELLA RENTHEIM: And *my* life, then?

BORKMAN: There you're to blame yourself, Ella.

ELLA RENTHEIM [*with a start*]: And *you* say *that*!

BORKMAN: You could quite well have been happy without me.

ELLA RENTHEIM: Do you believe that?

BORKMAN: If you'd only chosen to.

ELLA RENTHEIM [*bitterly*]: Yes, I know well enough that there was someone else ready to take me over –

BORKMAN: But you refused him –

ELLA RENTHEIM: Yes, I did.

BORKMAN: Time after time you refused him. Year after year –

ELLA RENTHEIM [*scornfully*]: Year after year I refused happiness, I suppose you mean?

BORKMAN: You could perfectly well have been happy with him instead. And then *I* should have been saved.

ELLA RENTHEIM: You –?

BORKMAN: Yes, then you'd have saved me, Ella.

ELLA RENTHEIM: How do you mean?

BORKMAN: He thought it was I who was at the back of your refusals – of your obstinate denial. And so he took his revenge. For he could do that so easily – he had all my frank, confiding letters in his hands. He made use of them, and so it was all up with me – for the time being. You see, all that's your fault, Ella!

ELLA RENTHEIM: Really, John Gabriel – when it comes to the point, *I* seem to be the one who's in *your* debt.

BORKMAN: It depends how you look at it. I know very well how much I have to thank you for. You had this place, the whole estate, bought in for you at the auction. Put the house entirely at my disposal and – and your sister's. You took charge of Erhart and looked after him in every way –

ELLA RENTHEIM: – as long as I was allowed to –

BORKMAN: – allowed to by your sister, yes. I have never meddled in these domestic matters. As I was saying – I know what you've sacrificed for me and for your sister. But you were in a position to do it, Ella. And you must remember that it was *I* who made it possible for you to do it.

ELLA RENTHEIM [*indignantly*]: You're quite wrong there, John Gabriel! It was my deep and warm affection for Erhart – and for you too – it was *that* that made me do it!

BORKMAN [*interrupting*]: My dear, don't let us discuss feelings and things of that kind. I mean, of course, that even if you did do what you did, yet it was *I* who gave you the power to do it.

ELLA RENTHEIM [*smiling*]: Hm, the power, the power –

BORKMAN [*hotly*]: Yes, precisely; the power! When the great, decisive stroke was to be struck, when I couldn't spare either family or friends, when I had to lay hold of – and did lay hold, too, – of the millions that were entrusted to me – then I spared everything of yours, everything you owned

328

and possessed – although I could have taken and borrowed that – and used it – just like all the rest.

ELLA RENTHEIM [*cold and calm*]: That's perfectly true, John Gabriel.

BORKMAN: It is. And that's why, when they came and took me, they found all your money untouched in the vaults of the bank.

ELLA RENTHEIM [*looking at him*]: I've so often thought of that. Why did you spare precisely what was mine? And only that?

BORKMAN: Why?

ELLA RENTHEIM: Yes, why? Tell me.

BORKMAN [*hard and scornful*]: You think, I suppose, it was so as to have something to fall back on – if things went wrong?

ELLA RENTHEIM: Oh no, I'm sure you didn't think of that in *those* days.

BORKMAN: Never! I was so absolutely sure of victory.

ELLA RENTHEIM: Well, but why, then?

BORKMAN [*shrugging his shoulders*]: Good gracious, Ella – it's not so easy to remember motives that are twenty years old. I only remember that when I was alone, struggling in silence with all the vast undertakings that were to be set in motion, I seemed to feel as though I were the captain of an air-ship. There I was, in those sleepless nights, inflating a giant air-ship, to sail out over an unknown, perilous ocean.

ELLA RENTHEIM [*smiling*]: You, who never doubted your victory?

BORKMAN [*impatiently*]: Men *are* like that, Ella. They both doubt a thing and believe it. [*Looking straight before him.*] And I suppose that was why I didn't want to have you and what belonged to you with me in the air-ship.

ELLA RENTHEIM [*in suspense*]: Why, I want to know! Tell me why?

BORKMAN [*without looking at her*]: One doesn't want to take one's dearest possession aboard on a voyage like that.

329

ELLA RENTHEIM: But you *had* your dearest possession on board. The whole of your future life –

BORKMAN: Life isn't always the dearest thing.

ELLA RENTHEIM [*breathless*]: Was that how it was with you then?

BORKMAN: I rather think it was.

ELLA RENTHEIM: That *I* was the dearest thing you had?

BORKMAN: Yes; something like that comes back to me.

ELLA RENTHEIM: And yet years and years had passed since you'd deserted me – and married – someone else!

BORKMAN: Deserted you, you say? You know perfectly well it was higher considerations – well, *other* considerations, then – that compelled me. Without *his* support I couldn't make any progress.

ELLA RENTHEIM [*controlling herself*]: Deserted me, then, from – higher considerations.

BORKMAN: I couldn't do without his help. And he made *you* the price of the help.

ELLA RENTHEIM: And you paid the price. In full. Without dispute.

BORKMAN: I hadn't any choice. I had to win or fall.

ELLA RENTHEIM [*with a trembling voice, looking at him*]: Can it be true, what you said, that at that time I was the dearest thing in the world to you?

BORKMAN: Both then and after – long, long after.

ELLA RENTHEIM: And yet you sold me, all the same. Bargained with another man over your right to love me. Sold my love for a – for a directorship!

BORKMAN [*gloomily and with bowed head*]: Utter necessity drove me to it, Ella.

ELLA RENTHEIM [*getting up from the sofa, fierce and trembling*]: Criminal!

BORKMAN [*starting, but controlling himself*]: I've heard that word before.

ELLA RENTHEIM: Oh don't think I'm speaking of any crime

330

against your country's law. Whatever use you may have
made of all these share-certificates and bonds – or whatever
they were – what do you think I care about that! If I'd had
the right to stand beside you when everything crashed about
you –

BORKMAN [*tensely*]: What then, Ella?

ELLA RENTHEIM: Believe me, I would have borne it gladly
with you. The disgrace, the ruin – everything. I would have
helped you to bear it all –

BORKMAN: Would you have wanted to? *Could* you?

ELLA RENTHEIM: I both would and could. For then I didn't
know about your great, your terrible crime.

BORKMAN: Which? What do you mean?

ELLA RENTHEIM: I mean the crime for which there's no for-
giveness.

BORKMAN [*gazing at her*]: You must be out of your mind.

ELLA RENTHEIM [*coming nearer*]: You are a murderer! You
have committed the deadly sin!

BORKMAN [*shrinking back towards the piano*]: You're raving,
Ella!

ELLA RENTHEIM: You have killed the power to love in me.
[*Coming nearer to him.*] Do you understand what that means?
It speaks in the Bible of a mysterious sin, that there's no for-
giveness for. I've never been able to see till now what it
could be. Now I do see. The great, unpardonable sin – it's
the sin of killing love in a human creature.

BORKMAN: And you say I've done that?

ELLA RENTHEIM: You *have* done it. I've never really known
till this evening what it was exactly that happened to me.
Your deserting me and turning to Gunhild instead – I took
that just as ordinary inconstancy on your part. And the
result of heartless scheming on hers. And I almost think I
despised you a little – in spite of everything. But now I see
it. You deserted the woman you *loved*! Me, me, me! The
dearest thing you had in the world – you were ready to

hand it over for gain. *That's* the double murder you made yourself guilty of. The murder of your own soul and of mine.

BORKMAN [*cold and controlled*]: How well I recognize your passionate, undisciplined nature, Ella. It's no doubt reasonable enough for you to see the thing as you do. You're a woman. And so, of course, it seems as though you know nothing else, value nothing else in all the world.

ELLA RENTHEIM: No, I certainly don't.

BORKMAN: Only your own heart's concern –

ELLA RENTHEIM: Only that! Only that! You're right.

BORKMAN: But you must remember I'm a man. As a woman, you were the dearest thing in the world to me. But if it has to come to that, then one woman can be replaced by another –

ELLA RENTHEIM [*looking at him with a smile*]: Was that your experience, when you had taken Gunhild as your wife?

BORKMAN: No. But the tasks of my life helped me to bear *that* too. All the sources of power in this land – I wanted to make them subject to me. Everything that earth and fell and wood and sea contained and all their riches – I wanted to subdue it all and create a kingdom for myself and through it the well-being of many, many thousands of others.

ELLA RENTHEIM [*lost in memories*]: I know that. So many evenings we talked of your purposes –

BORKMAN: Yes, I could talk to you, Ella.

ELLA RENTHEIM: I joked about your schemes and asked whether you wanted to waken all the slumbering spirits of the gold.

BORKMAN [*nodding*]: I remember that phrase. [*Slowly.*] All the slumbering spirits of the gold.

ELLA RENTHEIM: But you didn't take it as a joke. You said, 'Yes, yes, Ella, that's just what I do want.'

BORKMAN: And it was, too. If I could only get my foot into the stirrup –. And *that* depended then on that one man. He could get me the controlling interest in the bank, and was prepared to – if I on my side –

ELLA RENTHEIM: Just so! If you on your side gave up your claim to the woman you loved – and who loved you so immeasurably in return.

BORKMAN: I knew his devouring passion for you. Knew that he'd never on any other condition –

ELLA RENTHEIM: And so you made the bargain.

BORKMAN [*vehemently*]: Yes, I did, Ella! For the desire for power was irresistible in me, you see! And so I agreed. Had to agree. And he helped me up half-way to the heights that drew me to them, where I longed to be. And I climbed and climbed. Year by year I climbed –

ELLA RENTHEIM: And *I* was like something wiped out of your life.

BORKMAN: And in the end he flung me down again into the abyss. Because of you, Ella.

ELLA RENTHEIM [*after a short, reflective silence*]: John Gabriel, doesn't it seem to you as though a curse had rested on the whole of our relationship?

BORKMAN [*looking at her*]: A curse?

ELLA RENTHEIM: Yes. Don't you think so?

BORKMAN [*uneasily*]: Yes. But why, exactly –? [*Breaking out.*] Oh, Ella, I hardly know any longer which is right – I or you!

ELLA RENTHEIM: You're the one that has sinned. You killed all the human joy in me.

BORKMAN [*in anxiety*]: Don't say that, Ella!

ELLA RENTHEIM: All a woman's joy, at least. From the time your image began to grow dim in me, I've lived my life under an eclipse. All these years it's grown harder and harder for me – quite impossible in the end – to love any living creature. Neither people nor animals nor plants. Only this single one –

BORKMAN: Which single one –?

ELLA RENTHEIM: Erhart, of course.

BORKMAN: Erhart?

ELLA RENTHEIM: Erhart, – your son, John Gabriel. Yours.

BORKMAN: Has he really been so near to your heart, then?

ELLA RENTHEIM: Why else do you think I took him? And kept him, as long as ever I could? Why?

BORKMAN: I thought it was from pity. Like all the rest.

ELLA RENTHEIM [*in strong inward emotion*]: Pity, you say! Ha, ha! I've never known pity – since you deserted me. I simply couldn't. If a poor, starving child came into my kitchen, freezing and crying and begging for a little food, I let the cook look after it. Never felt any desire to take the child in myself, warm it by my own stove, enjoy sitting and watching it eat its fill. And yet I'd never been like that when I was young; I remember that so clearly! It's *you* who've made that empty, barren desert in me – and around me, too.

BORKMAN: Only not for Erhart.

ELLA RENTHEIM: No. Not for your son. But for everything else, every thing that lives and moves. You have cheated me of a mother's joy and happiness in life. And of a mother's sorrows and tears too. And perhaps *that* was the worst loss for me, you know.

BORKMAN: Do you think so, Ella?

ELLA RENTHEIM: Who knows? Perhaps it was a mother's sorrows and tears that I needed most. [*With stronger feeling.*] But I couldn't bear the loss with patience then! And that's why I took Erhart. Won him entirely. Won the whole of his warm, trusting child's heart for myself, – until –. Ah!

BORKMAN: Until what?

ELLA RENTHEIM: Until his mother – his mother in the flesh, I mean – took him away from me again.

BORKMAN: He had to leave you, after all. And come into town here.

ELLA RENTHEIM [*wringing her hands*]: Yes, but I can't bear the

334

solitude, John Gabriel! The emptiness! The loss of your son's heart.

BORKMAN [*with an evil expression in his eyes*]: Hm. I don't suppose you've lost it Ella. Hearts aren't easily lost to anyone downstairs here – on the ground-floor.

ELLA RENTHEIM: I *have* lost Erhart here. And *she* has won him back again. Or someone else has. That shows quite clearly in the letters he writes me from time to time.

BORKMAN: Then it's to take him home with you that you've come here?

ELLA RENTHEIM: Yes, if only *that* could be done, then –!

BORKMAN: Oh, it can be done, if you really want it. For you've got the strongest and first claim on him.

ELLA RENTHEIM: Oh, claim, claim! What's the good of a claim here? If I haven't got him of his own free will – then I haven't got him at all. And it's *that* that I must have! I must have my child's heart all to myself now, not shared!

BORKMAN: You must remember that Erhart's in his twenties. You wouldn't be able to count on it for long, you know – keeping his heart and not sharing it, as you put it.

ELLA RENTHEIM [*with a sad smile*]: It wouldn't need to last so very long.

BORKMAN: Wouldn't it? I should have thought that what *you* want, you want till the end of your days.

ELLA RENTHEIM: Yes, I do. But that doesn't mean it need last long.

BORKMAN [*starting*]: What do you mean by that?

ELLA RENTHEIM: You know, surely, that I've been ill all these last years?

BORKMAN: *You* have?

ELLA RENTHEIM: Don't you know that?

BORKMAN: No, not exactly –

ELLA RENTHEIM [*looking at him in surprise*]: Hasn't Erhart told you about it?

BORKMAN: I can't really remember at the moment.

ELLA RENTHEIM: Perhaps he's never talked about me at all?

BORKMAN: Oh yes, I believe he's talked about you. But the fact is, I so seldom see anything of him. Hardly ever. There's someone downstairs who keeps him away from me. Well away, you understand.

ELLA RENTHEIM: Do you know that for certain, John Gabriel?

BORKMAN: Yes, I know it all right. [*Changing his tone.*] Well, so you've been ill, then, Ella?

ELLA RENTHEIM: Yes, I have. And this autumn it got so much worse that I had to come into town and get the advice of more experienced doctors.

BORKMAN: And I suppose you've already seen them?

ELLA RENTHEIM: Yes, this morning.

BORKMAN: And what did they say about it?

ELLA RENTHEIM: They confirmed absolutely what I'd long suspected –

BORKMAN: Well?

ELLA RENTHEIM [*evenly and calmly*]: It's an incurable disease I have, John Gabriel.

BORKMAN: Oh, don't believe anything like that, Ella!

ELLA RENTHEIM: It's a disease there's no help or cure for, you see. The doctors don't know any remedy for it. They must let it take its course. They can't do anything to stop it. Only perhaps ease it a little. And that's something, after all.

BORKMAN: Oh, but it may take a long time yet, believe me.

ELLA RENTHEIM: It may possibly take the rest of the winter, they told me.

BORKMAN [*without thinking*]: Oh well, the winter's pretty long.

ELLA RENTHEIM [*quietly*]: It's long enough for *me*, at any rate.

BORKMAN [*energetically, turning it aside*]: But what in the world can have caused this illness? You who've always lived such a healthy, regular life –? What can have caused it?

ELLA RENTHEIM [*looking at him*]: The doctors thought that

336

perhaps I'd once had to go through some great distress of mind.

BORKMAN [*flaring up*]: Distress of mind! Ah, I understand! It's to be *me*, who's to blame!

ELLA RENTHEIM [*with increasing agitation*]: It's too late to go into *that* now. But I *must* have the child of my heart again, my only child, before I go! It's so terribly hard for me to think of, that I've got to leave everything in life – to leave the sun and the light and the air, without leaving behind me a single person who will think of me, remember me kindly and sadly – the way a son thinks of and remembers the mother he has lost.

BORKMAN [*after a short pause*]: Take him, Ella – if you can get him.

ELLA RENTHEIM [*eagerly*]: Will you consent to that? *Can* you?

BORKMAN [*gloomily*]: Yes. And it isn't such a great sacrifice, you know. Because he isn't mine in any case.

ELLA RENTHEIM: Thank you, thank you for the sacrifice all the same! But then I've one more thing to ask you for. A great thing for *me*, John Gabriel.

BORKMAN: Well, just say what it is.

ELLA RENTHEIM: Perhaps you'll think it's childish of me – won't be able to understand it –

BORKMAN: Well, tell me. What is it?

ELLA RENTHEIM: When I die, quite soon now, I shall leave a fair amount –

BORKMAN: Yes, I suppose you will.

ELLA RENTHEIM: And I mean to let it all go to Erhart.

BORKMAN: Well, you haven't really got anyone nearer.

ELLA RENTHEIM [*warmly*]: No, I certainly have no one nearer than him.

BORKMAN: No one of your own family. You're the last.

ELLA RENTHEIM [*nodding slowly*]: Yes, that's just it. When I die, then the name of Rentheim dies too. And that's a very bitter thought to me. To be wiped out of existence – even to your name –

BORKMAN [*flaring up*]: Ah, – I see what you're getting at!

ELLA RENTHEIM [*passionately*]: Don't let that happen! Let Erhart bear the name after me!

BORKMAN [*looking sternly at her*]: I understand you all right. You want to save my son from bearing his father's name. That's what it is.

ELLA RENTHEIM: Never! I would have borne it myself, proudly and gladly, together with you! But a mother, who's soon to die –. A name is more of a bond than you realize, John Gabriel.

BORKMAN [*coldly and proudly*]: Very well Ella. I shall be man enough to bear my name alone.

ELLA RENTHEIM [*seizing and pressing his hands*]: Thank you! Thank you! Now the debt is cancelled between us. Yes, yes. So be it. You have made good what you could. For when I'm gone from this life, there'll be Erhart Rentheim living after me.

[*The tapestry door is thrown open.* MRS BORKMAN, *with the large shawl over her head, stands in the open doorway.*]

MRS BORKMAN [*in violent agitation*]: Never, to all eternity, shall Erhart be called that!

ELLA RENTHEIM [*shrinking back*]: Gunhild!

BORKMAN [*harsh and threatening*]: No one has permission to come up here to me!

MRS BORKMAN [*coming a step further in*]: I give myself permission.

BORKMAN [*going towards her*]: What do you want with me?

MRS BORKMAN: To battle and fight for you. Protect you against evil powers.

ELLA RENTHEIM: The most evil powers are in yourself, Gunhild!

MRS BORKMAN [*harshly*]: Let that be as it may. [*Threateningly, with upraised arm.*] But this I tell you – he shall bear his father's name! And bear it aloft to honour again! And I alone will be his mother! I alone! My son's heart shall be mine. Mine and no one else's.

[*She goes out through the tapestry door and shuts it behind her.*]

ELLA RENTHEIM [*shaken and overcome*]: John Gabriel – Erhart will be wrecked in this tempest. There must be an understanding between you and Gunhild. We must go down to her at once.

BORKMAN [*looking at her*]: We? I too, do you mean?

ELLA RENTHEIM: Both of us.

BORKMAN [*shaking his head*]: She's hard, you know. Hard as the metal I once dreamt of hewing out of the mountains.

ELLA RENTHEIM: Then try it now!

BORKMAN [*does not answer; he stands and looks doubtfully at her*].

ACT THREE

Mrs Borkman's living-room. The lamp is still burning downstage on the sofa table. Beyond, in the garden-room, the lights are out and it is dark. MRS BORKMAN, *with the shawl over her head, comes in by the hall door in great distress of mind. She goes across to the window and draws the curtain aside a little; then she goes across and sits down by the stove, but jumps up again at once and goes over and rings the bell-pull. She stands by the sofa and waits a moment. No one comes. Then she rings again; harder this time. In a little while the* MAID SERVANT *comes in from the hall. She looks cross and sleepy and as though she had dressed in a hurry.*

MRS BORKMAN [*impatiently*]: What's become of you Malene? I've had to ring twice.

MAID: Yes, ma'am, I heard you all right.

MRS BORKMAN: And yet you didn't come.

MAID [*aggrieved*]: I had to put a few clothes on first, I suppose.

MRS BORKMAN: Yes, you must dress yourself properly. And then you must run over at once and fetch my son.

MAID [*looking at her in amazement*]: I'm to fetch Mr Erhart?

MRS BORKMAN: Yes. You're just to say he must come home to me at once, because I want to talk to him.

MAID [*sulkily*]: Then I suppose I'd better wake the coachman at the manager's.

MRS BORKMAN: Why?

MAID: So that he can harness up the sledge. The snow's awful outdoors tonight.

MRS BORKMAN: Oh, that doesn't matter. Just hurry up and go. It's only round the corner.

MAID: Oh but, ma'am, it isn't round the corner, not by no means.

340

MRS BORKMAN: Yes of course it is. Don't you know where Mr Hinkel's house is?

MAID [*spitefully*]: Oh, I see. Is it *there* Mr Erhart is tonight?

MRS BORKMAN [*surprised*]: Yes, where else should he be?

MAID [*hiding a smile*]: Well, I only thought he was where he usually is, that's what I thought.

MRS BORKMAN: Where do you mean?

MAID: At this Mrs Wilton's, as they call her.

MRS BORKMAN: Mrs Wilton's? My son doesn't go *there* very often.

MAID [*muttering to herself*]: There's them as says he's there every blessed day.

MRS BORKMAN: That's nonsense, Malene. So go across to Mr Hinkel's and see about getting him.

MAID [*tossing her head*]: Oh, all right. I'll go. [*She is just going out through the hall, but at that moment the hall door opens.* ELLA RENTHEIM *and* BORKMAN *appear on the threshold.*]

MRS BORKMAN [*staggering back a step*]: What does this mean?

MAID [*frightened and folding her hands instinctively*]: Heaven help us!

MRS BORKMAN [*whispering to the* MAID]: Say that he must come this very minute!

MAID [*in a low voice*]: Yes, ma'am.

[ELLA RENTHEIM *comes into the room, with* BORKMAN *after her. The* MAID *slips round behind them out of the door and shuts it after her. There is a short silence.*]

MRS BORKMAN [*again in command of herself, turning to* ELLA]: What does he want down here in my room?

ELLA RENTHEIM: He wants to try and come to an understanding with you, Gunhild.

MRS BORKMAN: He's never tried to do that before.

ELLA RENTHEIM: He's going to, tonight.

MRS BORKMAN: The last time we stood face to face – it was during the trial. When I was called to give an explanation –

BORKMAN[*going nearer*]: And tonight it is *I* who will give an explanation.

MRS BORKMAN [*gazing at him*]: You!

BORKMAN: Not about my wrong-doing. All the world knows *that*.

MRS BORKMAN [*with a bitter sigh*]: Yes, that's true enough. All the world knows it.

BORKMAN: But it doesn't know *why* I did it. Why I *had* to do it. People don't realize that I *had* to do that because I was myself – because I was John Gabriel Borkman – and no one else. And it's *that* I want to try and explain to you.

MRS BORKMAN [*shaking her head*]: It's no use. Impulses don't acquit anyone. Nor fancies, either.

BORKMAN: They can acquit one in one's own eyes.

MRS BORKMAN [*throwing out her hand in protest*]: Oh stop talking about it! I've thought quite enough about all these dark affairs of yours.

BORKMAN: So have I. In those five endless years in the cell – and other places – I had time for that. And in the eight years up there in the gallery I had even more time. I have opened up the whole case for fresh investigation – by me, myself. Time after time I have re-opened it. I have been my own accuser, my own defence, and my own judge. More impartially than anyone else at all – that I *can* say, I have walked the floor of the gallery up there turning over and over every one of my actions. Considered them on every side just as unsparingly, just as pitilessly as any lawyer. And the verdict I come back to every time is *this*, that the only person I have sinned against is myself.

MRS BORKMAN: How about me, then? And your son?

BORKMAN: You and he are included in what I mean when I say myself.

MRS BORKMAN: And what about the many hundreds of others? Those that people say you have ruined?

BORKMAN [*more vehemently*]: I had the power! And the call

within me that allowed of no doubt. The imprisoned millions lay there all over the country, deep in the mountains, and called to me! Cried to me for freedom! But no one, none of the others heard it. Only I alone.

MRS BORKMAN: Yes, as a brand for the name of Borkman.

BORKMAN: How do we know that, if the others had had the power, they wouldn't have acted just as I did?

MRS BORKMAN: No one, no one but you would have done it!

BORKMAN: Perhaps not. But that was because they hadn't the abilities that I had. And if they *had* done it, they wouldn't have done it with *my* goal before their eyes. The deed would have been quite different. To put it briefly, I have acquitted myself.

ELLA RENTHEIM [*gently and beseechingly*]: Ah, but can you say that so positively, John Gabriel?

BORKMAN [*nodding*]: Acquitted myself on that point. But then comes the great, crushing accusation from within.

MRS BORKMAN: Which is *that*?

BORKMAN: I have stayed up there and thrown away eight whole, precious years of my life! The very day I was set free, I should have gone out into reality – out into the iron, hard reality in which there are no dreams. I should have begun from the bottom and climbed up all over again to the heights – higher than ever before, in spite of all that lay between.

MRS BORKMAN: Oh, that would only have been to live the same life over again – believe me.

BORKMAN [*shaking his head and looking at her, as though instructing her*]: Nothing new happens. But the thing that *has* happened – it doesn't repeat itself either. It's the eye that changes the deed. The new-made eye changes the old deed. [*Breaking off.*] But you don't understand that.

MRS BORKMAN [*shortly*]: No, I don't understand it.

BORKMAN: No, that is just the curse, that I never have found understanding in a single human soul.

ELLA RENTHEIM [*looking at him*]: Never, John Gabriel?

BORKMAN: Except in *one* – perhaps. Long, long ago. In the days when I didn't think I had need of understanding. Otherwise, since then, never in anyone! I've had no one watchful enough to be on hand and rouse me – to ring as it were a morning bell for me – rouse me up anew to glad toil. And to instil into my mind that I had done nothing irreparable.

MRS BORKMAN [*laughing scornfully*]: So you do need it, after all, to have *that* instilled from outside?

BORKMAN [*in rising wrath*]: Yes, when the whole world hisses in chorus that I can never rise again, why, then there may come moments when I myself am near believing it. [*Lifting his head.*] But then there rises up again my innermost, triumphant conviction. And *that* acquits me!

MRS BORKMAN [*looking at him with a hard expression*]: Why did you never come and ask me for what you call understanding?

BORKMAN: Would it have been any use – if I had come to you?

MRS BORKMAN [*warding off the idea with a gesture of her hand*]: You have never loved anything outside yourself – that's the core of the matter.

BORKMAN [*proudly*]: I have loved power –

MRS BORKMAN: Power, yes!

BORKMAN: – the power to create human happiness far and wide about me!

MRS BORKMAN: You once had the power to make *me* happy. Did you use it for that?

BORKMAN [*without looking at her*]: Someone has to go down as a rule – in a ship wreck.

MRS BORKMAN: And your own son? Did you use your power – did you live and breathe to make *him* happy?

BORKMAN: I don't know him.

MRS BORKMAN: No, that's true. You don't even know him.

BORKMAN [*hardly*]: You've taken care of that – you, his mother.

MRS BORKMAN [*looking at him with haughtiness in her expression*]: Ah, you don't know what *I've* taken care of!

BORKMAN: You?

MRS BORKMAN: Yes, I myself. By myself.

BORKMAN: Well, tell me then.

MRS BORKMAN: I've taken care of the name you will leave behind you.

BORKMAN [*with a short, dry laugh*]: ... I leave behind me? Well, well! It almost sounds as if I were dead already.

MRS BORKMAN [*with emphasis*]: And you *are*, too.

BORKMAN [*slowly*]: Yes, perhaps you're right. [*Flaring up.*] But no, no! Not yet! I've been very near, very near to it. But now I'm awake. Refreshed again. There's life before me yet. I can see this new, shining life waiting and quickening – And you'll see it yourself, too.

MRS BORKMAN [*lifting her hand*]: Don't dream about life any more! Stay quiet where you lie.

ELLA RENTHEIM [*indignantly*]: Gunhild! Gunhild! How can you –!

MRS BORKMAN [*without listening to her*]: I will set up the monument over the grave.

BORKMAN: The pillar of shame, perhaps you mean?

MRS BORKMAN [*in rising emotion*]: Oh no, it won't be a tablet in stone or metal. And no one shall be allowed to carve a scornful inscription on the tablet I set up. It shall be as though a ring, a living hedge of trees and bushes, were planted thick, thick around your buried life. All the dark things that once *were* shall be covered over. They shall hide John Gabriel Borkman in oblivion from men's eyes!

BORKMAN [*hoarsely and cuttingly*]: And this work of love – *you* will perform?

MRS BORKMAN: Not in my own strength. I wouldn't dream of thinking that. But I've bred up a helper to dedicate his life to this one aim. *He* shall live a life so pure and lofty and radiant, that your own life under-ground shall be obliterated up here on earth.

BORKMAN [*gloomy and threatening*]: If it's Erhart you mean, say so at once!

MRS BORKMAN [*looking him straight in the eyes*]: Yes, it's Erhart. My son. He whom you're ready to renounce – in payment for your own misdeeds.

BORKMAN [*with a glance at* ELLA]: In payment for my gravest sin.

MRS BORKMAN [*brushing it aside*]: Only a sin against a stranger. Remember the sin against me! [*Looking triumphantly at them both.*] But he won't listen to you. When I call on him in my need, he will come! For it is with *me* he is to be! With me and never with anyone else – [*Listening suddenly and calling.*] I can hear him there! There he is – there he is! Erhart!

> [ERHART BORKMAN *opens the entrance door hurriedly and comes into the room. He is in his overcoat and has his hat on his head.*]

ERHART [*pale and anxious*]: Why, Mother – what in heaven's name –! [*He sees* BORKMAN *who is standing by the doorway to the garden-room, starts, and takes off his hat. He is silent for a moment and then asks.*] What do you want me for Mother? What's happened?

MRS BORKMAN [*stretching her arms out towards him*]: I want to see you, Erhart! I want to have you with me – always!

ERHART [*stammering*]: Have me –? Always! What do you mean by that?

MRS BORKMAN: I want to have you, to have you, I say! There's someone who wants to take you from me!

ERHART [*falling back a step*]: Ah, – you know that then!

MRS BORKMAN: Yes. Do you know it too?

ERHART [*starting and looking at her*]: Do *I* know it? Well, of course –

MRS BORKMAN: Ah, a deliberate trick! Behind my back! Erhart, Erhart!

ERHART [*quickly*]: Mother, tell me what it is you know!

MRS BORKMAN: I know it all. I know that your aunt has come here to take you away from me.

ERHART: Aunt Ella!

ELLA RENTHEIM: Oh, listen to *me* for a moment first, Erhart!

MRS BORKMAN [*going on*]: She wants me to give you up to her. She wants to take your mother's place with you, Erhart! She wants you to be her son and not mine in future. Wants you to inherit all her property. To give up your name and take hers instead!

ERHART: Aunt Ella, is this true?

ELLA RENTHEIM: Yes, it's true.

ERHART: I didn't know a word of this till now. Why do you want me to come back to you again?

ELLA RENTHEIM: Because I feel I'm losing you here.

MRS BORKMAN [*harshly*]: It's to me you're losing him – yes! And that's only as it should be.

ELLA RENTHEIM [*looking at him with entreaty*]: Erhart, I can't bear to lose you. For I'll tell you, I am solitary – and dying.

ERHART: Dying –?

ELLA RENTHEIM: Yes, dying. Will you be with me till the end? Join yourself to me entirely? Be for me as if you were my own child –?

MRS BORKMAN [*interrupting*]: – and desert your mother and perhaps your mission in life too? Do you want to do that, Erhart?

ELLA RENTHEIM: I am doomed to die. Answer me, Erhart.

ERHART [*affectionately and moved*]: Aunt Ella, – you've been so wonderfully good to me. With you I was able to grow up without any troubles, as happy as I think any child could be in its life –

MRS BORKMAN: Erhart, Erhart!

ELLA RENTHEIM: Oh, what a blessing that you can still see it like that!

ERHART: – but I can't sacrifice myself to you now. I can't possibly make a hard and fast promise to be like a son to you.

MRS BORKMAN [*in triumph*]: Ah, I knew it all right! You won't get him! You won't get him, Ella!

ELLA RENTHEIM [*sadly*]: I see that. You have won him back.

MRS BORKMAN: Yes, yes, – he's mine and mine he'll stay. Erhart – it's true, isn't it? – we two have still some way to go together.

ERHART [*fighting with himself*]: Mother, – I may just as well tell you straight out –

MRS BORKMAN [*in suspense*]: Well?

ERHART: It's only a little way now that I shall be going with you, Mother.

MRS BORKMAN [*standing as though struck*]: What do you mean by *that*?

ERHART [*plucking up his courage*]: Good heavens, Mother – I'm young! I feel as if this close, indoor air will suffocate me in the end.

MRS BORKMAN: Here – with me!

ERHART: Yes, here with you, Mother!

ELLA RENTHEIM: Come with me, then, Erhart!

ERHART: Oh, Aunt Ella, it isn't a scrap better with you. It's a different kind *there*. But that doesn't make it any better. No better for *me*. It's roses and lavender – close, indoor air, there as much as here!

MRS BORKMAN [*shaken, but having got back her composure*]: Close air at your mother's, you say!

ERHART [*with growing impatience*]: Yes, I don't know what else to call it. All this morbid solicitude and – and idolatry – or whatever it is. I can't stand it any longer!

MRS BORKMAN [*looking earnestly and seriously at him*]: Are you forgetting what you have pledged your life to, Erhart?

ERHART [*breaking out*]: Oh, call it rather what *you* have

pledged my life to! You, you've been my will! I've never been allowed to have one of my own! But now I *can't* bear this slavery any longer! I'm young! Do remember *that,* Mother! [*With a courteous and considerate look at* BORKMAN.] I can't dedicate my life to atone for someone else. Whoever that other person may be.

MRS BORKMAN [*seized by a growing dread*]: Who is it that has changed you, Erhart?

ERHART [*disconcerted*]: Who –? Well, couldn't it be I myself who –?

MRS BORKMAN: No, no, no! You have fallen under the influence of some outsider. You're not under your mother's any longer. Nor under your – your adopted mother's, either.

ERHART [*with forced defiance*]: I am under my own influence, Mother! And obeying my own will!

BORKMAN [*going towards* ERHART]: So perhaps my hour is come at last, for a change.

ERHART [*with distant and measured courtesy*]: What –? What do you mean by that, sir?

MRS BORKMAN [*scornfully*]: Yes, that's just what I'm wondering.

BORKMAN [*continuing unchecked*]: Listen, Erhart – would you like to join with your father? It's not through another person's life that a man can raise himself up when he has fallen. Those kinds of things are only empty dreams, stories they've told you – down here in this close air. Even if you were to order your life so as to live it like all the saints put together, – it wouldn't help me in the least.

ERHART [*formal and respectful*]: That's quite true, put like that.

BORKMAN: Yes, it is. And it wouldn't help either if I gave myself up to wither away in penance and contrition. I've tried to help myself out of it with dreams and hopes – all these years. But that sort of thing's not for me. And now I'll have done with dreams.

ERHART [*with a slight bow*]: And what will – what will you do then, sir?

BORKMAN: Lift myself up again, that's what I shall do. Begin from the bottom again. It's only by his present and his future that a man can atone for his past. By work – by incessant work for all that stood, when I was young, for life itself. But now a thousand-fold more than it did then. Erhart, – will you join me and help me with this new life?

MRS BORKMAN [*raising a hand in warning*]: Don't do it, Erhart!

ELLA RENTHEIM [*warmly*]: Yes, yes, do it! Oh, do help him, Erhart!

MRS BORKMAN: And *that's* what you advise! You, who are solitary and dying!

ELLA RENTHEIM: It doesn't matter about me.

MRS BORKMAN: Yes, just so long as it isn't *I* who take him from you.

ELLA RENTHEIM: Just so, Gunhild.

BORKMAN: Will you, Erhart?

ERHART [*in painful distress*]: Father, – I can't now. It's quite impossible!

BORKMAN: But what do you want to do, then?

ERHART [*with a blaze of feeling*]: I'm young! I want to *live*, for once, like other people! I want to live my own life!

ELLA RENTHEIM: Not to sacrifice a few short months to bring light into another life, that is going empty into the darkness?

ERHART: Aunt, I *can't* do it, however much I want to!

ELLA RENTHEIM: Not for someone who loves you so deeply?

ERHART: Upon my life, Aunt Ella – I can't do it.

MRS BORKMAN [*looking keenly at him*]: And your mother has no hold on you any longer either?

ERHART: Mother! I'll always love you! But I can't go on living for you alone. It's no life for me, that.

BORKMAN: Then come and join with me, after all! Because

life, life is work, Erhart. Come, and we two will go out into life and work together!

ERHART [*passionately*]: Yes, but I don't *want* to work now! Because I'm *young*! I never realized that I was before. But now I feel it hot and racing through me. I *won't* work. Only live, live, live!

MRS BORKMAN [*with a cry that shows she has guessed*]: Erhart, – what do you want to live for?

ERHART [*with glittering eyes*]: For happiness, Mother!

MRS BORKMAN: And where do you expect to find *that*?

ERHART: I've *found* it, already!

MRS BORKMAN [*screaming*]: Erhart!

[ERHART *goes quickly across and opens the hall door.*]

ERHART [*calling*]: Fanny, – you can come in now!

[MRS WILTON, *in outdoor clothes, appears on the threshold.*]

MRS BORKMAN [*with uplifted hands*]: Mrs Wilton –!

MRS WILTON [*a little timidly, with a questioning glance towards* ERHART]: Can I, then?

ERHART: Yes, you can come now. I've said everything.

[MRS WILTON *comes into the room.* ERHART *shuts the door behind her. She bows formally to* BORKMAN, *who returns it silently. There is a short silence.*]

MRS WILTON [*in a quiet but firm voice*]: So the word has been spoken. And I can well believe that I must seem to have brought great unhappiness upon this house.

MRS BORKMAN [*slowly, looking fixedly at her*]: You have destroyed the last remains of what I had to live for. [*Breaking out.*] But this – this is absolutely impossible!

MRS WILTON: I quite understand that it must seem impossible to you, Mrs Borkman.

MRS BORKMAN: Yes, you must be able to see for yourself that it's impossible. But then what –?

MRS WILTON: I'd say rather that it's quite improbable. But there it is, all the same.

MRS BORKMAN [*turning*]: Are you in real earnest about this, Erhart?

ERHART: This is happiness for me, Mother. All the great and glorious happiness of life. I can't tell you anything else.

MRS BORKMAN [*to* MRS WILTON, *clenching her hands*]: Oh, how you have bewitched and infatuated my unhappy son!

MRS WILTON [*with a proud lift of her head*]: I have not done that.

MRS BORKMAN: You've not done that, you say!

MRS WILTON: No. I've neither bewitched nor infatuated him. Erhart has come to me of his own free will. And of my own free will I've met him half-way.

MRS BORKMAN [*looking her scornfully up and down*]: Yes you, indeed! I can well believe it.

MRS WILTON [*controlling herself*]: Mrs Borkman, there are forces in human life that you seem not to know very well.

MRS BORKMAN: What forces, may I ask?

MRS WILTON: The forces that call two people to bind themselves together for life, inseparably – and without fear.

MRS BORKMAN [*smiling*]: I thought you were already bound inseparably – to someone else.

MRS WILTON [*shortly*]: That someone else has left me.

MRS BORKMAN: But he's still living, they say.

MRS WILTON: For *me* he's dead.

ERHART [*intervening*]: Yes, Mother. For Fanny he *is* dead. And in any case this other man doesn't concern me in the least.

MRS BORKMAN [*looking sternly at him*]: You know it, then – about this other man?

ERHART: Yes, Mother, I know it perfectly well, the whole thing – all about it!

MRS BORKMAN: And yet, it doesn't trouble you, you say.

ERHART [*brushing it aside petulantly*]: I can only tell you that it's happiness I want! I'm young! I want to live, live, live!

MRS BORKMAN: Yes, you are young, Erhart. Too young for all this.

MRS WILTON [*firmly and seriously*]: You mustn't imagine, Mrs Borkman, that I haven't told him the same thing. I've laid the whole of my past life clearly before him. I've reminded him repeatedly that I'm a whole seven years older than he is –

ERHART [*interupting*]: Oh nonsense, Fanny – I knew that from the start.

MRS WILTON: But nothing, nothing's had any effect.

MRS BORKMAN: Really? Hasn't it? Then why didn't you send him away without more ado? Shut your house to him? That's what you ought to have done, and in good time!

MRS WILTON [*looking at her and speaking quietly*]: That's just what I couldn't do, Mrs Borkman.

MRS BORKMAN: Why couldn't you?

MRS WILTON: Because my happiness, too, lay in this one person.

MRS BORKMAN [*contemptuously*]: Hm, – happiness, happiness –

MRS WILTON: I've never known before what happiness was in life. And I can't bring myself to turn away my happiness, just because it comes so late.

MRS BORKMAN: And how long do you think that happiness will last?

ERHART [*breaking in*]: Short or long, Mother – it doesn't matter!

MRS BORKMAN [*in wrath*]: You blind creature! Don't you see where all this is taking you?

ERHART: I'm not bothering about looking ahead. I don't want to look round me in any way! I only want to be allowed to live my own life for once!

MRS BORKMAN [*in deep pain*]: And you call this life, Erhart!

ERHART: Why, don't you see how lovely she is!

MRS BORKMAN [*wringing her hands*]: And so this crushing disgrace – I'm to bear this as well!

BORKMAN [*in the background, harshly and bitingly*]: Ah, well –
you're used to bearing things of that kind, you know, Gunhild.

ELLA RENTHEIM [*imploring*]: John Gabriel –!

ERHART [*in the same tone*]: Father –!

MRS BORKMAN: Here I'm to go about seeing my own son,
every day, before my eyes, with a – a –

ERHART [*interrupting sternly*]: You won't have to see anything, Mother! You can be sure of that! I'm not staying
here any longer.

MRS WILTON [*firm and controlled*]: We're going away, Mrs
Borkman.

MRS BORKMAN [*turning pale*]: You're going away, too! Together, I suppose?

MRS WILTON [*nodding*]: Yes, I'm going south. Abroad. I'm
taking a young girl. And Erhart is coming with us.

MRS BORKMAN: With you – and a young girl?

MRS WILTON: Yes. It's this little Frida Foldal, that I've taken
to live with me. I want her to go abroad and learn more
about music.

MRS BORKMAN: And so you are taking her with you?

MRS WILTON: Yes, I can't very well send the child off down
there by herself.

MRS BORKMAN [*suppressing a smile*]: What do *you* say to that,
Erhart?

ERHART [*a little taken aback, shrugging his shoulders*]: Why,
Mother, if Fanny really wants it that way, well –

MRS BORKMAN [*coldly*]: When is the party setting out, if I
may ask?

MRS WILTON: We're going at once. Tonight. My sledge is
waiting down in the road – outside the Hinkels' house.

MRS BORKMAN [*looking her up and down*]: Ah – so *that* was the
evening party!

MRS WILTON [*smiling*]: Yes, there wasn't anyone there but
Erhart and me. And little Frida, of course.

MRS BORKMAN: And where is *she* now?

MRS WILTON: She's sitting in the sledge, waiting for us.

ERHART [*painfully distressed*]: Mother – you understand, don't you? I wanted to spare you this – you and everyone.

MRS BORKMAN [*looking at him, deeply wounded*]: You meant to go away from me without saying good-bye?

ERHART: Yes, I thought that was best. Best for both sides. Everything was settled. The luggage packed. But when you sent for me, of course – [*Trying to hold out his hands to her.*] Good-bye Mother.

MRS BORKMAN [*turning away and repelling him*]: Don't touch me!

ERHART [*gently*]: Is *this* your last word?

MRS BORKMAN [*sternly*]: Yes.

ERHART [*turning*]: Good-bye to you, then, Aunt Ella.

ELLA RENTHEIM [*pressing his hands*]: Good-bye, Erhart! Live your life and be as happy – as happy as ever you can!

ERHART: Thank you, Aunt Ella. [*He bows to* BORKMAN.] Good-bye, Father. [*He whispers to* MRS WILTON.] Let's get away – the sooner, the better.

MRS WILTON [*in a low voice*]: Yes, let's.

MRS BORKMAN [*with an evil smile*]: Mrs Wilton, do you think you're really acting wisely in taking that young girl with you?

MRS WILTON [*returning the smile, half ironically, half seriously*]: Men are so changeable, Mrs Borkman. And so are women. When Erhart is through with *me* – and *I* with *him* – it'll be as well for us both if he, poor dear, has someone to fall back on.

MRS BORKMAN: But what about yourself?

MRS WILTON: Oh, I shall manage all right, you know. Good-bye, everybody. [*She bows and goes out through the hall door.* ERHART *stands a moment as though he is hesitating; then he turns and follows her.*]

MRS BORKMAN [*letting fall her folded hands*]: Childless.

BORKMAN [*as if waking up to a resolution*]: Out into the storm alone, then! My hat! My cloak! [*He goes quickly towards the door.*]

ELLA RENTHEIM [*stopping him in acute anxiety*]: John, where are you going?

BORKMAN: Out into the storm of life, I tell you. Let me go, Ella!

ELLA RENTHEIM [*holding him fast*]: No, no, I won't let you go! You're ill. I can see you are!

BORKMAN: Let me go, I tell you! [*He tears himself free and goes out into the hall.*]

ELLA RENTHEIM [*at the door*]: Help me to keep him, Gunhild!

MRS BORKMAN [*cold and hard, remaining in the middle of the room*]: I don't want to keep anyone in the world. Let them leave me, all of them. One after another. As far away – as far as they want to. [*Suddenly, with a piercing scream.*] Erhart, don't go! [*She starts forward with outstretched arms towards the door.* ELLA RENTHEIM *stops her.*]

ACT FOUR

An open space in the grounds outside the main building, which lies to the right. A corner of this, with its entrance door and a flight of stone steps, juts out on to the stage. Along the background, and nearly reaching the grounds, stretch steep slopes overgrown with fir-trees. On the left, the beginnings of a small scattered wood. The snow-storm is over, but the ground is thickly covered with the new-fallen snow. So are the fir-trees, heavy and loaded. Dark night and driving clouds. The moon gleams faintly from time to time. The surroundings catch only a dull light from the snow. BORKMAN, MRS BORKMAN, and ELLA RENTHEIM are standing out on the steps. BORKMAN, faint and weary, is leaning up against the wall of the house. He has an old-fashioned cape thrown over his shoulders; he holds a soft, grey felt hat in one hand and a thick, knotted stick in the other. ELLA RENTHEIM is carrying her cloak on her arm. MRS BORKMAN's large shawl has fallen back over her shoulders so that her hair is uncovered.

ELLA RENTHEIM [who has planted herself in MRS BORKMAN's way]: Don't go after him, Gunhild!

MRS BORKMAN [in dread and agitation]: Let me go, Ella! He mustn't go away from me!

ELLA RENTHEIM: It's absolutely no use, I tell you! You can't catch him up.

MRS BORKMAN: Let me go, all the same, Ella! I will cry aloud after him all down the road. And surely he'll hear his mother's cry!

ELLA RENTHEIM: He *can't* hear you. He'll be sitting in the sledge by now –

MRS BORKMAN: No, no – he can't be in the sledge already!

ELLA RENTHEIM: He's been in the sledge for some time, believe me.

357

MRS BORKMAN [*desperately*]: If he's in the sledge – then he's there with her, with her – her!

BORKMAN [*laughing grimly*]: And so he certainly won't hear his mother's cry.

MRS BORKMAN: No. Then he won't hear it. [*Listening.*] Hush! What's that?

ELLA RENTHEIM [*listening too*]: It sounds like bells ringing –

MRS BORKMAN [*with a low cry*]: It's *her* sledge!

ELLA RENTHEIM: Or someone else's perhaps –

MRS BORKMAN: No, no it's Mrs Wilton's sledge! I know the silver bells! Listen! Now they're driving right by here – at the foot of the hill!

ELLA RENTHEIM [*quickly*]: Gunhild, if you want to call after him, then call *now*! Perhaps after all, he'll – [*The ringing of the bells is heard close at hand in the wood.*] Be quick, Gunhild! They're right below us now!

MRS BORKMAN [*standing irresolute for a moment; then stiffening herself, hard and cold*]: No. I won't call after him. Let Erhart Borkman drive away from me. Far, far out into what he now calls life and happiness.

[*The sound is lost in the distance.*]

ELLA RENTHEIM [*after a moment*]: Now we don't hear the bells any more.

MRS BORKMAN: I thought they sounded like funeral bells.

BORKMAN [*with a dry, quiet laugh*]: Ah – they're not being rung over *me* yet!

MRS BORKMAN: But over *me*. And over him, who went away from me.

ELLA RENTHEIM [*nodding thoughtfully*]: Who knows if they're not ringing in life and happiness for him, after all, Gunhild.

MRS BORKMAN [*starting and looking hard at her*]: Life and happiness, you say!

ELLA RENTHEIM: For a little while at any rate.

MRS BORKMAN: Would you let him have life and happiness – with her?

ELLA RENTHEIM [*warmly and sincerely*]: Yes, with all my heart and soul I would!

MRS BORKMAN [*coldly*]: Then your power of loving must be richer than mine.

ELLA RENTHEIM [*looking far ahead*]: It's perhaps being starved of love that preserves its power.

MRS BORKMAN [*fixing her eyes on her*]: If that's so – then mine will soon be as rich as yours, Ella. [*She turns and goes into the house.*]

ELLA RENTHEIM [*standing a moment and looking in distress at* BORKMAN, *then laying her hand cautiously on his shoulder*]: John, you come in too. Come now.

BORKMAN [*as though waking up*]: I?

ELLA RENTHEIM: Yes. You can't stand the bitter winter air. I can see you can't, John. Come along; go in with me. Indoors, where it's warm.

BORKMAN [*angrily*]: Up into the gallery again, I suppose?

ELLA RENTHEIM: Better into the living-room to her.

BORKMAN [*with a start of fury*]: Never in my life will I set foot under that roof again!

ELLA RENTHEIM: But where will you go then? So late at night, John?

BORKMAN [*putting on his hat*]: First and foremost I'll go out and see to all my hidden treasures.

ELLA RENTHEIM [*looking anxiously at him*]: John – I don't understand you!

BORKMAN [*with a laugh interrupted by a cough*]: Ah, I don't mean stolen property that I've hidden. Don't be afraid of that, Ella. [*Stopping and pointing ahead.*] Look at that man there! Who's that?

[VILHELM FOLDAL *in an old, snow-covered overcoat, with his hat turned down and with a large umbrella in his hand, comes towards the corner of the house, struggling with difficulty through the snow. He is limping heavily on his left foot.*]

BORKMAN: Vilhelm! What have you come back to me for?

FOLDAL [*looking up*]: Good heavens! Are you out on the steps, John Gabriel? [*Bowing.*] And Mrs Borkman too, I see!

BORKMAN [*shortly*]: It isn't Mrs Borkman.

FOLDAL: Oh, I beg pardon. As a matter of fact, I've lost my spectacles in the snow. But why are you, who never go out of doors –?

BORKMAN [*carelessly and lightly*]: It's time I began to be an open-air man again, you see. Nearly three years in custody, five years in the cell, eight years up there in the gallery –

ELLA RENTHEIM [*troubled*]: John Gabriel – I beg you –!

FOLDAL: Yes, yes, yes –

BORKMAN: But I want to know what you came for?

FOLDAL [*still standing at the bottom of the steps*]: I wanted to come up to you, John Gabriel. I felt as if I *must* come up to you in the gallery. Dear, dear – that gallery!

BORKMAN: Did you want to come up to me, who'd turned you out?

FOLDAL: Good lord, yes; that doesn't matter.

BORKMAN: What have you done to your foot? You're walking lame.

FOLDAL: Yes, just think – I've been run over.

ELLA RENTHEIM: Run over!

FOLDAL: Yes, by a covered sledge –

BORKMAN: Ah!

FOLDAL: – with two horses. They came down the hill like the wind. I couldn't get out of the way quick enough; and so –

ELLA RENTHEIM: – and so they ran over you?

FOLDAL: They drove right on top of me, Mrs – Miss –. Right on top of me, so that I rolled over in the snow and lost my spectacles and got my umbrella smashed [*Rubbing himself.*] and my foot hurt a little too.

BORKMAN [*laughing inwardly*]: Do you know who it was in that sledge, Vilhelm?

FOLDAL: No, how could I see that? It was a covered sledge

360

and the blinds were drawn. And the coachman didn't even stop a moment, when I went rolling over. But *that* doesn't matter, because – [*Breaking out.*] I'm so wonderfully happy, you know.

BORKMAN: Happy?

FOLDAL: Well, I don't really know what to call it. But I think I might almost call it 'happy'. For something so extraordinary has happened! And that's why I *couldn't* do anything else – I *had* to come over and share my happiness with you, John Gabriel.

BORKMAN [*roughly*]: Very well, share the happiness then!

ELLA RENTHEIM: Oh but take your friend in with you first, John Gabriel.

BORKMAN [*sternly*]: I won't go into the house, I tell you.

ELLA RENTHEIM: But surely you heard he's been run over!

BORKMAN: Oh, we all of us get run over – once in our lives. But one must pick oneself up again. And behave as if it was nothing.

FOLDAL: That was a deep saying, John Gabriel. But I can perfectly well tell you outside here in a moment.

BORKMAN [*more gently*]: Yes, please do, Vilhelm.

FOLDAL: Well, now I'll just tell you. Now just think – when I got home this evening from you – I found a letter. Can you guess who it was from?

BORKMAN: Perhaps it was from your little Frida?

FOLDAL: Exactly! Fancy your guessing at once! Yes, it was a long – rather a long letter from Frida, you see. A servant had been there and brought it. And can you think what she wrote about?

BORKMAN: Could it possibly be to say good-bye to her parents?

FOLDAL: Precisely! It's wonderful, how you can guess, John Gabriel! Yes, she writes that Mrs Wilton has got so fond of her. And now she wants her to go abroad with her. So that Frida can learn more about music, she writes. And Mrs

Wilton has engaged an excellent teacher who will go with them on the journey. And read with Frida! For unfortunately she's rather backward in certain subjects, you understand.

BORKMAN [*laughing inwardly, with a chuckle*]: Well, well. I understand it all uncommonly well, Vilhelm.

FOLDAL [*going on eagerly*]: And think, she only knew about the journey for the first time this evening. It was at that party, you know. Hm! And yet she found time to write. And the letter is so warmly and prettily and kindly written, I assure you. Not a trace of contempt for her father there. And then such a delicate idea, you know, that she wanted to say good-bye to us in writing before she went. [*Laughing.*] But there's not going to be any of *that*!

BORKMAN [*looking enquiringly at him*]: Why not?

FOLDAL: She writes that they're starting early to-morrow. Quite early.

BORKMAN: Oh indeed – to-morrow? Does she write that?

FOLDAL [*laughing and rubbing his hands*]: Yes, but here's where I'm being cunning, you see! I'm going straight up to Mrs Wilton's now –

BORKMAN: Now, this evening?

FOLDAL: Good gracious, yes. It's not so very late yet. And if everything's locked up, I'll ring. Without more ado. Because I will and must see Frida before she goes. Good night, good night! [*Is going out.*]

BORKMAN: Listen, my poor Vilhelm – you can spare yourself that bad stretch of road.

FOLDAL: Oh, you're thinking of my foot –

BORKMAN: Yes, and you won't get into Mrs Wilton's in any case.

FOLDAL: Oh, I certainly shall. I'll go on ringing and ringing at the bell till someone comes and opens the door. For I must and will see Frida.

ELLA RENTHEIM: Your daughter's gone already, Mr Foldal.

FOLDAL [*standing as if struck*]: Is Frida gone already? Do you know it for certain? Who did you hear it from?

BORKMAN: We have it from her future teacher.

FOLDAL: Oh? And who's he, then?

BORKMAN: It's a certain Mr Erhart Borkman.

FOLDAL [*radiantly happy*]: Your son, John Gabriel! Is he to go with them?

BORKMAN: Yes. It's he who's to help Mrs Wilton to educate your little Frida.

FOLDAL: Now God be praised! Then the child's in the best of hands. But is it quite certain they've already gone away with her?

BORKMAN: They went away with her in the sledge that ran over you in the road.

FOLDAL [*clasping his hands*]: Just to think that my little Frida was sitting in that grand carriage!

BORKMAN [*nodding*]: Oh yes, Vilhelm, your daughter's come to driving about now. And so has our Mr Erhart. But – did you notice the silver bells?

FOLDAL: Oh, yes. Silver bells, you say? Were they silver bells? Real, genuine silver bells?

BORKMAN: You can be sure of that. The whole concern was genuine. Both outside and – and in.

FOLDAL [*with quiet emotion*]: Isn't it wonderful, how happily things can work out for a person! It's my – my little gift for poetry that's turned to music in Frida. And so I haven't been a poet in vain, after all. For now she'll go out into the great, wide world that I used to dream so eagerly of seeing. Little Frida, travelling in a closed sledge. With silver bells on the harness –

BORKMAN: – and running over her father –

FOLDAL [*happily*]: Oh, nonsense! It doesn't matter about me – so long as the child –. Well, then I came too late after all. And so I'll just go home and comfort her mother who's sitting in the kitchen crying.

BORKMAN: She's crying?

FOLDAL [*with a little laugh*]: Yes, just imagine it – she was sitting crying her eyes out when I came away.

BORKMAN: And *you're* laughing, Vilhelm.

FOLDAL: Yes, yes, I am. But she, poor dear, she doesn't know any better, you see. Well, good-bye. It's a good thing I've got the tram so near. Good-bye, good-bye, John Gabriel. Good-bye, Miss! [*He bows and goes out with difficulty by the way he came.*]

BORKMAN [*standing still for a moment and looking ahead of him*]: Good-bye, Vilhelm! It's not the first time in your life that you've been run over, my old friend.

ELLA RENTHEIM [*looking at him with suppressed anxiety*]: You're so pale, John, so pale –

BORKMAN: That comes of the prison air up there.

ELLA RENTHEIM: I've never seen you like this before.

BORKMAN: No, because I don't suppose you've ever seen an escaped prisoner before, either.

ELLA RENTHEIM: Oh, come along, John, and go in with me!

BORKMAN: Stop that coaxing tone. I've told you –

ELLA RENTHEIM: But when I beg you to? For your own sake –

[*The* MAID SERVANT *comes half-way out on to the steps.*]

THE MAID: Excuse me; Madam says I'm to lock the front door now.

BORKMAN [*in a low voice, to* ELLA]: You hear; now they want to lock me in again!

ELLA RENTHEIM [*to the* SERVANT]: The master isn't very well. He wants to have a little fresh air first.

THE MAID: Yes, but Madam herself said that –

ELLA RENTHEIM: I'll lock the door. Just leave the key in the lock and –

THE MAID: Oh well, all right. I'll do that, then. [*She goes into the house again.*]

BORKMAN [*standing still a moment and listening, then going quickly down on to the open space*]: Now I'm outside the walls, Ella! Now they'll never get me again!

ELLA RENTHEIM [*going down to him*]: But you're a free man in there, too, John. You can go and come just as you like.

BORKMAN [*in a low voice, as in terror*]: Never under a roof again! It's so good to be out here in the night. If I went up to the gallery *now* – the ceiling and the walls would crowd together. Crush me. Flatten me out like a fly.

ELLA RENTHEIM: But where will you go to?

BORKMAN: Just go on and on and on. See if I can reach freedom and life and people again. Will you go with me, Ella?

ELLA RENTHEIM: I? Now?

BORKMAN: Yes, yes – at once!

ELLA RENTHEIM: But how far?

BORKMAN: As far as ever I can.

ELLA RENTHEIM: Oh, but think what you're doing. Out in this wet, cold winter night –

BORKMAN [*in a rough, hoarse voice*]: Ah, my lady is troubled about her health? Well, it is delicate, of course.

ELLA RENTHEIM: It's *your* health I'm troubled about.

BORKMAN: Ha, ha, ha! A dead man's health! I can't help laughing at you, Ella! [*He goes further on.*]

ELLA RENTHEIM [*going after him and holding him fast*]: What was it you said you were?

BORKMAN: A dead man, I said. Don't you remember Gunhild saying I was just to stay quiet, where I lay?

ELLA RENTHEIM [*making up her mind and putting on her cloak*]: I'll go with you, John.

BORKMAN: Yes, we two, we do belong together, Ella. [*Going on.*] Come, then!

[*They have gradually made their way into the low wood on the left. This hides them bit by bit until they are no longer seen. The house and the open space disappear. The land-*

scape, with its slopes and shoulders, changes gradually and becomes wilder and wilder.]

ELLA RENTHEIM'S VOICE [*heard in the wood on the right*]: Where is it we're going, John? I don't know my way here.

BORKMAN'S VOICE [*higher up*]: Just keep in the tracks I've made.

ELLA RENTHEIM'S VOICE: But why've we got to climb so high?

BORKMAN'S VOICE [*nearer*]: We must go up the winding path.

ELLA RENTHEIM [*still hidden*]: Oh, but I can't go on much longer.

BORKMAN [*on the edge of the wood to the right*]: Come along! We're not far now from the view point. There was a bench in the old days –

ELLA RENTHEIM [*coming into sight through the trees*]: Do you remember that?

BORKMAN: You can rest there.

[*They have come out on a little open space, high up in the wood. The slope goes steeply up behind them. On the left, far beneath, is a wide-spread landscape with fjords and high, distant mountain-ranges one behind the other. On the left of the open space is a dead fir-tree with a bench under it. The snow lies deep on the ground.* BORKMAN *and after him* ELLA RENTHEIM *come in from the right and make their way with difficulty through the snow.*]

BORKMAN [*standing by the steep edge on the left*]: Come here, Ella, and you shall see.

ELLA RENTHEIM [*joining him*]: What is it you want to show me, John?

BORKMAN [*pointing outward*]: Do you see how the land lies free and open before us – far and wide?

ELLA RENTHEIM: We often sat there on the bench, in the old days, and saw far, far further out.

BORKMAN: It was a dreamland we looked out over then.

ELLA RENTHEIM [*nodding sadly*]: Yes, it was the dreamland of our lives. And now the land is covered with snow. And the old tree is dead.

BORKMAN [*without listening to her*]: Can you see the smoke from the great steamships out on the fjord?

ELLA RENTHEIM: No.

BORKMAN: I can. They come and they go. They carry the spirit of unity all round the world. They shed light and warmth over the souls in many a thousand homes. It was *that* I dreamt of creating.

ELLA RENTHEIM [*quietly*]: And it remained a dream.

BORKMAN: It remained a dream, yes. [*Listening.*] And listen, down there by the river! The factories are at work! *My* factories! All those I would have built! Listen to them at work. It's the night-shift. So, they work night and day. Listen, listen! The wheels whirling and the cylinders flashing – round and round! Can't you hear it, Ella?

ELLA RENTHEIM: No.

BORKMAN: *I* can hear it.

ELLA RENTHEIM [*anxiously*]: I think you're wrong, John.

BORKMAN [*more and more exultant*]: Oh, but all this – this is only like the outworks of the kingdom, you know!

ELLA RENTHEIM: The kingdom, did you say? What kingdom –?

BORKMAN: *My* kingdom of course! The kingdom I was just about to take possession of that moment when I – when I died.

ELLA RENTHEIM [*still and shaken*]: Oh John, John!

BORKMAN: And now it lies there – without defence, without a master – abandoned to robbers to take and plunder. Ella! Do you see the mountain-ranges *there*, far away? One behind another. They rise up. They tower. *That* is my deep, unending, inexhaustible kingdom!

ELLA RENTHEIM: Yes, John, but there's a freezing breath coming from that kingdom!

BORKMAN: That breath is like the breath of life to me. That breath comes to me like a greeting from imprisoned spirits. I can see them, the millions in bondage; I feel the veins of metal that stretch out their curved, branching, luring arms to me. I saw them before me like shadows brought to life – that night when I stood in the cellar of the bank with the light in my hand. You wanted your freedom then. And I tried to do it. But I hadn't the strength. The treasure sank into the abyss again. [*With outstretched hands.*] But I will whisper it to you here in the stillness of the night. I love you, where you lie as though dead in the depth and in the dark! I love you, you treasures that crave for life – with all the shining gifts of power and glory that you bring. I love, love, love you!

ELLA RENTHEIM [*in silent, but rising emotion*]: Yes, your love is still down there, John. It's always been there. But up here in the daylight, my dear – here there was a warm, living human heart, that beat and throbbed for you. And this heart you crushed. Oh, more than that! Ten times worse! You sold it for – for –

BORKMAN [*shivering, as though a chill went through him*]: For the kingdom – and the power – and the glory – do you mean?

ELLA RENTHEIM: Yes, that's what I mean. I've said it once tonight. You've murdered the power to love in the woman who loved you. And whom you loved in return. As far as you *could* love anyone. [*With uplifted arm.*] And therefore I prophesy this – John Gabriel Borkman – you'll never win the reward you asked for murder. You will never march in triumph into your cold, dark kingdom!

BORKMAN [*staggering back to the bench and sitting down wearily*]: I almost fear you're right in your prophecy, Ella.

ELLA RENTHEIM [*crossing over to him*]: You're not to be *afraid* of *that*, John. That would be the best thing that could come to you.

BORKMAN [*with a cry, clutching his chest*]: Ah –! [*Dully.*] Now it's let me go.

ELLA RENTHEIM [*shaking him*]: What was it, John?

BORKMAN [*sinking back against the back of the seat*]: It was a hand of ice that took hold of my heart.

ELLA RENTHEIM: John! Did you feel the hand of ice?

BORKMAN [*murmuring*]: No. No ice hand. It was a metal hand. [*He slides right down on to the bench.*]

ELLA RENTHEIM [*pulling off her cloak and laying it over him*]: Lie quietly where you are! I'll go and get help for you.

> [*She goes a few steps to the right; then she stops, goes back and feels his pulse and his face for some time.*]

ELLA RENTHEIM [*quietly and firmly*]: No. It's best so, John Borkman. Best so for you.

> [*She wraps the cloak closer round him and sits down in the snow in front of the bench. There is a short silence.* MRS BORKMAN, *muffled in outdoor wraps, comes through the wood on the right. In front of her comes the* MAID *with a lighted candle.*]

THE MAID [*throwing the light on the snow*]: Yes, yes, ma'am. Here are their tracks –

MRS BORKMAN [*looking about her*]: Yes, here they are. They're sitting over there on the bench. [*Calling.*] Ella!

ELLA RENTHEIM [*getting up*]: Are you looking for us?

MRS BORKMAN [*harshly*]: Yes, I have to.

ELLA RENTHEIM [*pointing*]: Look, here he lies, Gunhild.

MRS BORKMAN: Asleep!

ELLA RENTHEIM [*nodding*]: A deep and long sleep, I think.

MRS BORKMAN [*breaking in*]: Ella! [*Controlling herself and asking in a low voice.*] Did it happen – by his own will?

ELLA RENTHEIM: No.

MRS BORKMAN [*relieved*]: Not by his own hand, then?

ELLA RENTHEIM: No. It was a freezing, metal hand that took hold of his heart.

MRS BORKMAN [*to the* MAID]: Get help. Fetch the people from the estate.

THE MAID: Yes, yes, ma'am. [*In a low voice.*] Merciful heavens –! [*She goes out through the wood on the right.*]

MRS BORKMAN [*standing behind the bench*]: So the night air has killed him –

ELLA RENTHEIM: That's probably it.

MRS BORKMAN: – him, the strong man.

ELLA RENTHEIM [*crossing to the front of the bench*]: Won't you look at him, Gunhild!

MRS BORKMAN [*putting it aside*]: No, no, no. [*She lowers her voice.*] He was a miner's son – the bank director. Couldn't stand the fresh air.

ELLA RENTHEIM: It was more likely the cold that killed him.

MRS BORKMAN [*shaking her head*]: The cold, do you say? The cold – that had killed him long ago.

ELLA RENTHEIM [*nodding to her*]: And turned us both to shadows, yes.

MRS BORKMAN: You're right in that.

ELLA RENTHEIM [*with a sad smile*]: A dead man and two shadows – *that's* what the cold has done.

MRS BORKMAN: Yes, cold at the heart. And so we two can take each other's hands, Ella.

ELLA RENTHEIM: I think we can now.

MRS BORKMAN: We two twin sisters – over the man we both loved.

ELLA RENTHEIM: We two shadows – over the dead man.

[MRS BORKMAN, *behind the bench, and* ELLA RENTHEIM *in front, stretch out their hands to each other.*]

NOTES

I have added here a few notes on passages where the original has provided its own peculiar problems for the translator and particularly for the translator, the modern reader or the producer who wishes to think in terms of a modern setting. Obviously many more notes should have been written for the proper elucidation of certain passages, but these may perhaps serve as specimens.

Rosmersholm

1. p. 30. 'that's the Principal!' Kroll is described in the list of characters and in the text as 'Rektor', the normal title for the head of a university or school. 'Rector' bears a quite different connotation in England (though not in Scotland) and some other title must be found. 'Principal' is perhaps the best equivalent. But it cannot be repeated constantly, as 'Rektor' can in the original, and I have therefore invested the worthy headmaster with an honorary doctorate as the nearest English equivalent to the qualification proper to his position at that date. [See also Introduction, p. 26.]
2. p. 32. 'the civic dispute ... that's raging here.' William Archer gives a clear account of the political situation in his Introduction to Heinemann's edition of the translation. (vol. ix. pp. viii–xi.)
3. p. 32. 'I've tasted blood now.' A quotation from the almost proverbial line in the old National Anthem. The English loses something of its grimness, which Kroll closely adopts.
4. p. 35. 'Will you stay to supper ...?' Rebekka actually invites Kroll to take tea with them that evening. A nineteenth-century English public would have understood evening tea, but the twentieth-century equivalent is a light supper. For a production in the costume and setting of the nineteenth century the words 'Will you take tea with us' might be used and the corresponding modifications made in the three earlier references in this act.
5. p. 37. *The Lighthouse*. Mortensgaard's paper has given his translators some trouble. The original 'blinkfyret' is literally a revolving light, a thing usual only in lighthouses, lightships, and light-buoys. The alternatives sometimes used are 'Searchlight' and

'Beacon', which are represented by quite other words in Norwegian and, by their very nature, could not use revolving lights. Mortensgaard's paper seems to have been intended primarily to guide and illuminate the new 'liberal' party and only incidentally to search out and expose the weaknesses of such opponents as Kroll who had already attacked it. 'Lighthouse' therefore seems fairly just.

6. p. 39. 'Yes, my dear fellow'. Kroll sets us a problem often met in translating from languages which possess a special pronoun ('du') for intimate use. He addresses his brother-in-law as 'Rosmer' throughout (not 'John', as Brendel, the tutor, does) and this, shorn of the 'du' which accompanies it, gives the wrong impression of distance in English. The only thing that can be done in translating is to add a phrase, as here, which may serve to do the work of 'du' in a roundabout way. (Incidentally Kroll never changes from 'du' to the formal 'De', even after the quarrel.)

7. p. 40. 'expose yourself to the treatment one gets there.' This is a tame and unsatisfactory translation of an original which literally means 'the confectionery which is served out there.' Kroll's racy metaphor is not easily transferred whole and alive to English.

8. p. 45. 'a storm-tossed solstice.' Brendel's mixed metaphors at the climax of his enthusiasm are hard to distinguish from the naive blunders which characterize his culture and his scholarship. The original here is literally 'solstice'; we can only presume that he meant 'equinox', since, rightly or wrongly, the two equinoxes are associated with storms and the two solstices are not. Brendel is equally unfortunate with, for instance, his 'A la bonheur' (p. 47). Many translators silently correct this for him, but it is characteristic and should stand. Without any direct comment, Ibsen succeeds all through this scene in throwing a quietly destructive light on Brendel's value as a tutor.

9. p. 46. 'ROSMER: The only thing.' The French translator, Prozor, gives this speech to Brendel, but the three principal Norwegian editions consistently attribute it to Rosmer. This is of the utmost importance, as taking the speech from Rosmer might acquit him of the impulsive and slightly sentimental blindness with which Rebekka has accepted Brendel's preposterous travesty of the artistic process.

10. p. 55. 'dressed in a house-coat.' This is the nearest modern equivalent to the 'morning-dress' of the original. For a production in nineteenth-century setting, the necessary substitution will be made.

11. p. 57. 'talk to the Rector.' Rosmer is addressed and referred to as 'pastor' or 'herr pastor' throughout, a word whose English counterpart would give a false impression. As Rosmer has formerly held a clerical office the equivalent of a rector's or a vicar's in England, I have allowed Mrs Helseth to speak of him as though he still held it (as old servants sometimes do). The only other people allowed to commit this solecism are Mortensgaard, in a moment of ingratiating servility, and Kroll when carried away by a mood of spiteful irony. The other possible rendering of 'pastor' is 'the Reverend Mr Rosmer', too cumbersome for general use, but sometimes serving the same purposes as 'Rector'. In certain other cases, where the speaker is neither uneducated nor vindictive, 'pastor' or 'herr pastor' must be rendered by plain 'Mr Rosmer' or 'sir'.

12. p. 73. 'REBEKKA: John!' Rebekka uses the name 'Rosmer' throughout when she is alone with him, but this would almost certainly give a misleading impression of the relationship if it were carried over into English and especially since he always calls her 'Rebekka' when they are alone. I think 'John' is the better term in modern English, but a producer using a nineteenth-century setting would be justified in restoring the 'Rosmer' of the original and might gain something by doing so.

13. p. 96. 'we use each other's Christian names.' I attempt in this way to give the effect of the use of the intimate pronoun in Norwegian. Literally translated, this and the two previous speeches would run: 'REB: He would much rather not have met thee (= dig), Rosmer. KROLL [*involuntarily*]: Thou! (= Du!) REB: Yes, Principal, Mr Rosmer and I – we say 'thou' to each other.' This is in fact the first time she has said 'du' or 'dig' to him in front of Kroll.

14. p. 103. 'Her coat.' The original is 'cloak' and a cloak should, of course, be used in a nineteenth-century setting.

15. p. 104. 'Mortensgaard's religon.' Mrs Helseth's speech, though not illiterate, has occasional blunders such as characterize Gina

Ekdal's in *The Wild Duck*. Here, for instance, she says 'reglion' instead of 'religion' (not a native Norwegian word). I gratefully adopt R. Farquharson Sharp's adroit invention 'religon', which appears to give precisely the right seasoning of illiteracy to the respectable Mrs Helseth's discourse.

16. p. 110. 'I'm changed, so that my own past bars my way.' This is a rather free translation of a passage that might be rendered literally: 'now am I become such that my own past bars it out [the "happiness" mentioned above] for me.' I think the important point here is the irony that she recognizes. What she wanted is at last within her reach, but now she has become the kind of person who cannot take it, who cannot forgive herself the past she once thought nothing of.

The Master Builder

17. p. 134. 'have supper with us.' Mrs Solness, in the original, invites Dr Herdal to come back and 'drink tea with us'. This meal is here, as in *Rosmersholm* and elsewhere, better rendered in English as 'supper'.

18. p. 148. 'Orangia.' In the original this is 'Appelsinia', which, as Archer points out, comes immediately from 'appelsia' ('orange'). There is perhaps no need to translate here, but 'Orangia' seemed to justify Hilde's distaste better than a word which would have no associations for an English audience.

19. p. 175. 'A little while before dinner.' This meal ('middag'), which cannot quite be translated by 'lunch', takes place in the middle of the day. The drive, therefore, would be at noon.

20. p. 177. 'upon the ministrants either.' It is perhaps hardly necessary to mark the distinction between 'minister' and 'ministrant', but Ibsen does in fact do it in the original (ed. 1930 p. 58) with his 'tjenende' and 'tjener' and I have attempted to follow.

Little Eyolf

21. p. 215. 'locked brief-case.' The brief-case is of course an anachronism. The 'mappe' which Asta Allmers carries is of a different design from either the modern despatch-case or brief-case.

22. p. 229. 'your gold and your green forests.' Though this describes literally enough the inheritance which Rita brought to Alfred, the phrase is commonly used to describe great wealth or extravagant promises.

23. p. 238. 'You had champagne, but you touched it not.' A quotation from the concluding couplet of J. S. Wergeland's 'Republikanerne'. ('De saae paa hverandre. Han vandred sin Vei/De havde Champagne, men rørte den ei.')

24. p. 241. 'The evil eye.' Ibsen uses the plural throughout, both here and in Act II. The English habit of using the singular makes the reference back less effective in the later passage, but it seemed better to use the customary phrase as far as possible.

25. p. 248. 'the blue blouse and the shorts.' This is of course a modern rendering. What Asta actually says is 'knee-breeches' and that picture should be retained in a costume production, even though we are only to see the knee-breeches of the little boy in the mind's eye, by restoring the older word here.

26. p. 278. 'two good travelling companions.' Alfred's phrase (here translated literally) is a common one, but taken in conjunction with 'death and I', it calls to mind legends such as that of Sintram and his Companions in La Motte Fouqué's well-known tale.

27. p. 282. 'a hard day's work before us.' Almost an echo of Karsten Bernick's words at the end of *The Pillars of the Community*.

John Gabriel Borkman

28. p. 316. [Stage Direction]. Borkman sits on the sofa and invites Foldal to take a chair, in defiance, I think, of contemporary manners. And so the point, slight as it is, had better be made in a costume production. The sofa is the position of honour and for Borkman to take it alone gives to the interview a faint suggestion of a royal audience which should not be lost. When, later, Ella Rentheim visits him, he has the grace (p. 327) to invite her to the sofa.

29. p. 325. 'No poet.' Foldal actually says 'Ikke noget digterkald', which is, literally, 'No poetic vocation', but the English phrase lacks the brevity and dignity of the Norwegian and so I have preferred to let him echo Borkman's words on the previous page,

'Du er ingen digter, Vilhelm'. This is one of those cases in which the significance of the original is perhaps best preserved by modifying the actual phrasing. Any producer would also, I think, draw the line at using the phrase 'poetic vocation' at the height of one of the most moving passages in this act.

Discover more about our forthcoming books through Penguin's FREE newspaper...

READ MORE IN PENGUIN

PENGUIN AUDIOBOOKS

A Quality of Writing that Speaks for Itself

Penguin Books has always led the field in quality publishing. Now you can listen at leisure to your favourite books, read to you by familiar voices from radio, stage and screen. Penguin Audiobooks are ideal as gifts, for when you are travelling or simply to enjoy at home. They are produced to an excellent standard, and abridgements are always faithful to the original texts. From thrillers to classic literature, biography to humour, with a wealth of titles in between, Penguin Audiobooks offer you quality, entertainment and the chance to rediscover the pleasure of listening.

You can order Penguin Audiobooks through Penguin Direct by telephoning (0181) 899 4036. The lines are open 24 hours every day. Ask for Penguin Direct, quoting your credit card details.

Published or forthcoming:

PENGUIN AUDIOBOOKS

READ MORE IN PENGUIN

A CHOICE OF CLASSICS

Lord Macaulay	**The History of England**
Henry Mayhew	**London Labour and the London Poor**
John Stuart Mill	**The Autobiography**
	On Liberty
William Morris	**News from Nowhere** and **Selected Writings and Designs**
John Henry Newman	**Apologia Pro Vita Sua**
Robert Owen	**A New View of Society and Other Writings**
Walter Pater	**Marius the Epicurean**
John Ruskin	**'Unto This Last' and Other Writings**
Walter Scott	**Ivanhoe**
	Heart of Midlothian
Robert Louis Stevenson	**Kidnapped**
	Dr Jekyll and Mr Hyde and Other Stories
William Makepeace Thackeray	**The History of Henry Esmond**
	The History of Pendennis
	Vanity Fair
Anthony Trollope	**Barchester Towers**
	Can You Forgive Her?
	The Eustace Diamonds
	Framley Parsonage
	He Knew He Was Right
	The Last Chronicle of Barset
	Phineas Finn
	The Prime Minister
	The Small House at Allington
	The Warden
	The Way We Live Now
Oscar Wilde	**Complete Short Fiction**
Mary Wollstonecraft	**A Vindication of the Rights of Woman**
	Mary and Maria
	Matilda
Dorothy and William Wordsworth	**Home at Grasmere**

READ MORE IN PENGUIN

A CHOICE OF CLASSICS

Leopoldo Alas	**La Regenta**
Leon B. Alberti	**On Painting**
Ludovico Ariosto	**Orlando Furioso** (in 2 volumes)
Giovanni Boccaccio	**The Decameron**
Baldassar Castiglione	**The Book of the Courtier**
Benvenuto Cellini	**Autobiography**
Miguel de Cervantes	**Don Quixote**
	Exemplary Stories
Dante	**The Divine Comedy** (in 3 volumes)
	La Vita Nuova
Bernal Diaz	**The Conquest of New Spain**
Carlo Goldoni	**Four Comedies (The Venetian Twins/The Artful Widow/Mirandolina/The Superior Residence)**
Niccolò Machiavelli	**The Discourses**
	The Prince
Alessandro Manzoni	**The Betrothed**
Emilia Pardo Bazán	**The House of Ulloa**
Benito Pérez Galdós	**Fortunata and Jacinta**
Giorgio Vasari	**Lives of the Artists** (in 2 volumes)

and

Five Italian Renaissance Comedies
(Machiavelli/**The Mandragola**; Ariosto/**Lena**; Aretino/**The Stablemaster**; Gl'Intronati/**The Deceived**; Guarini/**The Faithful Shepherd**)
The Poem of the Cid
Two Spanish Picaresque Novels
(Anon/**Lazarillo de Tormes**; de Quevedo/**The Swindler**)

READ MORE IN PENGUIN